Field of View is a work of fiction. All names, characters, places, and incidents, are either the author's imagination or are used in a fictitious manner. Resemblance to real persons, either living or dead, events or locales is purely coincidental.

Copyright © 2013

Published in the United States by Jack Pirtle Author
www.jackpirtleauthor.com

Registration Number TXu 1-875-413

ISBN: 978-0-615-95431-8

All book designs by Jared Nichols
www.vitech.org

For Klaire, my true companion.

Acknowledgements

A genuine thank you to Bonnie for her expertise and keen eye. Thanks to Maureen for pointing me in the right literary direction. I'm indebted to my sister Fair, who knows the rhythm and flow of east Texas as well as I do. I thank her for lending an ear when I was ready to throw in the proverbial towel. I owe so much to Sally and Kayri, even though I thought their red ink would never cease flowing. My gratitude to Klaire, who never wavered in her belief that my late-in-life story telling would bear fruit. To my children who cheered me on as I attempted to ascend an uncharted mountain of words. To Jim and Buz for their old car IQ's. To Tim and Janna for extending a helping hand. Lastly, I owe thanks to Jared, whose technical wizardry made the e-publish goal a reality.

"Man was made at the end of the week's work,
when God was tired."

—Mark Twain

Field
of View

by

Jack Pirtle

Prologue - The Doll in the Green Dress

A stout Negro woman with freckled, light skin walked awkwardly in the direction of the bus stop, her legs bowed as if from the weight of her lot. Her plan was to catch the noon bus to south Dallas. There, she would spend the weekend with her four grandchildren and her recently abandoned daughter-in-law. Her son, unfortunately, like his father before him, was seemingly bent on a self-destructive path to nowhere worthwhile.

As she had done many times before, she made sure her plans for travel were not to be upset by the rude arrival of an early bus. Buses, like a lot of things in life, were not to be trusted. Buses were either late or early. Experience had taught her that they were never on time. An early arrival was by far the riskier of the two scenarios. Satisfied she had beaten the bus to its mark, she took a deep breath and settled in on a sun-ravaged wooden bench whose faded sign urged her, or anyone else, to take out a loan at a nearby First National Bank. *"We have high interest in our customers,"* the sign read, *"but only low interest for our loans."*

As comfortably as she could manage, given the heat and humidity, she adjusted the broad brim of her hat. The last thing she needed was more sun on her face. Too much of it brought freckles, like rain nourishes the worst of seedlings. Any fool knew that.

From the corner of her eye, the woman saw what appeared to be a doll falling from a tall nearby high-rise building. Squinting and shading her eyes with her hand, she turned toward the building hoping to bring the falling doll into sharper focus. The doll was wearing a green dress. It fell upright at first, its light-colored hair lifted up and away from its porcelain face by the rapid descent. Then, in agonizingly slow motion, the doll rotated over on its back. Suddenly its arms were alive, thrashing about wildly as if reaching for some unseen cord that would halt its free-fall to the unforgiving earth below.

Then, as if it had never been there in the first place, the doll vanished from her view. A loud, mechanical rush of noise signaled to the woman that her bus had arrived. She blinked several times and for a few moments, remained motionless. Finally, she gathered herself, rose stiffly from the bench, and walked toward the open door of the bus. She paid her fare and moved toward the back of the bus where seats were reserved for people of her kind. Amid the whine and thrust of the bus as it lurched forward, the woman tried to make sense of what she had seen. She thought it in order to pray.

*　　*　　*　　*　　*

Willis Sturm had great difficulty trying to explain to his supervisor why it had taken so long to situate the hotel's guest. Supervisor Culpepper's inquisition and subsequent lecture, Willis observed, resulted in formation of spittle on the corners of his much-disliked supervisor's mouth.

"Shit, Sturm, what did y'all do up there for all of what was it, an hour 'er so? If I get as much as a complaint from what's her name, the Fields' guest, y'all 'er fired."

"Couldn't have been that long," the bellboy responded weakly. "Thirty minutes, maybe a little more...she wanted the windows open."

"Thirty minutes shit," Culpepper countered. "Dammit boy, since when does it take so long to settle a guest? Anyway, why 'fer God's sakes did she want the window open? Got air conditionin' don't we? Paid a fortune for it."

Hoping the reprimand would be the end of it, Willis departed in the direction of another arriving guest. As he stepped through the revolving plate glass door of the hotel which led to a parked car outside, he mulled over Culpepper's mad-as-a-wet-hen muffled, but audible, parting shot: "Sorry excuse of a poor performin' bell-hop."

As Willis entered the harsh, reflected light of day, he took note of a crowd that had gathered. Marble, polished concrete and people obscured the newly-arrived car. Oddly, it began to rain. No clouds were directly overhead. The sun was shining yet it was raining. What a strange day. Willis could recall none stranger. Now, the Devil was whipping his wife. Or so the wives' tale said. What were so many people doing in front of the hotel? Why was a woman with two small children running from the crowd? Was that a woman screaming? And why did the faces he could see look like they had just seen the grim reaper or worse?

From somewhere within the unsettled crowd of people, another shrill voice sliced hard into the thick, traffic-laden air outside the hotel. Other screams followed in its terrifying wake. Tires squealed as cars came to a sudden halt.

Willis jerked his head in the direction of a car that was rear-ended by a delivery truck. He then returned his view to the chaos of the crowd. Audible above the discordant voices, Willis heard someone exclaim, "Christ Almighty!" Then, as if in a choreographed play, the crowd began to move back almost in lock-step from something that remained unseen and unknown by Willis.

Pushing past several onlookers, Willis caught sight of a patch of green contrasted in color by a pool of crimson liquid. Was it a green dress? Was it "that" green dress? Finally, managing an unobstructed view, he gasped and fell back involuntarily as he made the ungodly connection. It was "that" green dress. It was "that" girl, although her face was turned from his perspective. Her blond hair was soaked in blood. Her feet were bare. The girl who had asked him to keep her company, and who had so perplexed him with her looks and bizarre ways, had jumped to her death; her earthly form rendered into a bloody, disjointed, and lifeless heap.

A man in a fedora shouted for someone to call an ambulance. Another man stepped forward and covered the girl's face and upper body with his newspaper. Blood spilled from beneath the newspaper in a tenacious and gravity-driven meander toward the curb. Willis noticed the wrist of an exposed hand was still adorned by the cheap drug store watch she had referenced so many times. Unknown by Willis, the timepiece had stopped on impact. It had stopped within seconds of Rita Anne Fields' nineteenth birthday. *"Not one minute more,"* she had affirmed to her mirror the day she made up her mind to end her life. *"Not one minute more."*

Willis needed fresh air. "Fresh air's good for you," she had said in the hotel room as she requested Willis to open the window of the 22nd floor. "People don't get enough fresh air," he remembered her saying. "It is my birthday," she had volunteered. And how many times had she referenced her watch, he asked himself, as tiny heat-driven needles assaulted his face and arms. There was less light now. The clouds must have moved in. The clouds would put an end to the strangeness of rain while the sun shone. The Devil would have to stop his crazed whipping of his wife. Or was that just an, an...old wives'....

Field of View

With the forced blessing of a mind-numbing escape full upon him, Willis fell to his knees, then face first to the polished concrete. Prone on the concrete until a time when he would regain consciousness, he was once again destined to keep company with the girl in the green dress. As he lay unconscious, a distant siren marked the approach of an ambulance. The rain had stopped.

Chapter 1 - Dearth of Knowledge

"A documentary photograph makes an important statement about something or some person or some event, whatever. Whether it's worthwhile or not depends on the photographer but mostly on the viewer, doesn't it?" Carl asked, looking over at James Ray to make sure he was paying attention. *"Take the Hindenberg when it crashed and burned...in what was it...thirty-seven? Now that's a classic, time-honored documentary photo.*

The photographer, what's his name, had the patience to wait and trip his shutter at the exact moment the doomed airship struck the ground. The blimp was all aflame and coming in at forty-five degrees," Carl continued, using his left hand to portray the airship's angle of descent while his half-consumed cigarette, deftly suspended between his thumb and middle finger, served as a visual substitute for the Hindenberg. *"Killed a bunch of people. Everyone on board, actually. Made for a hell of a good documentary photo. Marked the end of passenger blimps filled with hydrogen gas, too, if you are interested in the history part of it."*

*   *   *   *   *

James Ray thought it to be the first worthwhile picture taking opportunity that had bothered to come knocking. What with his school and his part-time work at the *Mayweather Tribune,* he didn't have time to seek out such an image, he had to have the good fortune of stumbling over one. And on this blessed-do-nothing Sunday afternoon, an incoming tornado had presented him with the chance of a lifetime. Unburdened as he was by any responsibility, self-imposed or otherwise, the teenager with a newfound curiosity for the craft of photography first caught sight of the weather disturbance from the family's planked front porch. He had been observing the darkening sky for several minutes. He was on the lookout for streaks of lightning. Once witnessed, he would count to himself one thousand one, one thousand two, etc., until a clap or roll of thunder ceased his counting. Having counted to five one thousand and ones, James Ray estimated the last flash of lightning was five miles away. He figured the lightning to be somewhere near Devil's Lake on the outskirts of town.

Suddenly, the sky began to roil overhead. Just as suddenly, snake-like, a tornado appeared out of the turbulence. It was in its beginning dust whirl stage. It quickly organized and then matured in mere minutes. The maelstrom first touched and then began ripping savagely at the earth beneath. James Ray was stunned. Motionless at first, he then spun into action and raced for the front door of the house. The camera. Where was the camera? Moving from room to room, he caught no sight of the family camera, a simple Sears Roebuck Tower box camera. A second trip into his mother's bedroom revealed the camera perched on her dresser. It was partially hidden from view by an eight by ten framed Turman family photograph taken ten years earlier in the fall of 1942.

*   *   *   *   *

Five of the six Turmans are pictured, smiling and content, as if there weren't a care in the world. Hope, however, the youngest and all of two years old, had decided a scowl was in order and tenaciously held to her look despite cajoling from her parents, her siblings, and an increasingly frustrated photographer.

"Smile darlin'. Lookie here now. Smile, darlin'. Can y'all do somethin' to get the little one to smile? One smile is all I need."

The door-to-door encyclopedia-salesman-photographer had decided to use a large overstuffed living room chair for his prop. Dark-haired and pert Sarah Mae, on-again, off-again elementary school teacher, and mother of four, was directed to sit in the chair and hold the hard to manage Hope on her lap. Sarah Mae had just completed an agonizingly long home perm for the portrait and was looking her best. At times when she was less prepared, she was still an eye-catching, attractive woman who looked younger than her years. She was pleased with her hair, the pin curls removed only minutes prior to the arrival of the photographer. Faith, age four, blonde and blue-eyed like her little sister, was assigned a position on the chair's armrest. As she snuggled close to her mother, she was asked by the photographer to place an arm around her mother's neck. Seth, the oldest of the two boys, was eight. He stood upright and to the right of the chair. Seth was tall for his age and on more than one occasion, folks had questioned where such height came from given the fact that Turmans weren't known for hitting their collective heads on ceilings. At age eight, Seth was almost as tall as his mother.

James Ray, age six, was small in stature and he possessed many of the striking visual characteristics of his mother. His eyes were close set, his hair coal black. The angularity and sharpness of his facial features evidenced the ample supply of Coushatta Indian blood that coursed through the veins of his mother's side of the family. If provided a bonnet of feathers and a bow or rifle, the boy could easily have passed as Indian. Without either, he and his mother's physical characteristics were recognizably Native American. In the photo, he is staring beyond the lens of the camera and even beyond the photographer. In his time-frozen gaze he seems to be looking at a point photographers refer to as infinity, the point where two parallel lines converge. J.B. called his son's propensity to look beyond what was directly in front of him as his "hundred-yard stare." The boys, the photographer had decided, would serve as bookends for the females of the family and stand beside the chair, slightly turned, each with a hand on the chair's upholstered arms.

The father, William Jennings Bryan Turman, was told to stand and lean forward from the rear of the chair. "Be the guardian, Mr. Turman", the photographer ordered. J.B., as he was known throughout the Mayweather community of some seven thousand people, disliked the posed position because he felt it was too revealing of what little he had left of his hair. On the subject of hair, J.B. liked to take credit for the blond hair and blue eyes of his two girls. That, he was oft to say, was "a gift from the Turman side." He, after all, was once blond and he would remind anyone of this salubrious fact although his head no longer held sufficient evidence to prove it. He could, however, lay claim to blue eyes. His eyes, unlike his hair, had not fled the scene. The father, fit for his mid-thirties age at the time the photograph was taken in 1942, was in his second year as Mayweather County school superintendent.

"Now lean forward Mr. Turman...that's right. Forward a little more. Good. Now hold it. Y'all, everybody smile and we'll get this thing done. Can someone get the little one to smile? Anyone?"

J.B. held his position leaving Sarah Mae to try to coax Hope into a smile. Half a smile would do. Oddly positioned as he felt he was, he was reminded of a time when he was in the Navy, trying to maintain his balance on the deck of his wave-tossed, displacement-hulled PT boat.

Despite the agonizing effort to get everyone ready and dressed for the photo session, including Hope's grumpiness, his own discomfort, and what J.B. thought to be bossy ineptness on the part of the photographer, the photo worked. It documented a moment in time and space that in years to pass, everyone in the group, other than Sarah Mae, would see as representative of the time when the family was at its best. Sarah Mae's view of the family portrait was uniquely different. Pleased yes, but only to a point. Something was awry. The photo held a mystery which only Sarah Mae could bring to the light of the day.

Two years prior to the family photo, J.B. and Sarah Mae lost their fifth child, a girl, due to complications of childbirth. In the traumatic touch and go process, Sarah Mae almost lost her life as well. If another girl, they were to name the child Charity, thereby completing what Sarah Mae viewed as some kind of latter-day biblical trilogy. The loss of Charity still stung all the Turmans but Sarah Mae suffered longer and deeper. Moody and often depressed, Sara Mae was yet to recover from the emotional trauma. Instead of questioning her God following such a loss, she became even more religiously resolute and dogmatic. As the days and years passed, God and Jesus played an ever-increasing role in her life. The change was so pronounced that J.B., when he bothered with a thing called reflection, sometimes thought he was married to a stranger.

*   *   *   *   *

James Ray rushed from the house and upon inspection, saw that the hard-to-find camera had but one exposure left. The other eleven frames had been utilized to document a recent family reunion at Devil's Lake State Park. Only one exposure left with a tornado approaching! "For crap's sake!" he said out loud as he ran for the aging cedar tree in the family's side yard. His ascent of the sixty-foot fragile branched tree was both unpleasant and challenging. As he mounted the tree, the camera was switched from one hand to the other as he proceeded branch by gnarly, sap-laden branch. He climbed as far up the tree as his weight, and the branches that supported him, would allow.

Satisfied with his position and the expansive field of view, the sixteen-year-old waited patiently to document the tornado much like, he thought, the photographer who captured the demise of the Hindenberg. James Ray recalled portions of Carl's lecture on documentary photos: *It makes an important statement...whether it's worthwhile or not depends on the photographer's skill, but in the end it's up to the viewer.*

The boy's subject, the incoming tornado, should it be cooperative and head his way, would serve as his *center of interest.* Carl had lectured about that as well. James Ray liked his photography mentor. He was gruff, yes. He was strange in a lot of ways but he was also helpful and patient. He would check for understanding, a thing a lot of teachers at his high school didn't do. Given his experience with many of his teachers, a lesson presented was a lesson complete, done, over, whistle blown. More often than not, there was no follow-up questioning, no attempt to reinforce the concept or lesson. In Carl's case, however, if James Ray didn't show working knowledge of the concept, Carl would come at it another way. Through the back door, as Carl put it. And despite James Ray's pleading, Carl refused to introduce another concept until James Ray had shown mastery of the previous one.

James Ray repositioned himself in the tree for more comfort although none was forthcoming, all the time keeping a wary eye on the tornado. Much to his delight, it had touched down and was now close enough that he could see debris being strewn from its violent contact with the earth, like an angry finger of God. James Ray waited and as he did, he recalled another lesson on photo composition when Carl had taken a smoke break from his duties as photographer for the Mayweather Tribune.

"Don't take a photo that lacks a center of interest," Carl said while pointing to the Mayweather courthouse. "See, look down the street to the courthouse. In this photo situation we will use the courthouse as our center of interest. Center of interest is what first catches your eye. It's the most important visual part of the photo. So our quarried stone, proud-as-can-be-courthouse with all of its honorable people coming and going is our center of interest in our photo. It's framed by both the adjoining buildings and the elm trees on the east and west sides. It's also supported by the parked cars on Main street. From our perspective, Center Street serves as a leading line taking the viewer's eye to the courthouse, our center of interest. Get it? See how the visual elements combine to help you make your statement?"

James Ray nodded in the affirmative.

"Now, take away the courthouse from the scene. What do you have now?"

James Ray shrugged, trying hard to follow the lesson.

"Well," Carl continued, lighting another cigarette. "nothing much, do we? Take away a photo's center of interest and the photo is a little of nothing. Something in every photo should command the viewer's attention, capture their interest."

Carl inhaled deeply and turned in the direction of the courthouse.

"Your daddy still work at the courthouse?" he asked.

"Yes," replied James Ray. "He had two terms as county school superintendent and then got booted, but then he became county auditor. Still in the same courthouse after all those years but in a different office."

"Got booted?"

"Got voted out. Had somethin' to do with school consolidation or somethin'. Daddy was for consolidation and the other guy, I can't remember his name. Anyways, he was against it, and since it's a county job I think...at least my Daddy says, that the town of Mayweather was for consolidation, and the rest of the county was against it."

The courthouse clock tolled four in the afternoon.

"How do you do a silhouette?" James Ray asked as the two moved toward the paper's darkroom.

"Show me several pictures you take that display a solid, eye-grabbing center of interest and I'll teach you. Simple, actually. Something even a flea brain like you might be able to comprehend," Carl jested, gently bumping James Ray into a wall dividing the darkroom's two doors.

If the tornado cooperated, and that was a big if, given the fickle nature of such a weather event, and if James Ray made the right decisions compositionally, he held high expectations that his recorded image would possibly be one of the best ever documentations of one of the most feared of severe weather events. He would employ every compositional technique Carl had taught him. He would place the center of interest in the frame according to the *rule of thirds*. He would apply the *horizon rule* to include one-third land and two-thirds sky. He would allow *go room* so as to provide   space for the tornado to move within the frame.

James Ray felt that he possessed enough compositional knowledge that he could easily manage the photo opportunity. Carl, had he been present, would have perhaps thought otherwise. If he did everything right, he might even get published. How great would that be? It would be the beginning of a lifelong career in the world of photography. He would document important things like grand openings and ground breaking ceremonies such as the proposed veteran's hospital being built on the east side of town. Or, perhaps dramatic moments such as the time the Mayweather townspeople had gathered around the square to celebrate the surrender of Japan. Camera in hand, he would artfully capture the *peak action* moment of a football game or document the fun and frolic on yearly display at the county fair. In his mind, there would be no end to his photographic heroics. Maybe he would get published by *Look* or *Life* magazines, front cover perhaps.

As a typical teenager, however, he gave little thought to his own mortality and gave far more thought to living for the moment. His thoughts of future fame and glory moved quickly back to real time and the approaching tornado. For now, tomorrow was tomorrow and a lifetime away. He gave no thought to his personal safety or the untenable position in which he had placed himself. He had but one exposure. He had but one opportunity. He was determined not to botch the effort. The teenager gave no thought to the hard, cold fact that descent from the cedar would be as time-consuming as the ascent.

Chapter 2 - Prurient Interest

On the dawn of her nineteenth birthday, Rita Anne Fields was satisfied she had left no detail of her three, monthlong plan unattended. She was ready and even confident despite her lingering fatigue. She would do today what most people would find impossible to even imagine, let alone plan and execute.

Noting her reflected image on a wall-mounted-mirror, she managed a smile. It wasn't a smile intended to convince, it was rather more of a smile of capitulation; I've lost the race but at least I ran it, she thought. Give me credit for that. Everyone should manage a smile when their birthday rolls around. Perhaps the smile was unconvincing given the importance of the day. Rita, however, felt she had few peers when facial expressions were designed to feign ecstasy. Practice, her mother had offered on many an occasion, made for perfect.

Rita moved to the window of her apartment facing the street. She parted the venetian blind slats so she would be positioned to see the arrival of the taxi. In doing so, she noticed a thick layer of dust had taken residence on the slats. Were she destined to remain in the apartment, she figured she would do a lot of things differently. Keeping things more orderly would be a big priority; although, like her mother, she wasn't big on housework. What was the opposite of living in an apartment that was a total mess? A place for everything and everything in its place? In another life, she would keep a clean apartment, fix the broken mirror in the hall, mend the fences of some relationships gone awry, and above all, figure out a different way to earn a living. As a reinvented person, maybe she would take up churchgoing. If she put her mind to it, perhaps she would even be one of those persons who claimed to have found Jesus and having found him, would cling tenaciously to his teachings.

Rita recognized that when she had begun to let little things go, inconsequential as they seemed at the time, she had also begun to let issues of much greater personal impact pile up. And when a big, dirty thing or two arrived at her life's doorstep, although uninitiated and uninvited, coupled with the fact she had done little or nothing to put those things right or call a halt to much of anything, problems had gotten complicated so fast it seemed that no amount of effort could fix them.

Field of View

She realized she was leading a reckless, morally compromised life. Her existence was akin to a bunch of loose logs awash on a swollen river, all cattywampus, and lacking in purposeful direction. Nothing could stop them on their disordered journey, unless they stopped themselves. Forget order, forget meaning, forget life itself for that matter. The logs were loose and moving, she among them.

*   *   *   *   *

Having maneuvered his 1952 DeSoto, with its time-honored waterfall grill into the unloading lane of the Lamar Hotel in downtown Dallas, the impish driver with stooped shoulders and pock-marked face pulled hard on the emergency brake, and killed the engine. As often as possible, without being noticed, he had furtively observed his fare's nice-looking, but sad face, in his rearview mirror. The mirror framed her face perfectly.

"Here's the Lamar," he announced in foreign-accented English. A pretty picture he reflected. A pretty picture worthy of framing. Had he ever transported someone finer? He was sorry the ride was over.

The trip from Greenville to the Lamar had ended all too soon for the taxi driver. Even so, he would hold thoughts of his fare's attractive face for days or weeks. When he was in one of those seemingly never ending, waiting-to-be-ushered-into-service modes with little else to occupy his mind, he would think of the lovely girl in the green dress.

Maybe the girl was an actress of some kind? An actress, however, who had said nothing for the entire ride except where her destination was and seemingly more importantly, when she expected to arrive. Although she hadn't smiled and had barely spoken, the roomy confines of the four-door DeSoto overflowed with her presence. Her dress seemed the happier of the two, the driver recalled.

Rita beat both the bellboy and the driver to their objective in opening the taxi's rear passenger door. As the door opened, two well-defined legs probed beyond the car's interior running board, descending in unison to the asphalt below.

"I'll get y'all's bag," the bellboy said.

Rita didn't answer, instead she turned to face the driver and handed him a generous tip.

Field of View

"Thank you for the ride," she offered, looking beyond the man who had been watching her in his rearview mirror. Rita turned to follow the boy who displayed maroon slacks with matching shirt, topped by a cap with an embroidered silver "L." She walked purposefully to the entrance of the hotel, her heels clapping a cadence on the polished concrete.

The taxi driver stared at the girl. She was engulfed first by the dark shadow of the hotel's entrance and then by its revolving plate glass door. He marked to memory the curvature of her hips and what could be seen of her legs. He wondered what it would be like to have such a woman and who would have her today at the hotel. Perhaps some rich oil man. And, why hadn't the girl simply taken the bus from Greenville? The bus would have been a ride that cost less. Perhaps, he thought, a rich man was paying for her and money was of no consequence.

* * * * *

The copper-clad mustang stood proudly atop the twenty-nine story Lamar Hotel in downtown Dallas. Facing west, for the moment, the mustang reared upright. Its mouth was agape while its two front hooves maintained a constant and dramatic pose, as if taking the offense against some perpetually unseen opponent. The horse's two rear hooves were bound securely to a large rectangular platform of steel and reinforced concrete. Designed to rotate slowly on its thirteen-ton platform, the horse stood 450 feet above street level.

The stately beige brick building with its guardian mustang above, paid homage both to the hustle and bustle of cosmopolitan Dallas as well as to the Lone Star State's seemingly unlimited supply of fossil fuels and commercial success. The Lamar Hotel dominated the city's landscape by day. At night, it was the mustang's turn to dominate the skyline. The horse and its platform were lit by over one thousand feet of red neon. The image was further highlighted on all four sides by two dozen floodlights, enabling the iconic horse to be seen for miles in any direction. Occasionally, the movement of low-lying clouds would couple with the light of a full moon. This created a lock-step image in which the copper horse appeared to gallop upright and unaided through the east Texas sky. The optical illusion provided even greater muscle to the ever-unfolding mythology of Texas and its stand-alone uniqueness.

*　　*　　*　　*　　*

Inside the hotel, Rita registered. She wrote her name slowly and purposefully. A bald, pug-nosed clerk with a severe outcropping of liver spots peered unabashedly at the hotel's guest. He broke his stare only when she completed her signature and looked up at him. Rita had proudly signed her name as if it meant something, not like the majority of people whose signatures were poor examples of their early school training in cursive.

In diametrical opposition to her life, her signature was neat, controlled and precise. Her letters were of the correct slant and height, while maintaining a stylized and proper relationship between upper case and lower case. No fancy swirls or other sloppy, nonsense cursive for her. Regardless of any situation calling for her signature, each letter and each word from beginning to end would, to the best of her ability, resemble some ideal inscription recorded on master pages somewhere in an unseen, cursive heaven.

"Are y'all expectin' company?" the clerk inquired.

"No," Rita answered curtly, annoyed by the question and aware that both the ugly clerk and the absurdly-dressed bellboy were watching her. "It's my birthday, though," she added, although she had had no intention of revealing such a fact. Now out, what actual difference did it make?

"Congratulations," offered the clerk.

The taxi driver had watched her during the entire ride to the hotel. She knew he had stared at her when she had walked to the entrance of the hotel even though she never cast a backward glance. She remembered the time when her stepfather had begun watching. Then came the time when watching wasn't enough. In all fairness, upon reflection, the watching in and of itself was relatively harmless. Watching, in one form or another, had paid the rent. More than the rent, actually. It was when the watching became doing that all her troubles had begun. The watching, of course, had led to the doing and the doing, was when, one by one, the logs had begun their random and unpredictable journey down the swollen and unforgiving river.

The bellboy ordered the elevator door open with a push of a button. He invited the hotel guest inward with a wave of his hand, and he directed the elevator to the twenty-second floor. As was his habit should the elevator ride take more than a few floors, he broke the uncomfortable silence.

"Goin' to be in Dallas long?" he asked.

"Not really," Rita responded as she turned to face the bellboy. She thought him to be nice looking, and she guessed, innocent. Most men weren't nice looking. Women either, she reflected. The bellboy was tall, had large blue eyes and Rita supposed him to be somewhere near her age. His face was pleasantly sharp and masculine. His body type and facial features would easily meet the requirements for the type of male model she had worked with over the last couple of years. Especially so, if he were well endowed.

"Y'all seem a friendly type. Nice lookin' too. Ridiculous outfit, though. What's your name?" Rita inquired, forcing a hint of a smile.

"Willis. Willis Sturm," he answered weakly. Willis held hope for some kind of inconsequential chat from the good-looking hotel guest but in no way did he expect words evaluating his appearance. Off balance, he turned his gaze to the safety and security of the elevator door.

Glancing at her watch, Rita noted that she was a good thirty-five minutes ahead of her schedule.

"Look at me Willis," she ordered. "That's your name, right? Willis?"

Willis obeyed and turned in Rita's direction. His eyes met hers. He swallowed hard, reaching upward with his right arm to reposition a wayward strand of well-oiled black hair to its proper place.

"I like your eyes," Rita said.

Willis took a half-step backwards, his face still flushed from her earlier observation.

"Whatever brings 'em to be that color?" she asked, recalling a lesson from a high school science class that had something to do with peas or beans or some such and how things like genes get passed on from one something to another and how the mixing and passing on of different or similar genes produced all kinds of results, some good, some bad, some altered forever.

Willis had yet to answer Rita's question when she dropped a verbal bombshell bringing Willis to take an immediate step deeper into the limited space of the hotel elevator.

"Y'all a virgin, Willis?" she asked, as the elevator neared the twenty-second floor.

From his more defensive position, Willis swallowed again. And once more, he reached to reposition the recalcitrant strand of hair.

"We're here at your floor," he answered instead.

"Don't open the door until you answer my question. Are you a virgin, Willis the bellboy? Are you or are you not?"

Willis was dumbfounded. Never, if he lived to be one hundred, did he figure he would be so questioned by a hotel guest or anybody else for that matter.

Trying to gain his composure, Willis nodded in the affirmative. "Well, I...I'm not a virgin, actually," he replied, telling the truth. At the ripe old age of twenty, he had lost his virginity a scant two weeks before.

"OK, you can open the door."

As the two departed the elevator, Willis thought he needed to qualify his admission that he was no longer a virgin. "I have a girlfriend," he blurted into the hallway.

"Well, Mr. Lamar Hotel Milky-Blue-Eyes, goodie for you. Now listen closely to what I'm askin' you. I want you to spend thirty minutes with me in my room...thirty minutes, thirty-one actually," she said, checking her watch. "Can y'all do me that favor?"

"What?" Willis asked incredulously.

"You can't be hard-of-hearin' at your age, now can you? I'll ask you one more time. I want you to spend thirty-one or so minutes with me in my room. Fate has brought us together and I can't explain more than that except to say I need company for the time I asked you for. That's all I'm askin', a little company." Rita gave light to one of her three remaining cigarettes.

Willis noted that Rita's voice had softened, weakened even, and there was noticeably less braggadocio and assertiveness.

Rita inhaled deeply with the realization she was on the verge of losing composure. "Look at me Willis. Willis with the big blue peepers. It's a simple request. What's so Goddamn difficult about keepin' a good payin' customer of this hotel satisfied? That's what y'all are here for, right? Y'all are here to serve, right? Besides, Willis, I've found that tellin' yourself that somethin' is hard is what makes it hard. Tell yourself you can do it, and well, you can do it." To give credence to her words, she blew smoke in Willis' direction.

In an effort to figure out how to properly respond to the hotel guest's outlandish request that he spend time with her in her room, Willis noted how light her small single luggage bag was. Did it hold anything at all? Maybe it held stuff a woman uses when she goes to bed or wears before some kind of lovemaking. Maybe someone is going to meet her for her birthday.

Willis gathered his courage and turned to face Rita directly. They were now at room 2206. Her room. The room she had reserved for one night only. The room in which she had extended a strange and most unusual invitation for him to join her.

"I'll get fired if I go into your room and stay any time beyond just getting you situated," he managed, thinking that would settled the issue.

He waited for Rita to respond. She looked intensely at him. He patiently held her look with the anticipation that she would call off her request.

Framing Rita's straight and well-sculpted nose were two catlike, seductive green eyes. Any light within those eyes, Willis reflected, seemed locked inside by some kind of unrelenting gravitational force. Her lips were full and well-defined. The lower lip, the larger of the two, pursed forward as if in a perpetual, red-accented pout. Willis didn't know much about makeup, or women for that matter, but he figured whatever it was she had done to herself to enhance her looks had been worth the time and whatever cosmetic expense had been worth the effort. Willis figured she would be physically striking with no makeup whatsoever.

He soon abandoned his effort to maintain eye contact with Rita. He looked down and once again began to repeat the defense of his position not to remain in her room.

"Like I say, I greatly appreciate y'all's askin' me to..."

Rita cut him off. "Open the door, Willis," she commanded.

Once the door was opened, she grabbed Willis by an arm and pulled him inside. She then ordered him to shut the door. He found himself standing near the room's light switch. He flipped the switch and a lamp near the bed became illuminated.

With a slow sweep of her head, Rita surveyed the room. It was spacious and well-appointed. Heavy dark curtains draped the room's two side-by-side windows.

"The windows face the street, right?" she asked Willis.

"Yes, they do. Good view of the city from the twenty-second floor."

"Good. Then go and let some light in and open one of the windows."

Willis pulled back the curtains and daylight flooded the room. He began to sweat as he struggled to open the nearest of the two windows. He was already taking too much time getting his guest settled. Any unnecessary lingering beyond the official and undefined efficiency of much more than seeing a guest to his or her room would be held to high scrutiny, up to and including, he feared, being fired.

Rita walked to the dresser mirror. With her makeup expertly applied and her bleached-blond, page-boy hair in perfect hairspray fit, she turned to ask Willis how she looked. Her shirtwaist, green silk dress sported a Peter Pan collar, accented by large ceramic buttons, bearing painted images of birds in flight. She had left the top buttons unsecured, thereby not only revealing cleavage of her ample breasts, but also a visually tantalizing leading-line that first, having followed the uplift of her breasts, spilled downward until they reached a tuck highlighting her waist. The dress's straight skirt, designed as it was with a demure kickpleat, created the illusion that even when in full stride, she wasn't moving at all. Her brown suede pumps, although the season would have suggested otherwise, nicely accented the green dress and trim of her ankles. Willis continued struggling with the hotel window. He wished he could remain in the room with the beautiful, yet hard-talking guest, without negative consequences for doing so. He wished he could go beyond staying in the room. He wished he could touch her, smell her, make love to her; or, given her emboldened ways, perhaps she would make love to him.

Rita didn't acknowledge his comment. Instead, she checked her watch yet another time and then silently returned to her reflection in the mirror. She was, as Willis had observed, very well put together. However, there were those in her world who preferred her naked as the proverbial jaybird as opposed to being dressed and put together. When she was in her disrobed state, the only adornment she wore was her trademark cultured pearl necklace. That, and the dark blotch of a birthmark occupying prime real estate on the fleshy and rounded right cheek of her backside.

"Go ahead and open the window, for God's sake," Rita commanded.

"But the hotel has air-conditionin'. Put it in a couple of years ago."

"Doesn't matter, folks need fresh air. I need fresh air. Is that good enough for you?"

"Of course...I just...the window's hard to open since the trim was last painted, I guess. They went through a complete remodel..."

"I don't give a shit about paint or air-conditionin' or remodelin' or anything else you can think of as an excuse to not open the window. Get the Goddamned window open!"

The reluctant, wooden-encased window finally yielded to Willis's urging, suddenly and harshly jerking upward and open. The room instantly flooded with traffic noise from below.

"All the way open."

"All the way?"

"We already know y'all aren't hard of hearin'. We've been through that already."

Willis obliged. He wondered if he should bother mentioning the air-conditioning again and how to work it or would doing so cause her to begin cursing sailor-like.

"I'll go now. Ice is down the hall to the right and..."

"Sit down, Willis. There. In that chair."

Willis had turned to exit the room. He stopped, looked back at the hotel guest, and reversed direction in compliance with her command. He sat, and immediately began to worry about what might be coming next. He knew he was in some kind of trouble but was unable to fathom what kind, or how much.

Rita sat on the bed and deftly launched a shoe in his direction. The shoe landed at his feet.

Willis noted that her remaining shoe was delicately suspended by a nylon- encased foot and primed for its launch as well. Within seconds, it too, was at his feet. He nervously swallowed and sank ever more deeply into the soft cushioning of the chair.

"Reckon y'all would be good at horseshoes," he managed, despite his emotionally diluted state.

"You play shoes?" Rita questioned.

"I do. Reasonably good, I reckon."

"As good at shoes as you are at makin' love?"

Willis looked to the ceiling then to the open window, and then back to the ceiling. He sought safety in any object that might be neutral and non-threatening.

"Y'all's place or mine?" Rita asked, breaking the silence.

"What?"

"Jesus, Willis-the-Lamar-bellboy. Horseshoes. I'm just making small talk. You must think I'm goin' to jump you or somethin'. Y'all's place or mine...horseshoes for Christ's sakes."

Look, I really have to be goin'. I'm goin' to lose my job... they'll come lookin' for me and..."

Rita held up her hand, palm facing Willis, in a non-verbal order to remain seated. She referenced her watch. She now had only fifteen minutes to wait. Time had passed quickly. The bellboy had been useful.

Willis lapsed into silence, his mind a mix of emotions so tangled he couldn't make sense of anything; the crazy, good-looking guest, what he would do after he was fired, what was yet to befall him, anything. He began to despair, to feel that empty, no-way out-feeling he had felt last year when his mother remarried and within days ordered him out of the house.

"Smoke?" Rita asked, reaching for a cigarette.

"No, thank you."

"I allow myself six a day. Tryin' to cut down. Have actually. Used to smoke a pack a day. Smokin' yellows your teeth, you know. Can't see evidence of it in a black and white photo though. Anyways, tell me about yourself, Willis. What do you have on y'all's plate?"

"Well, like I said, I have a girlfriend," he offered, wishing he hadn't for fear Rita would make some kind of sexual comment in return. "She works over to Neiman Marcus."

"Needless Markup?"

"Yes, she's in lingerie." That, too, was something he thought would have been best left unsaid.

"Do tell. That oughtta be fun. Different panties for each night of the week. But you aren't sayin' anythin' about yourself. How's your life been up to now? A screwed up mess like most folks?"

"I suppose so. I have some good days and some not so good, you know like...well, anyway, my Dad left when I was three and..."

"Men are assholes, 'ceptin' for you, Willis-the-bellboy. Is that the case? Y'all bein' the exception to the rule? Is that right? After all, you did honor my request. That's good, but given enough time, maybe you would fall into line with the rest of the males of this world."

"I try to be..."

"Tryin' don't answer the question. Are you tryin' not to be an asshole or are you tryin' to be an asshole? Anyways, it's time for you to leave, Lamar Hotel-King-of-the-Bellboys. I do thank y'all for visitin' with me. I really do appreciate it and I'm sorry if I scared the shit out of you which I can plainly see I did," she said, blowing smoke in Willis's direction.

Willis quickly rose from the chair. "Well, thank you, too. I'm all right, I just..."

"I know, you need to be goin'. So go. Seems everybody has a schedule to meet one way or another."

Rita watched Willis as he hurriedly left the room, softly closing the door behind him. As he entered the refreshing safety of the hallway, Willis figured if he moved fast enough, and put enough distance between him and room 2206, he could return to the emotional blessing of a less bizarre and confounding world. Later, he thought, perhaps he could make sense of what had just happened. Then, again, maybe not.

Rita rose from the bed and once again faced the mirror. The hotel mirror, she noticed, was in much better condition than the hall mirror back in her apartment.

Chapter 3 - Athwart

Below the stately cedar, Sarah Mae called for her son at the top of her voice but to no avail; the force of the wind swept her anguished plea in the direction of the family's barnyard and beyond, far from the earshot of her son whose senses had obviously abandoned him. She saw that he was near the top of the tree, that he was peering through a branch of the tree, that he held a camera to his face. He and the camera were aimed at what appeared to be an approaching tornado. Of all things that frightened her most, a tornado would rank high among them. Also counted at the top of the list, would be the Devil. Another, the loss of a child. At the moment, she was confronted by all three.

"Mercy Lord, mercy," she muttered to herself as she tried to maintain her balance given the unrelenting force of the wind. From the ground, she figured James Ray was holding the camera J.B. had given her a Christmas or two ago. It was, after all, the family's only camera.

"James Ray!   James Ray, for heaven's sakes...come down! Please come down now!" Sarah Mae shouted. She began to cry.

Trying a new strategy, she took off her apron and waved it wildly back and forth. "James Ray, come down! Come down now! You'll be killed!" she screamed. "Have mercy Lord, please have mercy," she repeated to herself.

The tornado was now in full sight. It appeared to be only a mile or so distant from their street and house and worse, seemed headed in their direction. Her son's brainless act of trying to take a photograph from the top of the cedar convinced her that he had lost what little common sense he had. On an upswing of her apron, the wind snatched it from her grasp and sent it sailing hundreds of feet into a neighbor's yard. Grimacing, she turned and with both hands holding her hair close to her head, she retreated to the rear of the house where there was less wind but where she could still see her son in the tree. She began to silently pray.

"Dear Lord, please don't take my son, James Ray...he's a good boy and he has had enough difficulty already in his young life. Please spare him, Lord." In her one-way conversation with her personal deity, she acknowledged her son had often displayed recklessness, thinking that an honest appraisal of his behavior might in some small way affect the possibility of his safe deliverance.

Too emotionally weak to continue standing, Sarah Mae fell to her knees. She began quoting her favorite Psalm, Psalm 25, the Psalm of David. "...guide me in your truth and teach me, for you are my God and savior and my hope is in you all day long."

Her prayerful thoughts were rudely interrupted when a section of corrugated metal roof was ripped from the barn. Apron-like, it too flew in the neighbor's direction. With great discipline, Sarah Mae entered into a meditative state. The wind ceased to howl and a great calm came over her. She revisited a storm from her childhood when her Native American grandmother, a full-blooded Coushatta, held her safely in her arms while rocking in a cane bottom chair. Her grandmother spoke to her in her native language. Sarah Mae knew not what the words meant but the words were emotionally meaningful, regardless.

Despite Sarah Mae's pubescent age, her grandmother had bundled her with blankets and held her closely, rocking, rocking. Like lost souls, wind whistled from cracks around the weathered door as the frail, wooden-frame, two-room house creaked and groaned from the push of the wind. On a nearby rough-cut oak table, a coal oil lamp cast large and distorted shadows on the walls. While in the security of her grandmother's arms, Sarah Mae felt no harm could come to her.

In the tranquil depths of Sarah Mae's dream state, despite the approaching storm, despite the insanity of her son, the recall of the clipped cadence of her grandmother's unknown but soporific words washed over her, calmed her, and gave her hope.

As the tornado labored ever closer, James Ray was startled to see lightning rip from the center of its rope-like funnel to the earth below. The attendant thunder clap was immediate. Suddenly, he perceived the approaching maelstrom as more of a personal adversary, rather than a collection of visual elements suitable for a documentary black-and-white photo.

The entire sky turned an absorptive black and the wind rose to even greater heights, its velocity pitching a fierce roar through the web of the cedar's branches. James Ray was shocked to see a house taken by the tornado. Now was the time to trip the shutter. Now was the time to capture the storm's rude assault on the town of Mayweather. Having recorded his image, it was also high time to seek shelter from the storm.

Although he had heard nothing of his mother's plea from beneath the cedar, nor had he caught sight of the frantic wave of her apron or anything else other than the approaching storm, James Ray, satisfied he had recorded a documentary photograph of importance, began his difficult descent from his perch in the tree. He had done what he had intended to do. People would note his photographic skill as well as his bravery. He would soon become famous. His career as a photojournalist was launched. He couldn't wait to tell Carl before developing and enlarging his hard-earned image.

As James Ray ran for the house and some semblance of shelter, the tornado, as if sensing it was no longer needed to meet James Ray's subject matter requirement, lifted and altered course. Random chance made the nearby town of Honey Grove the storm's greatest victim in terms of property loss. An article in the *Tribune* claimed seventeen homes were completely destroyed by the tornado, three in Mayweather and fourteen in Honey Grove. Over a hundred homes were damaged to one degree or another. Injured also, was Honey Grove's business district, anemic though it was. Miraculously, no one was killed in either town, although a farmer claimed loss of two cows, a mule and a goat. Many people in Mayweather thanked the Lord for his mercy and divine intervention. A few Mayweather and several Honey Grove residents, their homes torn asunder, seemed exempt from the intervention.

*   *   *   *   *

Randi Trimble, a reedy wisp and a go-getting summer intern for the *Dallas Morning News,* was assigned the story. Since the apparent suicide was the second at the Lamar in four months, her editor thought a person similar in age and sex would be a good investigative fit.

"*Another Death at the Lamar,*" ran the headline, much to the chagrin of the hotel's management. Neither Randi nor her supervisor placed any credence in the circulating rumor that the hotel was jinxed, or under some kind of curse, or that Dallas teenage girls were more likely to jump to their deaths than girls in other big cities. Two female teen suicides were certainly worthy of note and introspection but they were not a trend, not yet anyway. And why would someone commit suicide on one's birthday? Further, despite the initial police report, was it truly a suicide?

Randi's editor figured the girl who jumped from the twenty-second floor was perhaps a copycat and the birthday coincidence could be irrelevant.

The autopsy had revealed that a 116-pound female human life had been terminated by falling from twenty-two floors onto concrete.

"A free fallin' object plus gravity does it every time," the examiner mused.

Unlike the previous death at the Lamar, the victim's body contained neither alcohol nor drugs. Yes, it was another death or suicide or whatever at the same hotel, although initiated from a different floor. Same tragic result.

"Most interestin," the examiner informed Randi, "is the fact the young lady was pregnant. About twelve weeks is my best guess."

Armed with the knowledge that two deaths had occurred rather than one, Randi was more motivated than ever. If she could come up with enough information, perhaps the paper would have a print-worthy piece of investigative journalism. Perhaps not.

Randi gladly accepted the challenge. She figured many lives were askew to one degree or another, and askew or not, the vast majority of people kept on living their lives. After all, the world was chock-full of unhappy people. Her older sister Eileen, was a case in point. And as miserable as Eileen claimed her existence to be, she hadn't jumped out of a high-rise building. Most likely, people who are miserable and depressed, Randi reflected, might think about taking their own lives but few had the gumption or courage to pull it off.

She would need to talk to the bellboy who lost his job over the whole mess. She had been informed that he had been questioned extensively by the Dallas police but no charge had been made. When she left the newspaper building to drive to the suicide victim's former high school--if, in fact, her death was a suicide--the hotel's former bellboy, a Willis Sturm, had yet to return her phone call.

"Hardly knew her," the Plano High School principal said. "Got sent to me once or twice as I remember. Once slapped a boy so hard his nose bled, if I recall correctly. Best to talk to some of her teachers, although as you know they're on summer break."

"Could I have their telephone numbers?"

The principal laughed. "Confidential. Probably out of town or on vacation anyway, like I say."

"Do you have a yearbook when she was a senior? I could try to contact some of her former classmates."

"I believe so. Wait a minute."

After departing high school, Randi decided to drive to the home of Humphrey A. Harlow, a retired chemical salesman believed to be the dead girl's stepfather. It was an hour or so to Sherman. Her effort, so far, had largely been a goose chase. The scenic, wild Texas bluegrass and scrub oak would be a diversion that would give her time to think.

"That there rocker's sturdy enough for me, I reckon it'll hold what little y'all put in it," Rita's stepfather offered. "Sit, go ahead and what do y'all want? I ain't got time fer a bunch of small talk."

"Well, I just wanted to get to know your daughter, what she..."

"Wasn't my daughter. Stepdaughter was it. Dead now anyways, ain't she?"

Randi was taken aback, thinking she might have stumbled into some kind of oppositional interview situation with a person she immediately held to be stupid and uncaring. Why she had said daughter when stepdaughter was called for, she didn't know. Involuntarily, she drew a straight line across her note pad and blinked several times as she fought to maintain the courage necessary to continue the interview she had only just begun. Although one of the most talented interns the paper had hired recently, she was still raw and inexperienced in dealing with people who were uncooperative or worse, just plain mean. She suddenly stood, craned her neck and fiddled with a glass bead on her necklace. Then, she sat again. The frayed and fragile rocking chair voiced its resistance. How it would support the expanse of someone the size of Mr. Harlow without immediate collapse was beyond her.

"I apologize if I misspoke. Look, Mr. Harlow, I have been given a job to do for the *Dallas Morning News*. I have been asked to put together a story, a bio sketch of..."

"What the hellfire is a bio sketch?"

"Biography. A brief summary, if you will, of someone's life. In this case, y'all's stepdaughter Rita."

"Well, then. From where I sit, a bio whatever is a heap different from tryin' to get to know a dead person."

"They're pretty much the same actually," Randi replied, wishing she hadn't. She feared that the calloused and insensitive man might see her as highfalutin' and toss her from the house.

"Be that as it may," he calmly replied and reached for a water glass perched on an end table. The glass contained some kind of amber liquid.

"Looky, I don't know why she did what she did. Don't make sense to me now, didn't then," he said, taking a goodly sip from his water glass. "Y'all can have what she left here when she moved out if that'll be of any use to you. She must not have thought any of it had much worth, I reckon. Suppose she didn't think much of her life either."

"She said nothin' to you? Y'all had no idea what she was thinkin'?"

"None."

"The Dallas Police searched her apartment. They found no note, nothin'. There was no note left in the hotel either. The detective said it's unusual for someone to take his or her life and not leave a note of explanation of some kind. The why of it all."

"Maybe so. I have no knowledge how things like that work. If I rightly recall, her yearbook is in with a box of other stuff, mostly junk, I reckon; but if y'all think that would be of some help, you're welcome to it. The police investigator feller didn't seem interested."

"Thank you. With y'all's permission, I'd like to take whatever you have back to the paper. We'll either mail it back to you or I'll return it personally."

Harlow stood, went into another room and returned carrying a weighty cardboard box. "Here it is. I don't care whether or not you return it. Don't give a God bless either way. Y'all can see I don't have a lot of extra space around here."

Having already looked at Rita's yearbook, Randi quickly located the page displaying her senior portrait.

"She was a very pretty girl," Randi offered, noting Rita's wide smile, perfect hair, and what appeared to be a pearl necklace.

"Indeed she was. Took after her mother. Her mother was a looker, too. A looker until Mother Nature and bad habits went to work on her, anyways."

Harlow walked over to a shelf and retrieved an unframed 5" x 7" black and white photo. It was dusty. Time and high humidity had caused the photo paper to curl into itself. It was Rita's senior portrait, the same photo that had been used for publication in the yearbook. "Y'all can have this also," he said, handing the photo to Randi.

"Thank you. I appreciate that. You're sure you don't want it back?"

"Nope, keep it, toss it, I don't care."

"Could you tell me how to locate her mother?"

"Nope. Ain't got no idea. Pretty much a whore as far as I'm concerned. After she up and left me, she remarried not once but twice. Last name could be anythin' by now. And who Rita's real father is, suppose y'all are goin' to ask me that next, God only knows. Her mother never talked about it and I didn't give a shit. Rita lived with me off and on, then with her mother off and on and so on and then, all of a sudden, she seemed to be doin' well money wise. She mentioned, as I recollect, somethin' about a modelin' job. Went and bought herself a nearly new car, got an apartment, paid me back some money she had borrowed and started dressing all spiffy-like."

Randi took note that Harlow's water glass was nearly empty. That, in combination with his slurred speech, signaled a need for her to stand, conclude the interview, offer thanks, and hightail it back to Dallas. She asked for Harlow's phone number and he reluctantly gave it to her.

"One last question, Mr. Harlow. Did y'all know Rita was pregnant?"

Randi judged her trip to Sherman as reasonably successful. Stupid and calloused though Mr. Harlow was, he had in the end been helpful. He had seemed surprised, shocked even, that Rita was pregnant at the time of her death. And the photo was priceless. A photo such as the one in her yearbook had already been screened for reproduction and wouldn't hold up to another reproduction in the paper. The original photo now in her possession, thanks to Mr. Harlow, would suffice nicely. Hopefully, she thought, the yearbook would be a roadmap connecting her to some of Rita's high school peers. Armed with the photo, the yearbook, and any iota of possible information the box might hold, Randi felt she might be able to flesh out Rita Anne Fields as a person; who she was and more importantly, what drove her to take her own life. Randi was now more convinced than ever, that her death was indeed a suicide.

Chapter 4 - Separate but Equal

"It's where the South begins," J.B. explained to Faith. "if you're drivin' east, that is. Not that that will help you in any particular way with your slave history project. Interestin' place, the town you live in. Northeast Texas. Texas as a whole. Let me put it this way. Indians were here first. They're native to the country. They were here for thousands of years but how they got here is another story. Anyway, about five-hundred years ago, the Spanish came poking around after their so-called discovery of America, explorin' here and there but that's neither here nor there for y'all's assignment. Anyway, they, meanin' the Indians, mostly were hangin' out in the southwest in places like Texas and New Mexico and Arizona and California and elsewhere throughout the United States of course, but for your assignment, we'll focus on Texas and its neighbors. 'Course, those places weren't states like I just called them, they were places the Spaniards wanted to themselves. Although the Indians: the Comanches, the Apaches, the Cheyenne and a bunch more tribes—too many to mention, didn't like the Spaniards acting like they owned the land for a lot of reasons includin' that Indians were there first and anyway, they never thought anyone could actually own the land.

Then, lo and behold, here came the Mexicans after the Spaniards pretty much lost interest and they went about pesterin' the Indians just like the Spaniards had done, but of course, the Indians pestered back all the while the Mexicans, like the Spaniards before them, claimed that they actually owned the land and just when you thought things couldn't get worse, from everywhere you could shake a stick at, here came the white people bringing their colored slaves with 'em. See, we're gettin' close to y'all's assignment. They, the Europeans, were the folks who had settled the eastern part of our nation and when that began to fill up, they marched into Texas which still belonged to Mexico at the time. These people were hunters, trappers, merchant men, church preachers, sodbusters...."

"What's a sodbuster?"

"It's what a farmer was called in the early days. That's what a farmer was called because he busted up the soil in order to plant his crops."

"What does all this have to do with Texas once bein' a nation all to itself and then bein' a Confederate state, all the time keepin' slaves?"

"I'm gettin' to that part."

*   *   *   *   *

If one ignored the ubiquitous "White Only" or "Colored Only" signs in Mayweather or Mayweather County or the rest of Texas or throughout the south for that matter, in almost all the cases, colored people in the early 1950s were considered by the white majority as convivial, although a solemn part of the larger community. A part of the community, that is, as long as colored residents knew their place and knowing it, acquiesced to the strictures of Jim Crow.

In Mayweather, ninety miles northeast of Dallas, nine miles south of the the Red River, and only a two hour drive to Arkansas, crosses weren't burned and stones weren't thrown. The last time a colored person had been hanged in Mayweather was over fifty years removed from the fact; a thing of the past, gone and largely forgotten, at least by the white majority. The town's culture in things social, economic and political, strongly resembled its yesterdays and would mirror virtually the same values and behaviors in its tomorrows and seemingly for all the tomorrows that were destined to follow. Things were especially slow to change, if at all, in colored town. The festering sore of racism, under the yoke of separate but equal, was mostly hidden from view by the opaque undergarment of southern racial norms.

"Most folks in Mayweather," J.B. intoned from his chair at the kitchen table, "are good people but like people most anywhere, they have their opinions when it comes to race." J.B. was speaking mostly to himself as he neatly folded the *Tribune* and placed it on the table, leaving it to appear undisturbed and unread since its arrival toss into the Turman front yard earlier that morning. He was half hoping that Sarah Mae might be inclined to join the conversation. The subject of race had come to his mind since helping Faith with her homework the previous evening. That, and the fact that James Ray was now over at the Johnson's house in colored town hanging out with Sammy, the Johnson's son. The thought also occurred to him at times when he reflected on the racially mixed blood of his wife and children.

Field of View

Sarah Mae didn't answer. She was busy slicing vegetables from their home garden for two chicken pot pies.

"Have any more carrots?" she asked.

"I do. How many do you need?"

"A couple will do." She would hold one pie for the family's consumption at supper that evening. The other she would hold in abeyance and freeze in her new Frigidaire.

J.B. walked outside to the garden, located two carrots, uprooted them, and tossed their leafy green tops into the chicken pen.

"Here, darlin'," he said, offering the carrots to Sarah Mae upon his return. As he did so, he patted her gently on her behind.

"Thank you and keep your hands to yourself."

"You mean the way I didn't used to when we were intent on makin' babies?"

"Hush, J.B. for heaven's sakes! The children might be listenin'."

"Not a child in sight as far as I can see. Girls are in their room, Seth is at the library or so he says, and James Ray is over to Sammy's house."

"Here's the question," he said, returning both to his seat and to the subject of race. "Why is it that someone like Sammy over in colored town, who obviously has some white blood in him from somewhere back in the days when some white-as-cake-frosting slave owner pounced on some black-as-chocolate Negro slave, producin' as a result, a child of mixed race and then, lo and behold, everyone goes and says he's Negro. Why is that?"

"Because he's Negro."

"Not completely so. He's only mostly Negro and some white. So at what point does enough white blood...let's say now the white frostin' is now a majority...take precedence? And how about this? When y'all's grandmother, a full-blood Indian, married a white part-time dirt farmer, part-time preacher and when they had children, y'all's mother bein' the case in point, what is that situation called?"

"Half-breed I suppose," J.B. said, answering his own question. "However, one can only be a half-breed once, right? And why isn't a half colored, half white person called a half-breed instead of a mulatto? Some so-called Negroes are obviously as much white or more white than they are Negro. When does one stop being Negro? That's what I'd like to know. If someone has a drop, a tiny insignificant drop of Negro blood, does that go and make him Negro regardless? So then, if a person is more white than black, when does he get to move out of colored town and take up residence in a house next to ours? Or are they forever damned because of one drop and therefore destined to be marked and subservient 'til he goes toes up? Doesn't make sense to me. Not a whit."

Sarah Mae drew a deep breath. J.B. was off again on one of his philosophical tangents and although she tried hard not to show it, she was sensitive to her mixed-race heritage and even more so for her children. Her second son, she knew, was the largest recipient of all. It was a subject that was little referenced by anyone save J.B., who seemed not to know when to keep his insensitive mouth shut.

"And what about our kids? They've got Indian blood in them, but they are considered white. What about that? How come they aren't considered Indian?"

"J.B., I have news for you," Sarah Mae said, turning to face her husband. "I'm busy tryin' to put food on the table and you are tryin' as hard as y'all can to rile me. Aside from providin' me with two carrots and all the energy that took, you've done nothin' constructive to move things forward here in the kitchen other than go on and on about race and such. It's a subject of which I have no interest."

J.B. voiced an apology and offered Sarah Mae help with her continued preparation. She thanked him, but declined his offer.

He left the kitchen for the bathroom where he intended to put his Gillette single-edge, copper-blade razor to useful purpose. His face well-lathered, he recalled a time when Morris Wickware, perhaps the town's leading racist, should there be such a category, had so annoyed J. B. with his racial comments that he recounted his tirade with Sarah Mae when he returned home.

Upon hearing J.B.'s account of the verbal tiff, she declared that from hence forward, they would identify a decent auto mechanic who had the sense to recognize that "all God's children are created equal."

Although J.B. couldn't have disagreed more with Morris regarding race, he was not looking forward to searching for a new mechanic; and worse, explaining to Morris at some Sunday morning Methodist service why Morris was out and someone else was in.

*   *   *   *   *

"Gapped 'em wrong to begin with," Morris said, putting a spark plug so near J.B's face that J.B. couldn't muster a good focus. Were he able, he figured he wouldn't know a correctly gapped plug from an incorrectly gapped plug even under the scrutiny of a microscope.

"Same, I suspect," Morris continued, "with the points in the distributor. Y'all ought to stick with crunchin' numbers down to the courthouse."

"Probably so...I know I'm no mechanic but I thought at least I might be able to put a little more spring in the old gal's step."

"The way she's runnin' now it's a wonder y'all made it to the shop."

On a bench burdened with a miniature junk heap of old car parts silhouetted by a dingy, fly speckled window, a radio squawked a play-by-play re-creation of a major league baseball game. J.B. turned his attention to the game hoping he wouldn't be in for further car repair criticism from his prejudiced and rub-it-into-your face auto mechanic.

"Hear that?" Morris questioned, looking up from beneath the hood of J.B.'s Oldsmobile.

"What?"

"The Goddamn ball game, Turman. Giants and Dodgers 'er playin' a game called baseball. The score's one to one in the eighth. Guess who has gone and done the scorin' for both teams?"

"I don't rightly have any idea. Wasn't listenin' on the way over."

"Well, Robinson stole home in the third for the Dodgers. In the fifth inning, Mays homered, tyin' the game. See what's happenin' to America's pastime?"

"I guess I don't follow..."

"Shit, Turman. The Goddamn niggers are takin' over, that's what. I'm tellin' you, first Mr. Break-the-Color-Barrier Robinson and then there's Mr. Roy, what's his face, the nigger catcher fer the Dodgers."

"Campanella. Nickname's Campy."

"Who gives a rat's ass what his nickname is? Anyways, look around, for God's sakes, niggers are coming out of the cracks everywhere. Don't know their place anymore."

J.B. remained silent hoping Morris's outburst would soon run its course.

Having worked himself into a good racist lather, however, Morris eased his upper body from beneath the hood of the car, turned to face his tune-up ignorant customer, and began scratching the air with a feeler gauge.

"Mark my words, Turman, baseball has been taken over, or will be over time, by the darkies. Tomorrow, it'll be football or basketball and so on down the line. Imagine a bunch of niggers playin' ice hockey. Now that would be a sight."

"Good Lord, Wickware," J.B. managed, finally deciding he had to put up some kind of defense of a group of people he held to be a beleaguered and mistreated minority. Failure to do so, he figured, would be an abject display of cowardice. J.B. folded both arms across his chest. "No need to get so riled. I don't think the way you do about race and I suppose you know that; but, I don't go and give light to my feelin's unless someone asks, and I don't for the life of me remember askin' you about how you felt about Negroes in sports or anywhere else for that matter. I came in here askin' y'all to tune-up my Olds. I expect to pay a fair price for your rescue but not to have you sermonize me about colored people in baseball. I say give 'em a break. If a Jackie Robinson is good enough to play for the Dodgers in place of a white player, then good for him. Good for the colored race for that matter."

"Now look who's riled," Morris responded, stepping in J.B.'s direction, still armed with the feeler gauge. "Just y'all watch and see. Next thing you'll know, we'll have a colored person for president. And what makes for a nigger lover anyways? I've always wondered."

J.B. felt like he'd been hit with a left hook flush to the jaw, hard and mind-numbing. To his credit, as he tried to craft some kind of response, he felt he had largely stood up to Morris's nonsensical and hateful harangue. He also thought he had scored at least a point noting that Morris had used the term *colored* instead of *nigger*. Still, Morris had just called him *nigger lover*.

"I...you just...let me see if I understand you, Morris. Did y'all just call me a nigger lover?"

"Did no such thing. Just asked y'all what makes for a nigger lover, that's all."

Satisfied he had won the round if not the entire bout, Morris returned to the car's engine compartment leaving J.B. to get off the mat before the count of ten.

In his attempt to cope with the sting of Morris's verbal assault, J.B. stepped toward the safety of the radio broadcast hoping that the non-threatening play-by-play of the baseball game would come to his mental rescue. Standing by the radio, J.B. noticed a copy of the Dallas Morning News on top of a nearby shelf. The Turmans had ended their subscription to the paper a month or so ago due to one of his and Sarah Mae's many attempts to get their financial house in order. His perusal of the paper's front page revealed a picture of the girl who had recently jumped to her death at the Lamar Hotel in Dallas. The girl was pretty, J. B. noted. He was saddened, but pleased, that he could now connect her name with her likeness. Why her death seemed important, J.B. didn't know. Maybe it was because he had two girls; and, as he had repeated many times to parents complaining about changing diapers or some such: you feed them, you clothe them, you put a roof over their heads, you school them, you tuck them in at night, and sooner than you think, they become teenagers.

*   *   *   *   *

Sarah Mae had learned of the girl's death at Bible study and she used the girl's fate to lecture all four of her children for a half hour or so about the sanctity of life. The lecture had been delivered at supper time. Sarah Mae, J. B. recalled, had conducted a value-of-life session so disciplined and controlled that even a squirming James Ray was unable to leave his seat at the table.

After church the following Sunday, J.B. had wrung the neck of a young hen. After all the blood, the plucking, the boiling, the dismemberment, the frying and the carnivorous consumption, Sarah Mae rounded up all four children and drove them to Mayweather cemetery for a continuation of her sanctity of life lesson. There, she prayed for her little Charity who never saw the light of day, let alone felt the warmth and security of her mother's breast. She prayed also for the girl who died in Dallas.

"...and dear Lord Jesus, we pray for the dead girl's soul, and we..."

"Rita Fields," Seth offered. "That's what the paper said."

"You interruped my prayer."

"Sorry, but that's her name."

"It would be nice if you were more meditative."

"I wonder how many girls are out there with the name of Rita and how many of 'em have taken their own lives?" Seth questioned. "She may be the only one."

"You sound like your father," Sarah Mae replied. "Count your chickens, record the transactions, ponder the likelihood."

Sarah Mae returned to her lecture. James Ray was only half listening. He found the cemetery stimulating, ripe with visual elements, a challenging feast of photographic subject matter. He had saved almost enough money to buy a decent camera. He knew he couldn't afford a camera like the Graflex Carl used at the paper, but whatever he bought, it would be head and shoulders better than the family Sears Tower.

The deceased girl's picture and the article's text were located on a bottom right column of the newspaper. J.B. had learned that the girl's death had been officially ruled a suicide and that she was with child at the time of her death. Seeing that Morris was still busy under the hood, J.B. separated the front section from its remaining parts, casually walked over to the Olds, and tossed the confiscated portion of the paper through the open passenger side window into the back seat.

Wickware would charge him enough for the tune-up and in doing so, J.B. rationalized that his adept, but racist mechanic could spare a few pages of a newspaper that was three days old.

As J.B. wrote a check to Wickware Auto Repair, Morris began cleaning his hands of engine grease.

"One thing's for sure, J.B.," Morris intoned, "although they might take over the game of baseball, the coons ain't gonna go and break Cobb's record for stolen bases, or Ruth's home-run record, single season or career. Mark my words, Turman. Mark my very words."

J. B. elected not to respond, instead he thanked Morris for his effort, entered his smoothly idling Oldsmobile and drove in the direction of home. On the way, he tried to get into Morris's mind. What drove him to such racial dislike and hatred?   He thought maybe it was the fact that even though few Negroes had found their way into the major leagues, the few that had had possessed skill equal to or superior to that of white players. Why would Willie Mays be on the field if some manager or owner didn't feel he was talented enough to be there in the first place? So, J.B. reasoned, that very fact would run contrary to Morris's belief that Negroes were inferior to whites. In the grind and grunt of Morris's dim and feeble mind, he held expectations for a kind of reality that was at odds with the change he was witnessing.

In a way, however, J.B. figured Morris was right. Things were bound to change, although nothing much seemed to change in Mayweather other than the seasons. One could bet against change in Mayweather and win every time. And should change be on some kind of social or political horizon, what would be wrong with that? It wasn't like America was going to be occupied by Imperial Japan or Nazi Germany. That had been settled. And if Negroes were at some point in the future going to play a larger and thusly more important role in American society, then good for them.

Immediately after leaving the shop, J.B. noticed the renewed vigor of his '38 Oldsmobile. "Fellow has talent, you have to give him that," he said as much to his Olds as to himself. J. B. patted the dash of his Olds. *Sorry, old-timer, y'all have been a good and reliable friend but I'm going to replace you some day. Got my mind on something bigger and stronger. A car with colors more in keepin' with the fifties. Sorry, my friend. Sorry.*

As he eased his faithful but aging car onto the crunch of the family's gravel driveway, J.B. smiled, imagining a day when the Johnsons and the Turmans might even live on the same block, drink out of the same water fountain, and even sit together while breaking bread at Linde Bee's Cafe. And if such a day did ever come to pass, a certain racist auto mechanic, should he too be alive at such a time, would have been brought along kicking and screaming the entire way.

Chapter 5 - Perplexed

Carl Malone was an enigma, J.B. thought. Sure, he was a mentor to his youngest son, James Ray. He was thankful for that, and James Ray seemed buoyed by his part-time job and Mr. Malone's tutoring at the *Tribune*. After all, James Ray's day was lengthy and hard. He needed all the help that might come his way. When school was in session, basketball practice was held at 5:30 a.m. sharp. No tardiness, no absences were tolerated. His Mayweather Warrior morning basketball coach was the afternoon's football coach as well, performing both jobs in tandem or independently, depending on the ebb and flow of the athletic nature of the season. Then, after a full day of school, James Ray reported to the *Tribune* for three hours as darkroom assistant, then home to supper, homework, and finally, bed.

James Ray was beyond thankful for summer vacation. He had time to think, to experiment with all things photographic, to spend time with Sammy, and to enjoy the youthful uplifting that leisure time spent at Devil's Lake State Park provided. There was no admission fee to the park and, best of all, no adult direction. There was nothing but the water, the junipers, the hackberries, the jukebox, the foxtrotting with a seemingly endless number of girls. Most of the teenagers who gathered at the lake were from Mayweather but some came from other county outposts. The locations were small in the grand sweep of Mayweather County. Small and inconsequential. They were places he had never visited. Places like Telephone, Bug Tussle, Monkstown, Ivanhoe and Wolf City.

What troubled J.B. most was what he judged to be an overt display of material well being by James Ray's mentor. He and Sarah Mae struggled to make ends meet, drove an aged car, and charged their groceries at Piggly Wiggly. They also possessed a mortgage they had a difficult time honoring on the first of each month. Carl, though, drove around town in a brand-spanking-new, canary yellow 1952 Cadillac.

J.B. was good at a lot of things, but he was at his very best when making things add up. He believed that things, numbers, situations, people, and relationships were all subject to analysis and could be broken down into root causes and summations. What didn't make any sense whatsoever to him was how a newspaper photographer, no degree required, who earned a modest newspaper salary, could parade around the square in a new model Cadillac.

"I'm tellin' you Sarah Mae, it just doesn't fit. I don't see how it's possible."

"Maybe the Malone fellow has inherited money or somethin'," Sarah Mae replied.

"Possible, but not likely. Possible, but not probable. A fellow could be struck by lightnin' because it's possible, but the odds are against it. It's not probable. I could be run over by a Mack truck tomorrow afternoon walkin' home from the courthouse. Again, it's possible, but not probable. Understand what I'm sayin'?"

"Well, he's nice to James Ray and that's good enough for me. James Ray has a hard time focusin' and my observation is that he is more motivated right now than he has been at any other time other than when it's basketball season. Are y'all lookin' to go out and buy a new car? A Cadillac maybe? We'd better talk about that, if that's what you're thinkin'."

"Of course not. I'm just tryin' to make sense out of a situation that doesn't seem right to me, that's all. He's a Yankee, too. What in the fool tarnation would bring a forty-year-old man, or however old he is, from some back east big city to Mayweather of all places?"

"Well, I do declare," Sarah Mae shot back. "Y'all go on and on about the stupid Wickware fellow and his prejudiced nonsense and then you go and have hard feelings for Mr. Malone because he's from north of the Mason-Dixon line."

J.B. shrugged his shoulders, choosing not to respond. Years of experience told him that engaging in a verbal battle with Sarah Mae was a losing endeavor. Instead, he picked up a *Time* magazine with an article featuring Dwight D. Eisenhower, a retired general, a Republican, and the party's choice for the next President of the United States. He wondered if the country could wean itself from two decades of Democratic leadership. And once weaned, what would the new status quo look like? Maybe Jim Crow would be out and improved race relations would be in? That would be good but he couldn't imagine himself voting Republican. He loved presidential elections. The upcoming contest would make for some good verbal sparring, regardless of who was elected.

Sarah Mae saw that she might lose J.B. to the magazine, so she reintroduced the topic of the suicide in Dallas.

"Speakin' of a situation that doesn't seem right, that girl who jumped to her death at the hotel in Dallas...why would she go and do such a thing? What was so wrong in her life that she would, of her own volition, end it? Now that's a question more worthy of discussion than what kind of a car Mr. Malone drives around town or where he comes from."

"I don't know," J.B. replied, putting down his magazine. "In all honesty it bothers me too. Two suicides in the space of a few months seems improbable to me as well. Who knows? The article said she was troubled and had a hard upbringin'. And it wasn't just her who lost her life. The autopsy revealed she was pregnant. I told you that, remember? Goin' on three or four months. She left no note. How will we ever know?"

It was now time for Sarah Mae to remain silent. After praying silently for the girl and her baby, she took up another subject, one that had caused tension between the two but one that had to be addressed nonetheless.

"And since we have a moment to ourselves, when are y'all goin' to begin on the storm shelter?" Sarah Mae asked. "It's been a week since the tornado and I don't see an ounce of progress yet. Y'all are goin' to build one aren't you, J.B.? Build one before the next tornado, right? The Lord only knows when he'll send another our way. Could be several at once for all I know and then where will we be? It's the old stitch in time thing."

"'Stitch in time may save nine,' but it'll take a toll on our pocketbook."

"Or," Sarah Mae added, ignoring J.B.'s retort, "the old sayin' about fixin' the leaking roof when the sun is shinin', not waitin' for the rain to fall."

"I don't think the Lord goes about decidin' when and where to send a tornado, Sarah Mae. Got far more important things to do than bothering with the affairs of us mere earthly mortals at all. Maybe he's not there in the first place."

"Don't start with y'all's agnostic talk. I don't want to hear it and I won't stand for it."

J.B. reached for his *Time* once again. It seemed that corruption in the Truman administration was being used to hammer Adlai Stevenson, the Democratic nominee.

"Show me a government that isn't." J.B. said aloud.

"What?" responded Sarah Mae.

*   *   *   *   *

Field of View

The darkroom was his sanctuary, his place of worship. James Ray loved the smell and mystery of darkroom chemicals. He didn't mind the redundancy of mixing the developer, the stop-bath and the fixer. Further, he didn't mind the cleanup. That was a small price for the joy of witnessing latent photographic images as they were coached into abstract black and white two-dimensional forms. That transformation, that chemical rendering of the unseen to the observable, was what he loved most. The totality of the darkroom, combined with the red hue of its safelight, was a transformative and spiritual experience.

Under the harsh light of an incandescent bulb, the darkroom was ordinary and lacking in visual stimulation. It was nothing more than a twelve-by-twelve four-wall room. There were shelves containing photo paper and bottles of unmixed chemicals, a bench to hold trays used in the developing process, an enlarger, a drum dryer for enlargements and a wall-to-wall string of wire purposed with air-drying negatives. However, when lit by the safelight the darkroom instantly became another world, a world so exciting and new that James Ray thought he had had the good fortune to stumble across an earthly nirvana.

"I can't seem to get it sharp as I'd like," James Ray complained to Carl. Carl looked up from touching up an enlargement to be used in visual support of an editorial plea for renovation and subsequent county use of an abandoned WWII air base facility north of town.

"Y'all's tornado picture?"

"Yes, I've tried to enlarge it twice now and..."

"Let's see the enlargement. You're right. It isn't completely sharp. You made sure you had tight focus when you were enlarging?"

"Yes."

"Let's see the negative."

James Ray carefully removed the negative from the enlarger and handed it to Carl. Using a hand held magnifier, Carl studied the grain of the negative. "Try a 5x7 and see what happens. It's likely to stay sharper with less enlargement. Looks to me though, the problem is more camera shake than being out of focus. Hard to have a fixed focus camera like yours be out of focus. Most likely when you released the shutter, what with the wind and sway of the tree and all, the bugaboo of camera shake has bitten you on your teenage ass."

Field of View

Despite the disappointment of the image not being sharp to James Ray's satisfaction, or Carl's for that matter, Carl was complimentary of the way the photo was composed.

"Good placement of the center of interest. Tornado's got some go-room. I see the rule-of-thirds, too. Your horizon is off, though. Appears to me like the town of Mayweather has lost its balance, tilting like a ship at sea."

James Ray corrected for the photo's poorly rendered horizon by adjusting the easel and enlarging his image to a 5x7 only. His work day had come to an end. He wished he could stay, but supper would be waiting. He cleaned up, said goodbye, and offered thanks to Carl. As he walked the seven block distance to his house, he gave more attention to his documentary photo than he did to where he was stepping.

"Fuck you, Turman!" a voice shouted out from the window of a decrepit and paint-peeled four-door Dodge.

James Ray jerked his head in the direction of the passing car. The voice belonged to Rusty Wickware, Morris Wickware's bully of a son. Why Rusty had taken such a sordid dislike to him, James Ray had little idea. He could think of no words he had spoken, nor actions taken that would bring Rusty to harass him so. Maybe it was because Rusty was cut from the basketball team and he, James Ray, was the team's starting point guard. Maybe it was because of his polio tainted right leg that was a half-inch or so shorter than his left, leaving him with a slight, but noticeable limp. Although he had survived the affliction of polio largely unscathed, the limp was a lingering reminder. Maybe it was because of his colored friend, Sammy.

As one might imagine, Rusty, known since his elementary years for his threats and means of intimidation, was also well-schooled in the art of prejudice. Having been served heaping plates full of racial prejudice, Rusty more than lived up to the expectations his father had set for racial superiority. His mother, as well. Racial discourse in the Wickware home was a common and seething pablum of dislike for anyone with dark skin or a different kind of dress or a strange manner of speaking. Anyone or anything that deviated from their definition of what was and was not acceptable, was not only open to criticism but in most cases, subject to the piggyback of demonization.

Rusty's reputation had grown over time. It was reinforced when and where a situation opportunistically presented itself. He was pleased that in most cases, he didn't have to create one, they just seemed, as if by luck, to materialize.

His best and most creative intimidation, sans the gift of opportunity, was one he proudly created all by himself. It was back when the two boys were in the fifth grade. It was recess, and it was James Ray's turn to pitch in a softball game. Rusty, who had struck out at his last turn at bat, decided to lay flat on the ground between James Ray, the pitcher, and George Lightfoot, the batter. Should a ball hit him while prone in front of the batter, Rusty had the option of either going after the batter or the pitcher, depending on who was the perpetrator. James Ray's first pitch was short and landed smack on Rusty's backside. Had Mrs. Poundstone not been on playground duty, James Ray would have gone home after school much the worse for wear.

As Rusty and his gang drove to Devil's Lake, the group continued yelling obscenities from the car's open windows. They cursed anything that moved and some things that didn't. The Jax beer the boys were consuming in behavior-altering abundance, had run out and no more was to be found in the town of Mayweather or its general vicinity due to what was referred to as *local option*. At each election, Mayweather citizens were afforded the option of voting up or down the sale of alcohol and each time the measure was on the ballot, the measure fell miserably short. Given the town of Mayweather's religiously-rooted, anti-alcohol intransigence, a person with a desire and thirst for anything alcoholic was forced to drive across the Red River to Oklahoma or to Dallas or eighteen miles to the town of Leonard. Leonard was in Mayweather County but in the view of some, it was a far more enlightened place, if not to live, at least to wet one's whistle. Or, one could always develop a friendly relationship with a bootlegger. Several Mayweather residents supplemented their day jobs with just such enterprises.

As recent testimony to Rusty's claim to be someone to be avoided at all costs, he had removed the front teeth of a farm boy who was in town for a bit of weekend socializing. The fifteen-year-old boy, Artis Tillman, although a strapping and fit youngster, severely overestimated his muscular prowess when he took on Rusty. Tossing bales of hay into the back of a pickup and slopping hogs were different kinds of activities when compared to a bare-knuckle fight with someone as crafty and experienced as Rusty.

Artis not only found himself minus two of his front teeth, he had to be treated for a ruptured groin as well. Rusty fought with what was available and his feet and legs were as readily available as his fists.

The reason for the rumble in front of Nicely's Drug was quickly retold. In the retelling, Rusty's myth of invincibility grew faster than a plot of chicken manure-nurtured vegetables. Artis made the unforgivable mistake of flirting with a girl that Rusty had conveniently and arbitrarily decided belonged to him. His second equally unforgivable mistake, was his decision to take his comb to his hair while seated in a booth having a cherry Coke with Reba Bottoms, a sophomore cheerleader at Mayweather High. It was an opening wide enough for Rusty to have driven his Dodge through.

"It's plain rude to comb y'all's hair where food is served," Rusty said, deftly snatching the comb from Artis's hand. "Want y'all's comb back? Come outside and get it." Shoving the comb in question into the right rear pocket of his Wrangler jeans, Rusty turned and left through the front door of the drug store.

Rusty didn't have to wait long. He was soon joined by one angry and red-faced farm boy. Without saying a word, Rusty smiled as he retrieved the comb from his jeans pocket with his right hand, and offered it to Artis. As Artis glanced down at the comb, his mind an emotional thicket, Rusty hit him square in the mouth with his left fist. Artis stumbled and fell backwards, stopping only when he met the drug store's quarried stone foundation. Wounded but enraged, Artis charged Rusty, only to be met with a kick to the groin. Artis fell to the cement walkway in more pain that he had ever felt in his life. More than when he had broken his ankle jumping from an apple tree and more than when he had severed the tip of his pinkie finger while using his mother's butcher knife to whittle a sling-shot from a forked branch of an ash tree. The fight was over in less than thirty seconds. Victorious yet another time, Rusty left to round up some of his cohorts. He couldn't wait to share the good news.

"Should I call the sheriff?" Reba inquired.

"No," Artis answered, wiping blood from his mouth with his handkerchief. "Too late for that, I reckon. Should have had the sheriff around from the start of it. Y'all could do me a favor, though."

"Sure, what is it?"

"My folks are parked on the north side...of the square. It's a black Ford truck. If they ain't in the truck doin' their people watchin'...I don't know, they might be in Spivy's or Penneys somewhere. I don't know. I'm hurtin' pretty bad. I think somethin's wrong 'cause I can't get up...please, I do...I do need y'all's help. Tillman is my folks' names. Joyce and Artis. And...and thank y'all for helpin' me. Sorry...sorry about how everythin' turned out. I'm sorry."

Chapter 6 - Help Wanted

It was two o'clock in the afternoon when thirty-four year old Judith Marie Chambers asked the operator to connect her to the *Daily Tribune*. She could wait no longer.

Damned dry town, she reflected, knowing not to make such a judgment out loud for fear of being overheard by the operator. Maureen Sumwalt, Mayweather's only full-time operator was a nosy, nuisance of a woman who was famous for remaining on the line well past the point of a decent disconnect. Although Judith had yet to hear of spinster Sumwalt's reputation, she knew the possibility existed and was duly cautious.

As she waited for someone to answer her call, the long, perfectly manicured red nails of her right hand drummed impatiently on the thick, beveled glass top of an end table. Reaching for a cigarette, the drumming ceased. Once lit, Judith inhaled deeply and then launched a fine example of a smoke ring into the interior of the Chambers' living room.

"Tribune," answered a female voice, barely audible above the clamor of a nearby printing press.

"Yes," Judith replied, pausing for the audible click of the operator's disconnect. "May I speak with Carl Malone?"

"Sorry. Say again."

"Carl Malone."

"Oh, him. Hang on, he's probably in the darkroom and if he is I can't...he won't open the door. I'll go see if I can find him," the voice replied in obvious irritation. The phone was set down harshly.

"Well, excuse me," Judith said into the voiceless, staccato sound of machinery tasked with meeting yet another endless number of drop-dead deadlines.

As she waited, Judith commenced drumming once again. For as long as she could remember, she had coped with being a kind of male magnet. In first grade, a boy had drawn a crude representation of her bottom and signed his creativity with a heart. Maturing early, she leap-frogged past puberty, becoming a woman almost overnight. Judith Marie Chambers was taller, more shapely and more attractive than her peers and thus she found herself in a position where she was forced to play defense, to learn to avoid eye contact, to walk in the opposite direction, to say no repeatedly. In school, boys fixated on her aspects, in the singular and in the totality: her breasts, her legs, the fullness of her lips, the flip and curl of her hair, her expansive hazel eyes.

At a church outing, Arnold Higgenbotham had the good fortune to have taken a picture of Judith in her bathing suit. He used the photo for self-gratification as often as the mail got delivered. Another boy, Jimmy Brown, was far more fortunate. For reasons Judith herself couldn't explain, Jimmy was able to break through her sixteen-year-old wall of defense. He found himself with the precious and irrevocable gift of being given permission to touch her breasts for a brief moment. No more than a few days later, Jimmy had parlayed his and Judith's petting into full-blown sexual conquest of epic proportion. In a vivid but completely untruthful recount of their one night of sexual exploration, with Jimmy doing all the exploring, he had the two making torrid love in a wood shed, on a tractor seat and even at home on her family's couch with her parents in and out of the kitchen oblivious to their sexual mischief. Although Judith was still a virgin in good standing, Jimmy's titillating re-creation of his encounter with her, outright fabrication though it was, made for a reputation she didn't deserve. Over time, Judith became aware of Jimmy's colossal truth-stretching. One day she found him bent over the school's water fountain. Approaching him from the rear, she scratched the back of his neck so severely that blood wicked through the back of his shirt collar.

Judith had been in Mayweather no longer than a week when word of her arrival was all over town. A trip or two to the post office and a visit to the hardware store to purchase a light switch cover was all it took. Given her presence anywhere in town, heads turned, both male and female. In her wake, conversations were a spicy mix of admiration, lust or jealousy, depending on who was doing the talking.

The phone at the *Tribune* remained off the hook. The woman who said she would look for Carl had not returned. Judith had waited for over five minutes, hearing nothing but the clatter and clang of machinery, no impatient female voice, no Carl Malone. Disgusted, Judith slammed her receiver into its cradle, snuffed out what remained of her cigarette, and lit another.

*   *   *   *   *

"Y'all diggin' to China, J.B.?" asked Elsie Cornforth, the Turman's neighbor.

"Reckon so, Elsie. Once I get there we'll have some fortune cookies. Maybe I'll visit a little with Confucius if he has the time."

"Y'all do have the best sense of humor, J. B. but I expect y'all have somethin' else in mind diggin' the way y'all are along with the help of y'all's two boys. Mornin', boys."

Seth ignored her greeting. Instead, he launched a shovel full of dirt in Elsie's direction, causing her to take a step backwards. Neither of the Turman boys were pleased to be asked to remove several tons or so of dirt so their daddy could begin framing a storm shelter for their mother. Although the three had been at their digging for less than two hours, their progress had been considerable. The black loamy richness of soil in and around Mayweather made for easy removal and also for successful cotton farming and backyard vegetable growing.

James Ray looked up at Elsie and in doing so, noticed she was silhouetted by the morning sun. Just as Carl had said, back lit as she was, there were no revealing details to her person as she stood by the excavation site. He marveled at the imagery devoid of anything other than the shape of her cane, the shape of her hat, the shape of her spindly legs and the shape of her aged and bent body. Carl was right. James Ray, without any other supportive visual information, would know that shape anywhere.

When Elsie had approached the work site, Seth and James Ray were shoveling at a depth of some three feet. J. B. was at ground level, moving the soil the boys had removed farther from the excavation site. The soil was destined to be transferred a final time to the shelter's top. Once the shelter was complete and roofed, the mass of its rounded, soil laden dome would signal to anyone familiar with such construction, that it was an upstanding, albeit new, member of the storm shelter fraternity.

"Shape outlines the subject, makes it recognizable," Carl lectured. *"Got to be backlit. Your source of light comes from behind the subject, not from the front or the side. Underexposing helps silhouette the image also. We'll talk about shutter speed and aperture settings another time. Anyway, a backlit wintering tree is recognized by way of its trunk and extended branches. You don't need anything else, like the color and texture of the tree's bark or the color of its leaves, whatever. Its shape is the important thing, in and of itself. In a silhouette, a tall ship, you*

know, the kind most people think of as a pirate ship, is recognized not by its detail but by the uniqueness of its shape. Same thing with form. Form occupies space and by occupying space, the subject is seen as real by the viewer. A rock is a rock. A cup a cup and so on. A woman's form is different, hopefully, than a man's form and you, sex-starved teenager, would recognize the difference between a female form and a male form a mile away. Right? Now go and combine a female's shape and form together and you'll have some delicious and satisfying work cut out for you. Adam had some rib didn't he? Some rib indeed."

Throwing another shovel of soil up and to the side of the shelter's boundary, marked by a footprint, James Ray again referenced Elsie's trademark straw hat with a feathered plume of some sort. The silly hat added interesting visual information despite the lack of any detail.

So that's how it's done, James Ray thought. *Select your subject, your center-of-interest, and just like Carl says, have the light source located behind the subject, not from the front or from the side. That way, the image's shape becomes the most important visual element. It's the information the photographer intends to reveal, nothing more. Details like color, or things that reveal texture like the softness or hardness or the rivers of wrinkles on Elsie's face are missin'.* James Ray figured he could now take a silhouette on purpose, not by accident. He was so pleased with his revelation, that he saw his busybody neighbor in a new light, both literally and figuratively.

Elsie Cornforth was the Turman's neighbor on the east side. The south and west sides were free of neighbors because the Turman house was on a corner parcel. The north side neighbor was an elderly and ailing bachelor who, in his working life, had been a policeman, a jailer, a bailiff, and after retirement, developed a reputation for being one of the town's most consistent and noisy drunks. A mere two years ago, he accidentally set fire to his house, almost causing a conflagration of epic proportion. Now, well into his seventies and suffering from liver failure, he had become well acquainted with the inside as well as the outside of a jail cell.

From his perspective, J.B. noted that Elsie had her very toes on the invisible line separating her property from the Turman's. How she was able to identify such a demarcation interested him as he wiped perspiration from his forehead. Was it on accident or by purpose? If by purpose, J.B. reasoned he and the boys were in for a long morning. She was on her property, they on theirs. If she chose, she could stand there all day observing, questioning, and commenting like an announcer at an athletic event of some kind. Turning back to his work, J. B. recalled that no resident, regardless of economic status, had the backbone to fence off his or her property from another's. That would be surefire testimony that the property owner was harboring dark and lurid secrets.

Around mid-morning, Sarah Mae brought out some sweet tea and passed it around. Thankfully, Elsie had long ago retreated to the shade of her front porch swing. She was happily joined by her tail wagging, scruffy, mixed terrier. J.B. took advantage of the break in shoveling to mention a family who had just moved to town.

"New family's in town. Chambers is the name. Just moved in a week ago from Fort Worth into the old Wainwright house. The brick one on East Fifth. The one with the two giant magnolias. The one with the trees that are liftin' up the sidewalk. Know that one Sarah Mae? Three houses down from..."

"Yes, I do. Now get on with it. What's the family like? How many children do they have and what does he do? What does the wife do? Are they churchgoers? Hope they aren't Catholic."

"Well, what if they are Catholic? Are we goin' to send them back to Fort Worth?"

"Of course not. It's just that there are no Catholic churches in Mayweather. Have y'all noticed that J.B?"

In an effort not to be derailed, J.B. returned to his accounting of Mayweather's newest residents.

"As I was sayin', Bud, he's the head of the house..."

"So the wife, whatever her name is, she doesn't have a say in who runs the house?"

"For God's sakes, Sarah Mae, may I finish without an interruption?"

"Forge ahead. Get on with it, appears to me y'all still have a lot of diggin' ahead of you."

"All right. The father, Bud is his name, like I said. He's the new manager of Reliant Pump. The wife is a homemaker, I suppose. Don't rightly know about church. One daughter only and she, I'm told, will be a junior next year at the high school. It's said she's a swimmer. A sprinter. Swims the 1500 meters or some such. Good enough for a college scholarship. So, looks like she's college bound. Where, I have no idea. Either one of you boys have any interest in makin' her feel welcome? Her name's Ruth Ann. Good lookin' I'm told. Any interest? Any at all?"

As both Seth and James Ray tried to fashion an answer to their daddy's question, Elsie, having spied Sarah Mae, left her swing and ambled over to greet her. Once her toe was planted squarely on the line dividing the two properties, J.B. thought she may as well have been toeing the 38th Parallel separating the two Koreas. Elsie offered a good afternoon and immediately pulled the trigger on her questioning.

"Now, Sarah Mae, tell the Gospel truth. Y'all's husband J.B., claims he and the boys aren't diggin' to China but are actually buildin' y'all a storm shelter. Is that so?"

"It's the gospel, Elsie. Want some iced tea?"

"No, thank you kindly."

"Truth is, Elsie," J.B. interjected. "Sarah Mae and I pretty much had a knock-down-and drag-out over whether to build or not build a storm shelter. Guess who did the knockdown and draggin'? Can y'all suppose who won the argument? Pay no never mind to the evidence in front of you, Elsie: the shovels, the hole, the stakes and twine markin' what might just be the exterior dimensions of a storm shelter and all. Now, be cautious though with y'all's answer. Just because the boys and I are diggin' like there is no tomorrow, don't go and take that or anythin' else as evidence a storm shelter is under construction. Could be we're headed for China after all."

"You go on so, J.B., that's why I asked Sarah Mae for the truth."

"J.B., I have no idea what to do with you," Sarah Mae said, hands on her hips, eyes in an intimidating squint aimed sharply at her husband. She knew Elsie. Whether a tidbit of gossip was the truth or something faintly resembling the truth or something without a particle of truth, it would be all over town by noon on the following day.

Chapter 7 - Of One's Own Choosing

"Would you like a ride home?" Carl inquired of James Ray. "You haven't ridden in my Caddy yet have you?"

"It's only a few blocks to home, but yes, thank you very much. I'd like to ride in it. Best lookin' car I've ever seen."

"None finer," Carl said, as the two walked to the rear door of the *Tribune*. Carl's car was parked, as always, in an angled and strategic position that occupied two parking spaces instead of one. This was so no one could inadvertently open one's car door and place an unwelcome and unsightly ding on the Cadillac's exterior sheet metal.

"You have your license yet?" Carl asked.

"I do. Got it when I was fourteen."

"Fourteen?"

"There's a law in Texas that says--I think it's because farmers need their sons to help with drivin' pickups loaded with hay or drivin' tractors and such--that kids can go and get driver's licenses when they are fourteen."

"Beats all. Too young if you ask me."

Carl's 1952 Cadillac was a remarkable piece of transportation. In both style and substance the car far transcended the usual and mundane utility of merely getting from one place to another. In 1949, when General Motors introduced its first major postwar automobile redesigns, both Cadillac and Oldsmobile were anointed with new, high performance, overhead valve, V-8 engines, coupled with an updated and efficient automatic transmission marketed as Hydramatic.

No production car in America could compete with the exhilarating acceleration of either car. In Carl's case, he cared less about speed than he did about the joy of wind in his hair, the luxurious look and feel of leather upholstery, the artful adornment wrought by the car's distinctive rear fins and of course, its honored and respected marque, Cadillac. Cadillac had gone head-to-competitive-head with Lincoln, Imperial, Packard, and other historical marques. Cadillac had not only survived, but had become a significant part of America's automobile lexicon. Cadillac was even more than that; the car's name existed as a metaphor for all things desirous and prized. All those things contributed to Carl's self-image as successful employee and businessman. The car's beauty and cachet also presented increased opportunity when he went trolling for opposite sex companionship.

"Ever been a hundred miles an hour?" Carl asked, blowing smoke in James Ray's direction.

"No, actually I haven't. My daddy's car is slow as a snail. Wouldn't go a hundred if you pushed it off a cliff."

"Let's do it then. There's a stretch on the way to the Red River. Might even hit a hundred and ten if some farmer isn't ploddin' along on a tractor. I'll drop you off at your house after we go for a spin."

Seated in Carl's Cadillac, James Ray thought he was in a kind of car heaven on earth. However, heaven could wait. He was pleased with his life at the moment. Good things had come his way. His tornado photo had been published by the *Tribune* along with their giving him personal credit for documenting the storm's mayhem. The high school yearbook editor, Francine Perkins, had called requesting permission to use it in the school's 1953 yearbook. The fact that the *Dallas Morning News* hadn't seen fit to publish the photo made little difference to James Ray given his breakthrough at the *Tribune*.

Another thing that added to his sense of happiness was the fact that his parents had ceased quarreling due to the progress of the storm shelter. In addition, his brother Seth was scheduled to move out since he had registered as a freshman at Texas Tech in Lubbock. That good news meant that James Ray would have a room all to himself for the first time in his life. Most rewarding of all were his new love of photography, his job at the newspaper and the fact he had purchased his first camera, an Argus C3! Carl had recommended the range finder camera since it was relatively inexpensive and had a reputation for rugged reliability. The Argus had been in production since 1939 and, given its popularity and ease of use, had virtually pioneered the 35mm format. Carl figured it would be a good beginning camera for James Ray.

"A photojournalist in World War II used an Argus," Carl shared. *"Developed his images in helmets he borrowed from soldiers. Given its similar shape and size, one day a soldier called it a 'brick' of a camera. The nickname caught on. The 'brick.' Now you own one. Treat it with the respect it deserves and congratulations."*

The other thing for which James Ray could give thanks was the fact that the Chambers invitation to supper was over. Neither he nor Seth had looked forward to the shared meal with another family, including the idle and inconsequential adult talk that was bound to come with it. Of the two, James Ray was the least impressed. Both of Ruth Ann's parents smoked and the Turman house smelled like smoke for weeks following. Sarah Mae also thought she smelled alcohol but wasn't certain who was the offender, Bud or Judith.

Judith Chambers didn't smile and seemed uncomfortable with the evening from its beginning. Mr. Chambers and J.B. had talked nonstop about the upcoming presidential election. Mr. Chambers owned up to be a Republican and J.B., claimed he was a Democrat with independent leanings. Things changed, however, when Sarah Mae offered up a hard question:

"Which church do y'all attend?" J.B. flinched and James Ray shut his eyes.

Bud answered immediately and unabashedly, "Not much of a churchgoer, actually. Never have been."

"Well, there's always time for a body to pick one's self up, isn't there?" Sarah Mae said into the awkward silence of the dining room. Seth asked for more gravy. Hope dropped her fork onto the floor. J.B. cleared his throat. James Ray sat silent, his hands folded. He had eaten and heard all he wanted.

"And you, Mrs. Chambers, what's y'all's view on church goin'?" Sarah Mae asked, having reloaded.

Judith turned to face Sarah Mae directly, placed her napkin in her lap and confidently quoted Henry David Thoreau, claiming that her own mind was her own church. "And please call me Judith."

Immediately following Judith's unconventional and religiously-loaded revelation, conversation around the table came to a halt like the sudden lifting of a record player's stylus.

J.B. too, remained silent but was struck by Judith's ability to quote Thoreau. If she knew something about Thoreau, perhaps she might be acquainted with Emerson or some other credible author of the time. Maybe she might even be familiar with Thomas Paine and his Common Sense call to arm's essay. Perhaps Poe. Yes, Poe. He would make for some good and stimulating supper time conversation, he thought.

Field of View

His evaluation of Judith Chambers had turned on a dime. He found her to be not only physically attractive, that was plain and undeniable, but also mysteriously aloof and, yes, intelligent. That was the surprising part. That was the part he had underestimated, hadn't even given it an ounce of consideration. Although she spoke little and failed to offer even a suggestion of a smile, when she did speak, J.B. found she managed some interesting retort or astute observation. Ordinary, she was not.

The whole supper thing had moved far too slowly for James Ray. Most of what was said was said by the adults. Seth and James Ray had offered little. Judith had offered even less until Sarah Mae asked another unfortunate question. That made for yet another conversational surprise of the evening.

"Y'all haven't touched your pork chops. Is somethin' wrong with 'em?" Sarah Mae asked Judith.

"I don't eat meat. Sorry."

"What?" asked Hope.

"She doesn't eat animals," explained Faith.

"Why not?" inquired Hope.

"Never mind girls, some people don't think meat is good for 'em," J.B. interjected in an attempt, Texas Ranger-like, to ride to Judith's rescue.

"Actually, it's more than that Mr. Turman," Judith said, thinking she had to come to her own defense now that the Turman supper table had been inconveniently converted to an examination table.

"I like the taste of a hamburger as much as anyone. I just don't see why an animal has to give up its life, mostly in a cruel way, to satisfy some hunger on my part."

All four of the Turman children, top to bottom, old to young, felt various pangs of guilt given Mrs. Chambers' explanation of why she was a vegetarian. Each of them, at one stage of growth or another, had witnessed, even danced around the flailing, headless body of a chicken whose neck had been wrung by their father. As if their mind's were one, they collectively recalled the almost every Sunday after church ritual of the wringing of a chicken's neck and the bloody, barbaric chaos that immediately followed the separation of the chicken's neck from its body.

"Well, I understand the sensitivity to the animal part but how do y'all get all the nutrients y'all need just eatin' vegetables and such?" Sarah Mae queried.

"Look at her." This time it was sixteen year-old Ruth Ann who rode to her mother's rescue. "She doesn't appear to be undernourished, does she? She's smart about food, knows how to put various food sources together in ways that create beneficial combinations of fat, protein and carbohydrates."

"Well," Sarah Mae replied, somewhat taken aback by what she felt to be an intelligent, but overly defensive, response on the part of Ruth Ann, "are y'all a vegetarian too?"

"I'll leave that answer to the pork chops," Ruth Ann said.

All eyes turned to her plate. The pork chops, gravy and all, were missing. Only bones remained.

"To each his or her own," Judith said. "I'm not about to tell Ruth Ann what she should or should not put in her mouth. I encourage her to make good decisions about all aspects of her life, but in the end, they're up to her."

"I'm goin' to become a vegetarian like Mrs. Chambers," Hope said into the introspective silence that followed. "So, Daddy, don't count on me eatin' any more fried chicken on Sunday."

After Seth had offered Ruth Ann a ride home ahead of what he projected to be more adult talk, James Ray asked if he could also be excused. His request was granted. He went to his room to continue familiarizing himself with his new camera. The girls had already taken to their room.

After the short drive to the Chambers' home, Seth had the nerve to ask her if she wanted to go see *Harvey,* showing at the American theater.

"Stars James Stewart," Seth offered into the vacuum of a non-response from Ruth Ann. "He's a lovable drunk and..."

"No thank you, I don't have time for movies and, for sure, don't care to go and watch a movie about an alcoholic," she replied, as swiftly as one would brush aside a crumb of cornbread from the supper table.

When goodbyes were finally said back at the Turman house, J.B. and Sarah Mae began the cleanup.

"Have you ever seen so much smoke? Interestin' evening, though. Smoke, vegetarianism, Thoreau and all. Served up a good meal, Sarah Mae. Pork chops, as you well know, are a favorite of mine. Green beans from the garden, mashed potatoes and gravy, pickled beets, biscuits, and then, pecan pie. My goodness. Loved every bite of it all."

Sarah Mae remained silent, other than to offer a thank-you in light of J.B.'s evaluation of her cooking.

"Judith doesn't appear to be a happy woman, does she?" J.B. asked, thinking perhaps he shouldn't have.

"How can an atheist be happy?"

"She didn't say she was an atheist as far as I heard."

"Well, if a body goes around claimin' one's own mind is one's own church, I don't know what else it's called. Y'all think she's pretty, don't you?"

"I, I think she's interestin' and she and her daughter could be sisters. She must have been a very young mother when she squeezed out her Ruth Ann."

"Y'all didn't answer my question. Do you or do you not think she's pretty?"

"Yes, Sarah Mae, my darlin'. She's pretty. There are a few pretty women around and you happen to be one of 'em. A person would have to be blind not to notice that fact; but, you're right, she's obviously unhappy, too. That marriage is one of convenience, if I ever saw one. I don't know what happened to Ruth Ann's real daddy. Maybe he up and left for all I know. Maybe they divorced."

"Maybe," Sarah Mae offered, "they were never married in the first place."

"Could be, I hadn't thought of that. Good thinkin' Sarah Mae."

"Anyway, seems that Mr. Chambers was kind enough to adopt her at some point. The Pearly Gates open wide for acts like that."

"Could be they do," J.B. said in response to the religious reference. "Be pretty much a shame if a fellow showed up and St. Peter informed the poor soul that there was no such thing as Pearly Gates."

Sarah Mae was too tired to take the bait and travel down some crooked road of philosophical nonsense with her husband.

"What about the boys?" Sarah Mae said, switching conversational gears. "Think either of 'em are interested in Ruth Ann?"

"Well, Seth offered her a ride home so I suppose he's interested."

"What about James Ray?"

"James Ray? He's in love with a camera."

As he and Sarah Mae worked their way to their bedroom, J.B. figured, correctly he thought, that Judith Chambers was unhappily married, trapped like so many were in an unfulfilling and sterile relationship. Bud looked unhappy as well. The two had given little attention to each other either at the supper table or later in the living room. An odd match, thought J.B. Bud was short and stout and his hair was combed straight back, lacking a traditional parting of the hair. Instead, he was like Richard Nixon, Eisenhower's cheesy choice for vice president. On any subject, his declarations or responses were straightforward and lacked both insight and imagination. Worst of all, J.B. judged him to be a stick-in-the-mud conservative. J.B. would perhaps have the opportunity to hoe that row with Bud Chambers at another time and in a more appropriate place. If he turned out to be a racist, he would introduce him to Morris Wickware. The two could moan and groan over what's happening to their beloved America while the Chambers' toothy black, 1949 Buick was having a radiator hose replaced. Perhaps Bud might invest in Morris's auto repair. They could rename the shop Birds-of-a-Racist-Feather Auto Repair.

J.B. thought his best line of the evening was when he criticized his own Democratic party for being exclusionary. It was as close as the evening's conversation came to the subject of race. "I think that politics is a matter of addition, not subtraction," J.B. pontificated. "Makin' it difficult for people to vote, regardless of color, is a losin' proposition long-term." He noticed that Judith had nodded her head in agreement.

The better half of the Chambers couple, J.B. reflected, was leggy, buxom, surprisingly intelligent, sullenly mysterious, and from what little he had learned, liberal. Why she would choose a man like Bud to be her husband was beyond him. It was just another of those things in life that didn't make an iota of sense; choices made, paths taken or untaken.

When J.B. and Sarah Mae were in bed, he placed a hand on Sarah Mae's hip and then began rubbing the lower part of her back. She lay still and didn't respond. Despite the lack of something resembling a sexual green light, he readjusted the sheet and moved closer to her. Their bodies were now together but the warmth that the coupling generated combined with an accumulated day's worth of heat in the bedroom, caused J.B. to throw off the sheet. Uncomfortable still, he got out of bed and repositioned the oscillating fan, hoping for some relief from the still, heat-laden air of the bedroom.

Once back in bed, he reached for Sarah Mae's face and kissed her cheek, then the back of her neck.

"It's late, J.B.," Sarah Mae said.

"I know. I, I just..."

Sarah Mae rolled over and felt his member. He was more than ready. She decided to allow for the lovemaking given the fact the two hadn't coupled in several months. She figured he would be spent quickly.

J.B. mounted Sarah Mae as was their usual position for making love. Sarah Mae thought the missionary position more than sufficient for any of their lovemaking sessions. J.B. could count the times on one hand when Sarah Mae had taken an authoritative position on top. He wasn't even sure what such a position was called. As their act progressed, J.B. tried hard not to give a sexually explicit thought to one Judith Chambers. If receiving a grade in school, however, his mental discipline would have warranted an 'F' for failure.

*   *   *   *   *

"Y'all already had two drinks before we went over to the Turman's for supper. Do you really think you need another?" Bud asked.

"I'll have as many or as few as I wish," Judith replied, pausing from the before-the-bed act of brushing out her hair. Given his reflection in her mirror, Judith could see Bud was watching her from the doorway of the bedroom. In spite of his observation, she took a goodly sip of vodka from her highball glass.

Judith had undressed from their torturous evening at the Turman's. She was wearing the pink nightgown Bud so adored. It was a flimsy, see-through, cotton gown affording Bud the opportunity to furtively observe the fullness of her breasts as well as the always arousing perk of her nipples. Given the short length of the gown, her legs, although partially hidden by the chair's seat, could be seen as well. She was barefoot. How long had it been? Bud asked himself. Two years? At least that long.

Field of View

The sound of Ruth Ann's radio trailed into Judith's bedroom. If Judith could hear Ruth Ann's radio, it was possible she could hear their conversation as well.

"Please keep your voice down," she said, returning to her hairbrush ritual. "It's past y'all's bedtime, anyway. Aren't you still reportin' to work early like you did last week? If so, it's y'all's bedtime."

"I was hoping...since we've moved to a new house and all, that we...that you might want to...that we might sleep together for a change."

Judith turned from the mirror to face her make-do husband. "Whatever gave you that idea, Bud? Comin' here to this backwater, no-nothin' of a place called Mayweather wasn't my idea of paradise, and you know it. If you hadn't gone and gotten yourself demoted, we'd still be in Fort Worth in a decent house with a decent opportunity for Ruth Ann to make somethin' out of herself, swimmin' wise and all. Now look at us, Bud, all of us misplaced misfits. Just look around. I don't know what you see but when I look around I see that we're in a shit-brick of a fallin' apart house built in some century past and you with a demoted job at the pump company, and me with nothin' whatsoever to do day in and day out. That's what I see, Bud. What do you see?"

"I see that y'all aren't keepin' your voice down, that's what I see. And I see that when you drink, you get defensive and angry, that's what I see."

Judith said nothing in reply to Bud's retort. Instead, she left for the kitchen, reached into the refrigerator's freezer, removed her bottle of precious vodka, and poured herself another drink. She was almost out. That was another thing. She now found herself in a town where the sale of alcohol was illegal.

Ruth Ann had finished writing to her boyfriend she had left behind in Fort Worth and had turned off the radio. Even though her door was closed, she had heard virtually everything her mother had said. Her stepfather, too. Wishing to hear no more from either parent, she turned to her side, pushed her head deeply into her pillow and covered her remaining ear with another pillow.

Bud walked to a hall closet and removed a blanket. He fetched a pillow from Judith's bedroom. He would sleep on the couch as he had done for what seemed like forever. He reached for a book he was reading. It was a book about men whose lives were changed forever by the chaos wrought by World War II. He located his bookmark. He resumed reading *From Here to Eternity.*

Chapter 8 - Disaggregation of Competing Factions

"What is it you call those old farts down at the courthouse?" Carl asked James Ray while examining James Ray's contact-sheet that pictured a motley group of four elderly men who were courthouse lawn regulars. The exposure Carl liked best among James Ray's photo essay was the one that pictured one of the men standing, the heavyset one, with two of the men seated on a bench. One of the aged men was leaning forward, head down staring at the ground. Another sat upright, his back pressed against the slats of the bench, a cigarette in his mouth. Yet another was captured walking into the scene from the background, stooped, cowboy hat, cane, and all. None of the men were looking at the camera's lens.

Acting on a suggestion from Carl, James Ray had asked them not to do so. Carl called it a "candid picture, one that captures a moment in time and space." To his credit, James Ray had spent time getting to know the group, also a suggestion from Carl. He knew them not nearly as well as his daddy knew the men, but enough that they were comfortable with him and his camera.

"My daddy calls 'em the Whittle, Spit, and Chew Club. Chewers for short."

"Your take on the group is good and, as a completely objective viewer, I like your photo essay and I'd say your daddy's description of the old farts fits. One, that one, he's whittling isn't he? The one walking into the scene is obviously in poor health. The one standing, I'll bet a pack of Camels that he's the leader, the captain of the ship. The one leaning back looks like he hasn't a care in the world despite his down-and-out luck. Good light, too. The direct overhead light casts shadows, adds drama. The use of hard light calls attention to hard lives. And that's but one of several you took from the oak, up-looking-down-camera angle. Gives the viewer a bird's-eye view of the group. Good job all around. You, young man, may make for a photographer after all. When we get some time I'll show you how to burn-in and darken the edges of the photo. That will add even more drama.

James Ray was more than lifted by Carl's comments. He was ecstatic. He hadn't felt so good about himself since the time he had been fouled with no time remaining in a basketball game. He had launched a soft floater in the lane which, if good, would have won the game. An opposing player, however, fouled him so hard he lost his footing and fell to the hardwood floor in a heap. He was afforded two free throws; one to tie the game and one to win it. He had made both.

"The thing I like most," Carl continued, as the two waited under incandescent light for a roll of film to develop, "is that all twenty-four of your exposures are dedicated to the same subject matter. Also, it's a fine collection of visual elements: the men, the environment in which they idle away their time, the obvious comfort of their togetherness, that and more. That's what I've been looking for. How in God's name does a photographer know that one exposure is the best exposure when he has nothing to compare it with? It's not unlike women. Take one to bed and what do you have? Take several to bed over time and you have a comparison. Understand what I'm saying?"

James Ray nodded.

"You were lucky with your tornado photo, though. To have taken twelve or a hundred for that matter, would have increased the odds in your favor. Always increase the odds in your favor, my young friend. Always."

Carl blew smoke toward the ceiling and sat down on the darkroom's bench. James Ray noticed that he coughed frequently. At first, James Ray thought the cough was a cold or something; but having spent three months or so with him on a regular basis, James Ray figured it might be something else. Having mentioned the persistent cough to his mother, Sarah Mae diagnosed the cough to be a "smoker's cough."

"The smokin' will kill him over time," she had added. "Every cigarette is a nail in his coffin. Maybe you can talk to him someday about quittin'. Does he ever go to church?"

Carl towered over James Ray. At 6' 4" tall, although clean shaven, he could be cast in a play as a modern day Abe Lincoln. Better yet, were he younger, he could play center for Mayweather's basketball team. His face was narrow with a sharp chin and deep set eyes. His black hair was well-oiled and his lips, thin and expansive. Decades of smoking unfiltered cigarettes had yellowed his teeth. His arms were long and his hands big, even for a man his height. Most striking to James Ray, however, was the authority with which he carried himself. He seemed to James Ray to be supremely confident in who he was and what he wanted. There were no ifs, ands, or buts with Carl Malone. Things would be done his way, period. To those who knew the real Carl Malone—the man who, four years back, had been burdened with the inconvenient but necessary task of reinventing himself—he occupied space in a nuanced, shades-of-gray-world, devoid of any moral code of behavior but his own.

*   *   *   *   *

The ride to the Red River in Carl's Cadillac was exhilarating. The loud trumpet and whip of the air at over a hundred miles an hour was, to James Ray, mind-altering. He felt free of constraint, free of parental control, free to follow his own dreams. In the brief but transformative minute that the yellow missile of a car sliced through the darkening afternoon air, James Ray, for the first time in his life, felt that he knew who he was and what he wanted to do with his life. After high school, he would attend a photography school somewhere. Then, he would someway, somehow make a living as a photographer. He would travel the world and ferret out images yet unrecorded and unseen. There would be no end to the pleasure and excitement of it all.

Having reached the demarcation between Texas and Oklahoma, to James Ray's surprise, instead of turning around and heading back to Mayweather, Carl crossed the river's expansive truss bridge into Oklahoma. Carl slowed the car, eased it off the highway's pavement onto a dirt road, and pointed its hood in the direction of a trailer some one hundred yards distant. Despite the slow creep of the Cadillac, dust swirled up and around the car coloring the ambient light of the setting sun.

"What are we doin'?" James Ray managed.

"How did y'all like the ride? A hundred miles an hour get you right down at your gonads?"

"I'll say. That was fun. Who's at the trailer?"

"Old friend of mine. You stay here and I'll just drop in to say a quick hello and we'll be on our merry way back to merry old Mayweather."

As Carl exited the car, a boy opened the door of the trailer and waved to Carl from the trailer's deck. Carl waved back as he began to walk the short distance to the trailer. He and the boy went inside, the door closed behind them.

As James Ray waited, his thoughts returned to having been transported, a few minutes before, to the rush and roar of an adrenaline-producing speed of over a hundred miles an hour.

He then contrasted that speed, that sensation, with the stillness and quiet of his current dead-stop-go-nowhere position in the very same magnificent, at rest, specimen of an automobile. Restless from waiting, James Ray decided to walk over to a bluff overlooking the river. The sun was setting. It had just broken through below a storm cloud and it seemed to James Ray as if he were witnessing an ideal rendering of a sunset in some kind of sunset heaven. Its brilliance—given the angle of the sun relative to the river—was mirrored in the water.

"The angle of incidence is equal to the angle of reflection," Carl had once said. James Ray would commit the scene to memory: the visual magnificence of the large, orange orb of a setting sun, its reflection as wave-chopped as the river, which was dutifully engaged in carting its immense volume of fresh water to the sea just as it had for eons of previous evenings. Moisture would be lifted to the heavens and from the heavens rained back to the headwaters of the Red over a thousand miles distant.

James Ray found himself completely surrounded by what Carl referred to as quality light. Owing to the sun's reflection, the river appeared to be on some kind of solar fire. The clouds were a mixed pallet of increasingly intense yellows, oranges, indigos, purples and more. The leaves of the trees were no longer green but had achieved a tint of color only an artist could conjure. Everything, even the trailer, was slowly but surely rendered into a canvas, its subject matter crafted by the hands of an unseen and unknown master painter.

James Ray was exhilarated yet remorseful. He was without his camera.

"Always have your camera with you. Always. Always have a full load of film and have an extra roll as back up. Always. A cop doesn't hit the street without his gun, does he? Not only does he have to have his gun, it has to be loaded, right? And he should have extra ammo beyond that, right? You never know what kind of photo opportunity you will run into. You might just walk into the visual opportunity of a lifetime. Remember the Hindenberg? Have I made my point?"

The transitory drama of the sunset having faded, James Ray remained at the river's bank in reflection of what he had been privileged to witness. As he waited, he recalled yet another lesson from his teacher.

"Light is measured in degrees Kelvin. Light has a temperature and its temperature changes as the sun moves throughout the day. The sun's temperature, its light anyway, is cool in the morning at sunrise, warm in the evening just before sunset. Those times are when light can be a photographer's best friend. It's a complete waste of film to photograph the Grand Canyon mid-day but that's when most knuckleheads do. After driving for hell knows how long, they get out, walk around, and snap away at one of the word's wonders at a time of day when the canyon is nothing more than a flat, lack luster, hole-in-the-ground. Direct, overhead light is worthless for that kind of a scene. A wiser person will wait for quality light. That's when the canyon comes to life visually. That's when the canyon reveals its best, most presentable self. That's when its shadows are cast and its texture revealed and when its colors are better than any technicolor you can imagine. That's the kind of sunset you see in Arizona Highways. If you are interested in the Grand Canyon as subject matter, get your teenage ass out of bed early or make sure you are available at sunset. After a storm is best of all."

"James Ray, you here?" Carl called into the increasing darkness.

"Here, over by the river. Comin'."

As James Ray approached, Carl, the boy and a man were loading what appeared to be heavy boxes into the cavernous trunk of the car.

"Like y'all to meet my good friend Rip...this is his son, Jake."

James Ray shook hands with both. Then Carl motioned James Ray into the car.

"Got to hightail it, boys." Carl said, slamming the trunk closed. "And thank you. See you in a couple of weeks or so." Carl brought the Cadillac's beast of a V8 engine to life.

*　　*　　*　　*　　*

J.B. had characterized Carl as "narcissistic," when a breakfast discussion with James Ray had turned to Carl Malone. As a general rule, J.B. felt that shared time spent with anyone would ultimately result in either a positive or negative influence in one's character development. James Ray had contributed little to the conversation. He worried there was a possibility that either his daddy's or mother's opinion of Carl would lead to his losing his job and, yes, losing time spent with a friend and mentor. He had learned so much from him. Carl had been kind to him. The thought of losing either his job or his relationship with Carl was both troubling and threatening.

Since narcissism was not in James Ray's vocabulary, he would have to look it up. He would find that the dictionary definition was reasonably consistent with J.B.'s explanation of the word, his daddy's the more colorful of the two. "Narcissistic," J.B. explained, "means thinkin' the sun rises and sets on you and you only. Means if Mr. Malone were to run for political office, say governor, he would put signs out all over the state proclaimin', 'Malone for Governor,' accompanied by words of encouragement readin', 'Texas and Narcissism Fit Like Gloves', or somethin' like that."

"You don't like him, do you?" James Ray asked.

"Whether or not I like him doesn't have anything to do with it. The question is whether or not he's a good influence on you. That's what's important. You'll be seventeen in a couple of months. Y'all are at the age when a youngster begins to look beyond his family for role models. All I'm askin' is for you to keep a sharp eye out for anything that might cause you to compromise on your principles, that's all. Make sure you keep good company and maintain a sharp eye. That's all your mother and I are askin'."

"Well, I think it's more than that."

"How so?"

"I don't think either of you like him and if I can be honest without gettin' in trouble, I think y'all are interferin' with my life," James Ray blurted.

"Interferin' with your life? Is that what you said?"

"I think you heard me..."

"Don't get disrespectful with me, James Ray!"

"Why is it Daddy, when either Seth or I try to defend ourselves, to try and explain what our thoughts and feelin's are, you up and claim it's disrespect? For some unexplained reason, you don't like Carl. Mother doesn't like him either. I'd like to know why."

James Ray was well into a good lather. His face was flushed, his eyes teared.

"And here I am lovin' my life and feelin' good about myself and all y'all want to do is to talk down Carl. What do you have on him? Is it because he's from back east? I heard you call him Yankee the other day when you were talkin' to mother. So what is it?"

J.B had risen from his kitchen chair but had remained silent in recollection of a time when he was in James Ray's position trying to defend himself from an onslaught of parental disapproval.

"You have a right to your opinions of your mother and me and Carl Malone for that matter but you don't have the right to be disrespectful. That I won't tolerate."

"Speakin' of disrespect, Daddy," James Ray shot back, "that's what I'm feelin', disrespect."

*   *   *   *   *

The club members met daily, even on weekends and Sundays, although their time together on Sunday was limited to a few hours in the afternoon. The vast majority of the town's residents were in church on Sunday mornings so people watching was severely limited. People watching and the spinning of outrageous yarns that came from the watching, was what they did best unless you counted all the knife swapping, the whittling, the spitting, and the chewing.

Eighty-two year old Ed Chip, known to his comrades as Chipper, was a member in good standing. In fact, he claimed the second longest tenure of the group. Chipper, never one to miss a good story-telling opportunity, had gotten good mileage from the tornado of a few weeks ago. In one fanciful story, he claimed that a chicken that had unfortunately been "sucked up" by the vortex had, while airborne, "shit" on his head. No one believed him, of course, but truthfulness wasn't the point. Truthfulness, according to their code of conduct, was a pure sign of some kind of personality weakness. The group operated on Don Quixote's belief that facts are but the enemy of truth. A clever lie, bold and outrageous, was far superior to the dullness of veracity.

Another lie, courtesy of the tornado, starring yet another airborne chicken, had to do with the chicken being so scared it had laid a hard-boiled egg from a thousand feet. "It was so hard-boiled that it didn't splat when it hit the courthouse steps," Chipper told another passerby. "It was good eatin', too. Just added a little salt and pepper. Dang good egg."

Most notable about Chipper, aside from his limitless ability to take something mundane and craft it into a clever fabrication, was the fact that he had eyes that looked in two opposing directions. If you were facing him, his right eye looked to his right, not straight ahead. His left eye, as if compensating for the poor performance of the right, tried to look straight ahead but was tilted slightly downward. Further confusing the situation was the left eye's tendency to correct itself and bob upward, hold its position for a few seconds, then, losing its grip, drop down again.

Early on, J.B. decided to simply look at Chipper's nose. His nose, after all, was going nowhere. J.B. and the WSC club were good friends. As was his custom, J.B. would take a mid-morning break from all of his office sitting and number crunching, purchase a Coke from the snack stand in the courthouse hallway, mosey down the flight of poured concrete steps to the outside lawn, and engage the club members in some idle chit-chat up to and including, perhaps, the give and take involved with swapping of knives. One knife had been passed back and forth so many times among J.B. and the men, that the knife had a name, Charlie. Poor Charlie, a once useful and artsy Gerber Scrimshaw, was such a wreck it became a kind of steel-bladed version of a hot potato. It was in such a sorry state of disrepair that it had lost almost all of its utility save for perhaps a game of hobo mumbly peg.

One sunny summer morning, Chipper accosted Louise Farley--a comely clerk employed by the post office--as she approached the courthouse to renew her driver's license. To his delight, she remained stationary while he recounted his tornado chicken shit story. He replaced the word "shit" with "crapped" thinking it more appropriate to his audience. She laughed and politely accused him of "pulling her leg."

"I'd never do that," he replied. "I'd leave that to a much younger man than I."

His retelling of that encounter made for lively conversation for several weeks what with one or another of the club members saying they would "pull more than her leg" or "gladly pull both of her legs" or "pull her clean into my bed," or voted best of all, "pull down her panties first, then commence pullin' on her legs."

Chipper's willingness to approach the post office clerk, and in doing so, josh her a little bit, not only gave the other members something to mull over, but more importantly, it was how one gained or maintained one's status in the group.

The group's titular leader was Wilfred "Winney" Bickerstaff. He was a couple of years younger than Chipper but he held his leadership position due to the fact he was the only member who had had some college, although that had been limited to a semester which he didn't complete. Nevertheless, he had a high school degree while the other members could only claim an eighth grade education, if that. When he felt he needed to reinforce his status by either overruling someone or working to gain consensus on one issue or the other, he would remind his colleagues of his extensive educational experience. Of importance also, was the fact that his grandfather had fought in the Mexican-American War. This tie to patriotic history, combined with the celebrity that came from a great, great uncle who had fought and died in the Alamo, made for credibility none of the others could begin to match by way of either truth or fiction.

"Wouldn't be a Texas without either of 'em," he proclaimed on many an occasion. Although he suffered from diabetes and didn't have feeling in his feet due to neuropathy, he would often stand. In standing, he felt he held a more distinguished and lordly position as compared to the lesser empowered individuals who remained seated. If being elevated above one's inferiors worked in India, he figured it was good enough for the courthouse lawn in Mayweather.

Interestingly, Winney had introduced the newspaper fellow's Cadillac for discussion on a day when J.B. had some extra time since his secretary was out of town attending a wedding and his audit of the books of the county treasurer's office had been completed.

As he approached, J.B. overheard Harold Rumph, better known as Soapy because he carved Ivory Soap instead of ash or pine, mention a "yeller Cadillac". J.B. figured the boys had chosen the *Tribune's* photographer for discussion.

"Good mornin' boys," J.B. said into the compromised summer freshness of the courthouse lawn. The compromise, of course, a direct result of an abundance of tobacco spit.
Individually, the men returned his greeting.

Field of View

"Just talkin' about the feller from the newspaper drivin' around town in his yeller Cadillac. Must pay well down at the paper fer him to have the money to up and buy a spankin' new Caddy, don't y'all think J.B.?"   The statement and follow-up question was spoken by Teddy Roy Thigpin, the youngest of the group at 75 years old. Teddy, or T.R., or 'Rough Rider' depending on who was doing the calling, had a disturbing tendency to challenge Winney for control of the group's conversation as well as to challenge his self-anointed authority.

Winney's brow became as furrowed as a newly-planted cornfield. After giving Teddy a hard stare, he turned to J.B. and spoke before he could respond to Teddy's out-of-order inquiry.

"Seems plain enough to me," Winney offered, "that a fellow can, since he's livin' in these here United States of America, go and drive whatever kind of a car he wants to. Right J.B.?"

"Suppose y'all are right, Winney. It is a puzzlement, though. I've actually given the subject some deep thought myself. My son, James Ray, y'all know him. He's my second son, Seth bein' the oldest. James Ray's the smaller of the two but athletic as all git out despite his minor handicap. Seth can't scratch his head and chew gum at the same time. Anyway, James Ray works for the Cadillac owner, interestingly enough. His name is Carl Malone. He's from back east somewhere."

"A Yankee?" asked Winney. "Here in Mayweather? Who let him in?"

"Good question. So here's my take on the situation if y'all have any interest."

"Please proceed," replied Winney, now fully in control of the meeting.

"Well, thank you kindly. A new Cadillac Coupe Deville is over four thousand out-the-door. Brand new, not used. That's a heap of money to almost anyone livin' in the county unless you're George Whipple, or Horace Southern, or a white Bloom descendant, or someone like that. Even then, none of 'em drive a Cadillac. Here's the thing, boys. The average wage in America...I've checked it out...is under three thousand. A teacher makes less than that and my Sarah Mae can attest to that very fact. So, here's a photographer of a small-town newspaper...we're not Dallas or Houston are we?"

"No, we ain't," replied Teddy. "I say it's good we ain't."

"Now to be completely honest, I don't rightly know what a small town newspaper photographer's salary is. I could ask Spencer Shoemaker. He's the paper's editor and owner, but I'd hate to do that 'cause it would look like I am a snoopin' busybody and he'd wonder why in the fool tarnation I would like to know such a thing in the first place."

"Y'all could say y'all was doin' a survey of sorts," Teddy suggested.

"Well, I don't think that pig would likely fly," replied J.B. "But back to my reasonin'. So we know that the price of his fine piece of transportation is more than the fellow makes in a year. Probably a goodly amount more. We also know that if he didn't pay cash for the Cadillac, he had to buy it on time. Interest rates for an auto loan are around five percent at any bank in town. Even if he bought the car on time, his payment on his Cadillac would be more than my mortgage payment. I'd say he would be far more likely, given his income at the paper, to afford a used Plymouth or a Ford, not a new car like a top-of-the-line Cadillac."

"Don't say," said Winney. "Y'all have done y'all's homework, hasn't he boys?" Once again, heads nodded in agreement. Chipper loudly expectorated in the general direction of a group of black birds. Winney decided it was time to stand. Soapy, completely deaf in one ear and hard-of-hearing in the other, leaned forward and cupped his good right ear hoping not to miss J.B.'s detective-like insight into the mysterious world of a Cadillac-driving newspaper photographer.

"Well, what's y'all's conclusion to it all?" Chipper asked. "Did he up and rob a bank? Did he inherit a heap of money? Maybe that's it."

"Good questions, Chipper. But I don't think those pigs fly either. Those things are possible but not probable. Understand my meanin'?"

This time there was no response to J.B.'s question. Winney, Chipper and Teddy were busy trying to get a handle on the difference between the concepts of possibility and probability. Soapy thought he had heard J.B. say something once again about pigs not being able to take flight, but nothing more.

"Here's what I think. I think our Carl Malone must have another source of income."

"What's that y'all said, J.B.?" asked Soapy in a squint. "He sourced his income?"

"Good Christ, Soapy. Y'all couldn't hear thunder," Winney interjected. "J.B. said he most likely has to have another job so as to support such luxury. Didn't say it in exactly those words but that there's the meanin' just the same."

"That's it?" inquired Teddy. "That's all we have to chew on? Nothin' more than the fact the feller has another job?"

"I'm afraid so, gentlemen. I, as you may know since I'm the county's auditor, like to come to conclusions based on facts and figures, not assumptions; and so in this case, I fear I don't have anythin', absolutely nothin' to go on but a guess. Y'all's guess that he's a bank robber seems as good as whatever I can come up with."

"Well, how about this?" Teddy asked. "Even if the feller has another job, don't it have to be part-time? And if it's a part-timer kind of a job, the extra pay ain't likely to be such that he can go out and afford a Cadillac does it?"

Winney recognized that Teddy's questions were sound but he resented what he nonetheless viewed as a kind of thorny conversational trespass. He decided he needed to remain standing.

"His Caddy has weak sprangs," volunteered Chipper. He had saved his pearl of observation for the last minute.

"Weak springs?" asked J.B.

"That's excactly right, weak sprangs."

"How so, Chipper?"

"Seen him come into town the other day. It wuz almost dark and he wuz comin' back from the direction of the Red. His Caddy was all stooped in the rear like it was carryin' a heavy load of some kind. I wuz walkin' home at the time. Seemed like y'all's boy James Ray wuz in the car with him. Y'all's boy smoke, J.B.?"

Chapter 9 - Can't Win for Losin'

Judith would have preferred a paper sack to the ridiculous excuse of a hat adorning her head. The black felt hat, half cap, was accessorized with a woven see-through mesh net that cascaded from the rear of its vestigial and tiny brim down over her entire face. The net was kept company by a host of equally-distributed, rounded black dots the size of pepper kernels. Hate the hat or not, it would serve its purpose in helping her avoid unnecessary attention up to and including being recognized.

What she was about to do was foreign to her and also against the law although her benefactor had assured her that half the county was engaged in bootlegging, either as a buyer or as a seller. Having to wait for her ride afforded her yet another opportunity to bemoan the reality of living in a town where almost everyone went to church, prayed to a Christian God, and voted against legalization of alcohol. "Three strikes and you're out," she mumbled to herself.

Judith peered up and down Maple Street but there wasn't a car moving in either direction that looked like the one she was told to seek out, a yellow Cadillac. Just when she thought she would have to remove the hat so as to have a cigarette, a car with a massive, chrome, egg-crate grill turned onto Maple from Second Street.

As the Cadillac came to a slow and smooth stop in front of Judith, Carl made   sure the car's pampered whitewalls remained a goodly distance from the curb. He leaned over and opened the car's passenger door from the inside.

"Pleasure to meet you, Judith Chambers," Carl said. "Careful with the door. Don't want it to hit the curb. Trying to keep this baby showroom fresh."

"You're late," Judith offered in return, as she stepped into the car and wrenched its heavy door closed. "May as well be robbin' a bank what with all this drama just to have some vodka on hand. Stupid, all of it."

Carl looked over his shoulder, and seeing no oncoming traffic, pulled the Cadillac onto Maple, made a left on Rayburn, and then a right onto Texas State Route 72.

Once out of town, Judith removed her hat and reached for her pack of cigarettes.

"Need a light?" Carl asked.

"No, thank you."

"How long have you been smoking?"

Judith looked over at Carl. She thought the question none of his business. The business of the day was to purchase some vodka, nothing more. No idle talk, no anything beyond the objective of securing enough vodka so that when she wanted a drink, she could have a drink and in doing so, say "go to hell" to the town's local option lunacy.

Given the speed of the car and the rush of air that attended it, Judith was unable to light her cigarette. Witnessing her inability to do so, Carl pulled a stainless steel lighter from his pant's pocket and placed it near her face. She accepted the offer, leaned forward, placed her left hand on his right, and drew his hand and the lighter closer to the tip of her cigarette. Handicapped by the movement of the car on the unevenness of the highway's surface, she attempted to mate flame to cigarette.

Carl enjoyed the warmth of flesh-on-flesh as he engaged in a brief game of visual tag, first focusing on the ruby-accented purse of Judith's lips as she tried to light her cigarette, then to the road, then back to Judith, and then back to the road again. He could easily have serviced her need in town but wanted her alone in his car and dependent. It was the first in several steps he would take to reel her in. He saw Judith Chambers as vulnerable. He figured she was unhappily married and knew she was addicted to alcohol. Given those factors, he calculated, she could be had over time. The woman would make for a much better-than-average sexual cavort in bed or in the candlelit inner sanctum of his stash cellar or in the backseat of his Cadillac, her nakedness illuminated by the soft radiance of a Comanche moon. Especially so, if she were tanked up and three sheets to the wind.

"Thank you, got it."

"You're welcome." Carl had taken note of Judith's wedding ring. Modest, he thought. Too modest an offering from someone who supposedly is a successful business manager. Maybe he wasn't back then when they consummated their vows. Regardless, if she had been the object of some kind of bride-to-the-highest-bidder auction, Carl figured she would have garnered the most accolades and the most amount of money. Looked to him like she had settled for something less than she deserved.

"Got a question for you. Just curious why you want so much vodka? You drink anything other than vodka? How can I help you with your need?"

"That's three questions. Which one do y'all want answered first? Or, do y'all want them answered in order? And it's 'may I' instead of 'can I,' just so you know. Of course you 'can' throw in somethin' else but the askin' permission to do so is the 'may I' part of it."

"Christ on a crutch, lady. Just trying to help here. Most of my transactions, all of them actually, I do in town without the bother and expense of driving out to my inventory in the country. You, Judith Chambers, are the first customer I've ever taken to my stronghold. I make the effort to please you and meet your needs and then you seem like you are above it all in some way and are happy to give me heartburn over something I didn't start in the first place. You called me, remember?"

"Sorry. Is that what y'all want? There, y'all have my apology. Look, I just don't like the situation. I've never done this before. It's a shitty situation no matter how you look at it. Here I am in a car with a stranger, someone I've only heard about, drivin' to God knows where so I can buy some vodka which is against the law thanks to some religious zealots who, it seems, are the vast majority of people in this sorry excuse of the town called Mayweather and the same sorry excuse of people go and make up 99% of the rest of the sorry county. Seems reasonable to me I ought to be able to buy what I want down the street from my house. Does that help explain some of my upset?"

Before Carl could conjure an answer, Judith took off again.

"And why didn't y'all answer the Goddam phone when I called three days ago? Called twice and the second time the asinine person who answered said you were there but couldn't come to the phone. Wouldn't was probably it. Y'all took 'till the next day to call me back. So much for customer satisfaction. If I were better acquainted with the stupid county and it's under-the-table, entrepreneurial bootleggin' goings on, I would have chosen someone else other than y'all."

"Told you to call me at home, that's why. Said any night but Thursday night. I called you when I was able. Don't call me at the paper, period."

Carl had enjoyed Judith's verbal onslaught. Not only was his passenger attractive, as an added bonus she was sassy and smart, too. Sexy, sassy, and smart, he figured, would make for a rollicking bedtime cocktail.

"Speaking of situations, how you're packaged is an unusual situation."

"What's that supposed to mean?" she answered, tossing the remains of her cigarette to the side of the road.

"Good looks and brains. Don't mind speaking your mind. Good package. Good combination. You ever modeled? You ever tried to leverage your good looks or have you wasted them and your brains on your businessman husband?"

* * * * *

The digging was taking what J.B. thought amounted to an eternity. True, he had help from his two boys although they were difficult to round up and invariably had an excuse of why they couldn't dig for an extended period of time. Booker T. Johnson, J.B.'s Negro friend, father of James Ray's friend Sammy and the courthouse's full-time custodian, had lent more help than the two boys combined.

"You and Eartha—Sammy too, if y'all can round him up —are more than welcome to take shelter here once it's finished. Hope I'm done before we take on another tornado or my marriage will be done and over."

"Doubt that, J.B., y'all's marriage to your Sarah Mae seems like a match made in heaven."

"Mostly," J.B. answered, recalling times when their relationship seemed less than one that would meet some kind of heavenly criteria for ideal. Their disagreement over the storm shelter was but one recent example. "Everyone struggles from time to time. Put two people together and over time they will figure out ways to pest each other. You and Eartha ever quarrel?"

"Never. I just up and do what she wants when she wants. Simple, J.B., just do what's expected and y'all's marriage will be as good as Ivory soap."

"Good advice, Booker. Ivory soap. Ivory soap. I'll commit that to memory and the next time my Sarah Mae makes up somethin' to fuss over, I'll say to myself, Ivory soap! Ivory soap! Now that, Ivory soap and all, is a subject that could make for a powerful sermon, don't you think? I wonder if there is a parable about Ivory soap?"

To complete the task of removing 144 square feet of earth to a depth of eight feet, J.B. was forced to buy two extra shovels at Roland's Hardware. What he would do with the extra shovels after the digging was done, he didn't know. He calculated after everything was said and done, the shelter would run a dollar or two over two hundred dollars. He wished he could pencil out an estimate down to a dime but Sarah Mae kept asking for upgrades.

"Henry Ford used to sell his Model 'T' for $240.00," J.B. said as much to himself as he did to Booker T.

"Beg pardon, J.B?"

"His Tinlizzy, the Model 'T.' Henry used to sell it for around what I'm goin' to be out buildin' this storm shelter."

"Well, two things, J.B. Firstly, y'all's marriage is worth at least two hundred dollars, I 'spect. Second, a Tinlizzy is mighty poor protection for y'all's family come tornado time."

Booker T. Johnson was the largest man in Mayweather; perhaps in the county. Standing at six feet seven inches, Book, as J.B. often called him, weighed 320 pounds, adding a pound or two following each year's Thanksgiving and Christmas holidays. He single-handedly moved Sarah Mae's newly purchased Speed Queen wringer washer from the storeroom's warehouse to the back of his Chevy pickup and then from the pickup to its final destination on the Turman back porch. The task would normally have required two warehouse workers to do what Booker T. managed by himself. By moving the washer himself, he saved the Turmans the delivery fee. Sarah Mae, as she always did after receiving help of some kind from either Booker T. or Eartha, baked a pie for the family. On that auspicious occasion, she pieced together two strawberry and rhubarb pies. One for the Johnsons and one for the Turmans.

Once the excavation was completed, Sarah Mae's Uncle Charles made sure the walls were plumb and square. He then began the framing necessary to receive the concrete. More concrete, J.B. surmised, than the WPA had used to construct the dam creating Devil's Lake State Park. Over time, however, J.B. became friends with the project, actually looking forward to the afternoon hours and weekend time he could spend working on the shelter. He stopped going to church on Sunday mornings claiming he had to complete the shelter before school started in September.

"Besides," he remarked to Sarah Mae, after selecting the 9th of September, James Ray's birthday, as the arbitrary date for the shelter's completion, "I don't have time to waste time singin' church hymns and listenin' to Pastor Pritchard drone on and on about salvation this or damnation that. If he should say somethin' I haven't heard a dozen times, you can share it with me while I sweat away workin' on y'all's salvation of a storm shelter."

"Once y'all are done I'll host an open house," Sarah Mae had responded. "That will be nice. I'll invite our good friends and neighbors."

"To a storm shelter open house?"

"Why not? Eartha and I will come up with some assorted finger food of some kind. My good friend Mindy from church can bring her ambrosia salad, and..."

"Lord alive, Sarah Mae, how many good friends and neighbors do you think y'all can stuff in one storm shelter?"

"Won't stuff 'em. You will lead 'em on a tour, one or two at a time."

*   *   *   *   *

One hot and humid summer Sunday afternoon, after the Turmans and Johnsons had completed their respective mid-afternoon dinners, James Ray and his friend Sammy got together. The two had taken to a tree house on the Johnson property they had built some eight years prior. The crude and aging tree house was located in an old pecan in the Johnson's back yard. Poorly constructed in the first place, the weathered planks of the tree house strained under the combined weight of two boys who were now in their teens as opposed to nine-year-old, would-be carpenters seeking solace from someone or something undefined.

"I ain't been in this tree house more than twice since we built it. When I was nine or ten? Somewhere around then," Sammy offered.

"I had just recovered from polio, if I remember correctly. I was eleven and y'all were about to turn eleven."

"You were lucky with the polio and all that."

"I suppose so. I didn't think so at the time. Six months is a long time to spend flat on your back not knowin' whether you'll walk again. And you were the only one who came to visit me in the hospital, the only one. I'll always remember that. None of my white friends came to visit. None."

"Scared mostly, I suppose. A girl in my class died from polio. She was in an iron lung and all and she still died."

The boys were four years old when they first met, too young to know that the color of their skin would soon divide them. Throughout the south, the segregated social wedge of racial preference would be driven at an early age, deep and hard and intractable, making such a friendship as theirs unthinkable, let alone possible. Despite the odds, despite the disapproving glances, despite the fact that Sammy was directed to "Colored Only" public drinking fountains while James Ray drank freely from "White Only" fountains, despite the fact that they attended separate and segregated schools, despite the fact that they worshipped at different churches--one in a colored slice of town-- the other cocooned in a far more socially privileged section of the same town, handicapped as their relationship was by all that, the two boys remained friends. Aiding and abetting the boys' atypical friendship was a salve of acceptance applied at every turn by their parents. Neither adult of either family had been able to fully articulate the why and how of their sons' defiance of social norms or theirs for that matter. It simply happened. It was what it was and there was no reason as far as anyone could articulate to bring it to an end.

In actuality, James Ray was closer to Sammy than he was to Seth. Sammy didn't have a brother. His only sibling had been lost one fateful and life-changing July fourth picnic six years prior. As her parents partook of their holiday feast, Wilma, playing with her older brother, slipped on a wet and slippery slope of a creek bank that was swollen from a previous week's downpour. The four-inch rain had flooded much of the county and Bois D' Arc Creek was just one of the county's many water-choked tributaries feeding into the Red. Sammy had watched in abject horror as she was taken by the velocity and weight of the creek's debris laden waters. Less than fifty yards from where he stood, the creek took a dogleg to the left. Wilma disappeared from view in less than the time it took her stunned brother to scream for help.

Sammy Johnson was taller, stronger, and a better physical specimen than his white friend. Sammy was destined to be an athlete and he knew it. Unlike many teens, regardless of the color of their skin, he knew what he wanted to be. He had decided he would become one of the greatest Negro players in all of baseball. Baseball would be his ticket out of Mayweather and the suffocation that came with the Jim Crow south. Unlike his father who was polite and docile and had conformed to southern society's expectations for his lot in life, Sammy figured he had a bone to pick with the white world and he'd pick it when and where he thought necessary.

"How are you doin' with y'all's 'way out' as you put it?" James Ray asked.

"Hard to say. My mother and I think we should move to California. The schools out there aren't segregated. Mother thinks I would have a better chance to make a name for myself."

"No kiddin'. My mother was just the other night talkin' about moving to California except it wasn't about segregation or anythin', it was that they would make more money. She wants my daddy to go back into teachin'. Mother's got family around Los Angeles somewhere. My Uncle Pirtle is a preacher at a Methodist Church. My grandpa on my mother's side was a principal of a junior high. He's retired now. My grandma's doin' well, health wise. Most all of my mother's sisters and brothers live in southern California. All of 'em are teachers as far as I know. Besides that, mother figures they would almost double their income by movin'. Imagine that. Us all livin' together in California."

"That would be somethin'. We might even go to the same school together. I'm not sayin' such a thing is goin' to happen. My daddy likes it here. He has a good job and he would hate to leave his church and his friends and all. I think he thinks he's here to stay. I don't think he can imagine a life outside of what we have here."

"How are y'all doin' with Rusty Shit-head Wickware?" Sammy asked, changing the subject.

James Ray laughed. "That's a good way of putting it. Shit-head. I'll have to remember that. How the shit are y'all doin', Shit-head?"

Both boys laughed, then fell into silence.

Eartha called from the rear of the house asking if they wanted anything to eat.

Sammy checked with James Ray. He answered in the negative but thanked her for the offer.

"Got some lovely mincemeat pie."

"Not now, mother, later maybe," Sammy called back. He was eager to hear how James Ray was coping with his nemesis.

"So has Shit-head left you alone lately? Tell the truth, Ruth."

"Honestly, I think about it more than I'd like. Seems like he pops up here and there when I least suspect it. Drives me crazy."

"Take a baseball bat to his head, that'll settle him."

"Well, I think I'd make a fool of myself goin' about town carryin' a baseball bat. My Daddy is teachin' me how to defend myself. He's givin' me boxin' lessons. He used to be pretty good. Boxed in the Navy and a little after that."

*   *   *   *   *

"What do you think we can do with James Ray?" Sarah Mae asked, joining J.B. on the front porch swing. She had finished a letter to her father and had folded the last of the Turman family laundry. Barefoot, she was carrying two glasses of sweet tea.

J.B. looked over at Sarah Mae as he tried to extricate himself from his thoughts pertaining to the storm shelter. Its door was the remaining problem. The door was so heavy, solidly-constructed, and at such an angle, that he could barely bring it to an open position. Once open, try as he might, he couldn't prevent it from slamming closed. He had decided to name the door, "The Door with an Attitude."

James Ray had tried to open the door and had failed. So too, had Seth. As strong as he was, even Sammy had great difficulty opening it. There was no way, J.B. figured, a woman the size of Sarah Mae would be able to manage to open the door in the face of an approaching storm. Some kind of cable and pulley and counter weights were in order but such a design was an engineering abstraction that was a stretch too far for J.B.'s mind no matter how hard he focused on solving the problem. In the end, he guessed he would have to hire someone to construct the door-opening contraption for him and that meant spending yet more money on the problem. Then, having opened the door and closed it, what happened when one was tucked away inside, the storm a thing of the past, and one wished to exit the shelter? What then? How did all that work?

"James Ray? I don't know that we can do anything with him or any of our children for that matter. You put a roof over their heads, you feed 'em, you school 'em, you tuck 'em in at night and you try to keep them safe. That's all you can do. I recall my Daddy saying that a parent has his or her children for life. You raise 'em the best you can and you hope for 'em the best you can but beyond that, they have lives of their own and they will live out those lives sometimes as you think they should and sometimes in opposition to what you think or wish or hope."

"I didn't mean to cause you so much anxiety, I was just wonderin' how the two of you are doin' after y'alls to-do the other day."

"We're fine. It's all passed. I think we need to give him a little space and I don't think he's in any danger with the Mr. Malone fellow, strange as he may be."

"Maybe so. I still worry about the relationship. I thought I smelled smoke on James Ray the other day."

J.B. remained silent, although given Teddy's comments the other day at the courthouse, he had to admit that James Ray's smoking was a possibility since Teddy thought he had seen him with a cigarette. Beyond that, his son was seen in the Malone man's car and even beyond that, the car seemed weighted in the rear and coming from the direction of Oklahoma. Bootleg liquor, perhaps? With James Ray in the front seat, of all things. Put it all together and J.B. figured it meant trouble. Regardless, he thought it best to keep all of it to himself until a time when he could broach the matter with James Ray in private. If let in on it before all the facts were known, Sarah Mae, J.B. calculated, would pitch a fit.

"Could be James Ray is more in danger from Rusty Wickware than from Mr. Malone."

"How so? Is that still goin' on after all these years?"

"Reckon so. James Ray was in to see me the other day. Hardly ever comes in to see me. I can count the times on one hand."

"What did he want?

James Ray had deliberately sought out his father while J.B. was working. He didn't want his mother in on the conversation. It was embarrassing enough that he would have to seek advice from his father and he wanted to avoid the likelihood of his mother's churchy and unproductive moralizing.

"Is this the office of the county auditor?" James Ray said, announcing his arrival.

"Well, hello, James Ray, I expect it is," J.B. said in instant recognition of his son's voice. "Look who's come to see me, Mabel. Miracles never cease."

Mabel Givens, long-time secretary of J.B's in both his courthouse positions, said hello and blew a kiss in James Ray's direction. "I changed y'all's diapers cutie-pie when y'all's daddy was county superintendent a hundred years ago. Y'all wouldn't remember and I suppose that's a good thing, isn't it?"

"I expect I don't and it is," James Ray replied, smiling.

"I just want to run somethin' by you, Daddy. Y'all have a minute? Carl said I could have a few minutes to run over and talk to you."

J.B. asked permission to leave the office as he always did when the need arose.

"Permission granted, Mr. Turman. Might you be back in a day or so?"

"I expect less than that, Mabel. Holler at us if need be. We'll be over on one of the north side benches."

Once outside and seated, J.B. broke the silence. "What's goin' on, young man? I hope it doesn't have to do with the conversation we had the other day. That's done and over with as far as I'm concerned."

"No, not that."

"What then, Hitler's alive and well and we're fixin' to have another world war?"

"Well, speakin' of a war, I need to know what's worth fightin' for. Do I keep ignorin' Rusty Wickware and his bullyin' ways or do I stand up and fight back?"

"He's still at it?"

"Never stopped. I can't exactly figure it out but I think it has to do with me likin' Sammy although he pestered me even before he knew about that. Been pesterin' me seems like all my life."

"If the boy is like his father, and I suspect he is, I'd guess he most likely is on your backside because of Sammy. That and the fact that he has bullied you since elementary git-go for whatever reason. What's to lead you to believe anything will change?"

"What do you mean?"

"I mean he's gotten away with the intimidation forever, why would he change his ways? You know about the sayin' about the leopard and his spots?"

"Well, yesterday I was in Woolsworth and..."

"It's Woolworth, not Woolsworth."

"Anyway, I'm mindin' my own business and he up and shoves me against a rack of hats. Says, 'Oh, excuse me', and walks away. I hear him mutter "asshole." He's the asshole."

"Mind your language, young man. You don't need to get down in the gutter with him."

"I could say worse."

"I expect so but that kind of language is more fit for a cow pasture. The question is what do you intend to do about the bullyin'. Seems to me it's time for you to put a stop to it. That movie's played longer than 'Gone With the Wind'."

"I agree, but I don't know how. Sammy says to hit him upside the head with a baseball bat."

"Might work if you happened to have the pure luck of havin' one in your hands when he comes callin'."

Both fell into an extended silence as they pondered the dilemma. A horn honked. The courthouse clock tolled three in the afternoon.

"Self-respect," J.B. said, standing up. "That's what's worth fightin' for. Self-respect."

Chapter 10 - The Ascension

James Ray and his on-again, off-again girlfriend, Melissa Martin, were in an off position, one that had held for almost a year. However, neither was worried about the relationship. James Ray was preoccupied with basketball, his new job at the newspaper, and now, his love for photography. Melissa was busy with yet another summer school. She was on schedule to graduate at the end of summer thereby completing four years of high school in three. Melissa was in too much of a hurry to waste time worrying about a relationship she had mentally set aside for a later date.

On his end, James Ray found it fun to be with Melissa. He thought her to be the smartest girl in the entire county, maybe Texas. Every time he was with her he learned something new and often useful. She had taught him about radio waves and why they traveled farther at night, she had schooled him on what made a basketball bounce when it struck a hardwood floor, and a host of other such things that James Ray had not bothered with, especially the science of it.

He had also seen her in her birthday suit. Her shape and form was like a slice of white bread, thin and delicate. Many other female classmates' bodies were also known to him and his lifelong friend, Bobby Joe Bosh.

The boys' outlandish voyeurism was a time-honored, summertime activity in which they were both skilled and experienced. On his part, James Ray felt the peeking, as they called it, should have stopped somewhere along the way while the two were still in grade school. Bobby Joe, however, found the activity—when it offered more than older, tub-shaped women—erotically stimulating. Plus, the peeking was free. After getting to Devil's Lake, the two would secretly approach the rear of the shower room and mount a quarried stone wall. The sturdy limbs of a mature black oak lent assistance. Once securely positioned, they would peer over and down to take in whatever gifts the day's view offered. Most important of all, was to not be caught in the act.

Both the men's and women's shower facilities were open air. Although no nakedness from the female side of the change rooms was ever brought into clear focus, WWII aviators from nearby Felix Field, would on occasion drop low and buzz the building hoping for a glance of a Mayweather rendition of Betty Grable or a reasonable facsimile. Although flightless, Bobby Joe and James Ray were able to obtain a much closer view point.

"One last time, that's all I'm askin'. One last time," cajoled Bobby Joe.

"I don't think so," James Ray responded. "If we get caught, we're long past bein' able to get away with a scoldin' or a reprimand. I expect they would haul us off to jail or worse."

"I hear you. It's just that I hear all the girls are headed for the lake today. That's what I hear anyways."

"Who makes up all the girls? All the girls at the high school? All the girls in the county? All the girls in Texas?"

"Maybe not all the girls from the high school but a bunch of 'em. I don't know exactly from where 'er how many. How many doesn't matter anyway for Christ's sakes. Naked is naked. Titties are titties, ain't they? A great ass is a great ass. And y'all ain't workin' today, are you? Come on, James Ray. For Christ's sakes come on! One more time and that's it, I swear on my mother's grave."

"She's not dead yet."

"She will be over time and that makes it a sacred vow no matter."

"If you promise to get off my back, one more time but no more. Jesus, Bobby Joe, you're a fat pain in the ass. Always have been."

"Thank you for the compliment. I aim to please."

*　　*　　*　　*　　*

It was none other than Melissa who walked Ruth Ann over to introduce her to James Ray at an evening session of Methodist Youth Fellowship.

"We've actually met," James Ray replied.

"We have actually," responded Ruth Ann, wishing the introduction hadn't taken place.

"My folks had Ruth Ann's folks over for dinner last week," James Ray said. "I found out her mother is a vegetarian."

Ruth Ann frowned.

"Interestin'," Melissa remarked. "Based on a sanctity of animal life or for personal dietary reasons as it relates to your mother's health and well bein'?"

"Everyone asks that question but not exactly in that way."

Following the awkwardness of the introduction, James Ray fled to the safety of friends near the water fountain as Melissa continued to question Ruth Ann about the ethics of vegetarianism. After all, Melissa was intent on becoming a doctor of some sort, most likely a general practitioner, and from what she understood, most medical training had little to do with a patient's nutrition.

"What makes him limp?" Ruth Ann asked at a point when Melissa had ceased questioning. "Is he a cripple of some kind?"

"He's probably as gifted an athlete as we have in Mayweather, limp or not and no, he's not a cripple in the general sense of the word. Had poliomyelitis when he was ten or eleven, I forget. He was fortunate, very fortunate. His affliction was transitory but it left him with his right leg slightly shorter than his left. Was in the hospital around six months or so. Y'all should go to one of his basketball games when the season rolls around. He's our startin' point guard. I don't know much about basketball but he has no trouble dribblin' around someone guardin' him. The impairment seems to throw off defenders somehow. He can out fake Houdini."

"Interestin'," Ruth Ann said, borrowing Melissa's term. "Excuse me, will y'all, I'm goin' to partake of some sustenance that awaits in the far corner, if I can locate a morsel that's sure to contain feathers, bone marrow, or possibly a kneecap."

Rude person, Melissa thought, as she watched Ruth Ann head for the finger food. Why would one athlete not hold interest in another? Despite Ruth Ann's unsocial behavior, however, Melissa had decided she would give extended study to the concept of vegetarianism. She might be missing something and that something might hold the possibility of changing herself, or later, her patients.

The boys caught a ride with a farmer hauling several large bags of chicken feed. There was plenty of room in the back of the pickup and the farmer, Otis Biggs, recognized James Ray. Thanking Mr. Biggs, the two vaulted into the back of the truck and settled in for the short, four-mile haul to Devil's Lake.

Field of View

Biggs let the boys out at the entrance of the park and they walked the remaining half-mile to the park's facilities: the concession stand, the pavilion and its concrete dance floor and jukebox, the man-made lake, and of course, the changing rooms.

Everyone had once assumed the park and its lake would be named after Sam Rayburn, Speaker of the House of Representatives and the town's most notable citizen; or after Roosevelt; or perhaps, James Butler Mays, a martyr of the Battle of the Alamo; or perhaps Bennett J. Bloom, an early east Texas pioneer.

Mayweather, however, was the first name to be cast aside at the city council meeting where naming the nearly-completed depression era New Deal project was but one item on the agenda. The naming alone occupied over two hours of the three hour meeting. It was believed by most in attendance that too many places were already christened Mayweather. There was the city and the county, of course, but also Mayweather High, Mayweather Drug, Mayweather Cleaners, the Bank of Mayweather, Mayweather Mercantile and Mayweather this and Mayweather that.

A younger J.B. Turman, in attendance, suggested the name of Bennett J. Bloom. At one time Bloom had owned almost half the county. If one drove from Mayweather to Oklahoma, his holdings in the mid-to-late 1800s bordered both sides of the road for the entire route. Labor from one of his enterprises cleared the timber from the road's path and although the Republic of Texas was largely penniless, he and others managed to create not only that roadway but other roads that even more efficiently connected Mayweather to its neighboring counties. Once there were decent roads, immigration increased from Germany, Ireland, England, and elsewhere. One family in four brought slaves with them. By the latter part of the century, Mayweather's population had increased to almost 7,000 residents. The numbers were shaky, but by then it was believed that some 30,000 people were living in the county. Business prospered. Cotton was farmed, timber felled, ornate Victorian homes were erected, and sturdy schools were built. Inversely, the local Indian population continued its steady march into oblivion.

Bloom also invested heavily in the Texas and Pacific Railroad. If one was in the timber business, one needed an efficient way to deliver one's product. He and three other Mayweather citizens formed the Bank of Mayweather in 1847, a mere two years after Texas joined the union. An elementary school was named for him and so, too, a cemetery. His great grandson, Orville, played an important role in implementing another New Deal program, the Rural Electrification Act.

To J.B.'s surprise, the time-honored name of Bloom received nothing more than the nod of a head or two. Into the silence, a person J.B. knew to be a Southern Baptist and an everyday bigot, rose to speak. Cheap fedora in hand, he calmly suggested Devil's Lake as a name. J.B. sank heavily back onto his chair.

"Seems harmless enough to me," Petis Farnsworth said. "Three people have died buildin' the park, haven't they? One from a heart attack. One fell off of the dam's scaffoldin', splittin' his head wide open, and another from a durn cottonmouth. The Devil's work all of it. And since y'all vetoed my suggestion of constructin' a place of worship at the park, small and modest though it was, seems Devil's Lake is as good a name as any. The name would be a reminder to any visitor from any part of the great State of Texas, that he needs to keep the Lord Jesus close to his side."

J.B. quickly countered with Coushatta. "Too hard to pronounce," the lone female council member said. "Well, then, how about Piney Ridge, named after the white rock outcroppin' and pine trees the lake will mirror at sunrise and sunset. How about that?" J.B. pleaded. "I don't frankly see how namin' the park after the Devil speaks well for any of us."

To J.B.'s dismay, the discussion returned to Petis's offering, a name for the lake J.B. held to be nonsensical and outright stupid. Perturbed, J.B. rose yet again to address a group whose collective brightness seemed dimmer than the glow from one of the vacuum tubes in his Zenith radio.

"I don't see, in all honesty, how you good people can name the park, paid for by hard earned tax payer dollars in hard times, after a religious myth of a creature. In my opinion, Devil's Lake, as a name, is first of all inappropriate given all the other good names we could confer on the lake, and second, it seems we get enough of the so-called Devil and his 'scare-the-pants-off-of-a-sinner' ways each Sunday at whatever church one attends. Seems to me, pure and simple, the good people of this county ought to be able to picnic, swim and hobnob at the park without havin' to pay any such homage."

Field of View

A motion was made and seconded. The vote was taken. Devil's Lake it would be.

* * * * *

It took no more than a minute for James Ray and Bobby Joe to climb the east wall and secure positions on various branches of stone and oak. The only thing the two boys were missing were prehensile tails. The building contained change rooms and showers on its west side and a concession stand on the east. Its west side was flanked not only by a mature black oak but a thicket of hackberry, juniper and tall grass.

The afternoon sun was to their backs and James Ray, given his beginning knowledge of photography, now knew they were almost invisible from the shower room below. The tree's limbs, its leaves, as well as their peeping Tom heads would be backlit and silhouetted, thereby lacking in visual detail.

Bobby Joe was the first to complete the ascension. "Oh my God, James Ray!" he whispered. "We've struck gold. It's the new girl. The one that's a swimmer. Good Christ, I can see her patch. Hurry!"

Upon hearing Bobby Joe's whispered exclamation, James Ray, who was behind him but nearly to the top of the wall, paused, turned and prepared to climb down instead. He felt like he'd been hit in the head with a hammer. He could feel his heart pounding the way it did before a game. He would have to take a deep breath, collect his senses, prepare himself for the battle ahead, but no, this time he would take flight, not fight. His face flushed as tiny, searing needles assaulted it. Now that fate had somehow chosen Ruth Ann Chambers--just recently a guest at his father's and mother's house--to be their voyeuristic target, he was beset with even more guilt. If found out, he was sure he would be disowned. Once released from jail or juvenile detention, he would have to move out of town disgraced and reviled.

Making sure he didn't fall and make things even worse than they already were, James Ray's right foot searched for a branch strong enough to bear his weight on the way down. His hesitation was all the time Bobby Joe needed. He reached down and grabbed James Ray by his shirt collar, pulling him upward.

"Git up here you ass-wipe," Bobby Joe whispered, too loudly, James Ray thought. "Y'all are missin' the sight of a lifetime. She's takin' a shower. God Almighty, what an ass. Jesus wept, there's her patch again. Great tits, too. That girl has it all. I don't know where the other girls are. Doesn't matter. She's all we need. I'm tellin' you, we've struck gold."

James Ray took another deep breath and against his better judgement, combined with the fear that Bobby Joe would create such a racket that they would be discovered, he gave in to the urgency of Bobby Joe's beckoning. Slowly, he moved upward to the top of the wall surrounding the shower room. After locating the same sturdy and voyeur-friendly limb that had held him all the other times, James Ray's head slowly rose like a teenage equivalent of a moonrise, his head finally high enough that Bobby Joe's academy-award-center-of-interest-celebrating was brought into his field of view.

What he witnessed was stunning. His emotions were a mulled mix of carnal lust, outright admiration for the beauty and athletic, but supple, litheness of Ruth Ann's feminine shape and form, and, of course, he felt a wagon load of guilt. From his perspective, Ruth Ann appeared Eve-like in her open-air garden of cascading water, falling upon flesh and then onto the stone below. The afternoon light scattered in measureless angles of reflection as the water caressed her short, black hair, and the curvature of her body.

Ruth Ann pivoted to her left and began soaping her legs. In doing so, she revealed not only the well defined sculpture of her legs but a here-again, gone-again, titillating view of her breasts in gravity induced descent. Then, she stood erect, reaching both arms upward to rinse her hair. Her nude, soap-and-water-slicked image was both breathtaking and exhilarating. Had he his camera, coupled with her permission, what wonder and magic would he be able to record on film. So blessed, he would employ a confederacy of reflected light and metal and glass and film, all acting in fine-tuned concert to capture and secrete away her latent likeness until acted upon by the chemistry of darkroom witchcraft. God would have nothing on him. He would create his own Garden of Eden. Ruth Ann would be his Adam's rib. His camera would document it all.

He had seen enough, however. The scene had been indelibly etched in his mind, camera or not. If he lived for a hundred years, he figured he would be able to instantly bring Ruth Ann's naked shower image into sharp focus much like hitting one of the cash register buttons at Nicely's Drug. Push any key, turn the crank and the drawer would pop open. But for now, he felt the urgent need to halt the proceedings much like the night when he and Melissa had parked and their usual pattern of petting had become so accelerated someone had to hit the brakes. It was Melissa who had brought the teenage passion-driven vehicle to a halt. This time, he surmised, it wasn't virginity at stake but simply one's dignity, what little of it he had left.

"I'm out of here," he whispered to Bobby Joe. "I'd suggest y'all come too, before the park ranger finds us out."

That evening, James Ray walked home in the dark. Carl had called to ask him to come in and help with a photo essay to be used in advertising the up coming county-wide Mule Day's celebration. It had taken longer than either had thought. On his way home his mind was full of Ruth Ann: her nakedness, the flower of her God-given beauty, dressed or undressed. Why he hadn't been interested in her from the beginning was beyond him. He had been a fool not to let her know he was interested. She had blown off Seth, but Seth was strange in many ways and had never displayed a winning way with girls. In all honestly, he too, had little experience beyond his several-year interest in Melissa and she in him. Suddenly, things had changed. He had seen the light and the light shone brightly on one Ruth Ann Chambers. Someway, maybe at the next Methodist Youth Fellowship meeting, he would find a way to express his interest. In the meantime, he would continue to nurture his newfound belief that Ruth Ann was a Mayweather incarnation of Wonder Woman.

As he turned onto his street, East 9th, a car slowly approached from his rear. Without turning, James Ray recognized the wheeze and rattle of the car to be Rusty Wickware's wreck of a Dodge. His thoughts of Ruth Ann suddenly turned to thoughts of survival.

The car pulled alongside him and stopped. Rusty leaned over toward the passenger-side open window and spoke in James Ray's direction.

"Been quite a day, ain't it Turman. I hear tell y'all were mighty lucky today. My, oh my. Gettin' a naked look at the new girl in town. What's her name? Ruth Ann is it? Y'all still got a boner?"

Laughter erupted from the confines of the Dodge. Without counting heads, James Ray surmised Rusty was accompanied with his usual brainless tagalongs. There would be three of them. Four counting Rusty.

James Ray swallowed hard, began his deep breathing and remained silent. Bobby Joe had obviously spilled the ascension beans. He and his big mouth. Their peeping Tom behavior at Devil's Lake was likely all over town by now. He was ruined. His life would never be the same.

"Think what y'all want, Rusty. It's late and I have to be gettin' home."

"Want a ride, Shithead? Three blocks is a long ways for a cripple."

"Fuck you, Rusty!" James Ray shot back. Turning from the car, he began to walk the three remaining blocks to home. He felt like running, but doing so would be both humiliating and cowardly.

Chapter 11 - Orbs of Light

"Happens on Thursday nights," Janey said, answering her husband's question. "Not every Thursday night but some Thursday nights. Anyway, the next day that's when I find things, personal like things. Some things I recognize like a make-up brush 'er somethin' like that. Once I found a lipstick. The kind a young girl uses. I know that 'cause it's a Tangee. Girls use Tangee. Our granddaughter Cecelia uses Tangee. And once I found a round glass like thing that I think might screw onto a camera lens or somethin'. Once I found a spent flashbulb."

"What's a flashbulb doin' up there?" Teddy asked. "That there hotel has hardly any customers anymore but y'all are sayin' the Honeymoon Suite is reserved for some Thursday nights come hell or high-water? And so on some Thursday nights the room's not only booked but folks are up there takin' flashbulb pictures? Flashbulb pictures of what? And why not Monday nights or Fridays or early some mornin' for God's sakes. Don't make an ounce of sense to me, Janey. Don't make no sense whatsoever."

"Might not, but it's true. Remember a Thursday night or so ago, I called y'all's attention to all the light flashin' that was comin' from the Honeymoon Suite and y'all had your head so stuck in your radio program you paid me no never mind? Remember?"

Janey worked for the Lone Star Hotel as a part-time, on-call housekeeper. Most days she had at least one or two rooms to clean, sometimes none. Once summoned, she would tote over her own Electrolux vacuum and labor away at however many or few rooms needed her attention. Once the rooms were clean and fresh sheets in place, she would lug the soiled bedding back across the street and do the laundry at her house. Over time, Janey had talked the hotel's penny-pinching owner into paying her for the vacuum's filters. After even more intense negotiation, she was finally reimbursed for use of her upgraded and favorite detergent, Duz, for the washing. She was on her own for the water and wear and tear of her washing machine.

The Lone Star was but one of two hotels in town. The other, the Blue Bonnet, was by far the hotel of choice as long as money was of little consequence. The Lone Star had long ago lost its competitive edge and had completed its fall-from-grace journey during the great depression. Its paint was peeling, its linoleum worn, its wallpaper out-of-date, and its parking lot a jumble of potholes and displaced gravel. The steps to the six rooms upstairs groaned under the slightest weight and the hotel's flooring throughout, save for the newly-installed carpet in the registration room, were but faint reminders of past glory. There was no money to install air-conditioning, ensuring that the hotel's rooms in the summer were as unbearable as they had been when the hotel was built in the early 1900s. Even its once proud, red and white neon lit marquee, a 1928 addition, was only half-functional. Its white outline of a star framed the words 'Lone Star' with the slimmest of flickers; whereas, in the red neon 'Lone Star' letters, only the Star was lit with its original nighttime radiance.

It was another random Thursday night when Teddy also observed the odd flashing of light coming from the hotel's second-story window. Given witness to such a strange event, his interest was fully stoked.

"You say all that there flashin' is comin' from the Honeymoon Suite?" Teddy asked.

"Indeed it is. That's the room facin' us. I know it like the back of my hand."

"Well, what fer bloomin' sakes could it be? The flashin' and all?"

"Don't know, but somethin' untoward is goin' on, I suspect."

"What?"

"I said somethin' untoward might..."

"Never heard that word before. Untoward. Where did y'all come up with such a fancy, highbrow word and what does it mean anyway?"

"Read it in a book. Means somethin' like bad things are likely to happen or somethin' like that. Leastways, bad things happened in the book. It was plain untoward through and through."

*　*　*　*　*

"Tell me what you know about composition," Carl said through the scatter of exhaled cigarette smoke.

The two had taken to Linde Bee's Cafe for some sustenance. James Ray figured it would be another long night given the fact they were still working on the Mule Day's photo essay. He had cautioned his parents he would most likely be home late.

"Take the street scene," Carl offered, nodding in the direction of Linde Bee's entrance, "tell me what you see, what's within your field of view, and we will go from there."

James Ray turned from the menu and looked to the front of the cafe and beyond.

"People walkin' about. Cars here and there. The courthouse beyond."

"That's all fine and good but what I want to hear from you is the language of the craft. Speak to me in the kind of language you would use if you were teaching a class in photography."

James Ray hesitated. Suddenly he felt inadequate, inarticulate, unable to answer Carl's question to any degree of satisfaction on his part or Carl's.

With no good way out, he would have to try. "Well, the street scene, the visual...the visual elements beyond, the people and the cars and so on, are framed by the cafe's window..."

"Good. Continue."

"And...should someone walk by or peek into the window, you might have your center of interest. Maybe it's you drivin' by in y'all's Cadillac and maybe y'all have someone ridin' with you."

"Go on."

"Well, if I took a picture from here, from our table, the people...the people in the foreground would be silhouetted because they're backlit while the folks runnin' around outside would be correctly exposed. Right?"

"Proceed, young man."

"I don't know. What if I changed my subject-to-camera distance and took the picture from the kitchen? What if I took the picture from the front door and eliminated the people near the window?"

"Now you're talking. You could do all those things and more."

"And what if I used a slow enough shutter speed so that y'all's Cadillac was blurred as it passed by but everything else in the photo was frozen? What about that?"

"All well and good. Here's the definition of composition. Composition is the creative arrangement of visual elements within the frame. Now, mark it to memory. You're the artist.

You're in control. You're the creator when it comes to composition. Whatever visual elements are out there, anything and everything are at your mercy. Well, almost. You can't move the Grand Canyon but you can make a million compositional decisions using the canyon as your subject matter."

Betty Smith, a long-time waitress at the cafe, approached to take their order. Carl ordered a chicken-fried steak. Although a foreign menu option at first, he soon developed a liking for the bottom-round, batter-dipped, skillet fried, tenderized steak, smothered in gravy. James Ray ordered a cheeseburger devoid of onions, but with a side of french fries.

After Betty had scribbled their order in some kind of cafe shorthand, Carl watched her leave the table. "Seems old man Binkert didn't have enough lead in his pencil to bring on a boy child," he remarked to James Ray. "His three girls, though, I'd like to take them all on at the same time. Maybe you could help me?" he added, smiling.

James Ray didn't reply although the youngest of the sisters, Sally, was Seth's age and attractive. She had been a cheerleader when James Ray was a sophomore. He assumed if such a situation did occur, the five of them altogether in a hanky-panky hoopla of some kind, he'd opt for Sally and leave the two older sisters to Carl.

"But back to composition. What's the definition? Lay it on me."

James Ray recited the definition verbatim. To his great satisfaction, his photo of the old men around the courthouse had been published by the *Tribune* in its Around Town Sunday section. Although he was paid nothing for his work, given the fact he was employed part-time for the paper, he nonetheless felt he was well on his way to becoming a local photographer of note. He was even offered the job of photo editor for the *Coushatta*. He was flattered but he had reservations as to whether or not he could meet that responsibility, practice and play varsity basketball and still be available for some as-needed-work at the *Tribune*. All in all, it seemed a stretch too far.

Their food was served and Carl surveyed his plate. He looked over at James Ray. "All right, apply the definition to the photo of the old geezers at the courthouse. The one run by the paper. How did you arrange the visual elements?"

James Ray swallowed a bite of his cheeseburger and began describing the multiple ways he had arranged the visual elements within the frame: his camera angle, his subject to camera distance, and his insistence that none of the men look at the camera's lens. In the most striking and revealing of all his exposures, the one when he was in the tree, up looking down at his subjects, he explained how he had used the leaves of the tree as a framing device. It was a trick Carl had suggested. The out of focus leaves framed them as they whiled away the day. The photo spoke of a sense of mystery surrounding them in their while-away-the-day-do-nothing-constructive courthouse environment.

"They're called circles of confusion," Carl interjected, hearing James Ray mention the leaves.

"What?"

"Circles of confusion. The lens of the camera can't resolve the incoming light rays because they are too close to the film plane to be sharply focused. Everything that is rendered sharp is the result of light rays falling precisely on the film's plane. The other rays, the ones that come to focus ahead of or behind the film plane fall flat, out of focus, unrecognizable in most cases. They are orbs of light, mysterious and unrevealing in visual detail. Anyway, start looking closely at pictures in magazines—Look, National Geographic, Arizona Highways, and so on. Look for elements in the foreground or background which are unsharp. They are unsharp because they are circles of confusion, out of focus light rays. Your job as a photographer is to know what causes them and to apply the techniques that manage the effect. I'll get around to teaching you about depth of field and use of circles of confusion at another time. Master that concept and you can call yourself a photographer. If you can't get a handle on depth of field, you may as well be posing as a point and shoot dirt farmer with no idea how to till the soil. Or maybe you'd be a fry cook at Linde Bee's, a person who doesn't know a roux from a finished gravy."

*   *   *   *   *

Judith had been saving for several years. Her getaway wasn't complicated and the move to Mayweather hadn't altered her plan. She would wait out Ruth Ann's senior year, and continue saving money from her house allowance so that she could move to Austin to be with her sister. Then she could dissolve her stagnant, miserable marriage. The only reason she agreed to move to Mayweather in the first place was the singular fact that Mayweather High had an Olympic-size swimming pool, which, for the greater part of its existence, had been seldom used. Fortunately for Judith and Ruth Ann, Cindy Stillwaters, a science and physical education teacher, who had been hired at the beginning of the 1950-51 school year, was on a mission to restore the pool and renew a swimming program. She was also a former All-American swimmer at Texas Christian University in Fort Worth. Her employment at Mayweather, coupled with her desire to utilize the uniqueness of the pool, might put an end to the period of its non-use.

Judith didn't know that she could credit the grandson of pioneer Bennett Bloom for the atypical and expensive olympic-sized pool. The pool was a late addition to the new Mayweather High School when it was planned back in 1927. The school board's president at the time was Bennett J. Bloom, and what a Bloom wanted, a Bloom got. What the good Mrs. Ann Carolyn Bloom wished for her son was an opportunity for him to participate in the 1932 Summer Olympics to be held in Los Angeles. The beneficiary of the budget largess, sixteen-year old Jack James Bloom, never made the Olympics. Traveling at a speed, estimated to be eighty miles an hour on a dirt and gravel country road, he lost control of his Indian Scout, was thrown, and killed. The motorcycle had been a birthday present from his parents.

Ruth Ann had come to Mayweather highly touted. Stillwaters, eager to revive the high school's swim program, had willingly taken on Ruth Ann upon her arrival at the beginning of summer. Both were eager to begin the training and Stillwaters volunteered to conduct the lessons, uncompensated for her time and effort, until school started in September. Reconditioning the pool meant convincing the school board to pony up the money necessary to resurface the entire fifty by twenty-five meter pool, re-stripe the ten lanes, refurbish or replace the boiler and pump, then fill and heat the 660,000 gallon pool to a temperature of at least seventy-seven degrees. All that for one student with outstanding promise plus a handful of hopefuls.

Stillwaters and Ruth Ann, along with Ruth Ann's mother, had made a personal pool opening appeal at a special session of the school board only to have a motion by Wisdom Wheelwright, a newly-elected member, suggest the item be rescheduled at a later date.

Field of View

"That there pool," Wisdom said, "probably holds as much water as Devil's Lake 'er more. And why in tarnation does the pool have to be, what did y'all call it? Resurfaced? Can't that be put off 'til later? That and the stripin' and all? Then there's the boiler. Money don't grow on trees around here, leastways as far as I've seen."

"The pool, Mr. Wisdom, if it's filled now and we put off the resurfacin' 'til later, will have to be drained and refilled. It's far more economical to do what has to be done now, not later," Stillwaters countered.

Judith Chambers felt the need to speak given the motion to table the issue. Time, she felt, was of the essence. Delay was unacceptable.

"We came to this fine city based on the fact my husband had a good job offer but also because of the reputation of Miss Stillwaters. That, and the fact that Mayweather High has an asset of unique value to the community and its students. Surely y'all recognize the value of such a thing. I dare say no other high school in Texas has such an asset. For an Olympic-size pool to be left unattended and in disrepair, is, I'm sorry to say, unbecomin'. I am fully confident that Miss Stillwaters will, in less than a year or two, put Mayweather back on the swimmin' map. That's all I have to say except to say thank y'all kindly for hearin' us out."

Although there were no more than two dozen people in attendance--six of them high school student swim possibilities, brought to the meeting by Stillwaters--all heads turned in Judith's direction and remained so as she spoke. A critic would have had a hard time deciding whether the mother or daughter was the finer example of a female.

Ruth Ann had remained silent until asked by Wheelwright what she thought about the money necessary to undertake such a project.

"I know money is always a problem with most things," she replied, after rising from her seat. "But I don't think you get a solid football team or basketball team or tennis or whatever, without spendin' money. I suppose y'all will have to make the decision whether or not to reopen the pool based on what y'all think is right. I can promise you one thing, though. If y'all decide to fix the pool, I'll bring home a state championship. I'll work hard for you. I promise y'all that, and there are some other kids here who will do the same if you give us a chance. Yes, it's about money, but it's also about providin' us with an opportunity."

"Y'all are a junior next year? Is that right, Ruth Ann?" Sam Mifflin, the board president, asked casually.

"Yes, sir."

Stillwaters hoped her formidable threesome had hit the equivalent of an aquatic home run. Following their presentation, however, a motion was made, seconded, and the five-member Mayweather School District Board of Education, in its collective wisdom, voted three-to-two against the proposal. The Bennett J. and Ann Carolyn Bloom pool legacy was doomed to remain in a state of disrepair and disregard, nothing more than a cavernous, reinforced steel, shotcrete and tile reminder of a once hopeful and competitive swimming past.

Chapter 12 - Game Change

Teddy arrived early. After stopping for his usual doughnut and coffee, he sauntered across Main and worked his way to the courthouse's *White Only* restroom. Inside, he relieved his bladder, and for what may have been the 10th time that morning, felt inside his top overall pocket to make sure his object for the day's discussion was still there, patiently ticking away, waiting for the right opportunity to be seen in the harsh and revealing light of day. Everything would change after he revealed his treasure, his evidence, his graphic, two-dimensional black and white equivalent of an atomic bomb.

Relieved of his urinary discomfort, Teddy went back outside, located his customary wrought iron bench, sat and began the wait for the others. They would be along soon, Soapy first, then Chipper, and lastly Winney. Any discussion of the day's events would wait for their leader, or as Teddy called Winney to his back, *"His Royal Hind End."* However, today would be different. It was Teddy's turn to lead, to direct, and yes, to reveal.

The courthouse clock tolled eight in the morning. Numerous shop windows around the square began to read *Open* instead of *Closed*. In choreographed unison, people began moving about. Car doors slammed shut, interior lights were turned on, store doors opened, sidewalks were swept, and the myriad sounds of a city square's morning arousal rang discordant into the still of the morning.

Teddy missed his good friend Ollie. It would have been nice to have Ollie at his side today. Ollie would have been proud of his discovery. Ollie was always enthusiastic, eager to chew on the day's subject matter, and always had something insightful to say even though he was hard pressed to see past his nose. Ollie was a good friend indeed.

Orville Batterton had been a fifth member of the Whittle, Spit and Chew Club. Sadly, Ollie was hit and killed by an inbound Continental Trailways bus two years past. The afternoon when he was struck down on Main Street, Ollie, although legally blind, had just sat through a movie doubleheader.

Following his death, Winney explained to the group that Ollie's propensity to go to the movies despite his visual handicap was no different from the way normal people go about listening to the radio.

"Folks make up what they can't see in their heads," he offered. "Same difference with Ollie, if y'all ask me. He hears what they're sayin' and makes up the pictures in his head. Might see a better picture that way, who knows?"

After listening to his two westerns, Ollie sought to cross traffic-laden Main to access the courthouse lawn so he could tell them about what he had just heard. Once he managed the courthouse lawn, he was mere seconds removed from his bench and cohorts. The rude obstacle of a bus, however, hit him while he was in full stride, his chin pointed in the general direction of his destination while his cane swept a presumed safe back and forth path ahead of him.

Interviewed following the accident, the Trailways bus driver said the old timer had taken to the street like a *"cur dog after a cottontail rabbit"*.

Out of respect to the deceased family, the *Tribune* decided not to use the bus driver's quote. The paper remarked, however, that the death was *"a great and tragic accidental irony for a longtime and worthy Mayweather citizen."* The irony had to do with the fact the bus was carrying Batterton's daughter and three of his grandchildren. They were coming to town to visit him on a Thanksgiving holiday.

Soapy appeared at his usual time, a few minutes after eight. He sat and opened a fresh bar of Ivory. "Mornin', Teddy."

"Mornin' back to y'all. It's a mighty fine day for a discussion, don't y'all think?"

"Reckon so. Here comes Chipper," Soapy observed. "If he don't hurry, he might miss the day's conversational train."

"Are we in a hurry?" asked Teddy. "I do have somethin' of unusual note but it can simmer for awhile."

"Well, what is it?"

"Like I say, it's simmerin'. Y'all will see soon enough."

"Mornin' Chipper," offered Teddy, when Chipper was within hearing distance.

"Hi-de-do, Chipper," said Soapy.

"And the same back to y'all."

"Reckon we could start the meetin'," Teddy said.

"But Winney ain't here," replied Chipper, aghast at such a suggestion.

"Ain't a concern of mine," responded Teddy. "Today is a day unlike any of our yesterdays. And besides, I'm countin' on

J.B. to help solve the mystery of the day. I dare say the subject will be over Winney's head."

"What in the world, are y'all talkin' about?" questioned Chipper. "Y'all gone and had somethin' to drink this early in the day?"

"Heard my name called. Somethin' havin' to do with my head?" voiced Winney from behind the benches. Uncharacteristically, Winney had approached the group from their flank. He had been detoured from his regular approach due to sidewalk repair on the east side of the courthouse.

"Just mentioned that y'all were headed our way but from a different direction," Teddy lied.

"Well, then y'all must have eyes in the back of yer head, T.R. Mighty fine asset, eyes in the back of y'all's head."

"What's that y'all 'er carvin', Soapy?" asked Teddy, trying to change the subject. "Gonna up and carve another undersized alabaster peter, balls and all?"

"Maybe. Might just go and show it to the new redhead at the superintendent's office. Might get her all hot and bothered."

"Take more than a tiny little Ivory soap-of-a-dick to get the likes of her goin'. Need to be the size of one of them big ass cucumbers or some such," Winney offered, thinking it was time to fire the starting gun to their day's mishmash of mostly conversational hogwash.

Seeing that Winney was seated, Teddy stood erect and as authoritatively as if before an unseen lectern. "I will introduce the first and only item for the day's discussion," said Teddy confidently.

"What's that y'all said about first and only?" asked Winney. "Who in the hell put y'all in charge of our day's discourse? Is somethin' wrong with you? Y'all gone plain nuts on us, have you?"

"I put myself in charge. I have here in my pocket a thing of great importance to all of us. Meanin' everyone in Mayweather. The county too. Maybe the great State of Texas. It's nothin' less than the Devil's work and when you see it y'all will agree, I'm dead certain of that," he said, tapping away at his pocket.

"Good Christ, Thigpin, what the holy shit are ye talkin' about? Have y'all lost what little mind you have?" responded Winney.

"Criticize all you want to, makes me no never mind. Y'all will see soon enough."

"Well then, when the flyin' fuck do we get to see whatever it is hidin' in y'all's pocket? You want money first? Y'all want us to lick yer boots?"

Teddy stood his ground and remained silent. He surveyed the tops of the surrounding trees. He reveled in the mood he had created. He was pleased that Winney was off his spot and upset. Things were going swimmingly. He, and he only, was finally in charge. The churning sound of a cement mixer could be heard from the east side of the courthouse. Birds chirped. The redhead from the superintendent's office walked by. All heads turned in her direction. Soapy hid his still rudimentary Ivory phallus between his legs.

"We'll wait for J.B," Teddy finally said. "Then we'll proceed. In the meantime, I'm goin' fer another cup of coffee. I'm goin' to need it. Anyone wanna come with me? We'll all need to stay alert and focused. After y'all see what I have in my pocket, everythin' will change. Nothin' will ever be the same in Mayweather. Coffee, anyone? I'm off for coffee."

"Never seen anythin' like it," snorted Winney in Teddy's wake. He spat and reached for a plug of his Bull Durham. "Man's off his ever-lovin' rocker."

"Maybe he's got a famous baseball card in his pocket," suggested Chipper.

"What would the devil's work have to do with baseball?" asked Soapy. "Fer sure he's got a corncob up his ass."

*   *   *   *   *

James Ray made it all the way to his front yard before Rusty's gang pulled up in front. The maltreated and poorly maintained Dodge loudly backfired when Rusty killed its engine. James Ray jumped, thinking Rusty had pulled out a gun and fired it in his direction.

Doors opened and slammed shut. Rusty was good with drama but he was minus a decent drum beat to announce his grandiose presence. The slamming of doors would serve as a substitute.

Following James Ray's profane farewell three blocks away and five or so minutes earlier, Rusty had thrown the Dodge's floorboard stick shift into first gear, popped the clutch, and pressed hard on the accelerator. In doing so, he flooded the engine's carburetor. Once the car was nursed back to life, Rusty sped to James Ray's house, hoping to catch him before he was barricaded inside. He was in luck. James Ray was on his front lawn, looking sheepish and minuscule under the glow of the corner lamp post. Finally, Rusty figured he had James Ray cornered unless, coward like, he ran for cover inside the house.

"I wanted to apologize for upsettin' you, James Ray. No harm intended," Rusty said, stepping from the street onto the Turman front yard. Turning his head back to his gang of three, he motioned them to stay near the car.

"Sometimes I go and get carried away and I'd like to make amends. That all right with you? There was no need for me to go and make mention of y'all's...what's it called? Infirmity? Or y'all's Ruth Ann boner, either."

"For the life of me Wickware," James Ray shot back, "I don't get what makes you such a sorry asshole, son-of-a-bitch."

"Well, then. Looks like y'all aren't man enough to accept my apology. Is that right, Turman? Y'all have somethin' else in mind? Would y'all rather take a swing at me. It's all right if you do. I 'spect I have it comin'."

Rusty stepped closer to James Ray. No more than two yards now separated the two.

From the dark of the front porch, a figure appeared. Barefoot and clad only by his plaid boxer shorts, J.B. walked slowly toward the two boys, saying nothing, his arms folded across his barrel of a chest. He looked at his son, then to Morris Wickware's feeble excuse of a son, and then in the direction of the Dodge and Rusty's thugs.

J.B. took a deep breath, rubbed his chin, and exhaled into the night's bedlam of cricket courtship racket. Given the surprise wrought by his presence, neither boy spoke.

Finally, J. B. broke the awkward silence.

"Can't figure, Rusty, why y'all's daddy can't keep the Dodge you drive in any kind of drivin' condition. Here you have a mechanic for a daddy and yet that fine historic relic of a car would be hard pressed to outrun a farmer's tractor. What's that all about? And just for my information, what happened to the Dodge's hood ornament? Good example of a leapin' kind of a ram if I recall correctly. All ready to do some worthy head buttin' and all."

"Fell off I reckon. Anyways, my daddy says I have to learn to tune it myself. Don't rightly care much about cars. Rather focus on gettin' myself a good piece of ass." Rusty surprised himself by answering both of J.B.'s questions but felt somewhat redeemed by his "good piece of ass" declaration.

"Well, that's informative. Thank you for sharin' about y'all's skirt chasin' activities, but let's forget the car tunin' and the girl chasin' and get on with the evenin's agenda. Why exactly are you here Rusty? I suppose James Ray would like to know and since y'all disturbed my sleep by way of your backfirin'-out-of-tune-for-life Dodge, let's hear what you and your boys are about this splendid evenin'. Did I hear you say somethin' about an apology? For somethin' y'all did recently or an apology for all the stupid and asinine things y'all have said and done since y'all were bein' diaper trained?"

Rusty took an involuntary step backward. It was just like an adult to go and fuck up the evening, he thought. Adults held the power. They had resources kids didn't. An adult was also likely to up and call the sheriff. And they knew how to mess with a conversation until they gained the upper hand.

"So what is it Rusty? Is your real reason for bein' here on our lawn to kick a little ass as opposed to gettin' some ass? What is it? Speak up, Rusty. Let's hear what's on y'all's teenage and yet to be fully developed mind."

Rusty remained silent, fists clenched in frustration.

"Just in case you're confused," J.B. continued, "my James Ray here will take you on right now. Just you and my James Ray. Up to it Rusty? Is that the real reason you graced us with your presence? Fine evenin' for a brawl if that's the case. Let's see now, I'll do the refereein'. Your tag-alongs will keep to the car and if a man's down, he's down until he gets up. Fists only. Keep y'all's legs to yourself Rusty or I'll personally see to it y'all will wake in the mornin' minus one or both of 'em."

Without a word, Rusty turned and retreated in the direction of his gang and the Dodge. He got in and pressed the starter. The car wouldn't start. The battery possessed no more life than a tomato vine following an ice storm.

Saying nothing, J.B. went inside the house, grabbed the keys to his Olds, drove the car to the street, and maneuvered the car's grill flush with the grill of Rusty's Dodge. He opened the hood of the Olds and ordered Rusty to do the same to the Dodge sans its chrome action figure of a mountain goat. J.B. connected the jumper cables, re-entered the idling Olds, increased its RPM's, and motioned Rusty to try to start the Dodge. From the dim light of the lamp post, it appeared the two conveyances were engaged in a sheet metal nose-to-nose Kama Sutra.

"It won't be the last you'll see of him. You know that, don't you?" J.B. said after Rusty's departure.

"Yes, I know. Bobby Joe, he was there when Rusty kicked the shit...sorry, kicked the crap out of that country boy. He said Rusty always sucker punches. He'll be talkin' about this or that and all of a sudden somebody's missin' their teeth."

"What does that tell you then?"

"I don't know, what?"

"When it cones down to it, hit him first. Don't wait for your teeth to go missin'. Hit him first and don't let up. A man with a broken nose is often a man broken. Be calm about it. Keep your senses. Know that surprise will always work in your favor. He knows that. I suspect he thinks you're a coward, a pushover. You'll have to show him different but show him in a hurry, don't wait around for the afternoon bus to Sherman. Take it to him fast and hard but be calm and efficient all at the same time. Just like you do when the game's on the line. Focus. Be determined but keep your calm just the same."

James nodded in the affirmative but didn't speak.

"By the way, son of mine, I need to talk to you about your Mr. Malone. It's late, I know, but we need to talk. And after what we just went through, I don't want any additional confrontation. Just you and me, father and son. Your mother's asleep and we'll let her rest. I hope y'all can put me straight on a couple of concerns I have."

*　　*　　*　　*　　*

The shelter was finished ahead of time. J. B. was pleased with the effort but uncomfortable with the cost of an entity that might not fully serve its purpose in the family's lifetime. Beside the cost and the iffy utility of it all, he figured his property taxes would no doubt increase as well.

Sarah Mae's open house soured in a hurry. No sooner had she placed a vase of fresh daisies and petunias on the small table in her storm shelter than Seth announced he had joined the Marines.

"*Semper Fidelis*, means always faithful. I'll check in at Parris Island in South Carolina then on to Camp Pendelton in southern California," Seth announced proudly.

"How did you do that without our permission?" asked J.B., as Sarah Mae immediately hid her face with her hands. Saying nothing, she sat heavily on the shelter's bed, its coiled wire webbing voicing resistance to the sudden weight.

"Been eighteen for a spell now. I would have had to get y'all's permission, a waiver, while I was seventeen. Now that I'm eighteen, I could do it on my own. So I did. And thanks for holdin' me back in second grade. Couldn't have met the age requirement otherwise. I just felt like I needed to make somethin' of myself. I feel like I don't know who I am or where I belong and I don't mean to hurt y'all's feelin's but I know I don't belong here. There's nothin' for me here. I can be somethin' in the Marines. I'm gonna be somethin', Mother. Don't cry."

"You were going to go to college," Sarah Mae managed.

"Not any more, I'm not."

James Ray was thrilled by the announcement. How many ways could one spell freedom? Not only would he have his own room for the first time, but he figured he was getting rid of a lifelong pest. After all, Seth had been there from the beginning. There would be no more having to put up with Seth's reading for hours into the night when he, James Ray, craved sleep and the darkness that should accompany it. He would finally have the gift of isolation and the peace and quiet that came with it. There would be no more haranguing over whose turn it was to borrow the Olds. There would be more white meat chicken available on Sunday afternoons and maybe, just maybe, bacon would cease to be rationed at breakfast time. All that and more. His being rid of his older sibling was to him the equivalent of finding a buried treasure.

"Good job, Seth," James Ray said. "Hope y'all do well. Where exactly is Parris Island and how long do y'all stay there before headin' for California?"

Almost everyone who had been invited showed up. One neighbor left early when she realized she would be sharing food and the lawn with the Johnsons. No one else seemed to mind that a colored family was present. If they did, they didn't let it be known. It would make for fodder for later discussion. Pastor

Pritchard blessed the shelter. Elsie told everyone she could that she had been there for the first shovel of dirt.

"Thought they were headed for China," she cackled. "Now look. Ever seen a more spiffy storm shelter? Ought to name it for a famous hotel or somethin'."

Eartha had baked three pies for the occasion. Her apple, lattice-crust pie was J.B.'s favorite. His contribution to the festivities was what he judged to be his famous peach and pecan home-churned ice cream. When he and Pastor Pritchard were chatting outside the shelter, J.B. told of the time when he had added a few ounces of Sarah Mae's breast milk to some of his homemade ice cream.

"The breast milk couldn't be refrigerated forever," J.B recalled. "So I up and threw it in the mix. Believe my brother said the ice cream was maybe the best I'd ever made."

Both men laughed until they were red in the face. Sarah Mae had overhead J.B.'s telling of the special ice cream story. Upon hearing the laughter, she walked up to J.B. and gave him a frown forceful enough to fell a grown elephant.

"Glad y'all are havin' a good time," she said. "Pastor Pritchard, I need to talk to you about Seth when y'all are done with y'all's merriment."

Amid the cleanup following the open house when the conversational air was still torpid from Seth's announcement, James Ray brashly voiced his desire to convert his mother's shelter into a darkroom.

"A what?" Sarah Mae asked.

"A darkroom. I can't get all that I need to do done at the paper. For the most part we are workin' on newspaper stuff. I don't have enough time to do what I want to do. That's why I need to use the shelter. It'll be perfect for a darkroom."

"I don't know about that," J.B. countered. "It would be the world's most expensive darkroom. I do know that."

"Absolutely not," Sarah Mae interjected. "I hoped and prayed for my shelter for years and I finally have it after all the kickin' and screamin' of y'all's father and I'm not about to see it full of poison chemicals and such. Absolutely not."

"I didn't kick and scream."

"Yes, you did! I had to pitch a fit to get you to finally build it. And y'all moaned and groaned the entire time, claimin' this or that was too expensive or this or that couldn't be done or whatever. I wonder if there's a husband in the entire world who can do somethin' without complainin' about it?"

"Maybe, maybe not," J.B. replied in his defense. "But it's done isn't it? And it's bigger and nicer than any storm shelter in the county. Got shelves for y'all's cannin'. Got electricity. A coal oil lamp wouldn't do. Had to have electricity. Had to have a rug so y'all's feet would stay warm. Had to have a whiz bang of a pulley and gear door that ought to be in the next world's fair wherever that's scheduled to be. Had to have a shelf for more than one version of a Bible and pictures of anyone we've ever know in our married lives, some dead, some alive, some barely so. Good grief, Sarah Mae, just what does it take to meet y'all's high standards for performance?"

In error, James Ray decided to put in his two cents worth. He may as well have cursed in front of Pastor Pritchard or shown up butt-naked for the open house.

"What I don't get is why I can't use it for a darkroom. A shelter is only used once in a great while. How often does a person have to take to one anyway? Once or twice a season? In the meantime, it sits there vacant and all."

"You mention convertin' my shelter to a darkroom one more time and you'll have a blistered bottom so bad you won't be able to sit down for a week, even if I have to do it myself," Sara Mae said, sobbing. She turned to the shelter, wrestled the heavy door open and then closed it behind her, leaving J.B. and James Ray in her wake. It would be two hours before she decided her point was sufficiently made and therefore a reasonable time to make her exit.

"Didn't see that tornado comin." J.B. said to James Ray. "I expect that either you or your mother are better at spottin' 'em than I am."

From the corner of her front porch, Elsie had witnessed the entirety of the confrontation although she was unable to hear all of it. She was best able to hear what Sarah Mae had said given the emotional pitch and volume of her words.

Once the Turman brouhaha ran its course, she recalled times when she also had to use the tools in a woman's possession to bring a man to heel. No longer, however. Her recalcitrant example of a husband died ten years ago on their 44th anniversary. Relieved of the bother of reminding a husband of his shortcomings came at a price, and that price was loneliness. She thought Sarah Mae had been too tough on J.B.

After all, he had labored long and hard on the shelter during days when the heat and humidity were a burden on any creature, two legged or otherwise.

She rocked back and forth on her swing. She looked over to the Turman yard and the completed storm shelter. She had seen Sarah Mae take to the shelter after her tirade. She wondered how long she would remain. What would she do down there? Would she pray? If so, for whom? For Seth perhaps? He could be sent to Korea. That war that wasn't called a war. Would she pray for a husband who would more happily do her bidding? Would she come to her senses and pray for her salvation and forgiveness as well? Would she be humble enough to seek a divine answer to her inability to see the world in a more positive light?

Although she no longer had to worry about reminding a husband of his shortcomings, she thought Sarah Mae should be careful in the level of her criticism, thinking that more than one single woman she knew would take on J.B. in a heartbeat, shortcomings and all. She included herself in that group. So what if she were older than he? What did a dozen or so years matter when it came to companionship? Further, if she had someone as fine as J.B., she'd never ask him to build her a storm shelter. A little handholding would do just fine.

*　*　*　*　*

The talk with James Ray had gone reasonably well until the end. When pressed, James Ray admitted to having had a cigarette when he was coming back from the Red River with Carl. He also admitted to having had a few cigarettes when he was with Bobby Joe over a period of three years or so.

"Don't like 'em. I know they're bad for me. I just did it...I don't know, out of some kind of companionship, if that makes any sense."

"I suppose it does. People do a lot of things out of a sense of companionship. Some good, some bad. Some things, I would put cigarettes and alcohol in the same category, can be habit formin' in a hurry. First thing a person is smokin' or drinkin' for the companionship of it and then lo and behold, a person is doing it because he thinks he has to. Can't think of life without it. Becomes a crutch, pure and simple."

"I know that's true. Bobby Joe used to smoke every now and then. Now he carries his cigarettes everywhere he goes."

"Do y'all happen to know what Mr. Malone was carryin' in the trunk of his Cadillac?"

"No, just some boxes. I was over to the river watchin' a sunset. Why?"

"Just wondered. Someone said his Cadillac had weak springs, that's all.

"Why would a new car have weak springs?"

"Don't know. Why didn't you call and let us know you were goin' to be late home from work?"

"I did. I told you Carl invited me to supper at Linde Bee's."

"Yes, but you didn't ask permission to go to the Red River with him."

"He just asked me if I wanted to ride in his Cadillac. That's all."

"James Ray, I worry about your relationship with the Malone man. Your mother worries also. Most times bad company will corrupt good character. Please take that under consideration."

"Are y'all sayin' Carl is bad for me? Is that what you mean by my character bein' corrupted?"

"I didn't say it was corrupted. I just want to warn you that it could be. I don't know the Malone man well. Not at all, actually. All I'm tryin' to say, and I'm not sayin' it well obviously, is for you to maintain a head's up attitude. Be true to your principles. Keep a good grip on your behavior. That's all."

"I really don't think you have anythin' to worry about. Carl is good to me. He's caused me to figure out what I want to do in my life. I really don't see how that corrupts my character."

J.B. sighed. James Ray lapsed into silence. He knew it would be imprudent to tell his daddy how thrilling it was to be transported at over a hundred miles an hour: engine revving, wind rushing, heart pounding. He had never experienced anything like it. Someday he would have such a fine example of a vehicle. Someday he would have enough money to buy someone supper at Linde Bee's and then take them for a ride of a lifetime in some fancy car. Spacious. Chromed. Beautiful. Fast. Someday.

Chapter 13 - Come Sunday Morning

"Here's what we will do." Stillwaters said to Ruth Ann and her mother. "We'll fund-raise. We'll do whatever we have to do to raise money and after raisin' enough to impress the board, we'll go back to them and ask them for the rest."

"What do y'all have in mind for the fund-raisin'?" asked Judith.

"Car wash, bake sales and so on. Whatever. I'm open for suggestions. I'm confident that if we work hard enough and show enough intent, we can change their vote."

Cindy Stillwaters was not one to take no for an answer. She was competitive. As the youngest of six children, she fought for her mother's time and attention. She fought for her rights when denied by one or more of her older and stronger siblings. As a teenager, she struggled with her sexual identity. In college, finally comfortable with who she was as a person, she fiercely competed at the state and national levels. As a teacher and coach, her first principal thought she was too strict, too demanding. Failure was not a word in her vocabulary.

The fund-raising word spread. Students and their parents organized. Money began to come in. It was Sarah Mae who had the best suggestion of all to raise money.

"Ask a Bloom. Ask Lucinda. Ask her next Sunday."

"Well," replied J.B., "that's all and good but she's a Baptist and she's not a Bloom, she's a Godshall. Lucinda somethin' Godshall."

"Lucinda B. Godshall. B. is for Bloom. She'a direct descendant. That's who she is."

"Don't say."

"Do. Y'all aren't the only one who knows people in town, J.B. Turman. Lucinda is a great, great, somethin' or other to the original Blooms...the..."

"Bennett J. Bloom."

"Yes, him and his descendants. That group. Good people, too. Did you know he was the first to release his slaves?"

"I believe I knew that, yes."

"Well, I'll make it a point to go to the First Baptist service on Sunday."

"Why don't you pick her up and take her?"

"That's a good idea. We'll pick her up and invite her to Linde Bee's after church and then ask her to help."

"We?"

"Yes, we."

*   *   *   *   *

"You have a fine body line." observed Coach Stillwaters. "You could be one or two inches taller but I suspect you may have finished with growin'. Girls mature faster than boys. You're as tall as you will likely get. We are exactly the same height and I managed reasonably well. I know the sport has changed since I competed, but not that much. Girls now are taller and faster. That's a fact. My old marks have fallen over time, like apples from a tree. Anyway, what's most important is heart. I'll take heart anytime. You give me heart and I'll take you to a championship. Better put, you will take me to a championship. Talent and heart, Ruth Ann. That's what it's all about."

"I will give you all I have," Ruth Ann answered, adjusting her swim cap.

"I'll expect that and more. I'll push you to your limits and beyond. You'll wake up some days wishin' I didn't exist. I see we need to strengthen your upper body. Add a few pounds of muscle overall. Your lower body is fine. Great legs. I wish I had y'all's rear end. Did at one time. I don't know where it went."

"Y'all want me to add a few pounds?"

"Muscle weighs more than fat. You, young lady, by the end of this very summer, will be as fit as any high school athlete anywhere. I'm also goin' to put you on a diet."

"What kind of diet? I've been thinkin' about becomin' a vegetarian. My mother's a vegetarian."

"Not now. It's not a good time for a major diet change. After practice today we'll sit down and y'all will tell me honestly what you put into your mouth each day. We'll go from there. We'll draw up a good food list and a bad food list. More of the good and less of the bad until there's only good and no bad. If I catch you with a Coke or a Snickers, you'll never hear the end of it."

"I don't have a sweet tooth, anyway."

"Ruth Ann, it's all part of a whole. You, my young and promising swimmer, are going to be taken on a wonderful journey. You will accomplish great things. Start imagining them now. Get it fixed in your head. Never think of failure. If you should lose a race, the experience will better position you for winnin' the next one. Think only of success. Set goals and then reach out for them. It's the most satisfyin' thing in the world."

* * * * *

Only minutes after being rejected by the school board, Coach Stillwaters told Ruth Ann they would be training at Devil's Lake State Park.

"You're a sprinter, Ruth Ann, but you need conditioning. The lake will answer our need just fine. Water is water. You'll train there until we can somehow convince the board to gather the courage to say yes, as opposed to no. I'll provide the transportation. That all right with you, Mrs. Chambers?"

"Call me Judith. Yes, that's fine. Better than fine, actually. Y'all being in Ruth Ann's life has given me a glimmer of hope. I know she has talent and I'm encouraged that y'all have offered her your support. You need to know how much I appreciate that."

"Well, you're welcome. It's what I do. Frankly, I wouldn't waste my time if I didn't believe Ruth Ann could excel. Others, too. They just need an opportunity and somehow, someway, we'll create that opportunity. If we can put it all together, and we will, we'll make believers out of anyone and everyone."

* * * * *

"Good afternoon, ladies." Carl offered as a salutation. He and James Ray had taken off from work early and Carl had promised James Ray he'd teach him about filters and how filters could alter light's effect on film. Devil's Lake was chosen by Carl as the venue for the lessons. The day was bright and sunny with a slight breeze out of the southeast.

"Oh, hi," responded Ruth Ann, turning in the direction of Carl's voice and becoming aware of James Ray's approach.

"Hi," said James Ray.

"This is Carl Malone," James Ray said. "I'm his assistant at the *Tribune*. He's also my photography teacher."

"Hi, name's Cindy. Cindy Stillwaters. I'm Ruth Ann's swimmin' coach."

"So, seems like it's student and teacher day at the park. Good last name for a swimming coach," Carl offered.

Field of View

"Photography teacher?" asked Stillwaters.

"Not officially. I'm the *Tribune's* photographer. James Ray here, is my assistant. He's got real promise. I'm going to teach him a thing or two about filters today. Maybe you've seen some of his work in the paper? Are the two of you girls up to some practicing at the lake?"

"Yes," Stillwaters answered. "And we need to get to it, if y'all will excuse us."

James Ray hadn't seen Ruth Ann since the fateful ascension a couple of weeks ago and suddenly she stood in front of him in a one-piece bathing suit, a swim cap and funny looking goggles. He couldn't help observing the tantalizing outline of her nipples, visible as they were through the tight fit of her competition suit. He thought her beautiful without makeup and strangely outfitted as she was. In a vivid recall of her sun-and-water-reflected shower nakedness, he flushed, thinking that somehow she might be able to read his mind and realize he was a low-down, sneaky, and unworthy kind of a person.

"Nice meetin' you, Mr. Malone," Ruth Ann said. "Good to see you again, James Ray."

James Ray and Carl removed themselves to the front of the pier. Under the shade of an oak, they sat on a bench watching the swimmer and her coach from a distance.

"The pier. One of the best leading lines I've ever seen," remarked Carl as he lit a cigarette. "You see it? Takes your eyes right to the subject. You know Ruth Ann?"

"Yes. My folks had 'em over for supper."

"So you know her mother?"

"Yes. I met her that one time."

"How long will it take you to screw Ruth Ann?"

"What?"

"You heard me. Red-blooded boy like you and a shapely thing like Ruth Ann. You have to be thinking about how you're going to get it on with her. Come on, James Ray, let's be honest here. Both watched as Ruth Ann prepared to take to the water.

* * * * *

"How many laps?" Ruth Ann asked her coach.

"Ten. I'll keep track. The last lap will be as fast as you can manage. I'll time the last two. Slow and steady for the first four. Pick it up on the second four. Come in and rest for ten minutes and then hit the water again. Faster on the ninth lap and as fast as you ever have swum on the last one. Each time, turn on the buoy I set out yesterday and remember, you won't be able to turn, kick off a wall and flutter kick. Your time, under controlled conditions once we get the pool ready, will be much faster."

Ruth Ann nodded, adjusted her cap once again, positioned her goggles, and faced the water of the lake, her toes curled over the edge of the lake's wooden pier. She turned her head in the direction of Stillwaters and spoke over her shoulder. "You really think we will get permission to redo the pool?"

"Sure as the sun will rise tomorrow."

Ruth Ann took a deep breath and dove expertly into the lake's tepid water.

From his perspective, James Ray was again overtaken by his desire to somehow, someway, make her his as he watched the rhythm of Ruth Ann's strokes. She parted the water swiftly, stroke by confident stroke, as if she were conveyed by a kind of water-adapted conveyor. It was all beautiful: the reflected light, the wake of the water and its texture, the billowing clouds overhead, the leading line of the pier, the horizon lines where the lake kissed the far shore, and again where the trees yielded to the sky. And, most beautiful of all was Ruth Ann's shape and form.

* * * * *

Although only mid-morning, J. B's office was stifling. He had corralled two oscillating fans. One was a small, eight-inch, ancient Colonial, he had perched on the top of a shelf that also held large bound volumes of hand-recorded county transactions, some dating back to the mid 1800's.

The other, his favorite, was a large, black, cast-iron General Electric. It pushed air his way and sat a mere four feet from his desk. It was situated on the office's plank floor and tilted up toward his upper body. Mabel had a fan of her own. The ceiling fan was aiding the relief effort too, but it was largely ineffective at any time of the year, especially during the summer months.

Even then, even with the cross current and push of all four fans, he was sweating through his dress shirt. He first loosened his tie, then a few minutes later, removed it entirely.

"Y'all sufferin' from the heat?" Mabel asked, knowing he was.

"Couldn't be hotter if I were a pullet in a pressure cooker. How many months will it be before a good ice storm rolls in?"

"More days than either of us care to count."

"Excuse me, Mabel. I've got to get some fresh air. I'll be back in fifteen."

J.B. strolled out of the east entrance, the entrance adjacent to his office, skipped down the stairs, and sauntered around the corner of the courthouse to hobnob awhile with the old timers.

Teddy quickly stood at the sight of J.B.'s approach. Winney remained seated. He had decided to go along for the ride and watch Teddy make a fool out of himself.

"Mornin', J.B." Teddy said. "Y'all got a few minutes? I have somethin' of extreme and immediate urgency."

"Don't say. Mornin' gentlemen. No one up to swappin' knives this fine, toasty summer mornin'?"

"Like I say, J.B., I've got somethin' that will change our lives forever. Nothin' will ever be the same in these here parts."

"Well then, T.R., what's up y'all's sleeve this mornin'?"

"Is everybody ready?" Teddy asked, looking first at J.B., then to Winney, Soapy, and finally to Chipper. Periscope like, he surveyed the courthouse lawn to ensure no one might disrupt his act of revelation. All heads nodded except for Winney's.

"Been ready since last July 4th," opined Winney. "Teddy here says after he produces his whatever the fool it is tucked away in his pocket, there'll be no more bacon with our mornin' breakfast 'er no more popcorn at the movies and such. I expect he'll tell us the Mexican army is headed our way led by the ghost of Pancho Villa. Maybe it's a telegram announcin' that Truman did actually lose to Dewey. So go ahead, Thigpin, show whatever it is tucked away in y'all's fuckin' pocket if y'all have anythin' there in the first Goddamn place."

Chipper spat. Winney reached for a plug of tobacco. Disturbed by the tension of the morning, Soapy renewed his carving. His tiny, pale but erect phallus was almost complete, testicles and all.

Teddy ignored Winney's tirade. "Well, here it is boys," Teddy said, reaching into his overall pocket.

Teddy handed a photograph to J.B.

J.B. winced and did a double take. He reached for his glasses. He stared at the photograph, repositioning it until it was in good focus. He cleared his throat.

"Where in God's name did you come up with such a thing?"

"What the shitfire is it, J.B.?" Winney asked. "Let me see."

J.B. handed the photo to Winney. Chipper rose and positioned himself so he could see over Winney's shoulder.

"I want to see it, too." said Soapy. "Let me see the thing, whatever it is."

"My wife Janey found it," Teddy answered. "She works for the Lone Star as a maid. Mostly part-time due to poor business and all but..."

"Y'all say the Lone Star?" J.B. asked.

"The Lone Star."

"Do tell. My Sarah Mae and I honeymooned at the Lone Star. Of course, that was back when the hotel still had some spring in its step," J.B. replied.

"It wuz taken at the Lone Star. I know that to be a fact."

"Y'all sure about that? How so?" J.B. questioned.

"Dammit," Teddy said, "hand the photo back to J.B. so I can show him somethin'."

Once again J.B. was privy to the view of a boy and girl engaged in world-series level sexual activity. He had never witnessed such a photograph before although when in the navy, a fellow sailor had shared a cartoon, paperback equivalent of Teddy's black and white pornographic image.

"Here, Turman, educate yourself. Check this out. Daisy Mae in all her glory."

Young seaman Turman took the pocket-size cartoon depicting a busty and topless Daisy Mae with one of her hands tucked inside her trademark shorter-than-short skirt. J.B. figured she was comforting herself although he wasn't sure how all that worked. Maybe that was some of the education he was supposed to receive.

To be sure, Daisy Mae and her voluptuous charms had stirred J.B. since his youthful discovery of her and Li'l Abner's cartoon relationship in the funny papers. Her shapely and sexy form was now in front of him, pleasingly rid of the trappings of conventional apparel. On one page, Li'l Abner had mounted her from her rear. In another, she was prone in high grass with her legs splayed in come-hither invitation while Li'l Abner and his admirable example of manhood, readied for the intriguing task at hand. In another, the Dogpatch twosome became a threesome when joined by Moonbean McSwine, a swarthy and sexy pipe-smoking-straight-out-of-the-hillbilly-hills brunette who had somehow lost track of her clothes as well. Daisy and Moonbean were servicing Li'l Abner to a sexual degree that the young sailor had yet to fathom possible.

Back in J.B.'s hands, the abstract black and white image was not only graphic, it was disturbingly titillating. Had it really been taken at the Lone Star? How was that possible?

"Try not lookin' at the kids, look beyond 'em," Teddy suggested.

"What are y'all tryin' to say, Teddy?"

"See the headboard? Look to the bed's headboard."

J.B. adjusted the photograph and his head until he had the photo in as sharp a focus as possible.

"I'll be durned. Y'all are right, Teddy. There it is plain and simple, but not somethin' one would notice first off. My son James Ray has a word for things in a photograph that aren't clearly focused. Somethin' to do with light orbs or unfocused confusion or some such photo speak. Anyway, it's hard to notice the headboard given all the hoopla that first meets the eye."

"What's hoopla got to do with the nakedness of it all?" asked Chipper.

"Whose headboard are we talkin' about anyway?" queried Soapy.

"The Lone Star's," J.B. answered. "It's in the room upstairs that they call the Honeymoon Suite."

"Well, what I want to know is why it's of anyone's business in the first place?" voiced Winney. "Why all the fuss? Kids are doin' nothin' more than any of us here would like to be doin' if we were up to it and their age, our pistols still loaded and all."

"The kids aren't playin' a game of Sunday afternoon croquet, Winney. It's more than hoopla really. I just used hoopla as a kind word for what seems to me like pure law breakin' of a sordid kind. This photo is down and dirty pornographic and the

the girl and boy look like kids to me and that means one or both of 'em could be underage. Hard to tell, but possible. Even if they aren't, that kind of picture takin' could put someone in jail. Especially so, if they are underage. And yes, Teddy, y'all are right. Y'all's photo was taken at the Lone Star."

Hand carved into the bed's headboard were large, stylistic initials, *"LS,"* framed by a star within a star. When he and his Sarah Mae were at the Lone Star for their honeymoon, the afternoon and evening when the two were cast in their own version of sexual let's-have-at-it activity, J.B. had noted the carving. When they checked out of the hotel, he had questioned the clerk regarding the uniqueness of the headboard.

The clerk had explained that the headboard had been carved by some fellow who was passing by. J.B.was informed that the man carved the headboard, put a few dollars in his pocket and moved on. The clerk had asked if he noticed the fancy bluebonnets on either side of the initials. He hadn't.

Chapter 14 - Transactions

"I have two bottles of the finest vodka you can buy in Texas. Sobieski. It's said that Poland is the birthplace of vodka, although the Russians most likely say otherwise. As I recall, Sobieski is named after a Polish king or military leader. I dare say it's as good a vodka as you can get your hands on. Again, if you're a Russian, I suppose you'd differ. Anyway, Sobieski is distilled more times than you have fingers on one hand. I'm fortunate to have some in inventory. Won't last long, that's for sure."

"Good. That's fine. I appreciate the background information but I'm not buying a vacuum cleaner and I don't need to like vodka anymore than I already do."

"Don't be so defensive, Judith. Good Christ. I'm just trying to make your experience worthwhile."

"What else do you have besides whatever it is you mentioned?   I just need a plain Jane vodka, that's all. I don't need to like it anymore than I do."

"Well, nothing as good as Sobieski. Especially for the money. What are you drinking now?"

"Seagrams. I really could care less about dead Polish leaders. I'll have two bottles of Seagrams and one of whatever it was you held up as bein' the crown royal of Polish vodkas."

"Okay," Carl answered, reaching for two bottles of Sobieski and one of Seagrams.

"I said two of Seagrams and one of...whatever it's called," countered Judith.

"I always like to give a new customer a bargain. And I especially want you to be a returning customer. You have other options. I know that. But no one will treat you the way I will. Besides, truth be known, most of my customers come nowhere near meeting your standards."

"What's that supposed to mean?"

"Whatever you want it to mean."

"How did you find this place?"

"The farm? My stash? I inherited the place, actually. The place was in service to another bootlegging businessman and he died of liver disease. Pour soul drank more than he sold. Anyway, I took over his business. Let me explain it this way. I don't own the farm; I just rent the cellar. Old Harold, the fellow who let us in, he's a retired cotton farmer. I pay him nicely for the use of his cellar. He's got nothing much other than his social security. The cellar keeps everything nice and cold. Not cold enough for beer. I keep that at home. I have two refrigerators. Do you know anyone else who has two refrigerators?"

"No, I suppose I don't."

"It's a little bit of a drive but I enjoy coming out here. It's quiet and peaceful. Want a cigarette?"

*　　*　　*　　*　　*

It seemed to Judith that she had spent her whole life waiting. She waited for the only love of her life to come home from the Army. Once home, there was a chance they would get married. Why he was so hesitant to get married was beyond her. They were lovers. They had a beautiful child. Before joining the Army, he had a good-paying job as a long haul truck driver. Although he was both stubborn and defiant, Judith tried to see beyond his faults. Once he returned and she was out of school, she imagined things would be made right and respectable. They would live together, own a home, and maybe, just maybe, have another child. In the meantime, she would wait.

Ruth Ann's father was killed in September, 1943, during the allied invasion of Salerno, the place in Italy Churchill referred to as the "soft underbelly" of Europe. The allied victory would mark the beginning of the effort to wrestle Europe from Hitler's military grasp. A subsequent counterattack by the Germans, although unsuccessful, ended the life of Private John Kinsey Sterling, Ruth Ann's father. Ruth Ann was four years old.

Judith waited for a place of her own. She waited for a college degree that was economically beyond her reach. Had she been married, there would have been government support. Her goal was to become a teacher of English. She also waited for Ruth Ann to be old enough so that she would be in school while she worked. Now, given her marriage to Bud, she found herself waiting for a time when she could excise the bitter aftertaste of consummated vows. She waited for a time when she had money saved and Ruth Ann securely tucked away in college. Her education, hopefully, would be the result of a fully-funded athletic scholarship. That's when the waiting would be over. No sooner, no later. She reached for a cigarette and poured herself a drink. The vodka Carl had suggested was good. He had been right.

The next morning, Judith picked up the phone and asked the nosy Sumwalt lady, the operator she knew by now, for the Turman's residence.

"I'm not sure what the number is." Judith said.

"Hold on, I'll connect you. How are y'all likin' Mayweather?"

"Just fine, thank you."

"Sometimes it takes a body some time to get into the flow of things, you know. I suspect the town's different from livin' in Fort Worth."

"Could you please connect me to the Turmans?"

"Of course. Number's three-six-four. Be careful. It's a shared party line."

J.B. answered. "Turmans, J.B. here."

"Good afternoon Mr. Turman. This is Judith Chambers. I was..."

"And the same good afternoon back to you, Judith. Things goin' well for y'all and Bud? Y'all's Ruth Ann?"

"Just fine, thank you. Mr. Turman, is Sarah Mae...?

"It's just fine if you call me J.B. My daddy was a populist and I got named for William Jennings Bryan, J.B. for the short of it all."

"Well, I suppose the name works for y'all but Bryan's fuss about the teachin' of evolution and all hasn't spoken well for him over the years, has it?"

"I agree wholeheartedly. Some would differ, my Sarah Mae for one. Anyway, what a mess that whole trial was. First..."

"May I please speak to Sarah Mae? I'd like to know if she's talked with the Bloom descendent. Lucinda is her name, I believe."

"Well, wish you could. She's taken the train to southern California. Goin' to visit her mother and daddy, sisters and all. All of 'em are in California, the land of milk and honey. I'm left here on the home front. Our Seth is headed that way as well. He up and joined the Marines. Two generations of Turman sailors and he breaks rank and joins the Marines."

"Are y'all okay with his joinin'? Korea's still a hot spot."

"Indeed it is. Anyway back to y'all's reason for callin'. Lucinda Godshall, she's a direct descendant of a pioneering family in these parts, and has more money than she knows what to do with. So Sarah Mae and I corralled her at church a Sunday ago. She's a Baptist and I barely made it through the service. Those folks keep a place of worship hotter than the hell they warn a body about every five minutes or so. Anyway, Lucinda, she said she was interested. Not a full green light, but almost green. Said we should come out to the ranch and visit."

"How long will Sarah Mae be gone?"

"Two to three weeks dependin'. She makes it that way each summer."

"That's too long to wait. We need to get the board's approval to get started on the repair and get the pool open as soon as possible.

"I'm sure that's true. How is the fund-raisin' goin'?"

"We're making some money but more important, we're showing effort and enthusiasm; but truth is, we need a large donation. Somethin' the board can see as substantial. Somethin' that will convince them to give the go-ahead and then figure out a way to fund the rest."

"Well, I suppose I could ring up Lucinda and ask for a meetin' right away. I'm surprised Sarah Mae dropped the ball. Would it help if I called?"

"Most anything will help. Yes, that would be kind of you. If you can arrange a meetin', I suppose Coach Stillwaters should come along as well."

"Y'all's Ruth Ann, also. It's hard to say no to a motivated teenager. I know."

"OK, then call me when you find out somethin'."

"I will. And thanks for the call."

"No, thank you! I appreciate y'all's willingness to help."

"You're welcome. I'll mention what we are up to in a letter to Sarah Mae. We're tryin' not to do the out-of-state long distance thing while she's gone. Costs a fortune."

"I feel like I can trust you, J.B. If y'all promise to try and get a meetin' organized, I have high hopes you will. I'll let Ruth Ann and her coach know we're workin' on it."

"I'll get right on it. I'll let you know. Bye, now."

"Bye."

Maureen Sumwalt, curious and efficient operator that she was, heard almost every word passed between Judith and J.B. Who needed to listen to soap operas on the radio when Mayweather was as good an example as either *Portia Faces Life* or *Stella Dallas.*

Field of View

*   *   *   *   *

J.B. received a letter from Sarah Mae a day following the call from Judith. She had written most of the lengthy letter on the train. The letter started out hopeful with trivial but detailed facts about people she met on the train. She described the desert landscape, the majesty of saguaros and the difference between the dusty pale of desert green from the vibrance of east Texas green. However, the continuation of the letter revealed words that were the ominous equivalent of an approaching storm.

...it's Tuesday morning. An ill wind blows, J.B., Daddy is not well. He seems to have lost his will to live. Momma says he stopped making his wine and twice recently, he couldn't find his way home from the corner market. Another time, when he was driving, he made a wrong turn coming home from church and Momma had to direct him the rest of the way back to their house. He was so upset, he cried. I have never seen him cry in his life. It was a trip he had made hundreds of time. He doesn't look good. He also seems to have lost his appetite. He barely bothered with the cherry pie I made. It used to be his favorite. Momma is worried and so am I. I also discovered a strange lump on my upper back. I noticed it when I bathed the Friday before I left. I didn't want you to worry. I'll have our doctor look at it when I return. It's probably nothing. You need to know I may stay longer than I first anticipated. How are things there? Have you heard from Seth? How are the girls? I miss them. Did you remember to take Faith to Sally's birthday party? James Ray? Is he all right and hanging out with his new camera? Please call Judith Chambers. I forgot to contact Lucinda Godshall about the fund-raising. Maybe I'm losing my mind as well...

The meeting with Lucinda Godshall came about earlier than either Judith or J.B. anticipated. In her telephone conversation with J.B., she announced that she would come to them, not the other way around.

"I'm comin' into town to do some shoppin' tomorrow. No need for y'all to go to the trouble to come all the way out to the ranch. How about havin' tea at Linde Bee's? Say 9:00 in the mornin'?"

Judith was thrilled but Ruth Ann and her coach couldn't make the meeting. They had scheduled a chit-chat in Sherman to talk with city officials about using the city's public pool for training when fall rolled around and when water at Devil's Lake became frigid.

Lucinda arrived thirty minutes late in her elegant 1951 Lincoln Cosmopolitan.

"Tiny thing can barely see over the steering wheel. See her there? To the left. In the bullet shape of a Lincoln," observed J.B.

"Yes, I see her. She is a small woman, isn't she?"

"More coffee, y'all?" asked the waitress.

"No, thank you. My tank's full," J.B. answered. "Maybe later."

"Yes, please," replied Judith.

J.B. walked to the door of the cafe, opened the door, reached for Lucinda's ring hand and kissed it. Still holding her hand, he led her to their table. He pulled back a chair and motioned for her to sit.

"Y'all are a real gentleman, Mr. Turman. I can tell a gentleman a mile away."

"I thank you kindly for your assessment of my character, ill conceived as it may be. Lucinda, I'd like you to meet a good woman, Mrs. Judith Chambers. She's the mother of our young competitive swimmer, Ruth Ann Chambers. She..."

"Pleased to meet you, Mrs. Chambers."

"The same. I've heard a lot about y'all's family from J.B. I'm recently from Fort Worth and..."

"Fort Worth, the gateway to the west. The drive from Mayweather to Fort Worth is like endin' up in France, the two places bein' so different in their culture and all."

Seated, J. B. continued to romance Lucinda. He smiled, he laughed, he held her hand, he interpreted if she missed a word or a meaning.

The eighty-six year old responded in kind. She thought she hadn't been seated with such a handsome and charming man for years, if ever.

J.B. got up and ushered the waitress back to their table.

"Tea, please. Lemon and sugar," Lucinda requested.

"I'll fetch the lemon. Sugar's on the table. Y'all all right otherwise?"

"Yes, dandy. Thank you," said J.B. "Don't go yet though. Anyone here want somethin' for breakfast? Toast or eggs or a chicken fried steak?"

Lucinda cackled. "Chicken fried steak for breakfast? Good choice, but I do think I will pass. I'd have to nap the rest of the day and well into tomorrow."

J.B. laughed. Judith smiled.

Coffee and tea would do. J.B. would have loved to have ordered something substantial like eggs and bacon or buttermilk pancakes but, then again, he had just had breakfast three hours earlier. Another hour and it would be Coke and grilled cheese sandwich time.

"Funny thing about names," Lucinda offered. "Y'all's name Chambers for instance. What kind of chambers? Judge's chambers? The chambers of a double barrel shotgun? Godshall? God shall do what and to whom? Turman's German, of course. Bloom is Anglo-Saxon. The name has to do with ingots of iron, not flowers. Anyway, not many Blooms around now except for some colored folks with the Bloom name. Got it when they became free slaves back in the day. I was introduced to a colored girl just last year who could pass for white. Name was Amber Rose Bloom. Sweet girl. She could waltz in here to Linde Bee's and order anythin' she wanted off the menu and go plumb unnoticed as to her race. There's a Jill Bloom, too. She's a cousin, but she's actually white. Doesn't live here. Lives over to Little Rock. On her last leg, poor thing. She's got Parkinson's. We used to call it Shakin' Palsy."

"Well, sorry to hear that," J.B. responded. "I've always had an interest in surname's as well," J.B. offered. "Take the Bottoms lady over to the library. Who would in his right mind choose Bottoms for a surname? Or Bickerstaff, or Cornforth, or take the leather shop owner on the way to Honey Grove, his last name is a complete..."

"Sorry to interrupt, but I have to be at First National soon," Judith interjected. "Could..."

"Of course. Lucinda," J.B. said, as he moved his head close to Lucinda's and fixed as serious a look as he could conjure, "I suppose we have to cut to the chase. You, bless y'all's heart, Lucinda, voiced some willingness a Sunday or so ago that y'all would be willin' to perhaps help with the school's swimmin' pool and all."

"I did and I will. My late husband invested heavily in property in and around Dallas before the war ended. He saw things, you know, such as cotton farmin' endin' around here and big things happenin' in big cities, not rural outposts like our little Mayweather. So, like I say, he bought up buildings and land in the Dallas area."

"He must've been a smart man," J.B. replied.

"Smart and good. I miss him terribly."

"Does he, you, I mean, own anythin' in Dallas we would recognize?"

Well, there's the Lamar Hotel to start. Do y'all know the Lamar?"

J.B.'s eyes opened wide. "Well, yes. Most everyone knows the Lamar. Are you sayin' you own the Lamar?"

"All of the holdings are in a trust, but yes, I suppose I do. Anyway, how much do y'all need? I can't take it to my grave, now can I?"

*   *   *   *   *

J.B. thought Teddy's Lone Star pornographic photo would burn a hole in his pocket. Having been granted custody of the sexually-explicit image, he wrapped it in his handkerchief in an effort to keep it from view. Should someone see him with the photo, he imagined it would be quickly reported to the sheriff. He also imagined himself being arrested and thrown in jail. *County's Auditor Possesses Porn*, the *Tribune* headline would exclaim.

Mid-afternoon on the day Teddy had dropped his equivalent of a visual bombshell, J.B. left his office, walked across the street to the Bank of Mayweather and placed the photo, now in a sealed envelope, in his and Sarah Mae's safe deposit box. It would remain there until Sarah Mae's return from California. What he would do with it after her return, he didn't know. Perhaps he would hide it somewhere in her storm shelter.

J.B. was puzzled by the sordid shenanigan of a photograph in more ways than one. Was the photo one of a kind? Probably not. Had someone set up shop in the Lone Star? Was the kind of activity represented by the photo an on-going enterprise? Maybe so. And if so, what should or could be done about it? Would Mayweather's lazy and incompetent district attorney call for a grand jury investigation? Maybe, if someone put a gun to his head. How about Mayweather's hoghead of a sheriff? If pornography was just another business like bootlegging, then the sheriff was most likely in on it, taking his cut and sleeping sound as a baby at night.

Then, there was the nature of the photo. Not the bare flesh and the carnality of it all, but the substance of the picture itself. It was stiff. It felt like it had a backing of some kind of which he was unfamiliar. He would like to ask James Ray but couldn't bring himself to do so given the explicit nature of the picture's image.

After he secreted away the photo, J.B. asked a bank teller if Derwood Tyler, the bank's manager, was ready to see him. Given Sarah Mae's absence, J.B. thought now was as good a time as any to apply for the car loan.

"There she goes," Derwood announced, rising from his chair no sooner than he had sat in it, in an effort to catch a better view of a woman driving a black, slant-back Buick.

"Who?" asked J.B. turning his head in the direction of the bank's expansive front window.

"The new woman in town. What's her name? Chambers somethin'? Bud and..."

"Judith is her first name," J.B. volunteered. "Chambers is the family's last name."

"That's it. Bud and the sweet-as-pumpkin-pie, Mrs. Judith Chambers. They were in for some business just the other day. Y'all know her? In her panties yet, J.B.? If so, y'all 'er faster than one of those hot-rod kids down to the Ladonia drag strip."

"Derwood, I am a happily married man. I only know one set of britches. How about y'all? Got more than a few to choose from?"

"Well, I'd like to know a man who wouldn't want to poke her. I'd take a roll in the hay with her any day of the year. Married, unmarried, whatever my condition happened to be."

J.B. didn't like the direction the meeting had taken. All he wanted was a car loan, a loan that would put him behind the wheel of a nearly-new '52 Hudson Commodore Eight. The car would announce a new and improved J.B. Turman, a successful father and man about town. The spiffy Hudson was led by a massive, eye-catching chrome grill. A lengthy stainless steel spear rose from the car's rear fenders and thrust forward to the front wheel wells. Mounted on the tip of the spear was a Hudson marque shaped like a rocket ship folks at the company's marketing department had coined, "Badge of Power". Driving a Hudson was putting your living room on wheels. Finer, in most cases.

Much like Sarah Mae had when she and J.B. first met, the car captured J.B.'s interest the day he first laid eyes on it. The Hudson, at least in his mind, was as fine as any of its competitors. Let Mr. Malone have his garish, fish-finned Cadillac. J.B. would have his roadworthy, stately Hudson. The Commodore was Hudson's premier offering if one opted for a combination of comfort and elegance. In keeping with the times, J.B.'s new love sported two-toned paint, robin's egg blue on the bottom and ivory on the top. Another notable feature was the car's frame, marketed as "step down". Hudson hugged the road like no other. Its more muscular cousin, the Hornet, was busy making road racing history across America.

The Studebaker and Hudson dealership on the outskirts of town had a reputation for inventorying some of the best used cars in the area. As J.B. was told when he first inquired about the car, an elderly woman in nearby Ector had died within two weeks of her husband's passing, leaving the car's future to be decided by an estate auction. The Mayweather dealership had purchased the car. The odometer read an anemic 4,210 total miles. J.B. figured he had accrued that many miles walking to and from the courthouse over the past dozen years or so. The Hudson had to be his. It spoke to him. It was destined to become the new family car. He would explain the purchase to Sarah Mae when she returned from California.

Sighing, J.B. signed the loan and returned the papers to Derwood.

"Don't tell me you wouldn't like to take a turn with the Chambers woman."

"Look..."

"Just because both of us are pushin' fifty, doesn't mean we don't still have a pulse, does it?"

"Yes, Derwood, I have a pulse. Last time I looked anyway."

"Well, then, neither of us have had our sex organs shrivel up like a mud flat, have we?"

"I guess I don't get it, Derwood. Shouldn't we leave Judith Chambers to her husband, Bud? Would that be all right with y'all? I'm married. You're married. Doesn't 'no man put asunder' mean anythin' to you?"

"Hold your horses, J.B. I'm just jokin'. Tryin' to make y'all's need for money less stressful. If you had put more money down on the car or if y'all had traded in the Oldsmobile, y'all's payments would be a lot less and there would be less interest to pay as well. So don't go and get all riled."

"I will get riled if you take off and lecture me about the loan. I came in here to do honest business. I'm a customer. You're a banker. I was led to believe that, anyway. A customer should be able to apply for a loan without feelin' like he's a mule that needs whippin'. I'd like to leave the bank today feelin' good about what's just transpired, not feelin' like I've been taken to a banker's version of a woodshed. Is that okay with you Derwood?"

J.B. thought his outburst, although warranted, might cause Derwood to tear up the loan papers. Bankers, he reflected, were a touchy lot, much like librarians. Librarians lorded over their books like they, themselves, had written every word and bound every book. Mostly, though, he recalled from his days as county school superintendent, they spent their days messing with the Dewey Decimal System and shelving. A banker lorded over cash and its distribution as if he were some kind of monetary deity wielding sole power over lesser mortals and their niggardly need for money. Making things worse, J.B. reflected, it wasn't their money to begin with.

Chapter 15 - Original Sin

"We don't talk religion. How about you and y'all's Eartha?" asked J.B.

"No need to. We both be happy with the Lord."

"My Sarah Mae, too. I just think religion as a whole is a stretch too far, if y'all will excuse my sayin'. One minute the Red Sea is parted, the next, Lazarus is brought back to life after bein' dead for days and then there's the rib lady and the talkin' snake in the Garden of Eden. And what about Adam's and Eve's offspring? All of 'em in bed together so as to populate the earth. What's that all about?"

"Well, I don't think the Bible, its words and all, is a thing to go and bother yourself with. Just be acceptin' and humble. That's what I say."

"I'm buying today, Book. Y'all want your regular RC cola?"

"I do. I like to be consistent with my afternoon cola. Ain't about to hurt its feelings."

J.B. asked Jules Olander, in charge of the courthouse snack bar, for one RC and one Coke.

"You goin' ta go for y'all's puny Coke?"

"I am. As hot as it is, maybe I'll buy three of 'em."

"RC has almost twice the ounces. Better buy for y'all's nickel."

"I do know that. OK, you talked me into it. Jules, my good man, I'll go for an RC, instead. "

"See there, J.B. Y'all is a most flexible man. I figure if y'all can go for an RC, y'all can go be more acceptin' of the Lord."

"I don't equate the two, Book. A cola might be nourishin' to some, but religion, church, and all doesn't come close to quenching my thirst. I've been a church goer all my life and I find it dissatisfying, like bein' served oatmeal for breakfast. Oatmeal's supposed to be good for a body but give me a fried egg any day."

"Are y'all sayin' y'all is a nonbeliever?"

"Oh I believe, Book. I believe. I just believe in reality. I believe in science. I believe that the earth and the heavens weren't a week's worth of work by some supernatural someone who looks something like me. I don't believe that a person who's dead for three days or so can rise up, roll away a boulder and ascend upward into the heavens accompanied by a host of angels. That's all I'm sayin'."

"That's a lot to be sayin', J.B. No wonder y'all don't talk religion with Sarah Mae. That's hard talk all the way around."

"Well, maybe so. But to live one's life and not ask questions, that, to me anyway, is as bad as it can get. Maybe there is a God out there somewhere who's on call when someone needs to get a good grade on a test or needs to hit a home run or be healed of blindness, whatever. I don't know for sure, but I doubt it. What I do know is that someone claimin' for certain to know there's a God out there is goin' on blind faith, not facts. Who is this God who rewards and punishes, who intervenes in their lives whether they want him to or not, and who tells his followers to kowtow to his example even though he has blood on his hands? And who gets to tell one group you're in and another group, sorry folks, y'all don't cut the religious mustard? That's plain arbitrary, Book. If I believed in a God of Salvation, I'd want him to be fair and have a good head on his shoulders."

"Y'all are all wound up, J.B. What's put a bee in y'all's bonnet?"

"Ever read the *Old Testament*, Book? I have, and the God of the Old Testament is an ornery and arbitrary old salt who has little or no mercy for anyone who steps out of line. Jesus? Now that's another story. He was a good man. No doubt about it. But ascending into heaven after bein' dead for three days? Rollin' back the stone and all? That's simply a stretch too far. Manna from heaven? And then there's Lazarus of Bethany. Dead for how long? All of it makes for good story tellin', but that's all.

"J.B., y'all seem out of sorts lately if you don't mind me sayin. Seems to me y'all have been walkin' around in a cloud 'er somethin'. What's botherin' y'all so?"

J.B. looked at his watch. It was past time for him to get back to the office. "I don't know, Book. If I named all the issues I'm dealin' with these days, I'd be hard pressed to mention 'em all. I might just go and miss a couple. Anyway, thank you for the visit. Nice to have someone to talk to. Is tonight the night y'all clean at the *Tribune*?"

"Yes, indeed it is. Thursday nights and Sunday afternoons. Sunday's paper is done late Saturday night so I go in after church on Sunday. It's nice and quiet. No presses goin' yakety yak."

*   *   *   *   *

"Goin' to do a photo essay with Ruth Ann as the subject," James Ray pronounced. "They're savin' me a page in the yearbook when school starts. The problem is I haven't asked Ruth Ann if it's all right with her."

"What's holding you back?" asked Carl.

"Nothin' other than my lack of courage. I get up the nerve and then I chicken out."

"Women, girls too, love bein' the center of attention. Ask, and most likely you will receive. Did you ever see my photo of Trixie?"

"No. Who's Trixie?"

"Remember the night we drove to the Red? The boy who came out to greet us? That was Trixie's brother. The man isn't her daddy but anyway, Trixie and I met when I moved to Mayweather, two goin' on three years ago. I'll bring her picture in tomorrow. Or, you can drop by the house after work."

"Sure. Is Trixie cute?"

"You've never seen a better bumper of a rear end. I guarantee it."

"What's the best way to arrange five or six photos for a spread in the yearbook?" James Ray asked.

"Start by asking your leggy girlfriend permission to do the photography. Then we'll talk."

"She's not my girlfriend, actually."

"Well, make her so. What's holding you back?"

"She's got a boyfriend in Fort Worth."

"So?"

"She says they're goin' steady."

"So?"

"Well, I don't want to…"

"Christ, James Ray. He's in Fort Worth. You are in Mayweather. Maybe not your mind, but the rest of you is anyway, and Ruth Ann is in Mayweather, so have at her. Are you afraid of your own fucking shadow?"

"No, I just thought if she had a steady boyfriend she was, you know, off limits."

"Let me tell you something, my young friend. Never doubt yourself. Especially with women. Women can be had. They are there for the taking. With a woman, no doesn't mean no. No usually means yes. They just pretend they can't be won over, had, whatever. A little gall and a little patience is the key to winning over Ruth Ann. Her mother as well. Both of them..."

"Her mother's married."

"So?"

"Well, If she's married..."

"Being married, James Ray, doesn't mean she doesn't want better than she has. Now, there's a woman just waiting to be had if I ever saw one and I've seen a lot, had a lot. I bet she's so unhappily married that she plays with herself at night. I'd like to do the playing for her. I'd show her what a good orgasm is all about. I'd send her to the moon and back."

James Ray was often taken aback by Carl's boastful and sexually-descriptive language having to do with women, or girls for that matter. If it came to sex, nothing seemed to be off the table. In one way, Carl's talk was educational. James Ray felt he had a leg up when talking sexual shop with Bobby Joe or Sammy for that matter. Further, Carl's ruminations about all things sexual, although foreign to his ears, peaked his curiosity. How did a woman 'play' with herself? What was that all about? How could Carl 'play' with her better than she could 'play' with herself?

Somewhat encouraged by Carl's confidence that women of any age thought "yes" even though they were saying "no," James Ray felt he at least needed to try.

"May I borrow the car?" he asked his father.

J.B. looked up from his newspaper. "Sure thing." Amos and Andy would be on soon and he had taken to his armchair in anticipation of his favorite radio program. The girls would join him, although some of the situational humor was over their heads. Sometimes, much to his chagrin, he did more explaining than listening.

"Where are y'all off to? The beaches of Galveston or maybe San Antonio? If it's San Antonio, say hello to the Alamo for all of us."

"Probably Galveston. Actually, I'm on the way over to Ruth Ann's house."

"Don't say. You developed an interest in her? If I were y'all's age I'd be interested."

"Probably, but don't start talkin' like Carl."

"How's that?"

"Nothin'. He just talks a lot about women. Girls, too. He seems to have taken a fancy to Ruth Ann's mother."

"She's married."

"He knows that. Anyway, thank you for the car. I'll be back in a couple of hours or so."

"Have fun and be careful."

"Y'all said you would like to drive to Devil's Lake?" James Ray asked, both surprised and pleased she would suggest such an outing.

"I did. I've got to get out of the house. I need some fresh air. Livin' room's full of smoke. My parents are drivin' me nuts."

"What's wrong?"

"Everythin'. They argue when they're together. Have as long as I can remember. I don't know why my mother married Bud in the first place."

"Do y'all always call your daddy, Bud?"

"Yes, he's not my real father. My last name was Sterling 'til Bud adopted me when he and my mom got married. My real father died in the war. My mom and real father were never married, actually. I guess that makes me a bastard, doesn't it?"

"Can't see how. I have to admit I don't know much about adult relationships and how they work. Maybe someday. Anyway, Mayweather is pretty conservative, I think. Things are supposed to be on the up and up."

"Parochial, too."

"What does that mean?"

"It's a word I learned last year in English class. Means limited or sheltered or somethin' like that."

James Ray opened the car door for Ruth Ann. She was wearing tight-fitting jeans and a red blouse. She had recently washed her hair. It was still wet. Her wet hair reminded James Ray, yet another time, of the fateful ascension.

The two remained largely silent as James Ray directed the Olds to Devil's Lake.

As they approached the lake's entrance, Ruth Ann spoke. "Funny thing, I was just here this afternoon. No more than an hour or so ago. Just like that, here I am again. I'd be livin' here if I had a place to sleep."

"Y'all were here for practice?"

"Yes. Coach is goin' to wear me out, but I love it just the same. There is no feelin' like plowin' through the water with nothin' to hear but the splash of the water and your own breathin'. When I'm in the lake, nothin' can bother me. I have no worry. I have no fear of anythin'."

"That must be a fine feelin'."

Artie Shaw's *Begin the Beguine* was playing on the jukebox as the two teenagers approached the lake's dance pavilion that was surrounded by wooden benches.

James Ray led Ruth Ann to a bench with a view of the water. The two sat. Neither spoke. In Artie Shaw's wake, it was Lloyd Price's turn. His *Lawdy Miss Clawdy* had hit the top of the charts for weeks, if not months.

"Do y'all like rhythm and blues?" James Ray asked.

"I do, but I like a lot of music. I like the big band sound, Glenn Miller's *String of Pearls* and *Stardust* and so on. I like old romantic standards too, and even some hillbilly. You know, Hank Williams, Patsy Cline and such. I'd be hard-pressed to pick a favorite among the different types. It's interestin' how different people like different kinds of music. Like food or anythin' else I suppose. I don't know what the word is that stands for different groups of things. I'll have to look it up."

"You meant things that belong together? Things that share a common what...a theme? Anyway..."

Abruptly changing the subject, Ruth Ann said, "I hear that you are quite the basketball player."

"Who told you that?"

"Melissa. At fellowship. Says you scored 23 points out of 34 of y'all's team points in a playoff game last year. All-State honorable mention. That's pretty impressive."

"Well, I've had some good games and some bad ones. I missed the winning shot two years in a row playin' the Bloom Bulldogs. My ears are still ringin' from the tongue lashin' I got from my coach."

James Ray felt the time was right to pop the question. He took a deep breath the way he did when he lined up for a free throw. He would let the question fly, its rotational spin in a predetermined arc where, if the star's were aligned, ball would caress twine.

"Would y'all be up for me doin' a photo essay of y'all's trainin'?"

"A what?"

Field of View

"A photo essay. I'd like to take a bunch of pictures of you trainin'. Francine Perkins, the yearbook's editor, said she would hold a page for us, me that is, but featurin' you. You will be the subject. I'll just take the pictures."

Ruth Ann looked directly at James Ray but remained silent. She wasn't sure what to do with him. He was nice. He seemed harmless. He had that funny walk, although it was less noticeable over time. And he seemed from a normal family, whatever that was. At least his parents seemed happily married and didn't argue day-in-and-day-out. Neither of them smoked. She thought his little sisters were nice. Sometimes she wished she, too, had blonde hair and blue eyes. Or even a little sister period, regardless of the color of hair or eyes. Someone to laugh with, to teach, to have as a pillow-talk companion, to serve as a counterweight to the burden of her unhappy parents.

"No, I don't think so," she said in answer to James Ray's question. "Coach Stillwaters is on me 'cause of my boyfriend back in Fort Worth. She says I don't have time for anythin' other than trainin.' She's even got me on a new eatin' program. She watches my every move. I'm surprised she isn't here this evenin' watchin' me right now."

First, there was her no to his question. His well-intended question had resulted in an air ball. Then there was the "watchin' me" statement. He had been guilty of watching. He couldn't look at Ruth Ann without recalling her naked in the shower. A shower that was no more than fifty yards removed from where they sat.

"Sorry, y'all will need to line up somebody or somethin' else. Besides, I don't like bein' in the spotlight."

"But y'all are a competitive swimmer."

"That's different from someone takin' pictures of you. I'm a swimmer, not a model."

J.B. had waited for James Ray to arrive home. He had been gone four hours, not a couple.

"James Ray, good y'all are home. I was startin' to worry. Is Ruth Ann okay? Did y'all get to visit with her parents?"

"Yes, Ruth Ann's fine. No, I didn't get to visit with her parents. Ruth Ann said they were fussin'. Daddy, I don't feel like talkin'. I'm tired. I'm goin' to bed."

*   *   *   *   *

Field of View

The Mayweather School Board held yet another special session. Given Lucinda Godshall's bequest, an amount that would cover two-thirds of the estimated cost to refurbish the pool, the board voted to approve the project. Bids would be entertained, contractors approved, and work begun. The pool's projected opening was scheduled to be early spring, school year 1952-1953. Ruth Ann would be a junior and Coach Stillwaters would be the most satisfied swim coach in the state.

Cashier's check in hand, Lucinda was on hand to speak in favor of the project. She recounted the history of the pool, referring to it as "an asset" and a "legacy to the greatness of our cherished Mayweather community."

Unknown to any board member or any potential contractor, and several were present for the meeting, Lucinda had promised J.B. and Judith that she would cover any amount over the initial bid. The precious and generous fact had been kept secret even from Coach Stillwaters.

Following the board's approval, Lucinda rose to speak again. "I can't thank y'all enough for what you have done tonight. Bennet J. and Ann Carolyn Bloom thank you from the grave. You have made us all proud. Our young and gifted Ruth Ann and her coach will make us all proud. Others in the program, too. I say put us back on the map, Ruth Ann. Bring Mayweather home more swimmin' victories than the high school halls have to hold 'em. Go Warriors!"

J.B wished Sarah Mae had been there to witness it all. He was as proud of the community as he'd ever been. Progress had actually been made. Change had taken place and he was there to testify to it. Despite the pool's initial cost and the cost of on-going maintenance, the stick-in-the-mud board had actually looked beyond its collective nose and had taken a long view of things. The sow's ear of a pool would be born again as a silk purse.

James Ray had decided to tag along although he had never been to a school board meeting and had no idea what such a meeting involved. He knew, however, that Ruth Ann's quest for the reopening of the school's pool was the only agenda item.

Ruth Ann stood and hugged him following the board's announcement. She cried. He fought back tears as well. Judith hugged J.B. He received her hug willingly and gave her a full and long hug back. Coach Stillwaters managed to actually smile, an ability Ruth Ann thought she didn't possess. Her coach hugged anyone within reach including a couple of board members. When she wasn't hugging someone, she was clapping.

J.B. picked up Lucinda, held her in his arms as if she were a small child, and did a little ditty in front of everyone. Someone in the room shouted, *"Go, Warriors, go! Fight Warriors fight. Hit 'em to the left, hit 'em to the right. Go, Warriors Go! Fight Warriors fight."*

As if on cue, others picked up the chant.

On the way home, J.B. could still smell Judith's perfume, the warmth of her body and how different it felt from Sarah Mae's. He was disturbed by his thoughts. They were improper, illicit even. He needed to be more disciplined in his thinking. He had never had such thoughts prior to meeting Judith. He had been attracted to other women but had never bothered to think what it would be like to have them in bed. He would have to keep a good and close eye on his thoughts. He knew behavior often followed thoughts and he needed to stop the train before it left the station.

In his bed and alone in his room, thanks to the providential departure of Seth, James Ray gratified himself in a vivid reconstruction of the Devil's Lake shower scene. In his sexual fantasy, he joined Ruth Ann. The water caressed their naked bodies while the sun, given its low afternoon angle, highlighted their sexual exploration. They coupled and he and she became one in an age-old ritual of sexual submission to the other. His fantasy was over in minutes. Despite his effort to extend it, he submitted to an urgent volcano of satisfaction.

The very next day James Ray was introduced to Trixie. Once again, he was overcome with sexual longing. First Ruth Ann, now Trixie. He wondered if the bombardment would ever end.

Carl had posed Trixie on a hay bale. Sepia-toned, she was wearing chaps, boots and nothing more. She was a tantalizing two-dimensional abstraction, visually enhanced by the wash of the barn's diffused light. Carl had chosen a hay barn because it was both private and convenient, and because of the universal appeal of such a venue; animals, people, endeavor, longing, and the priceless opportunity for the secrecy of consensual sex. The soft, particle-laden light was perfect for the mood as well as the mischief at hand.

"Light is the prime mover. Light must fit the situation. Hard light's for texture. Soft light's for mood, for sensuality. Soft light is interrupted and diffused. It's indirect. Like I say, use light to complement the subject or the situation. Most point-and-shoot photographers aren't photographers at all. They have no more awareness or concern for light than does the stump of a dead tree."

Trixie was seated on a bale of hay, her legs crossed. Her arms were folded across her bosom. A cowboy hat covered her private part. She faced the camera at an angle away from the camera lens but her head was turned looking over a shoulder toward the camera in an inviting, come hither and seductive glance.

"I've always held a warm spot for small-breasted women," Carl said. "They make for better lovers. Trixie was one of the best I've ever had."

James Ray was stunned by Trixie's image as well as the revelation that Carl had "had" her. He had never seen a photograph of a nude woman, ever. His guilt-ridden but fortitudinous view of Ruth Ann's nakedness had been no abstraction. That was real. The day of the ascension, she had beautifully, albeit unknowingly, put that matter to rest.

The photograph of Trixie, however stimulating, raised questions for James Ray. In Carl's words, what had "come before and after" the photograph of which he now bore witness? Were other versions of Trixie available? Other poses? Were boots an on-again, off-again situation? Chaps? What of the cowboy hat? Knowing Carl, he had taken dozens of her seductive image. He most certainly would had changed the camera's angle as well as the subject-to-camera distance. He would have photographed his subject in a greater variety of poses than a chess set had pieces. James Ray would bet on that. Should he ask to see more?

"Want to see more of our cowgirl?" Carl asked, as if able to read James Ray's mind.

"Sure, you bet. Trixie's great lookin'. I love the light."

"Why?"

"Well, it fits the mood, as y'all once said. She's...Trixie that is, well, the setting and all calls for soft light. Makes you feel like you are in the barn with her."

"Good. Let me see," Carl said, moving to a desk with several drawers. He opened one drawer, then another. Then a third.

"Here she is. Take one of them. Keep it out of sight from your parents. I doubt they are liberal enough to accept the beauty and art of it all."

James Ray quickly thumbed through the dozen or so 8 by 10 inch glossy exposures. He selected one in which one of Trixie's breasts was revealed. She was standing at a 45-degree angle from the camera, her well-rounded buttocks in full and admirable view. She was looking, however, directly into the camera's lens thereby establishing visual rapport with her audience. Her hands were on her hips; the cowboy hat sat on her head in a downward tilt. As evidenced by the one breast, her breasts were small but firm, youthful, and enticing. Carl had made excellent use of his subject and attendant props. Her pose complimented her shape and form. She was lean and compact. Her telegraphed look indicated she was both willing and able to take on whoever might be lucky enough to have joined her in the barn.

"How's that for round and firm and fully packed? No need to answer. Want a ride home?"

"No thanks, I need the exercise. I need to start gettin' back into shape. School will start in a month or so. Thanks anyway and thanks for introducin' me to y'all's Trixie. She's somethin' all right."

"Was. Too bad she got married. That was the end of our hay barn days. I haven't tried to make a move on her since. Maybe I'll get around to it one of these days."

James Ray tucked his own private version of Trixie inside his shirt and began the walk home. He took a circuitous route hoping to avoid an ever-opportunistic Rusty Wickware.

Chapter 16 - The Eyes of Texas

"Here's what we'll do boys," J.B. said to the assembled men. "We'll stake out the Lone Star. Teddy says the dirty picture takin' happens on some Thursday nights. So does y'all's Janey, right Teddy?"

"Exactly. Every third Thursday night it seems to be. The flashin' and all. The last time, I seen a bunch of kids. They just parked in the rear of the hotel and sauntered on inside through the back door. Three of 'em, lest I counted wrong."

"See anybody else?"

"I think somebody, maybe an out-of-state person stayed the night. They parked in the front lot. I walked over and took a peep at the car's plate. It wuz from New Mexico."

"Visitors or travelers, most likely," J.B. offered.

"Did y'all see anyone other than the kids from the rear lot?"

"Nope. A couple of alley cats tried to kill each other but that was all."

"So the flashin' is still goin' on?"

"Most certainly. Here's another strange thing, J.B. There's a big closet in the Honeymoon Suite. Janey says it used to never have a lock but since for awhile it has a big combination kind of a lock on it. She says the lock's been there...maybe for the last year or so but she didn't give it no nevermind. Wonder what it's hidin' inside?"

"Maybe a dead body," speculated Chipper. "Nothin' but a durn skeleton by now, I reckon."

"I still say we're makin' a mountain out of a Goddamned mole hill," opined Winney." And who gives a shit if kids get naked and poke each other until their brains fall out? That's what I would like to know."

"Winney, we've been through that before," J.B. countered. "Pornography is against the law, pure and simple. And if kids are involved, under eighteen and such, it's an even bigger and more serious violation. Besides, are y'all suggestin' we turn our heads and do nothin' and let this sorry picture takin' business go on right under our noses? Let the fine hamlet of Mayweather go the way of New Orleans, all cranked up with loose morals, everybody cavortin' about without an ounce of decency? I personally don't think so."

"Have y'all talked to the district attorney yet?" asked Teddy.

"No, not yet. We need some time. I'd like to have more than the photograph before I go see him. He'll need some convincin' before he will get off his backside and call for an investigation or a grand jury maybe."

"Seems to me we ought to notify the sheriff," said Soapy as he turned and spat behind his bench. Chipper lit a cigarette. Winney farted.

"Remember, Soapy, our fine example of a sheriff is also in daily cahoots with the bootleggers. Y'all know I have zero respect for him. Gentlemen, I figure we have to pretty much solve this sorry affair on our own and if y'all will donate a pinch of y'alls precious time, we can at least get the ball rollin'."

Winney farted again. He had dined on pinto beans, sautéed collared greens and cornbread the previous evening. Chipper scratched the back of his head. Soapy opened a fresh bar of Ivory. Teddy stood.

"I'll help y'all," said Teddy. "It's all happenin' across the street from our place. I figure I have some responsibility in puttin' a halt to the low down business."

"Me too," said Soapy, raising his hand. "I'll help ye."

"All right, for shit sakes. I'll go along," said Winney, his arms folded. "Seems to me that we're a Goddamned posse without a Goddamned sheriff or even a deputy for that matter. And let me say this, I ain't gonna go and arrest somebody or up and get shot. If things turn sour, don't look for me to bail any of y'all out."

"I would hope you would at least come visit us in jail," J.B. answered. "Bring us a pimento cheese sandwich, maybe."

"I'd prefer peanut butter and jelly," said Soapy. "Marmalade and peanut butter. It's probably what a body would get if he's behind bars. The peanut butter, anyway. I don't know about the marmalade. I doubt the jail keeper would go to the trouble of a fixin' up a pimento cheese unless the jailed person wuz famous or somethin'."

"I seriously doubt it'll come to that," J.B. counseled. "We're not goin' to do anythin' illegal. Just gather evidence, that's all. Make notes. Bear witness. Where it all leads to, I have no idea. Anyway, here's my plan."

*   *   *   *   *

Field of View

Hello Sarah Mae darling. Things are going well here. The board voted to redo the pool. Imagine that. Lucinda Godshall is going to pay for most of the expense. Don't say anything, but she says she is willing to help with the on-going maintenance as well. Says she will even cover any initial overrun costs. That's all highly confidential. The girls are well. They miss you. No word from Seth.

When are you planning to come home? Sorry to hear about your lump discovery. I'm sure you will have it looked into. Sorry also to hear about your father. Losing one's senses must be a hard thing to deal with. Hope to hear back from you soon.

As ever, J.B.

P.S. I think James Ray may be twitterpated. Don't know about the Chambers daughter, Ruth Ann. Our James Ray's hot on her trail for sure. Now he has two loves, his camera and Ruth Ann.

*   *   *   *   *

Carlson Tinker was a former classmate of J.B.'s at East Texas State Teacher's College. J.B. became certified and went into the honorable profession of teaching. Carlson, an economics major, dropped out his junior year. Fate would determine his life's work when his father died of a heart attack at an early age. Someone had to take over the car dealership he owned. While J.B. tried to make financial ends meet, Carlson ate high on the proverbial hog and lived in one of the nicest homes in Mayweather. Post-war sales of Studebakers and Hudsons made him wealthy by the standards of the area. The demand for the style and craft of post-war autos often resulted in car dealerships with empty showrooms. A new car sold almost as quickly as it was detailed and marked for sale. The used 1952 Hudson Commodore Eight was the only car in Tinker's two-car showroom. All his new cars had been sold in less time than his accountant could record the profit.

"Tinker, we go back a ways," J.B. reasoned. "College and all. Our boys go to school together."

"What are y'all suggestin' Turman?"

"I'm merely suggestin' that y'all lower the price of the Hudson given the fact it's a used car, that's all."

"Almost new. Never driven in the rain. Not one time."

"Look, Tinker, don't go and tell me someone didn't drive in the rain if they needed to go somewhere. I wasn't born yesterday."

"You were. So was I. That's the truth and when we were born doesn't have anythin' to do with a car transaction. Look, J.B. I've got a business to run here. I've got kids who are headed for college and all and I..."

"So do we all. I don't know exactly what a spankin' new Hudson Commodore runs but I do know if I'm goin' to be the second owner, I don't want...I won't pay a new car price."

"Well then?"

"Well then what?"

"Where are you goin' to find another one as fine as this one, new or used?"

*   *   *   *   *

Smoke rose from a half-consumed cigarette in a slow, uninterrupted plume. It spread like a blanket to all four corners of the showroom's asbestos tile ceiling. Through a large section of plate glass, rays of late afternoon light entered at a diffused angle. The light, burdened as it was by the smoke, degraded the beauty of the Hudson with which J.B. was so smitten. It was a travesty, he reflected, for such a fine car to be treated in such an unbecoming way.

The air that reeked of cigarette smoke also held another all too familiar scent, the harshness of nail polish remover.

J.B. scanned the showroom for the perpetrator of both the smoke and the nail polish. He found her parked behind a small, corner desk, initially hidden by the bulk of the Hudson. He noticed that she had rid her feet of her high heel shoes. A pack of Chesterfields lay crumpled on the desk. She had been watching J.B. since he'd parked his car. She knew him from his days as a school superintendent. She had voted for Mosbacher, a Republican.

Given the angle of the sun, J.B. could trace the direction her shoes had traveled by the disturbance of dust on the showroom's floor.

"Hello, Wileen. It is Wileen, isn't it? You used to work down to Washerteria, if I recall correctly. Kept all the ladies in line. Made sure no one got away without payin' their rightful amount of money for the fabulous service rendered. How's the world treatin' you? Got a good grip on the auto business all tucked away in y'all's corner and all?"

Wileen didn't reply. Instead she reached for her purse and opened a fresh pack of cigarettes.

"Mighty fine example of a car you have here, if you don't mind me sayin'."

"Don't mind. That's what a lot of folks are sayin.' Sold a new Studebaker two days ago. Waitin' once again for a shipment. That's why the Hudson is where it is. No new cars to sell, Hudson or Studebaker."

"Don't say. I suppose y'all are saying business is beyond good. A land rush on automobiles."

J.B. thought Wileen's legs looked like spindles. So skinny were they that he questioned how such legs could support her weight. But then again, she wasn't much more than a spindle herself. Scant weight on spindles. It must work somehow.

"So y'all say there's interest in the Hudson."

"Appears so. Had a young feller in just this mornin' rubberneckin' and all. In the end, he wanted a two-door. A Wasp or a Hornet. With four-doors, he thought the Commodore looked too much like an old man's car."

"Don't say. Must've been a discriminatin' buyer and all."

"Then there was a feller from over to Dodd City. He was in yesterday." Wileen blew smoke directly at J.B. He turned his back to the smoke and from what he took to be a rude and senseless woman.

"May I have a look-see at the Hudson?" J.B. asked, turning back to Wileen.

"He looked old enough to drive around in an old man's car," Wileen volunteered. "The feller from Dodd City."

"I'm done with hearin' about the Dodd City man. The one with one foot in the grave. May I have a look at the Hudson?"

"Help yourself."

"Where's Tinker anyway?"

"He's fishing up to Coffemill Lake."

"When might he be back?"

"Don't rightly know. A week or so maybe. It's his summer vacation time. He packs up his fishin' gear, a load of whiskey, and off he goes. Just himself and the wilderness and the mosquitoes. I'm watchin' the showroom whilst he's gone."

"Good for him. May I have the keys so I can look in the trunk?"

J.B. gave the Hudson a good looking over. He opened the hood and marveled at the car's massive and lengthy flathead V-8. He opened the trunk and was impressed by the size of its interior, an interior with a volume perhaps twice that of his Olds. He sat in the front seat and surveyed the clever design of the dash and its instrument cluster. Occupying prime real estate in the middle of the dash was a push-button radio, one that could be tuned to any of six stations, although the local station, KMAY, was the only one that could be heard static-free.

J.B. moved to the back seat and reveled in the luxury of the upholstery and in the roominess of the car. It was wider, longer, sleeker, and more powerful than his nearly antique Olds. It also sported an automatic transmission, a HydraMatic like the one in Carl's Cadillac. The handsome Hudson had wide whitewall tires and it even had rear fender skirts. Unknown to J.B. at the time, the Commodore Eight had been outfitted with every available add-on in Hudson's plate of options.

"Don't go and start it," Wileen shouted, seeing that J.B. was once again in the car's driver's seat, keys in hand.

"Why not?" J.B. fired back through the car's open door. "Couldn't hardly put more smoke in the air than there is already."

"We'll die from the exhaust, that's why."

"I expect we'll die regardless, Wileen, my good woman."

J.B. got out of the car and turned directly to face the ignorant pest of a woman whom Tinker had charged with the responsibility of minding the showroom. "Both our lives are numbered given the quality of air in y'all's fine example of a showroom." He handed the keys to Wileen.

"Y'all don't smoke, do you?" she asked.

"Nope. I'd rather die of natural causes, like chokin' on the bone of a pork chop or a hearty slice of mincemeat pie or some such. Or maybe swallow an apple whole. How about you, Wileen? Ever given thought to how you'd like to pass? Or y'all goin' to let the cigarettes decide for you?"

"I don't think I've ever met someone so disrespectful."

"Well, Wileen, maybe you will if you live long enough. I won't bother you any more. Y'all have work to do. That's plain enough to see and I need to grab some fresh air before I start to reduce my days on the planet. I suppose I'll know when Tinker's back when I see his car parked in front. I'm sure it would be askin' too much for you, busy as y'all are, to give me a call."

J.B. turned and left the showroom.

Wileen remained silent. She inhaled deeply and blew smoke in J.B.'s direction. She returned the nail polish cap to its container. She would tell Tinker about J.B's   rudeness. She would tell Tinker that he threatened her, that she had stopped him from running the car's engine while in the showroom. That and more.

On the way home, J.B. thought Wileen to be as uncooperative as one person could possibly be. *Speaking of disrespect. She's a skinny-legged, walking toothpick of disrespect. It's like she's defending some kind of car dealership Maginot Line. She's a cigarette smokin', nail-polishin', lazy, disrespectful, and stupid woman.* In a fanciful reconstruction of their meeting, he imagined writing a check for the full amount of the car, tax, license and all. Having done so, he would open the showroom's expansive double doors, take possession of the keys, start the Hudson, ease it off the showroom floor and drive the car home. Maybe circle the square to let people know he had a new car.

Tinker,

Thanks for the excellent car shopping experience. I have had none better. Your Wileen is a wonder of a showroom keeper. You are fortunate to have such a competent person at your disposal. If I were you, however, I would take away her cigarettes and ask her to do something constructive, like dust. Better yet, simply have her bone up on a thing called common courtesy. Other than that, again, congratulations. I hope your fishing experience went well. Coffeemill Lake is one of my favorite places to fish. Nothing better than landing a bucketmouth bass. By far easier than trying to buy a used car at your place.

Regards, J.B.

*   *   *   *   *

So caught up was he in his car-buying fever, J. B. hadn't given a thought to what possessing a second car would mean for his walk to and from work. He had walked six blocks to the courthouse and back through the worst and best of weather. He had sauntered through sleet, snow, and rain. He had sweated as he walked home, given the summer's abundance of heat and humidity. He had slipped on ice and had been attacked by a cur dog. One unfortunate day following a severe overnight ice storm, a rude branch of an elm tree broke from the burdensome weight of the ice. The branch fell directly onto J.B.'s head, knocking him to the icy sidewalk below and ruining a perfectly good felt fedora. He felt the resulting soreness of the lump on his head for a good two weeks.

Once Tinker returned from his fishing trip, J.B. purchased the Hudson despite Tinker's refusal to reduce the price he had set on the car. J.B. immediately found himself missing his walk to work: the smells of the day, the acrid smoke from someone's barbecue, the aroma of someone's stew, the sweet smell of someone baking bread. Further, he found himself looking for a good place to park. A place where someone would not open their car door and ding the side of his cherished Commodore Eight. One morning, he found himself parking so far away in an effort to ensure the Hudson's sheet metal health, he figured he should have walked in the first place.

Most of all, he missed the time to unwind. His fifteen minute walk to and from work had afforded him an opportunity to put things into perspective while he switched hats from auditor to father, from the relative peace and quiet of the office to the more stressful and unpredictable role as head of the Turman house. Head of the house was in name only, though. At the office, Mabel would do anything J.B. asked of her. At home, Sarah Mae called the shots. There, he did anything she asked of him.

James Ray was thrilled with his daddy's car purchase. First, it was his good fortune that Seth was out of the house, forever he hoped. His daddy, without a word to anyone as far as he knew, came driving home one afternoon from work in a nearly new Hudson. It still had a new car smell. The Hudson's addition to the Turman stable left the Olds to James Ray. Hallelujah! Unbelievably, the Turmans had become a two-car family. Who else in all of Mayweather county owned two cars?

"You haven't told Mom about the Hudson?" James Ray asked, while experiencing how it felt to be in the driver's seat surrounded by a glorious example of a dash and an interior that was so luxurious as to be beyond his imagination. Was the Hudson equal to Carl's Cadillac? Maybe not as fast, but still a fine example of early fifties automotive design. Comparing the two would be like trying to differentiate between the bodies of Ruth Ann and Trixie. Different to the point of recognizing one body from the other, certainly. With or without adornment.

He also wondered how it would feel to compare both cars in an automotive face-off of design and performance. He wondered how it would feel to compare Ruth Ann and Trixie in a similar, bodily flesh-to-flesh comparison. Of the two, who was best accessorized? Of the two, who was the best sexual performer? Had such a limb-to- limb, flesh-to-flesh face-off ever taken place? If so, he fantasized he would be more than pleased to be there for the accounting.

Chapter 17 - Troubled Waters

"Camera Obscura. It means dark box or chamber. Aristotle himself once fretted over how to capture a permanent image when he noticed that a small hole in a wall created an upside down, reversed left to right image on a wall behind it. Are you following?"

"I'm tryin'."

"Okay, so light travels through the hole in the wall, right? I'll teach you how to make a pin hole camera. Same thing as what Aristotle messed with. Either way, pin-hole camera or hole in the wall, light rays travel in straight lines, right? So a light ray from say, the top of a tree, will travel through an opening from top to bottom, from the top of the tree to the bottom of the wall beyond. Think of Aristotle's wall as film in a camera. Light rays from the trunk of the tree also travel in a straight line so that they end up at the top of the surface whether it's the wall or film in your camera. Follow what I'm saying?"

James Ray nodded in the affirmative, although what Carl was saying was difficult to comprehend. He also knew Carl would not give up teaching the concept until James Ray understood his meaning.

"Now, not only is the light reversed top to bottom and bottom to top, it's also reversed left to right and vice versa. Why?"

"Well, if...if light travels in a straight line, I suppose light rays comin' from the right side of the tree would end up on the left side of the film."

"Good. What else?"

"What else what?"

"What of the light rays from the left side of the tree?"

"The same as before but they would fall on the right side of the film."

"Right. Good." Carl lit a cigarette.

"That's why when you make an exposure, you get a reversal of the image you see. With a view camera, say the kind Ansel Adams uses when he documents a winter scene in the Sierras, he is actually seeing the landscape reversed top to bottom and left to right and so on."

"Why don't I see the reversal of the light rays when I take a picture with my Argus?"

"Think about it. Are you looking through the camera's viewfinder or looking through the lens of the camera."

"The viewfinder."

"Right. So your brain corrects for the reversal. I'll talk to you more about that later and about types of different cameras and how they work and what you see and what you don't see. It's late and I need to be going. Here are the keys to the darkroom. Lock up after you're finished cleaning and give the keys to Booker T. He'll be here tonight. Make sure you give them to Booker T. I don't want anyone else messing with the keys. I have a set of my own. But, again, make sure Booker T. gets them."

"Sure."

"Strange thing, your family's relationship with a colored family. It's different, but admirable. Back east, Yankeeville and all, differences matter but they aren't limited to skin color. Yankees find reasons to hate Catholics, Jews, Irish, Italians, the list goes on. Seems people are able to come up with a way to discriminate regardless. I say live and let live. Let people be who they are. Anyway, got to go."

*   *   *   *   *

Motivated by Carl's insistence that James Ray not accept Ruth Ann's unwillingness to be photographed, he asked her a second, then a third time. The third time, as the saying goes, was the charm. Ruth Ann gave in to James Ray's persistence, just as Carl had predicted.

The next obstacle, a far more difficult one, remained. He had to convince her stern, no-nonsense coach that the effort would not interfere with Ruth Ann's practice. He would drive to Devil's Lake and seek Coach Stillwater's permission. Carl had urged him to move quickly given Ruth Ann's green light. He waited patiently for the two to complete the day's routine.

"Y'all won't even know I'm around," James Ray promised. "I'll need a head and shoulder photo of Ruth Ann and one of the two of you talkin' things over. The rest of the shots will be candid. You won't even know I'm takin' 'em. Maybe some of y'all's recountin' the day's practice. Maybe one of you, Coach, y'all pointin' to the buoy with Ruth Ann lookin' on 'er somethin' like that. I can do the head and shoulders of Ruth Ann after practice or right before."

"What was it y'all said you would do with the photos?"

"The photo essay will have a full-page spread in the yearbook. Probably the *Chatterbox*, too."

"What's the *Chatterbox*?" Ruth Ann asked.

"School newspaper. And speakin' of newspapers, I've got reason to believe the *Tribune* will run one or more of them. Probably not the whole essay but one or two or who knows? The paper is interested in Ruth Ann because of the school board sayin' yes to redoin' the pool and all."

"All right. We need as much publicity as we can get even though the yearbook doesn't come out until spring. That won't be much help but the pool will be open by then. The school paper could run it right away, right? What chance do you think the *Tribune* will run a story with a picture or two?"

"Good to excellent. Mr. Shoemaker, he's the editor and he's a friend of my daddy's. He likes me, too. At least I think he does. Anyway, I do things around the paper that I don't get paid for. I even gave him a ride home the other day when his car wouldn't start. Believe it or not, I even baby-sat their twin six-years olds last week when their parents were off to the movies. Got a whole dollar for the effort."

"Okay, but I'll tolerate no interference whatsoever. Here's what you will do. Arrive early. Each day y'all will let me know ahead of time what it is you will be doin'. When you develop your film, I want to see the pictures. You won't submit anythin' without my permission."

"Yes Ma'am, and thank you. Thank you for..."

"Don't thank me. Thank Ruth Ann and, if it all works out, we'll be thankin' you."

James Ray couldn't believe his good fortune. Lately, it seemed that everything was going his way. He walked from the pier up the steps to the parking lot and began his journey home.

With practice finished for the day, Ruth Ann would shower and Stillwaters would drive her home.

"You don't have plans for James Ray as a boyfriend, do you?"

Ruth Ann laughed. "No, I told you I have a boyfriend in Fort Worth."

"Well, it's time you got rid of him."

"What?"

"Get rid of him. The last thing you need is a whiny I-miss-my-girlfriend boyfriend."

"I don't see him that much, actually. He's only been here twice since we moved. We write letters and all."

"You know the take on the old sayin' about absence and one's heart?"

"I don't think so."

"Absence makes the heart grow fonder of someone else."

"What do you mean?"

"Y'all's boyfriend will most likely find another girl to fill the void. The sooner, the better—as far as your trainin' and concentration are concerned. And let's give thanks to the fact he is in Fort Worth and not in Mayweather. What I'm askin' you is, given y'all's boyfriend's absence, don't go and let your heart grow fond of someone else. There's time for that down the road."

"I don't have anyone else in mind, if that's what you mean."

"You don't have to. Someone else might just make up your mind for you. Keep James Ray in his place or he'll be history. I'll see to it."

Ruth Ann showered. Until Coach Stillwater's lecture, she hadn't given a thought to James Ray as a boyfriend.

Dear J.B.:

Things aren't going well here. Daddy's difficult for Mother to manage and even I have a hard time with him. Yesterday, he asked me in what part of Texas did I live? Mother has taken him in for some tests although he fought her every inch of the way. We don't have the results back yet, but I know it's some kind of dementia.

I don't know what it's all going to come to. Anyway, how are things there? Good news about the board's approval of the pool and Lucinda's very, very generous monetary assistance. If we were that wealthy, I'd hope we would be equally generous. Thank you for your help in the matter and thank you for the article and picture from the meeting. James Ray must be proud of himself for having another of his photos in the paper. I think Judith Chambers looks like Jean Simmons, the British actress. Pretty, but sullen. Remember her from "Great Expectations"? It was the first movie we saw after we lost our precious Charity. Anyway, I think they should plan a grand reopening of the pool. I'll pass on the idea when I get back.

Field of View

I think I'll be home in a week or so. I'll call and let you know of my arrival time. You need to know that I'm thinking once again that we should move to California. My family is here and I am needed here. I think it would be good for our marriage if there's a change. I'm sorry to say but I think we are in a rut, relationship wise. I've given a lot of thought to the situation. California is different and exciting. Mayweather, I'm sad to say, is stuck in a rut also. Please give our moving to California serious thought. We need a change. Let's talk when I get home.
My best, Sarah Mae

* * * * *

"How's that again?"

"I want to convert the shelter into a darkroom."

"That's what I thought you said. You will remember your mother pitched a fit when y'all mentioned it to her the last time."

"I remember, but she's not back yet and I only need it for a couple of days, that's all."

"Why do you need it period?"

"Coach Stillwaters, Ruth Ann's coach, she..."

"I know who she is. What does she have to do with turnin' your mother's shelter into a darkroom?"

"Well, let me finish. Ruth Ann's coach has given me permission to do a photo essay of Ruth Ann."

"What's a photo essay?"

"A picture story. It'll be in the yearbook. The school's newspaper. Maybe even in the *Tribune*."

"A picture story of Ruth Ann?"

"Yes. Her life as a promising teenage swimmer. Her trainin' at the lake. Her relationship with her tyrant of a coach. All coaches must be tyrants. You wouldn't believe how strict she is. Anyway, I can see it all in my head. It's goin' to be great, Daddy. I can only have just so much time at the *Tribune's* darkroom. I can set up a darkroom in less than an hour and tear it down when I'm done. Mother will never know it was there in the first place. The shelter will be perfect for what I need and I can work on my own schedule, not have to be all rushed tryin' to squeeze what I need in between the paper's jobs. I'll have to buy a safelight and some chemicals but I have enough money saved for what I'll have to have. The *Tribune* has an extra timer and there's an old enlarger they don't use. Mr. Shoemaker said I could borrow it and..."

"I don't know. Your mother..."

"She'll never know Daddy. Have you written to tell her about the Hudson yet?"

*   *   *   *   *

"I could be gone for maybe an hour, Mabel," J.B. said. He felt guilty leaving Mabel to mind the office while he had a powwow with Leon Sutters, Mayweather's do-as-little-as-necessary district attorney. Mabel hadn't been feeling well and J.B. didn't want to take advantage by leaving her alone too long.

"I hope not that long but I don't know, Mabel. Dealin' with Leon is a little like dealin' with a stubborn milk cow. Leon thinks he's God's gift to all things legal and a stubborn milk cow thinks it's up to her when and where she gets milked. Will you be all right? Y'all can go home after I'm back. I'd cancel it but I had a hard enough time gettin' Sutters to schedule this one."

"I'll be fine. Leon's a case, isn't he?" replied Mabel. "What if someone comes in lookin' for you?"

"Tell them to come back another time. Later today or tomorrow. I don't care."

"What's so important J.B.?   Y'all seem wound tighter than a ball of kite string."

"Can't say, Mabel. It's one of those times when a body doesn't know which way to turn. I see myself as a decision-maker. Give me a problem and I'll solve it. Ask me to come to a conclusion based on facts and figures and I'm your man. To be entirely truthful Mabel, I think I'm losin' my touch. I went and paid too much for a car and I haven't been man enough to tell my Sarah Mae I bought it in the first place. I suspect there will be severe consequences for that act of decisionmakin'. And speakin' of Sarah Mae, she's been gone for two weeks leavin' me to worry about unsupervised children with school bein' out and all, and then, we haven't heard a single, solitary word from Seth, whether he's alive or dead or has gone AWOL, who knows? All in all, Mabel, I've had a lot on my plate lately."

"Sounds like you do. Sounds like a smorgasbord of things are all piled all of a sudden. Life has a way of doin' that to a person every now and then."

"Then, there's this thing I have to be quiet about. I'm not sure I trust myself to do what's right or what should be done, period. I don't even know why I decided to ride this horse in the first place."

"Oh my, J.B., y'all are in a world of torment. Is there anythin' I can do?"

"No, Mabel. You've done the best thing you could have done. Y'all let me rattle on. Thanks for bein' such a good listener. My Sarah Mae would have stopped me after the first declarative sentence."

"Husbands and wives do that to each other, don't they? I used to do it to Horace and..."

"Well, thank you Mabel. I'm late to my meetin' with Leon. I should be back in less than an hour, hopefully. You plan on goin' home when I return, okay?"

On his way up to the second floor, J.B. stopped at the turn in the staircase. One could look down into the stairwell from the second floor, or anywhere from the curved and oak-adorned stair railings, all the way to the concrete basement below. He recalled when Seth and James Ray used the railings as a kind of indoor slide. They would start at the second floor and slide backwards, jean bottoms to mahogany, whooping like little Comanches. If one or the other had lost their grip and fallen, it would have been an unkind end to either of them. They had even tried to talk Faith into what the boys called, "courthouse slidin'." Upon overhearing such an invitation, Sarah Mae banned both boys from the courthouse for a month and chastised J.B. severely for his permissiveness in letting the boys have the run of the place.

"The death of one child in this family is enough," Sarah Mae had said to a humbled J.B. "I don't want the boys anywhere near the courthouse until you guarantee their safety and put some degree of sense into their heads. Y'all's too, for that matter."

J.B. looked down toward the basement. A fall from even the first floor would ensure one's demise, he figured. He reflected back to the death of the girl at the Lamar Hotel in Dallas. She had fallen not two, but twenty-two floors to her death. *What would it take for someone to take one's own life, no matter how sordid or out-of-sorts? Misery was one thing. Leaping out of a window at twenty two stories of one's own volition was yet another.*

In keeping with Teddy's behavior when he first introduced the Lone Star photograph to J.B. and the boys, J.B.

had the photo in his shirt pocket, its image facing inward. Today was the day. He would present his evidence portraying sexual shenanigans over at the Lone Star to the district attorney. J.B. figured no good would come from doing so but, if questioned later, he could say he tried to interest Leon in investigating the affair. He would, in baseball parlance, cover his bases.

Leon's door was ajar. J.B. peered through the half-foot opening and caught sight of Leon. The district attorney was seated, facing away from the door toward a wall full of framed black and white photographed renderings of Mayweather at its economic and social apogee during the last several decades of the nineteenth century and the first two of the twentieth century.

It appeared to J.B. that the ever-alert and stalwart district attorney was sleeping. Through the opening in the door, J.B. noticed his head drop to his chest. Then in an involuntary struggle to right itself, his head jerked upward, paused, and once again fell to his chest. Leon snorted. J.B. smiled. Leon was losing the battle to keep his pumpkin-sized head upright. He was sleeping.

J.B. entered, walked Indian-like up to his desk, and stood there silently. He noticed an open desk drawer. It contained a bottle of whiskey. J.B. smiled again. Not only was the good district attorney asleep while criminals ran amok in the streets of Mayweather, he was most likely tipsy as well. Ever so quietly, J.B. took a seat in a chair facing Leon's desk. Leon snorted another time. Remembering that he needed to relieve Mabel in an hour or so, J. B. coughed. Leon was startled into consciousness.

"Good Christ, Turman!" Leon said, after catching view of his office's intruder. "I could have shot you comin' in here unannounced and scarin' the pure shit out of me."

"I doubt that, Leon. You would've been too slow on the draw. Nice pictures y'all have on the wall."

"Well, they are. That one, the one with the white frame? That's my grandaddy. Guess what he's standin' besides."

"Standin' beside?"

"That's what I said. Guess what it is?"

"It's a wagon, I suppose, unless you are about to tell me that it's a Roman chariot instead."

"I appreciate y'all's sense of humor, as always, Turman. It's a Studebaker."

"Studebaker's a car."

"Studebaker went into makin' cars but first they made wagons. Made sense. Go from wagons to cars. Just put an engine in 'em and off you go."

"Well, that's an impressive tidbit of fact, Leon. I'm sorry to say the town's not the same as it was fifty or sixty years ago when Studebaker was still building its wagons."

"Time does move on," Leon said as he stretched and yawned.

"Yes, it does," J.B. remarked. "After Studebaker decided to make cars instead of wagons, here comes the first world war, then the depression. People walked away from their homes. The dust bowl left a bad taste in everyone's mouth. Then here comes WWII with our able-bodied boys fightin' here, there and everywhere overseas. And the young women they left behind joined the war effort in big cities like Dallas and Houston. So the war ends and hardly any of 'em come back to Mayweather. They put down their roots somewhere greener economically speakin'. And then what? The county's life-blood, cotton, is now but a ghost of its past. Everybody knows that. Only one cotton gin left in the entire county. Nowadays, our youngsters can't wait to leave for greener pastures. They're either off to college or off to some good payin' factory job or whatever, and they're gone forever. Our country mice become someone else's city mice. I'm here to tell you, Leon, our glory days are over. Without our youth and somethin' to keep 'em here, this town has become inconsequential socially and economically and it'll stay that way short of some kind of a miracle. And I'm not a big believer of miracles."

"Well, Turman, y'all seem full of piss and vinegar today. I have to say I have never heard such a negative accountin' of our fine and honorable town, ever. Are y'all depressed or somethin'?"

"No, but I do have somethin' I need to talk to you about."

"Must be a good somethin' since y'all bothered to come all the way up to the second floor today. Hardly ever see you up here, Turman. I suppose I should be flattered."

"It's not a good somethin', Leon. Hardly that at all and flattery has nothin' whatsoever to do with it. I guarantee you that."

"Well, stop guaranteein' and show me whatever it is for shit sakes. I'm a busy man. Y'all are tryin' to mess with me and I have a low tolerance for such behavior on a hot as Hades afternoon."

Field of View

Leon wished he could access his whiskey. His throat was dry and a little whiskey would go down nicely. It would help him tolerate the county's auditor, a man he had disliked ever since J.B. became the victor in an effort to round up a comely country girl named Sarah Mae Pirtle.

"How's y'all's whiskey?" J.B. asked, landing a solid verbal left hook to Leon's jaw.

"Whiskey is whiskey," Leon retorted, quickly closing the drawer to his desk.

"Thank you for the clarification. I thought Jim Beam was sort of a run-of-the-mill pedestrian offering. I don't know much about spirits and all, but I figured you, an esteemed member of our high-powered and vibrant community, would pal up with something a tad bit more prestigious."

Satisfied he had landed another solid blow, J.B. reached into his shirt pocket. He flipped the photo's image toward Leon. "I've got a pornographic picture that was taken here in God fearin' and law abidin' Mayweather."

"Pornographic, y'all say? Taken here in Mayweather?"

"Here it is. You may need your glasses."

Leon reached for his half-glasses and jerked the photo from J.B.'s hand.

"Jesus wept! Hang me by my balls! What the hellfire and brimstone is this?"

Leon fell back into his chair as he surveyed the photo's image. There were two participants. One girl and one boy. The girl, the photo's center of interest, was positioned on her hands and knees on a bed, breasts in a descending position, while the boy, standing at the side of the bed, readied to mount her from her rear. His member was in the full throb of alert. He looked down as if to calibrate his entry. The girl's head was turned. She looked directly into the camera's lens, her face reflecting the anticipated ecstasy of being taken.

"Girl's got a good set of jugs on her, don't y'all think, J.B.? And how about that boy's pecker. Long as an axe handle. Longer than the two of ours put together, don't you imagine Turman?" Leon reached for a cigar box, grabbed a cigar, and began the ritual necessary to light it.

"Here's the thing, Leon. And by the way, don't go and blow any of y'all's cigar smoke in my direction. I'm asking you as kindly as I know how."

"It's my office and I will do as I damn well please."

"All right, do as you please but then give me back the photo." J.B. stood. "I'm sorry I've used up some of y'all's precious time. Hand me the photo, Leon, or I'll come get it!"

"Sit down and relax, Turman, for God's sake! Don't go and get huffy. I'll give it back to you in just a minute. Y'all brought it in here for me to look at so let me do so without fear y'all are gonna leap over my desk and grab me by my throat."

Leon continued examining the photo, his chair swiveling left to right and back again. His eyes moved from the girl to the boy, then back to the girl with the pretty face.

J.B. sat down and attempted to wave away encroaching cigar smoke.

"I'll grant you that the picture isn't run of the mill but why are y'all makin' such a fuss over it? There's no way in hell you can up and say this photo was taken in Mayweather. Pornographic, I'll grant you. What proof do you have it was taken here?" Leon leaned over his desk and handed the photo back to J.B.

"Mind if I open a window?" J.B. asked. "Otherwise we're goin' to have to conduct the rest of our meetin' on the lawn."

The air of the office had been quickly burdened by a thick layer of cigar smoke. J.B. rose and opened both north facing windows to Leon's office although Leon had not given him permission to do so. Why Leon had them closed in the first place on such a miserably hot afternoon was beyond J.B. Why people smoked cigars was also beyond him. That and a few thousand other things that people did that didn't make sense.

Pausing at the window, J.B. took a deep breath of the fresh air. He surveyed the courthouse lawn below. He saw that Winney and the group had made their camp as usual. Winney was standing. James Ray would have liked the scene, its perspective. From his perch from the second floor, the men's bench arrangement looked like a group of circled wagons, defensively positioned to fend off a hostile Indian war party.

It was then, standing at the open window, that J.B. was struck by a lightning bolt of comprehension. The swift strike from nowhere stunned his senses. He stepped back from the window and then approached it once more. He looked down to the ground below. He looked at the photo from the Lone Star. He had made the connection. Now he knew. The girl in the photo, the one who was ready to be taken by the boy from behind, was Rita Anne Fields. She was the suicide at the Lamar. She, whose gift of a body had stirred him into a guilty torment of sexual longing. How could he have been so stupid not to put it together. It was all as plain as plain could be. The girl on the bed in the pornographic photo and the suicide-driven Rita Fields were one and the same. He looked closely at her image. She was wearing nothing but a pearl necklace, the same pearl necklace she was wearing in her senior portrait. He would bet his life on it. The girl in the photo was Rita Fields: her face, her body, her pearls.

"You all right, Turman. Looks like y'all have seen a ghost 'er somethin'."

J.B. returned to Leon's desk but remained standing.

"I'm perfectly fine, Leon. Cigar smoke must have gotten to me. I've got to be goin', I promised Mabel I wouldn't be gone long."

"So what are y'all goin' to do with y'all's porno of a picture?"

"Nothin'. Burn it, I don't know. Like you say, probably not worth my time and effort to pursue who took the picture or where it was taken. None of my business, anyway. Like you say, no need to make a fuss over it."

"Now you're talkin' sense, although I'd like to have a copy of the picture. I'd frame it and hang it on my wall of historic photos assumin' that it was taken in Mayweather. And we have no proof of that whatsoever, do we Turman?"

"You're right, Leon. No proof whatsoever. I will say this, though. I've lived long enough, Leon, to know that money speaks. That's what all this is about, someway, somehow. Money speaks a special language of it's own. Money speaks of ways out of economic distress. It speaks of survival. It speaks of power and authority and intimidation. And, it speaks in hundreds of other ways."

"Thank you for the lecture."

"You're most welcome. But like y'all say, who knows if the photo was taken here in Mayweather. Probably someone else's dirty laundry, not ours. Doesn't matter in the long run does it? A passerby might have dropped it on the courthouse lawn. Sorry I've taken up so much of y'all's time. I've got to be goin'. Like I say, I told Mabel I'd be gone less than an hour."

"By the way, How did y'all come by the photo?"

"Found it on the courthouse lawn."

Chapter 18 - When Less Is More

"How's the new telephoto lens working out?" Carl asked.

"Great. I'm so glad I have it, even though I had to drive all the way to Dennison to get it," James Ray replied.

"Told you that old man Naughton had a good inventory. Good thing Argus is so popular. Count on him to most likely have what you'll need for your camera."

"I got a tripod also. Used, but in good condition. A light meter, too, although I was doin' a pretty good job with exposures by followin y'all's sunny-sixteen rule."

"Still got to work some on your tendency to underexpose. Underexposure is a sure sign of a novice. The light meter will help. Continue to bracket. One exposure for what you calculate is best, another one f-stop above, and the next, one f-stop below. You're buying insurance that way. Of the three exposures, one will be the most ideal."

"Speakin' of the light meter, I will need some help what with all the f-stop and aperture and shutter speed settings. Looks complicated."

"F-stop and aperture are one and the same. Let's start there. Aperture is an opening. The opening is variable. It can be small or large. Light floods in through the opening and you have light entering the camera. As you adjust the f-stop, the aperture, you are determining how much light is allowed to strike the film. Here's where it gets confusing. The larger the opening of the lens's aperture, the smaller the f-stop number. The smaller the opening of the lens's aperture, the larger the f-stop number. Are you following?"

"I don't know. Maybe."

"Well, pay closer attention. You'll get it over time. Now, let's add a door. This door is called the shutter. It sits behind the aperture. If you open the door, the shutter that is, slowly, what happens to light entering the camera?"

"It receives a lot of light...at least it does if the door, the aperture is open."

"Good," Carl said, pleased that his student was working hard to grasp the all important relationship between shutter and aperture. He lit a cigarette.

"Want one?"

"No thanks."

"Okay, now what happens when the shutter is set to open and close as fast as it can?"

"The film isn't exposed to much light."

"Right. So aperture, the size of the lens opening...remember it could be a small or large opening or somewhere in between, that determines how much light is allowed to enter the camera. The shutter's fast or slow opening and closing is the length of time that amount of light is allowed to enter the camera. Put the two together and you have the total volume of light striking the film. Got a headache by now?"

*　　*　　*　　*　　*

James Ray had followed Carl's advice and tried to "crop within the frame" when he began recording his photo essay images of Ruth Ann, and her swim coach with Devil's Lake serving as the venue.

"Less is often more in photography," Carl had said. *"Crop out unwanted background and other details when you compose. Don't wait for the darkroom to make up for your laziness. Remember you're the creator. You get to arrange the elements to make whatever statement it is you wish to make. Just be sure to give yourself a leg up on composition. Do all you can do to make sure your images are up to your expectations. If you are disciplined and satisfied with your creativity, it's a good bet others will be as well.*

On day three of his effort, unsettled weather brought about a sudden and dramatic shift in the afternoon light of Devil's Lake. The ambient light flirting with the environs of the lake softened and became more diffuse. This was the kind of light James Ray had been hoping for when he shot the head and shoulders of Ruth Ann. He didn't want harsh shadows that would result from hard, direct sun.

Given the increased wind, Ruth Ann had struggled against the choppiness of the waves. Lightning struck in the distance. In the wake of a loud clap of thunder, Coach Stillwaters called off the training session. Ruth Ann had three more laps to complete her usual routine.

"No need to take chances, let's call it a day." Stillwaters ordered. "Think y'all are making progress James Ray?"

"I do. I'm pleased so far. I'll show y'all the contact proof sheets tomorrow. I'm finished settin' up a darkroom in my mother's storm shelter. I can now spend as much time as I need to complete the shoot. Should be done in another couple of days. I hope so, anyway. I need to be done before my mother returns from California. She wouldn't take kindly to my usin' it as a darkroom.

"Clever. So she's not okay with you settin' up a darkroom in her storm shelter? I wouldn't know how to begin to set up a darkroom."

"No, she's not, but I'll be done before she gets back."

'I'm goin' to grab a snack. You want anythin' James Ray?"

"No, thank you."

"I'll have a Coke and some Fritos," Ruth Ann said, smiling. Seeing that her coach turned back to face her, she rubbed her stomach as if hungry and made a sad face, her lower lip extended in the suggestion of a pout.

"Have some peas and carrots when you get home," Coach Stillwaters shot back.

Despite her intense training, Ruth Ann had lost little weight and when she made mention of the fact, Coach Stillwaters reminded her that muscle weighed more than fat.

When Stillwaters returned, James Ray asked her if he could take Ruth Ann home. "I haven't done the head and shoulder shots and the light is perfect right now. If that's all right with you."

"Fine with me," replied Coach Stillwaters. "If it's all right with Ruth Ann."

"Sure. Fine. Let's get it done before it rains," Ruth Ann replied.

"We should be okay. It looks like the storm is maybe passing," offered James Ray.

Coach Cindy Stillwaters had taken to James Ray. She wasn't exactly sure why. Nonetheless, she saw him as no threat to the training. He was polite, unobtrusive, and he possessed a characteristic rare for a teenager, insight into the needs of others. During the lengthy passing of time while Ruth Ann completed her training routine, stroke by laborious stroke, Coach

Stillwaters found herself on the receiving end of photography lessons. She became the student, he the teacher.

"The Greeks called it 'dynamic symmetry,'" James Ray said. "I wake up some nights with dynamic symmetry runnin' through my head. Anyway, photographers are less philosophical, at least that's what Carl says. Photographers call it 'rule of thirds.' So here's how it works. If I'm shootin' Ruth Ann, I don't want to place her smack in the middle of the picture. The frame, it's called."

Stillwaters smiled. There was no longer much of a cloud cover. The sun had moved along the horizon so that she had to move a foot or so beneath the oak to ensure more shade. The air almost dripped from the humidity. "Sorry for the interruption, professor Turman. I get enough sun without askin' for more."

James Ray joined her.

"My mother avoids the sun like it's the plague."

"Well, y'all are dark-skinned enough. I doubt you have to worry too much. But y'all's little sisters, that's another matter."

"You've met them?"

"Yes, at Piggly Wiggly's, a couple of days ago or so. Your daddy was doin' some grocery shoppin'. Faith, she the oldest?"

"Yes."

"Well, she claimed there wasn't a morsel in the house to eat."

James Ray laughed. "That's the truth."

"Your daddy asked if I was for hire. He asked if I could come over and put things in order while your Mom is gone."

James Ray laughed again. "That's my daddy. He can make a joke about anythin'."

"Anyway," Coach Stillwaters said, "get on with ya'll's lecture. I'm enjoyin' it. I might even take up photography when I retire from teachin.' Maybe I could come to work for you?"

"Love to have you. Well, so here's what you do. Ruth Ann is sittin' on the pier, her feet in the water. She looks in the photographer's direction. She smiles and waves. What we are not gonna do is place her in the middle. No, Greek-like, we'll have her in the lower third of the frame. Are you followin'?"

"What do you mean, Greek-like? The dynamic symmetry thing you were talkin' about?"

"Yes. So, in your mind, right now, picture Ruth Ann as your subject with the pier and the water and all and divide what you see into thirds, horizontally and vertically." Using his index finger, James Ray stroked the air both up and across. "At the points where the lines intersect, those are the places, the locations you should place your subject, Ruth Ann, within the frame. That's dynamic symmetry. Carl says if it's good enough for the Greeks, it's good enough for us. Dynamic symmetry, it's an ancient art principle. Carl says photographers borrowed hook, line, and sinker from the art world. Photographers just use a different form of namin' what they're up to. All the same, though, really. Does it make sense?"

"Indeed it does. I had never thought about such things when I've taken a picture. I'm a changed person thanks to you, James Ray. How much do I owe you?"

James Ray worked as quickly as he could given the unpredictable weather. Carl's insistence that he bracket his exposures slowed him. After loading a second roll of film, he ceased with the bracketing, confident that the light meter's rendering of the reflected light from his subject was good enough. When there was cloud cover, he was shooting at an aperture of f-5.6 with a shutter speed of 1/125th of a second. Without the cover, he shot at f-11 at 1/125 of a second. He was hoping for slight overexposure, not underexposure.

Ruth Ann was more than cooperative. She had become as interested as James Ray was in the project. She posed, she preened, she smiled, and she laughed.

"How about this?" she asked James Ray. Ruth Ann took her towel and held it high over her head, stretching it between her two arms. She positioned her body facing the lake away from James Ray but cocked one shoulder in his direction. She looked over her shoulder directly into the lens of his camera. She smiled.

James Ray tripped the shutter. "Good, that was great! Hold it. I'll take a couple more."

He did so. Then on her own volition, Ruth Ann folded the towel and applied it to her face as if drying herself. She looked away from the camera then toward the camera. She smiled for several exposures and then feigned seriousness. She took the towel and wrapped it entirely around her upper body as if right out of the shower. She tilted her head to her right shoulder and supported her chin with both hands, her fingers spread. She smiled coyly and looked directly at James Ray.

James Ray moved forward, then back. He changed camera positions several times and even used Carl's trick of placing some tree leaves several inches from the camera's lens. The leaves would frame her face and because of their proximity to the camera's lens, they would be rendered as circles of confusion, adding mood and mystery to some of the images. He changed lenses. He also employed his new telephoto lens to convert the choppy, background light from the water into mysterious orbs. It was his attempt to employ circles of confusion as an artistic backdrop to his most amazing and precious of subjects.

James Ray soon ran out of film. He had underestimated how much he would use in the day's shoot. Once again, Carl had been right. A gun with no bullets. A camera without film. He was ecstatic, however, with the session. If there was a heaven on earth, the thirty minutes at the edge of the lake with Ruth Ann as his willing subject and he with his camera, was it. He felt he had been good at what he had accomplished but she had upstaged him. She was better than good. She was great.

"Y'all finished? I've enjoyed watchin' the show."

James Ray froze. He knew the voice, high-pitched and feminine, girl-like. He turned. It was Rusty Wickware; red-headed, fat-lipped, and smiling ear to ear. If there was such a thing as a teenage devil, Rusty would be chosen to play the part before all others.

"What do you want, Wickware?"

"I'd welcome an introduction, to start with." he answered, pointing to Ruth Ann.

Ruth Ann remained wrapped in her towel. It was a good thing. Suddenly she felt on display. She began to shiver. The wind had picked up. It began to sprinkle. Lightning struck at the south shore of the lake. Thunder ripped instantaneously throughout the park. Evidently, the storm had yet to release some of its fury.

*   *   *   *   *

J.B. once again toyed with the idea of showing the Lone Star pornographic photo to James Ray. His son might be able to shed some light on the image, although he was uncertain how.

He thought that perhaps James Ray might see things he didn't, like the lighting necessary to make such an image. J.B. assumed, given Teddy's and Janey's testimony concerning the intermittent flashing from the Honeymoon Suite's window, that some sort of artificial light was being employed. But what kind? J. B. knew nothing about such technical photographic matters.

What perplexed him also was the question of what came before or after the image he possessed? He remembered James Ray saying that a photographer should never, ever, take a single photo. *If that's true in the case of the Lone Star situation, then there would be several, if not dozens, of photos taken. Who knew what kinds of positions and couplings took place as the kids responded to someone's orchestration? They obviously hadn't acted alone. Someone had chosen them as models. Someone had hired them and invited them to the Lone Star. Someone had said do this, and someone had said do that. Someone had said go and the same someone had said stop. Someone, the photographer, had directed it all and recorded the doing permanently on film. Here's the question: Who is the person who continues the shooting on those Thursday nights? What does, or rather did, that person have to do with Rita Fields? What was their relationship all about? And just what was the crooked journey Rita Fields had taken from being a high school student one day and a pornographic star the next?*

Having saved the *Dallas Morning New's* article of the suicide in Dallas, J.B secured the article from his desk drawer and compared the newspaper's photo of Rita to the one taken at the Lone Star. He was certain the pictures were of the same girl. Rita Anne Fields, a high school senior and Rita Anne Fields, the porn star. He would, however, travel to Dallas to talk with Randi Trimble, the person who had written the article about the suicide. If she was still employed, that is. Even so, he thought, the newspaper must keep files on such things.

Dear Sarah Mae,

Things are hectic here but not anything I can't handle. No word from Seth. I don't know whether to blame him or the Marines. He should have joined the Navy. The girls are fine. The house is a wreck, though. I'll try to get it in order before you return. I hope you are having better weather than we are. I'm dying from the heat. Why don't we think about moving to someplace cool like Alaska? Anyway, I'm not moving to

California regardless of weather. You need to know that so you don't get your expectations up. I'm happy where we are and besides, we've talked about that subject before so you know my position on moving. You seem to imply our marriage is in a rut. Well, I don't think so. A long marriage does lead to familiarity if that's what you're implying but I don't think familiarity is another word for rut. Anyway, I have a little surprise for you when you come home. You'll love it. It solves a lot of our problems. Let me know the exact time of your arrival.

     Take care, J.B.

Chapter 19 - Double Trouble

"Oh yes, I don't drive by the Lamar without thinkin' about it," Randi said. "I'm pretty sure I can locate the file. We archive stuff like you wouldn't believe."

"I had a hard time locatin' you, what with your new surname and all."

Randi laughed. I've been married for six weeks now. Trimble to Greene. Greene's got to be spelled with an 'e' at the end. My husband Wayne, he tells everyone that. Got to have an 'e' at the end."

"Why's that?"

"Good question. Here I am an investigative reporter and I've failed to ask him. Maybe I should look for another line of work."

"What does he do, y'all's Wayne the Greene?"

"Sells advertisin' for the paper. Works here too. He's in advertisin' and I'm a reporter. It's nice, although we hardly ever see each other durin' the day. The *Dallas Morning News* is so big and all. As big as some small towns, most likely."

"Do you ever get lost in here?"

Randi laughed. "Not now. A bunch at first."

"How long have you been with the paper? How long will it take you to be editor-in-chief?" J.B. asked, smiling.

Randy smiled back. "Probably another week or two. Anyway, I'm goin' on a year now. if you count when I was an intern. Went from an intern to full time. I love my job. Some stuff is hard to handle, like the suicide you're askin' about, but all in all, this is what I want to do with my life."

"Well, good for you. Satisfaction in one's work is mighty important, for sure. Workin' on somethin' good right now?"

"Yes. Got somethin' to do with accidents at oil refineries. Why so many? What are the rules governin' the work place and what role does management have to do with the rules and the accidents and such? Interestin'."

"Good for you, Randi. I'll look forward to y'all's reportin'. I suppose they'll put you in charge of the newspaper in a year or so. We need good women in high places, don't we, Randi Greene, with an 'e' trailin' behind caboose-like?"

Randi laughed. "You're funny."

"I know. I can't help myself."

"If you don't mind my askin', Mr. Turman, why are y'all interested in looking back at the suicide?"

"I'm not sure," J.B. answered, hiding the truth. "I, I just want...I've got two girls, one of 'em just turned fifteen last year and one is almost fourteen and, maybe because of them...I don't know, actually. Good question," J.B. nervously cleared his throat. "Did you ever figure out why she did such a thing?"

"No. Unhappy life mostly, I suppose. Wasn't a joiner in school, as I recall. Lazy, no good stepfather and all. Mother who wasn't a mother. For sure, all the kind of stuff that would lead one to a state of unhappiness. I don't really know. It's disappointin' I didn't find out more, but they had me jumpin' with assignments. Wait here, I'll be back. Might be awhile. Y'all don't mind waitin?"

J.B.'s drive into Dallas in the comfort and style of his Hudson should have been a relaxing and satisfying rural outpost-to-city-back-to-rural-outpost journey. He rolled down all four windows and opened the cowl on the car's hood, inviting the moist summer morning air inside. The air was fresh and cooled by the highway speed of his living room on wheels Commodore Eight. The air carried a roadside mix of scents: freshly cut alfalfa, composting manure, and smoke from a rancher's effort to burn an acre or two of summer parched grass. Patches of blue bonnets mixed with Blackfoot daisies lined both sides of the two lane highway much of the time.

Relaxed, however, he was not.

There's simply too much to worry about to enjoy one's self. What a waste of a fine summer mornin'. Here I go and buy a new car and now I have to figure out how to tell Sarah Mae why I did so without asking her permission. First payment's due on the fourth of next month. Good gravy, what have I done? Now the Lone Star thing. Same song, second verse. Same girl, could be better, but it's gonna be worse. Here I've gone and stepped up to the plate, adoptin' as I have the responsibility to get to the bottom of the porno mess. No district attorney, no sheriff, and no grand jury. What the fool am I thinkin'? Where is it all leadin' to? And if Sarah Mae finds out I gave James Ray permission to convert her storm shelter into a darkroom, there'll be heck to pay. And at what point does Rusty find it convenient to take on James Ray? What will be the outcome of that? Nothing good. That's for sure. And I can't keep from thinkin' about Judith Chambers. It's plain immoral to have such thoughts. The don't covet your neighbor's wife admonition and all is like a millstone around my neck. What in the world is wrong with me? And when will Sarah Mae be back and when she is, will she let go for once and for all about movin' to California? Seems there'll be heck to pay about this and heck to pay about that. Heck here, heck there, heck everywhere.

*   *   *   *   *

The girls were with Eartha at the Johnson's house. It seemed they loved her as much as their mother. She had taught them to bake and to sew. She had changed their diapers and curled their hair. She had nursed Hope when Sarah Mae came down with a severe breast infection. She and Sarah Mae had been with child at the same time, the two friends delivering their girls a mere eight days apart. Having lost her child in the swollen creek that fateful day, Eartha bestowed on the two blonde-haired, blue-eyed Turman girls her gift of abundant love and compassion. When either of the two offered up a seemingly endless number of childhood transgressions, Eartha could always be turned to for comfort and sanctuary. Given her warmth and forgiveness, contrasted with their own mother's hard line over almost anything, made Eartha a childhood shelter from the storm.

She was also a seamstress of regional note. Some people drove to Mayweather from as far away as Sherman to drop off everything from the need for cuffs on trousers to the repair of blouses, dresses, coats, and more. She specialized in sewing original children's clothes, dresses mostly. Her smocking was admired by anyone who had ever tried to sew such a tedious, but artful, item of clothing. Her handiwork was also admired by persons who possessed nary an iota of knowledge of how such skillful sewing was wrought.

She kept several large Mason jars chock-full of more buttons than the Bank of Mayweather had half dollars. Eartha was a pro-button, anti-zipper zealot. Buttons were one of God's gifts to a seamstress. If a button fell off, you simply replaced it. If a zipper failed, it was because zippers shouldn't have been invented in the first place.

When the Turman girls were small children, Eartha helped Faith and Hope construct dolls made of nothing but stuffing, cotton backing, and a layered dress of colorful and different-sized buttons. The buttons for the doll's eyes were the largest of them all. The dolls still held a place of honor in the girls' bedroom. Faith named her doll "Pinch." Hope's doll was simply known as "Buttons."

Both James Ray and Sammy made chess sets out of Eartha's used wooden spools of thread. The varied thread that the spools once held were now holding together people's clothing throughout Mayweather County as well as across several adjacent counties.

Other than a Turman, no one would think of driving into colored town unless it was to avail themselves of Eartha's skillful sewing. She refused to meet any of her customers in town. She was a proud woman. If someone needed her help, well then, they could come to her house. And they did. One day at the courthouse, J.B. remarked to Booker T. that his front yard looked like a "parkin' lot."

Eartha's cottage industry was so successful that two Christmases ago, she had given herself the gift of a used Singer sewing machine. Such a possession was prized not only because of its efficiency and utility, but during the war, Singer ceased production of its sewing machines altogether. Like the inability to purchase a new car during the war years, purchase of an off the factory floor Singer was impossible. The War Production Board forbade its manufacture. Singer, like other American manufacturers, retooled for the conflict. The company joined the war effort by making .45 caliber automatic pistols. The war's miscreants, the Germans, Italians and Japanese, would soon discover the Singer Manufacturing Company's pistols were as efficient and reliable as their sewing machines.

*   *   *   *   *

Randi soon located the suicide victim's senior portrait. It was the one that had been given to her by Rita's stepfather, the one that the paper had published along with the article's byline mentioning Randi Trimble.

"Do you know what kind of pearls she might be wearin'?"

"Not really. Cultured, maybe."

"Are cultured pearls somethin' that a high school student would wear?"

"For her senior portrait?"

"Yes, and other times as well."

"Hard to say. They are pricey. I don't have a string of cultured pearls, that's for sure. I suppose they could be...maybe her mother's 'er somethin' handed down to her by her grandmother, who knows? Maybe she got a good buy at a pawn shop."

"Well, maybe to all of that, but let's say none of that's the case. Would she, all by herself, a high school senior or even earlier in her school career, be able to afford a necklace like that?"

"I don't know. I guess I don't follow you. What are you suggestin'?"

"I don't know, really. I think I'm on a goose chase of some kind. To be truthful, I don't know why I asked."

When Randi had handed the glossy black-and-white photo of Rita Anne Fields to J.B., he asked her if he could step to the corner of the conference room.

"Of course."

There, he removed the Lone Star photo from his shirt pocket and compared it to Rita's high school senior portrait. *They are one and the same. Rita the high school senior. Rita the porn star. I'm absolutely 100% sure of it. Same face, same hair, same necklace. No doubt about it. But what does it mean? That's the question.*

He returned to where Randi stood. "Randi, you stellar investigative reporter, y'all have been helpful and kind as well. It's a wonder you didn't call security and have me thrown out. Would it be possible for me to keep the photo?"

"Not really. It's part of the file and all."

"No problem, and thank you again for the help."

"Well, Mr. Turman, let me know if I can help y'all chase any of y'all's geese. We'll conspire to catch 'em all."

"Thank you, Randi, and say hello to y'all's Mr. Greene, the proud man with an 'e' at the end of it all."

J.B. said his goodbye and left for his return to Mayweather. He'd stop along the way and have lunch somewhere.

Randi was uncertain what the man from Mayweather was about. She thought the man nice, yet troubled somehow. She wondered if there were some connection between him and the suicide victim? Why, she wondered, would he drive all the way from Mayweather to compare photographs? And why be so secretive as to walk to the corner of the room holding Rita's senior portrait? He had compared that picture with another picture. What was the other picture's subject? Was it also a picture of the suicide victim?

She shrugged and returned to her desk. Accidents, workplace rules and management. Were there safeguards? If so, why so many accidents? If there are guidelines, again, why so many accidents? Deaths too. And what are acceptable limits for such things, and who sets them? Does the federal government establish the regulations? If it does, are they strictly followed? If they aren't followed, are there consequences other than injury and loss of life? She sat and she wondered. Soon, she'd have to investigate.

*　　*　　*　　*　　*

The telegram arrived at J.B.'s office at noontime. J.B. wondered why Sarah Mae hadn't sent it to their home address. Probably because the girls would have been so engaged in whatever they were doing they wouldn't have answered the door.

"Well, now I know."

"What, J.B.? Somethin' good comin' y'all's way?" asked Mable.

"Sarah Mae's comin' home. She'll be in Thursday at 9:38 p.m., so it says. I'd like to know of a train that arrives the same day, let alone precisely on the very minute of projected arrival. That'll be the day."

"Well, it will be good to have her back. If you don't mind me sayin' so, y'all have looked the worse for wear with her bein' gone."

"I expect I'll be the worse for wear when she gets home, actually. The house is a mess and I have a stack of laundry to do. Maybe I'll have Eartha over. She's cleaned for us before. Then, I've got to explain to Sarah Mae why I bought a car without her permission and..."

"You went and bought your Hudson without her knowledge? Oh, dear J.B. Why did you up and do that?"

"I didn't mean to let that slip out. I don't know. The car was...it was such a good deal, almost new and all and we needed two cars. Sarah Mae will work again this comin' fall and what with James Ray's workin' and the girls will be drivin' in a year or two and I'm..."

"No need to explain anythin' to me, J.B. Save y'all's explainin' for Sarah Mae unless you want to practice on me."

J.B. thought the telegram to be strange. It was brief as telegrams were with no adverbs or adjectives or conjunctions or word trivia of any kind. But missing also was any salutation or "*I love you,*" or anything else other than the short announcement of Sarah Mae's day and time of arrival. *Home Thursday 9:38 p.m.*

"What does a telegram cost anyway? Do you know, Mabel?"

"Depends, I think. You're charged by the word, most likely. I suspect that the cost goes up if it's from California to Texas, but it's less if a body goes and sends one from, say Mayweather to Dallas. Maybe it costs more dependin' on how fast you want it to arrive. All in all, I don't know much about telegrams."

*   *   *   *   *

In two short weeks, Judith had but one bottle left of vodka. It was the good vodka. The one she couldn't pronounce. She had consumed one bottle of it first and saved the second bottle for last. She would need to contact Carl again. She had no intention of driving back with him to his stash in the country. She figured the whole thing had been a ploy, a come on of some kind. It was his way of being Cock of the Walk, Lord of the Realm, Master of Mayweather Bootleggin' Society. She sighed. She would have to answer her need somehow. If the somehow meant meeting with Carl again somewhere private, she supposed she would. He, after all, was the gate keeper.

"Well, how do you want to do it then?" Carl asked. "Me hand it to you on Main Street? Or deliver it to your house with your daughter and your executive of a husband in the living room? The bigger problem we have is that Sheriff Albertson is in the middle of a crack-down on bootleggers. He does this, I'm told, just before every election and at a time when he's got a bee in his bonnet. Arrest a few souls, put them in jail overnight or for a few days, get some much needed press, and lo and behold, he gets lifted up by the populace and reelected. We have to be careful here. I don't like jail anymore than anyone else does."

Judith remained silent.

"So, with all that in mind, what's your pleasure, Judith Chambers?" Carl asked, holding the phone to one ear by his shoulder and neck as he deftly lit a cigarette.

"I'm not drivin' back out to the country in y'all's Cadillac with you holdin' court."

"I didn't invite you to. Hope I didn't offend you by taking you out there. No harm was done as far as I can see. Was a beautiful day for a nice ride in the country. I got some fresh air and you got your vodka. We conducted a little business. That's all."

Judith lit a cigarette, saying nothing. She reflected that at least a person could buy cigarettes in Mayweather. Or Spam or Wonder Bread or cow's milk.

"How about this?" Carl offered into the silence. "On the way to the Red River north of town about six miles, there's a road called South Cow. There's an abandoned farmhouse on the left after a half-mile or so. I could meet you there. You drive your car. I'll drive mine. I've got to pick up some beer in Oklahoma. On the way back, I'll stop by the farmhouse and I'll provide you with your order. Speakin' of your order, what will it be this time?"

"Same as last time, I guess."

"I don't have anymore Sobieski if that's what you're asking for."

"I don't care, whatever."

"How many bottles of whatever, do you need?"

"Three, same as last time."

"Where do you hide three bottles of vodka?"

"I don't have to hide them," she lied. One guilty bottle in the freezer was all she allowed anyone to see. Especially Ruth Ann. The remaining bottles would be kept unseen in her panties drawer.

"When?"

"Tomorrow? The next day? No, sorry, I'm busy the day after tomorrow. Wednesday or Friday works for me."

"How about Friday?"

"Like I say, Friday's good."

"I don't want to get there ahead of you. You tell me what time you'll be there and how to get there and all and I'll arrive five minutes or so after you do. I'm not about to be hangin' around an abandoned farmhouse breakin' a stupid law."

"Fine with me. So, drive north to the Red about six miles after the city limits, turn right on South Cow. You take a left after maybe a couple hundred yards or so. You'll see the farmhouse after you go over a hill. You'll see my Cadillac. South Cow is marked. The road to the farmhouse isn't. You'll know it when you see it, though. There's nothing else out there. Got it? I'll be there at eight o'clock sharp in the evening."

"That late?"

"Are you early to bed or something? It's getting dark by eight. We don't need to go about our business with the sun directly overhead, now do we?"

"All right. But you had better be there at eight. I'll arrive at 8:05."

"Don't worry, Judith. I've got you covered. It's nice doin' business with you."

"The same," she found herself saying as she hung up the telephone.

Uncovered is the more likely scenario, Carl reflected, smiling. *I'll have one hard-drinking and sexy Judith Chambers in the backseat of my Caddy. It'll be a feast of the flesh. It'll be sumptuous supper time on South Cow Road.*

Carl was well on the way to a good stupor. He was near polishing off a half-bottle of a rare, hand-distilled whiskey from Tennessee. He blew smoke toward the ceiling. He rocked back and forth in his oak rocker. In his relaxed and mind-altered state, he worked on the details necessary to seduce Judith. He saw himself a master of seduction. And if seduction didn't work, there were other tried and true methods. Satisfied his plans were solid, he got up from his chair. He ran hot water for a bath. In the tub, he decided to forego seduction. No bunts, no sacrificed flies, no attempts to move the runner around the bases. He'd swing for the fence instead. Why waste time playing with her when he could spend that time between her legs?

Chapter 20 - Rumination

"We should be done before Sarah Mae's train arrives. If I have to leave early, you boys can maintain your duty." said J.B. "James Ray will continue his watch from his lookout as well. I can see Sarah Mae's train comin' from our perch. Train will be late anyway. Trains always are so I'm not worried about havin' to leave early."

"If we up and get arrested, y'all can say you don't know us from Adam. Is that it?" Winney countered.

"That's right, Winney. Never saw any of y'all, ever. Not on the courthouse lawn. Not spittin', not chewin', not swappin' knives, and certainly never did I see one of you take a knife to wood. Never. Or, to soap for that matter. All of y'all, a durn bunch of no good for nothin' strangers."

"Don't go and joke about it, J.B. This here is serious business, snoopin' on a gang of outlaw dirty-picture-takers," offered Chipper.

"If I'm correct, there'll be only one photographer. Maybe the photographer will have a threesome this time. Better titilates the intended audience."

"Better titties for an audience? asked Soapy. "Is that what y'all said?"

"Titilates," said Winney. "Means bringin' a body to such excitement that fornicatin' is all one can think about. Means boner time if you're a man, which y'all are mostly, but y'all are way past bein' able to get titilated, let alone..."

"Please, gentlemen. Let's get on with it," J.B. pleaded. "Let's get serious here."

J.B. had bought each of the men a cheeseburger from Linde Bee's and delivered the meal to them during his afternoon break. The four chewers sat on their respective benches on the north side of the courthouse lawn. J.B. stood.

"Let's review the plan once more. Please pay close attention. Teacher like, I'll quiz you for understandin' every now and then."

"Why do I have to stay home?" asked Teddy.

"Because you are going to testify, if you ever have to do so, that the flashin' from the Honeymoon Suite was happenin' on our stake-out Thursday night and on many a Thursday night before. You and Janey are invaluable. Y'all's house next door, her knowledge of the hotel, the Honeymoon Suite, and Janey knowin' of the installation of the window curtain. Then one day, lo and behold, there's a lock on the closet door. Then there's the photo, and all the other things she has noticed or found. All that's immensely valuable. She deserves an award if we ever get to the bottom of this mess."

"She'll take it. What might it be?"

"Somethin' good. All right. Let me begin again. Winney, you are goin' to waltz into the Lone Star at eight sharp. You'll tell Jimmy Friday, he's the owner, you'll know him, he's all bent and pockmarked and has rotten, yellow teeth. Eyes like a squirrel. You'll tell him y'all are there to make a reservation for the Honeymoon Suite."

"And he's gonna say no, or that the room doesn't rent anymore, or somethin' like that."

"Exactly. Then what do you say?"

"Excuse me while I rest myself. I have a weak heart and I'm feelin' faint."

"Right. Then what?"

"Then I pretend to doze off."

"No, first you start readin' y'all's magazine, remember? Then you doze off."

"Right, the magazine puts me to sleep but I'm really still awake, just sittin' there with my eyes closed pretendin' to be asleep. I got it."

"Right. And if anybody comes in, you wake up, of course, and make note of who's arrived. How many of 'em are there? You've got to keep a sharp eye out for it all. And notice if there's a photographer with the kids. He should be carryin' a bunch of equipment unless it's stashed in the closet, which it probably is. Anyway, we don't know for certain what he looks like although I have a pretty good idea. Should be our bootleggin' Cadillac driver. Anyway, he won't look like the kids in the photo. You'll know when you see him. He's tall and walks like he owns the sidewalk. And please pay close attention to how old the kids are. It's important."

"Could I just up and ask one of 'em?" Winney said. "Maybe I could..."

"No, absolutely not, although it would be good if you could. I know you can't tell for sure but try to guess anyway. Do they look under eighteen?"

"At my wizened age, most everybody looks under eighteen."

"Funny. Then what?"

"I don't hang around. I leave. I go home and write it all down. What I seen and heard."

"Good, now you, Soapy and Chipper. What's y'all's role?"

Chipper raised his hand to speak. "We show up at the same time, eight. We guard the parking lots. Soapy in front and me in the rear."

"Good. What do you do to make yourself inconspicuous, nonthreatenin'?"

"I act like I'm lost." Chipper promptly replied. "If someone gets out of a car, I notice whut they look like and try to make out whut kind of car they're drivin' and all. I walk up to 'em and ask 'em for directions to Fifth and Main. 'Can y'all please tell me how to get to Fifth and Main? I so appreciate it if'n y'all can? If they say they don't know, whur Fifth and Main is, we figure they are out-of-towners. Right?"

"Right. Best guess, dollars to doughnuts, they're not from here. Y'all are missin' somethin' though."

"Whut?"

"You tell me."

"Oh, yea. I write down their license plate number and notice if the car is from Texas 'er Oklahoma 'er Mississippi 'er maybe from Canada."

"More."

"More, whut?"

"Good grief, Chipper. You notice if anyone is carryin' anythin'. Like camera equipment and such. Does anyone open the trunk? Does anyone get somethin' out of the back seat? That kind of thing."

"Yes, of course. Certainly. I notice all that kind of stuff."

"Good. You, Soapy?"

"Me? Same as Chipper 'cept I'm in the front and I notice everythin'. Who's comin', who's goin', how many 'er how few, if there's somethin' in the trunk, is the radio on and so on. Why would they park in the front? Seems to me that they'll park in the rear so they won't be seen."

J.B. drew a deep breath. "They probably won't, but you need to be there in case they do. Now, since you're watchin' the front, don't go and hang out directly in front of the hotel. Jimmy-the-Lone-Star-Friday might see you and get suspicious. He's likely in on the sorry business. Next door is the Washateria. There's a wooden bench in front. Act like y'all are waitin' for y'all's dryin' and you sit there until someone pulls up. Then you casually waltz over and do y'all's investigatin'."

"Whut are you and y'all's boy doin' again from the top of the drug store?" Chipper asked.

"We're goin' to take pictures of anybody comin' or goin'. James Ray will use his camera with a fancy lens that can bring things close up, like a telescope. So, in the end, we'll have y'all's testimony and our picture documentation."

"How does he take a picture at night?"

"Good question, Winney. There's light from the hotel porch, the sorry excuse of the Lone Star sign, and light from the corner street lamp. If they arrive early enough, there will be some daylight left. He says he'll *push* the film or some such. I'm not sure how it works. He's got a tripod and what? A cable release, that's what. He says he'll use a slow shutter speed with...with a, with a wide open lens. Something like that. Go and let in as much light as he can. Anyway, he says he can do it so I suppose he can. He's got a darkroom set up in Sarah Mae's storm shelter. He'll do the developin' there. She'll skin me like a rabbit for me lettin' him take over her shelter but I I'll try to survive the skinnin'. What's the sayin'? Easier to ask for forgiveness than to ask permission."

*   *   *   *   *

"Who are you?" Ruth Ann asked.

"A friend of James Ray. Known him since forever. I'm still waitin' to be formally introduced. Y'all up to it, Turman?"

"Get lost, Wickware. You're as welcome as a turd on someone's doorstep."

"Speakin' of turds, Turman. Looks like to me that y'all are the turd. Does Ruth Ann here know you and y'all's friend, Bobby Joe, are low down peepin' Toms?

"Who are you and what are you talkin' about?" Ruth Ann questioned.

"Name's Ronald Wickware, Rusty for short. Nice to meet you. You should know...Ruth Ann, that's it, isn't it? Sorry, we still haven't been formally introduced like I say but anyways, a good friend of mine, a certain Bobby Joe...I forget his last name, anyways, he tells me that him and James Ray, watched y'all naked in the shower over there a few weeks ago. No clothes, nothin' but y'all nakedness and soap and water."

"What in the world are you sayin'?"

"Just what I said. Want me to say it again?"

James Ray stepped back. He felt heat rise to his cheeks. He knew the day was coming when the word would get to Ruth Ann. He just didn't know when, and he hadn't considered the sting of the unethical behavior would be passed on to Ruth Ann while he was with her. It was the worst of all possible scenarios.

"What's he sayin' James Ray? Is he sayin' that y'all, you and Bobby what's-his-face, watched me takin' a shower? Is that what he's sayin'? Is it true? How did y'all manage that?"

"We need to be goin'." James Ray replied weakly.

"No need to leave so soon." Rusty shot back. "Gonna be a lovely evenin' at the lake. Storm's passed. Got some quarters for the jukebox. I'll take you home, Ruth Ann. Be my pleasure."

"Take a flyin' leap!" Ruth Ann fired back. "You too, James Ray! Y'all are both assholes!"

*   *   *   *   *

"Y'all's mother will be here in a couple of days. Will you be done by then?" J.B. asked James Ray.

"I'm out of paper. I'm goin' to have to drive to Sherman for some more. I have to replace some paper Carl loaned me, too. Should I take the Hudson or the Olds?"

"I'll take off early tomorrow and I'll go with you if that's okay. I can't today. I've got a meeting about Mule Days I can't get out of. I'm the chairman, you know."

"I do. May I drive?"

"Of course. Unbelievable how well the car hugs the road. You'll love it as much as I do. I hope your mother likes it."

"I'll tell Carl I'll need to be off early tomorrow."

"James Ray."

"What?"

"I have somethin' to show you. It's hard for me...the picture and all is...well, it's pornographic."

"Pornographic? What picture?"

Field of View

"I have a picture and it's top-to-bottom, front-to-back and side-to-side pornographic. It was taken at the Lone Star hotel. I know that for a fact. That's why we, you and me, and the old coots at the courthouse are goin' to stakeout the hotel. Somethin' sorry is goin' on there the third Thursday of each month and we're goin' to get to the bottom of it. I need you...sorry I have to ask you to help, but I need you to answer some questions since y'all know about photography and all. We'll stop on the way to Sherman by that creek that runs along the highway and I'll show you what I'm talkin' about. Maybe you can shed some light on some of it.

"Can you just show it to me now?"

"No. It's too much to handle around here. I've had to guard it with my life. Teddy's wife found it while she was cleanin' up at the hotel. Teddy's one of the old timers down to the courthouse and he and his wife live next door to the Lone Star. Anyway, remember the girl who jumped to her death at the Lamar Hotel in Dallas? It was in the news and all."

"Yea, I remember."

"Well, that girl and the girl in the pornographic photo I have, the one I'm goin' to show you, is the same girl. Was, the same girl. I suppose that's the correct way of puttin' it."

"I guess I don't follow, Daddy. If it's the same girl or not, what difference does it make?"

"I can't answer that. It's a good question. Maybe there's a connection, maybe not. Anyway, I think, I worry, that the kids in the photo are underage kids. Kids your age. Kids Ruth Ann's age. There are laws against that kind of mischief. I want you to help me by taking some pictures from the top of the drug store. They'll be part of a total package of evidence I'll present to Judge Schmid at some point. I don't think...you should know I've already been to the district attorney, anyway, he's asleep at the wheel as usual, and the sheriff, well, I trust him as far as I can throw him and that wouldn't be far."

*   *   *   *   *

"We'd be most pleased to have you join our staff," principal McMann said to Sarah Mae. "I'll have a contract drawn up as soon as we receive your transcripts and the board approves. You'll love California. Our schools are the best in the nation. None better. Fullerton is growing by leaps and bounds.

Field of View

There won't be an orange tree left if they don't stop building houses, and it looks like they won't."

McMann stood. "Mrs. Turman, I dare say your contract will beat anything Texas can offer. Great retirement system, as well. You say you're bringing three kids with you? Good news all around."

He thought it imprudent to inquire of her marital status. Many marriages in California were fragile at best. He figured marriage, like the orange groves in a county named after oranges, may have seen its more fruitful days.

"Well, thank you. Will you send the contract by mail? I'll mail my transcripts as soon as I get home. Should be here in a week, hopefully, then, I'll look forward to receivin' my contract. And I thank you for the interview. You have been most kind."

Sarah Mae had never taught fifth grade but she readily agreed to do so. "A classroom is a classroom, Mr. McMann. And children are children. I'll teach them well."

Joyce, Sarah Mae's mother, was as excited as she had ever been, ever. Sarah Mae was coming to California after all the years she had encouraged, pleaded even, for her to do so. Sarah Mae would be good company and help with her father. Help her too, as she aged after her lifetime partner died. He would go first. He was eleven years older than she and of poor mental and physical health. Sarah Mae would be her rock of comfort, her joy, her care provider in her final years. Of her four children, she and Sarah Mae were the closest. They would go to church together. They would pray together. Sarah Mae would be her rod and staff of comfort. After all the years of many letters but few visits, they would, once again, be united.

Joyce prayed it would all work out. J.B. would cope. He was a strong and resilient man. However, there were consequences for a man who had ceased to lift up his woman. If their marriage had soured, he needed to be held accountable. It was the way of nature. If one ceased to give, one ceased to receive. Further damning him, she figured, was his godless view of the world. He had even refused to take communion when the family had visited California after the loss of their little Charity. A child lost in the act of birthing and he refuses communion, calling it a foolish flesh and blood pagan holdover from the past.

The train ride from Los Angeles was endless. Sarah Mae prayed. She cried. She ate little. She slept not at all.

Field of View

She rehearsed her confrontation with J.B. a hundred times. In an argument, he would always be the victor if one judged the performance on clever word usage and points of information. Despite his superior debating skills, she historically won confrontations between the two armed with the potent arsenals of emotion and intimidation. She would see to it that this conflict and its resolution would be decided in her favor.

In one of her rehearsal scenes, she informed J.B. of her intent to leave and he begged her to stay. *I'll say I'm leaving regardless and he, chastened to the core, will say he can't live without me, and agree to move to California.* In a lesser likely scenario, she agreed to stay but only if he substantially changed his ways to suit her and accepted God's loving and forgiving ways. Lacking that, she would take all three children with her. James Ray would be the hardest to convince but in the end, she would prevail. *God will see to it.* In yet another mental trial of performance, this one on the hardscrabble western side of El Paso, she took to her storm shelter until he, the-world-revolves-around-me-and-my-needs William Jennings Bryan Turman, sat outside, sobbing, as he begged for forgiveness.

But beg forgiveness for what? That was the unanswered question. To her knowledge he, unlike she, had not sinned. His sins, if he had sinned at all, were merely sins of omission; sins of selfishness, sins of putting other things ahead of his adoration for her. Then there was his on-going sin of disbelief, his nonacceptance of God in heaven.

In a rational moment, as her train neared Mayweather, she knew that in the eyes of the Lord, she too, needed the salve of absolution.

Chapter 21 - Terminus

Voyeurs. Bastards. Voyeurs. Bastards. Voyeurs. Bastards. Voyeurs. Bastards. Breathe. Voyeur. Bastards..."

As was her habit, Ruth Ann adopted a mantra as she swam, stroke by smooth and powerful stroke. Voyeurs, right stroke. Bastards, left stroke, and back to the right. Lost in her thoughts, on the second lap she passed the turnaround buoy in full rhythm.

Voyeurs. Bastards. Voyeurs. Bastards. In less than a dozen strokes, she noticed the increased warmth of the water. The water had also gained a brightness unlike the deeper portion of the lake. She stopped close enough to the lake's south shore to be able to stand. She was in foreign waters.

The reputation of the south shore of Devil's Lake was legendary. Pastor Pritchard even mentioned the Gomorrah side of the lake in a hellfire-and-brimstone revival meeting. The lake's ill-repute of a southern shore was the historic playground of the county's less principled and less inhibited residents. There, they smoked, drank, cavorted, and fornicated. More than one Mayweather girl had been compromised on a 'park-and-make-out visit' and one had only to look around to find evidence of such wanton behavior.

Ruth Ann removed her goggles. *It's peaceful here. The view is different, too. James Ray, the rat's ass, mentioned perspective often. How things looked different and fresh from another viewpoint. And he said that no two people saw the same thing even if they were standing in the exact position with the same whatever it was in front of them. I'm never going to forgive him. How crass can one person be? Two persons, actually. I'm sure it's all over town. Me, naked in the shower, while the two of them were watching me from a tree or however it was that they were able to see down into the shower room. Bastards. Both of them.*

Given the absence of her coach and the bite of her embarrassment, she lingered. Lost in her thoughts, she moved closer to the edge of the lake. She was now only knee deep in the water. It was invitingly warm. She recognized she needed to be careful. There was a possibility she might step on a shard of broken glass. She could see the shore line was callously burdened with discarded bottles, beer cans, and other litter. She sighed. She would return to her routine. She had six laps to go. She turned back to face the north shore.

The threat warning from the cottonmouth had been there for a good minute or so. Ruth Ann, however, had her back to the venomous snake and had no awareness of its presence. When she turned and found herself face-to-face with the poisonous, water-adapted snake it struck its target swift and certain.

Ruth Ann fell back. Her leg. She was bitten. She screamed. The water moccasin was in the process of giving live birth and Ruth Ann had rudely intruded on the private nature of the birthing. After striking, the cottonmouth again resumed a threat position; a full half of its body was upright and out of the water, its mouth agape. This time she saw the creature and the linen white lining of its mouth. Ruth Ann extended both arms in defense. The snake took the motion as aggression. It struck a second time. The strike was little more than a blur, the palm of her right hand the intended recipient of its wrath. A sudden and searing pain enveloped her nervous system. She stumbled backward. She fell bottom first into the shallow and tepid water.

Satisfied with its retribution, the cottonmouth swam away. Her young, eight in all, followed.

"Oh, God!" she cried. *I've been bitten. Oh, God. What will do I do? It hurts. Oh, I hurt. A snake has bitten me.*

"Someone help me! Help! Help me!" she screamed. "Oh, God, please help me! Am I going to die?" She gathered herself and managed to stand upright. She turned to face the southern shoreline. She stumbled forward. She would fight her way through the lake's thicket at the shore and to the road beyond. Once there, maybe someone would help her.

James Ray waited for Ruth Ann underneath the oak by the side of the pier. It had been three days since he had been humiliated by Rusty. He had decided to drive to the lake and hopefully make amends with Ruth Ann following her practice.

Ruth Ann had refused to ride home with him following Rusty's revelation that he and Bobby Joe were the worst of voyeurs. She used the concession pay phone and called her mother to pick her up. Rusty had left smiling and satisfied.

James Ray had driven home mortified, crushed, reduced to a form of life lower than a cockroach. He was in love with Ruth Ann and now he had lost her. He figured no amount of effort would be of the caliber necessary to win her back, but he would gather himself together and try. Carl had encouraged him to do so.

"Nothing ventured, nothing gained." Carl counseled.

In truth, he didn't have her in the first place. He was trying to have her, trying to win her over when the son-of-a-bitch Wickware had taken a blowtorch to his dreams. His dreams were now engulfed in flames. Like the Hindenberg, he was reduced to smoldering ashes in the short expanse of a couple of second hand, gossipy, tell-all minutes.

Coach Stillwaters was in Sherman. She was meeting with the town's mayor in yet another attempt to win permission to train at the town's municipal pool. Olympic size it was not, but it would do until the Mayweather pool was repaired. He seemed interested. Coach Stillwaters had upped the ante. She would train up to six interested Sherman High students for free in exchange for use of the pool for two hours on Tuesday and Thursday afternoons and four hours early Sunday mornings.

Having noted James Ray's absence at the training sessions, Stillwaters had asked Ruth Ann about his whereabouts. Ruth Ann shared nothing about the sordid revelation and resulting upset other than to tell her that James Ray was "through."

"Through what?"

"He says he's through picture takin'," she lied. "He has all the shots he needs."

"I see. I'm surprised he didn't tell me. We've gotten to be good pals. When do we get to see them?"

*　　*　　*　　*　　*

"Well, that's nice. Thank you," Sarah Mae said.

"Do I get a kiss? A hug maybe, or have you forgotten what I look like?" J.B. asked.

Sarah Mae accepted the bouquet of roses and gave J.B. a casual kiss on the cheek.

"How was the train ride?"

"Long and tedious. We need to talk."

"Okay. Here at the train station or in the car, or on the way home, or in the house, or sometime tomorrow?"

"I'm serious, J.B. don't start tryin' to make light of the situation."

"What situation? I thought I was pickin' you up at the train station and that y'all would be happy to be home and..."

"There's my luggage. Do you mind grabbin' it for me?"

J.B. accepted her suitcase from the porter and tipped him.

The two walked to the street where the family's Olds was waiting. They said nothing then nor on the way home. Both were lost in their thoughts.

J.B. and James Ray had driven both cars to the drug store for the stakeout. When J.B. saw the approach of the train from the roof of the drug store, he left James Ray taking his pictures. When finished, he would drive the Hudson home. J.B. would drive the Olds to pick up Sarah Mae. It was his plan to inform Sarah Mae of the Turman stable upgrade before James Ray's arrival back at the house.

Faith and Hope were overjoyed to see their mother. The threesome hugged, kissed, and Sarah Mae cried. Once the greeting calmed, Sarah Mae began to unpack and distribute gifts. She had been to Knott's Berry Farm and the children and J.B. were beneficiaries of the visit. She bought both the girls a new dress and James Ray would receive a new wallet from a leather shop. J.B. got a jar of Mrs. Knott's Boysenberry Jam.

The girls finally went to bed around 9:30. James Ray had not returned home. J.B. began to worry. That, coupled with the fact that he and Sarah Mae had yet to talk, whatever that was all about. Then, there was the pressing need to inform Sarah Mae that the Turmans were now a two-car family. The combination of worry drove him to the medicine cabinet for two aspirins.

When he returned, he found James Ray and Sarah Mae in the kitchen. Sarah Mae had that look on her face. The look that would freeze an entire summer vegetable garden in the expanse of a few seconds. The look that had brought him to his knees more times during their marriage than he could count.

"So, you bought a new car without askin' me? Without a word, J.B.? With no consideration whatsoever of how I might feel about such a purchase? And just how do you figure we're goin' to pay for the car, whatever it is? What is it anyway? Looks like an upside down bathtub."

"I...it's a Hudson. A Hudson Commodore Eight. The car...it's used, actually and I got a really..."

"A really good deal that probably cost upwards of three or four thousand dollars, most likely," Sarah Mae shot back.

James Ray thought it appropriate to leave the room. He had his roll of exposed film. Now, he needed to develop it. The next shoe to fall was the storm shelter shoe. Its conversion to a darkroom would have him in as much deep water as his daddy.

"Well, y'all will be employed full time in September. Last year you worked just halftime and we made it fine. I've looked at figures and..."

"I'll be workin' full time next year. You're right on that front, J.B., but I won't be teachin' here. I'll be teachin' in California."

"What?"

"I'll say it again. Soon as it arrives, I'm goin' to sign a contract to teach in California. Fullerton. It's only a twenty-minute drive from Mother's house. I'll stay with her until the girls and I can find a place of our own."

"Is that want you wanted to talk about? You're leaving me? And you're takin' the girls with you? Just like that? Have you lost your senses?"

"No, J.B. I feel like I have regained my senses. I'm goin' to start all over. I'll be paid double what I'd make here in Mayweather. California is growin' by leaps and bounds. Besides, I'm needed there. Momma needs me. Daddy does too, although he doesn't know it. You can be a part of it by comin' with me. It's your choice."

"I can't believe what I'm hearin'. I feel like I'm talking to a stranger."

"Lower your voice. We've been strangers for a long time, J.B. If we're honest with ourselves, the spark's been extinguished for a long time. We've just been goin' through the motions and..."

"The motions, is it? Good grief, Sarah Mae, how callous can you be reducin' our marriage to nothin' but a couple of people doin' nothin' but occupyin' space in the same house. Since when are four children just goin' through the motions? And what makes you think you can just uproot the girls like they were beets in a garden and take them with you without my permission or theirs? How does that work?"

"I said to keep y'all's voice down. You'll wake the girls and James Ray may hear us."

"What if he does? Y'all haven't mentioned what you've decided to do with him, considerin' no one has free will but you."

"I agonized over that but in the end I didn't figure he would come with me. He has his job, his basketball, and all. Maybe after he graduates next year. I'll want to have him at some point."

"Well, what if I say you can't have him. What about that?"

"He's not yours in the first place. I'll decide what he does or doesn't do."

"Now what in the world are you talkin' about? What do you mean he's not mine?"

"He's not yours, J.B.," Sarah Mae whispered, her eyes wide. "You're not his father. As smart as you think you are, I supposed you would have figured that out long ago."

Chapter 22 - South Shore Disentanglement

Rusty and his tagalongs had been drinking all afternoon. They crossed the Red River into Oklahoma and secured three six-packs of Lone Star beer. With libation in hand, they drove back to Mayweather and beyond to Devil's Lake. Earlier, Rusty had raided his daddy's freezer, taken some frozen boar meat, and packed it in ice. He then hit his mother's pantry and took an ample supply of spices. Next, he grabbed some vegetables from the refrigerator. Lastly, he went into the family's garage and fetched some camping utensils. Once at the lake's south shore, Rusty chopped onions and carrots while the others gathered wood to made a fire. They drank, they shouted, they cursed and they laughed. Rusty claimed that Ruth Ann liked him and that he'd be between her legs in a week or so. She thanked him, he lied, for telling her of James Ray and Bobby Joe's evil watching ways.

"Her nipples were hard while we were talkin'. I could see 'em clean through her swimsuit. Hand me the tomatoes, Will. Hey! We don't need a fuckin' bonfire, 'fer fuck sakes. We want to cook the chili nice and slow."

The chili was his mother's recipe. It was famous among the Wickware clan. Rusty, his mother often remarked, was "weaned on it."

"What was that?" Cecil asked, he of the hunched shoulders and egg-shaped head.

Smiley cocked an ear in the lake's direction although he said nothing. He possessed a hard stutter and mostly listened to conversation, almost never initiating it. Ask him a closed question and he would respond with a yes or no. Ask him an open question, and he'd pretend he hadn't heard the question in the first place. He was at his best when he was either nodding or smiling.

"Didn't hear anythin'," Rusty replied.

"Thar. Thar it is again." Cecil said. "Over by the lake."

"Well, what the shit? Y'all 'er right. That's a scream all right. Y'all stay here boys. I'll go look." Rusty finished off his can of beer and tossed it into the undergrowth adjoining the picnic area. He walked the twenty yards to the road that circled the lake. He waited. He looked left and right. Another scream ripped through the bramble of the lake's shore, this time closer.

Field of View

Rusty saw something move. Something was moving from the lake through the mess of spindly trees and cattails. What was it he wondered? Could it be a person moving? A person wearing a swimsuit? The person appeared to be a girl.

Ruth Ann stumbled heavily through the thicket and shallow water. Her arms and legs bled from the unkind abrasion offered up by the sordid mix of living and dead vegetation. She fixed her gaze on the barest outline of a clearing. *That would be the road. The road. I must reach the road. Oh, God, I hurt.* "Help!" *I have to reach the road or I'll die. I have to reach the road. Reach the road. The road...*

The tissues surrounding the cottonmouth's bites were on fire. The flames of the fire were fanned by the assault of the snake's poisonous and bacterial-laded venom on her hand and leg as well as her central nervous system. She plodded forward. She tripped on a stump of a long dead tree. She fell. She got up. *I'm up. If I fall another time, I don't know whether or not I'll have the energy to get up. I'm having a hard time seeing. Is it because I'm crying or because I'm dying?*

"Help! Someone help me!" *Why can't I see? My mouth is dry. I'm so thirsty. My heart is beating too fast. Oh, how I hurt. God save me.*

"Help...please...someone help me!"

She tripped on a vine and fell again. Too weak to stand, she managed to rest on her hands and knees. Then, she suddenly pitched forward into the muck. Realizing she might suffocate, she managed to roll over onto her back, legs spread, arms limp to her side. She looked up to the sky and tried to focus.

The willows and cottonwoods danced gaily in the mixed light and shadow overhead. Then, like a child on a merry-go-round, the trees began to move in a circle, rootless, and free of the earth's confines. The trees continued their circle, rising and falling, up and down and up again as the merry-go-round's music played, tinny and hollow.

It's silly, the music. It's playing too fast. Too fast for my merry-go-round. If it goes any faster, I'll fall off. The merry-go-round is in the lake. A snake will bite me if I fall off. What's that drumming in my temples? I don't like the drumming. Why do I hurt?

Oh, is that Jesus? That's nice. Jesus has come to save me. He will heal my wounds. He will make things right. He will make my pain go away. Thank you, Jesus.

In the blessed tranquility of her near unconsciousness, the merry-go-round slowed and came to a stop. It's music, however, still hammered discordant, hollow, tinny and grating. The drumming. The music. The incessant drumming. Ruth Ann wondered when it would end.

*   *   *   *   *

"Well, you can thank the Samaritan of a young man who brought her in. Even as young and strong as she is, I doubt she would have survived if he hadn't come along."

"I, we, can't thank you enough doctor," Judith replied as she reached for a cigarette.

"Please don't smoke in here," Dr. Solinski said.

Judith gave Solinski a good stare and put away her cigarette.

"What's her prognosis? She will live, won't she?" Bud asked.

"She'll live. The anti-venin is already at work. She's stable. We're treating her with antibiotics for possible infection. She's heavily sedated and her pulse rate is almost back to normal. She's breathing well. I think she'll be fine over time."

"Thank you so much," Judith offered. "I don't know what I would do without her." She began to cry.

"She'll be fine. Again, thank the boy who brought her in."

"Who was he?"

"I don't know. Check with the emergency staff. I'm sure they got his name."

"How poisonous is a water moccasin?" Bud asked.

"Well, their kind is the only poisonous water snake. The bite can lead to death but not in most cases. They, like all pit vipers, are very territorial. Any invasion of their territory will provoke them. The good news is that the water moccasin, this particular species of pit viper, does not contain neurotoxic components like its cousin the rattlesnake."

"What's neurotoixic mean?" Bud asked.

"Brain damage, muscular weakness, impaired vision, the list goes on. So, I guess we could say the bad news is she was bitten by a water moccasin. That's the good news, as well."

Field of View

"How do we know it was a cottonmouth?" Judith asked.

"Well, shallow water. Warm water. August is a prime birthing time for water moccasins. If the hospital gets a snake bite from Devil's Lake, its almost always a water moccasin. Maybe a copperhead if the bite is away from the water. Otherwise...that's what surprises me."

"What?" asked Judith.

"Well, a cottonmouth will adopt a threat position before striking much like a rattlesnake will warn an intruder with its rattle. I suppose, now that I'm thinking about it, perhaps your Ruth Ann didn't see its warning. If you've ever seen a cottonmouth with its body forward and its head tilted back, its mouth wide open, fangs extended and all, and being there mere feet in front of you, you'd have to be blind not to see it."

"Maybe she was wearing her goggles and her sight was limited?" Bud surmised. "Maybe she swam right into the Goddamn creature."

"Maybe. She was wearing her swim cap when she was brought in. Don't know about the goggles. Maybe there was more than one water moccasin. We don't know. We'll not know details until she regains consciousness. I'll let you know when that is."

"Will she be able to swim again?" Judith asked.

"Don't see why not. We have some worry about necrosis. Hopefully, that won't be the case."

"What's necrosis?" Judith asked, sighing.

"Death of tissue cells. It's possible, even likely, that there will be some tissue damage around the bites but nothing that would hold her back in her everyday life. Swimming either. If there is scarring, it will make for a good story for her children and grandchildren. Again, she's young and strong and will, in all probability, come through with flying colors. Let's hold thoughts for a good and complete recovery. "

"Her hand is so red and swollen." Judith said.

"That's a battle being fought. I'm counting on your Ruth Ann to win. You said she's a competitive swimmer. Well, let's assume she's in the swim contest of her life. I'm betting on her to win. She'll come out just fine in all this. Let's bet on it."

Judith looked at her watch. It was eight in the evening. She was supposed to meet Carl in an hour. That wasn't going to happen.

Field of View

*   *   *   *   *

James Ray couldn't figure out why Ruth Ann hadn't returned from one of her laps. He knew she was at the lake. Over on the bench by the oak tree was her towel and sandals. He had waited for a good half-hour. She could manage several of her trips to the buoy and back in that amount of time.

He walked back to the concession stand and asked Patty Craze, the attendant, if she had seen Ruth Ann.

"Did see her, maybe an hour ago. She's here most every day you know. She was headed in the direction of the pier. That's where she trains, you know. Dives into the lake and swims back and forth, back and forth. Such a thing would plumb wear me to a frazzle."

"Me, too. Thanks, Patty. You haven't seen her since, though. Is that right?"

"No. I could've been in the back or busy. She has to walk by here to shower. I'll let y'all know if I see her. She's one fine lookin' girl, ain't she, James Ray?   Y'all interested in her? Might there be love in the air?"

Dejected, James Ray walked back to the pier and sat on the bench by the oak. Storm clouds had gathered to the southwest of the lake. A thunderhead rose anvil like in the distance. The sky grew darker.

James Ray stood. Then he turned and bolted to the concession stand.

"Patty, may I borrow a nickel for the pay phone? Please."

"Y'all don't have a nickel? I can make change fer 'ye."

"No. Please. I only have my special silver dollar. It's my granddaddy's birth-year dollar. I'll pay you back. You know that. Please. Somethin' has happened to Ruth Ann. I don't know what. Somethin' terrible, maybe. Please, Patty."

James Ray slipped the nickel into the pay phone.

"Operator."

"Mrs. Sumwalt. This is James Ray Turman. Could y'all please connect me to the sheriff's office? Hurry, please."

Two deputies arrived fifteen minutes later, the Mayweather volunteer fire truck a few minutes after that. James Ray met the two sheriff deputies at the parking lot. He rode with them to the south shore and beyond. They stopped, turned around and circled back. They saw nothing. James Ray noticed smoke coming from a picnic area a few yards removed from the lake's shore.

"Over there. Maybe someone's havin' a picnic. Maybe they saw somethin'."

Cecil Cyrus, Mayweather's fine example of a long-serving deputy sheriff, questioned Rusty's three remaining erstwhile cohorts. Hank "Hankie" Brown, a deputy for less than a year, was assigned the duty of exploring the several hundred yards of the south shore's thicket. James Ray accompanied him as they slowly traversed through the muck and tangle of the shore. Two firemen commandeered a boat with an outboard motor and began searching the south shore from the water. Another waited on the north shore surveying the lake with binoculars.

"What you boys up to on a fine day like today?" deputy Cyrus asked. "Looks like it's gonna rain on y'all's parade. What kind of a parade is it, by the way?"

"We ain't paradin'. We're cookin' chili."

"That so? Looks more like hands-in-y'all's-pockets instead of chili cookin'. Beer drinkin' too, seems like. All these cans of Lone Star belong to y'all? How did y'all get out here? I don't see no car. Don't look like you boys are the kind to up and walk all the way to the lake and all. Who brought y'all here?"

No answer was forthcoming. The boys fidgeted, shuffled their feet, and looked around furtively as if caught stealing a box of chocolates from the five-and-dime.

"I ain't askin' twice."

Cecil found his voice. "We wuz brought out here by our friend Rusty."

"Rusty who?"

"Rusty Wickware."

"Morris Wickware's son?"

"Well," Cecil replied, "he can cook mighty fine chili and..."

"Why ain't he here with you fine upstanding citizens cookin' his award winnin' chili and kickin' back and enjoyin' the day? Why is that? What's y'all's name boy?"

"Cecil. Cecil Lovelady."

"Don't say. Another Cecil in the world. I'll have to say that y'all's last name hardly suits you, if y'all don't mind me sayin' so. The Cecil's good...but Lovelady? Fuck a duck. What a last name for a hunched over feller like you. Where's the chili maker?

How come he ain't here cookin' his fine chili? And why is y'all's meat all over the ground? Is that the secret to his chili?"

Cecil didn't know which question to answer first.

Given his hesitation, Will answered. "He's gone."

"I'll do the talkin'," Cecil said, frowning at Will. Cecil liked being in charge. He thought himself second in line if something should happen to Rusty. He was warmed by the feeling of self-imposed authority but was highly discomforted by being questioned by the stupid sheriff deputy. Aside from that, he was hungry.

"And I'll ask the questions. Where's the Wickware boy, Mr. Love-a-lady?"

"He...he up and left. Hardly said nothin' other than that he was on a...on a...mission of rescue 'er somethin' like that."

"Now we're gettin' somewhere. Do you know who he was rescuin'? How long ago did he leave?"

"Maybe an hour ago. We heard screamin' from over there."

"Was a girl scream," Will offered.

"Did any of y'all see anything? A girl swimmer maybe?"

"I, I, I, did," Smiley managed. I, I, I, seen...seen her ba, ba, ba, blue saaaaswimin' ssssuit."

Rusty had told his boys to remain at the picnic area. They obeyed his order as usual. Smiley, however, mounted the top of the picnic table and was able to catch a tree and thatch restricted view of Rusty's rescue of Ruth Ann. Unfortunately, he had consumed so much beer, he lost his balance and fell hard to the ground, severely spraining his left wrist. When he fell, he took the cooking pot containing the morsels of marinated boar meat with him. Rusty had pulled Ruth Ann from the thicket to the side of the road. He then ran back to his car and drove back to where Ruth Ann lay unconscious.

"How are we gonna get back to town?" Cecil had asked.

"I'll come back to get y'all later," Rusty said.

Now, Cecil asked the same question of the deputy sheriff.

"That's not my problem, that's y'all's to figure out. We don't run a taxi service. Y'all stay right where y'all are. I'm gonna arrest the sorry lot of you for underage drinkin'."

By the time Deputy Brown and James Ray worked their way back to the picnic area, the boys had vanished. After both deputies had given up looking for them, the beleaguered teenagers came out from their thicket of a hiding place, split the carrots and bell peppers among them and drank the last of the beer. None of the boys liked onions unless they were cooked in Rusty's chili. A couple of hours later and drenched by a downpour, the besotted and hunger-driven boys began the long walk back to Mayweather. Varmints of the night would help themselves to the largess of uncooked boar meat.

Chapter 23 - Asunder

Winney was relieving his bladder when the models for the evening session casually walked through the rear entrance of the Lone Star, climbed the stairs, and proceeded down the hall to the Honeymoon Suite. They knocked on the suite's door and the door opened. They entered. The door closed behind them. Someone locked it from the inside.

Chipper noted the arrival of the car in the hotel's back parking lot. It had Texas plates. He memorized the combination of letters and numbers after the passengers, two girls and a boy, were inside the hotel. The car was a well-worn, four-door, 1939 Studebaker Commander.

Soapy saw nothing. He chewed. He spat. He whittled at a fresh bar of soap. As a detective, he figured he had, like Casey at the bat, struck out.

James Ray was only able to take two exposures. The first documented the arrival of the car as soon as it was parked. The second time he triggered the cable release to the camera was when the three people, whoever they were, were walking to the rear entrance to the hotel. Even with his new telephoto lens, they were tiny, nondescript objects given the distance from the roof of the drugstore to the hotel parking lot.

*   *   *   *   *

The back and forth between Sarah Mae and J.B. lasted well into the night. They moved from the kitchen to the backyard, where Sarah Mae was bitten numerous times by mosquitoes, Then, they returned to the kitchen once they saw James Ray's bedroom light extinguished. While in the backyard, their discourse was accompanied by crickets, fireflies, and an owl J. B. disliked, even hated. On several occasions the barn owl had taken one of J.B.'s chicks for an evening meal. J.B. viewed his conflict with the owl as man against nature. It was a battle he was losing.

Once, seated on the front porch alongside Sarah Mae, he threatened to fetch his single-shot .22 caliber rifle and "pluck the durn thing from its perch." Sarah Mae put a halt to his vengeful thoughts by saying that the owl had to earn a living and a chick here and a chick there was a small sacrifice in God's scheme of all things nature.

This night's lengthy argument was sprinkled with Sarah Mae references to God this and God that and God willing and so on.

"What about you and your intentions to bring our family to its knees? Is it humanly possible for you to give me an answer that doesn't contain what God wants or God wishes? Is that possible?" J.B. asked.

"No. It's not possible. God is there to..."

"Jesus Christ, Sarah Mae, there you go again."

"Using the Lord's name in vain will get ya'll nowhere."

"I'm gettin' nowhere as it is. First you tell me my James Ray isn't mine and all that that implies and I don't...I don't want to know anythin' more than that. Period. No more. I can't take anymore than you have already dished up. Keep that sorry business to yourself and y'all's God. Let him deal with it and with you for that matter."

"He's been dealin' with me since it all happened. I ask for forgiveness each and every day."

"Well, good for you. Good you have such a friend to turn to. I notice, however, you haven't asked for my forgiveness. How does that work, Sarah Mae? You go and ask your God each and every day for forgiveness but you've yet to humble yourself enough to ask for my forgiveness."

"Telling you wouldn't have helped. I didn't want you to turn your back on James Ray. Or me, for that matter. And what good would it have done, J.B.? You knowin' I sinned. You knowin' I was unworthy for all these years. You knowin' James Ray wasn't your boy child. It was my cross to bear."

"I suppose my idea of marriage is different," J.B. countered. "I thought that when two people joined hands and problems reared their ugly heads, like they always do in a marriage, the problems were to be worked on by both man and wife. Maybe I could have helped you with your cross. Maybe I would have understood. You didn't give me that opportunity, though. You left me in a tunnel of darkness for sixteen years. That, to me, is the bigger of the two sins. You left me adrift in some kind of ocean of ignorance. Some gift, Sarah Mae."

"And there you go, always got a smart thing to say. Y'all are always ridin' some kind of high horse of sarcasm. That's what I've had to put up with. You and y'all's belittin' and sarcastic remarks. Well, J.B. you were absent in our marriage from the beginning. That's what you don't understand. Pure and simple, y'all have been absent. How does a person share with another person when all they will get back is some sassy remark about bein' in a tunnel of darkness or wallowin' in an ocean of ignorance?"

"Did I hear you say I've been absent? Absent from our marriage? Was that it? How can you honestly say that? If I've been absent it's because I didn't know what our marriage was undergoin', under attack as it turns out."

"Yes, that's what I said. Y'all have been absent from our marriage. There, I said it again. You've yet to ask me about the lump on my back. Hardly a word in a letter, not when I got off the train, not since I've been home, nothin'. That's what I'm talkin' about when I say you've been absent. Absent to help around the house. You mow the lawn and you tend the garden and that's about it. You've been absent to help with the children and listen to their problems. You've never listened to my problems. And you've always had a quick solution when what I desperately needed was someone to listen. I don't have anyone to talk to but God. You've been absent to any of my needs but always present when some group needs a chairman or someone to volunteer for this or that. You see J.B., y'all's job and everythin' else you think is important to you and what you want and what you need, has been your marriage. You've had little or no time for me and the children. You don't believe in God. You don't like church. You don't like Christmas."

"Maybe so. You're right about the religious part, actually. On your end though, you're married to your church and your God and Jesus and Christmas, too. How's that for a marriage? The father, the 'wife' and the holy ghost? So here's the question, Sarah Mae. In the eyes of your Lord and Savior, I wonder if he sees what you call 'my bein' absent in our marriage' as better or worse than y'all's rendition of infidelity? And I'm sorry about not askin' about y'all's lump or whatever it is...it's just that I've been so preoccupied what with..."

"That's just what I've been talkin' about. Mr. J.B. Preoccupied Turman. Just so you know, the thing is cancerous, J.B. I had it checked out in Los Angeles. I'm sick with a kind of cancer. The doctor said it's a...a deep, some kind of a high grade liposarcoma. I think that's the way it's pronounced. It's a fatty tissue kind of cancer. The lump is on my back near my neck."

Field of View

Sarah Mae turned and showed J.B. the tumor. "The doctor says usually the tumor is found on a person's thigh but it can pop up elsewhere. It's not good, J.B. The five year survival rate is only fifty percent. That's another reason I'm goin' to California. I'll get the treatment I need. And, I'll have someone to talk to. Someone who'll listen. Someone who'll hold my hand. God will be right there with me."

"I'm sorry..."

"You're always sorry, J.B. I have to say that's one of your redeeming values. You mow the lawn, you're an honorable chairman of this or that, and you do say sorry. If you could just get ahead of havin' to be sorry so often. That would be nice."

"Well, at least when I say I'm sorry, at least I'm askin' you for forgiveness, not lookin' skyward for some fatherly lookin' soul, up in the clouds, sittin' cool as a cucumber, watchin' us poor, confused and weary mortals struggle with a thing called life. My head hurts, Sarah Mae, I'm goin' to bed. I am truly sorry about your cancer. You need to know that. Maybe I'm not the husband you wish me to be but I'm sorry for your health situation. Sorry, too, for the mess we're in. Sorry for you. Sorry for me. Sorry for our family. Just plain sorry for it all."

Bed meant the couch in the living room. It wasn't the first time in his marriage he'd sought shelter from the storm on the living room sofa.

But sleep, he could not. He sat by the radio and tuned it to faraway places, marveling at a technology that was beyond his grasp. He took two more aspirins. After Sarah Mae had retired, he went into the kitchen and made himself a ham sandwich. Maybe he wouldn't sleep at all. When he was a sailor, he had pulled some all-nighters and he could do it again.

He sat at the kitchen table and stared at the checkerboard table cloth until the red and white checkered squares became visually transfixed, as if occupying another dimension, another reality. He wondered what his world would look like in the days to come.

A splintered family? Life without my wife and two girls, Seth already gone and in harm's way. Now, I'll have to deal with an estranged wife with cancer and a fifty percent chance of surviving. What will I do with a house too large for James Ray and myself? Will Sarah Mae take the Olds to California? She will need a car. She hates the Hudson. Can I stop her from leaving? Do I want to stop her from leaving? What are people going to say? How can I make ends meet without the benefit of Sarah Mae's economic contribution?

At four in the morning, barefooted, J.B. stepped to the bathroom and shaved. He would escape to the safety and sanity of his office. He stared into the mirror. *I'm old,* he thought. *Old and tired. What has my life become? Where is all this headed? I've never felt so alone and miserable in all my life. I'm both a fool and a failure. Who was Sarah Mae's lover, anyway? And was it just a one time fling? I have always marveled about how much James Ray looks like his mother's Indian side. The other children are obviously Turmans. No question about that. So, I'm not his father. Good grief.*

He quietly went into the bedroom and secured a shirt, trousers, and tie. His shoes and socks were in the living room. He would bathe when he came home after work. J.B. wondered how the stakeout of the Lone Star went. He would find out when he talked to the chewers.

*   *   *   *   *

"Well, J.B., y'all look pretty much like a train wreck."

"I expect so, Winney. Thank y'all for the compliment. It was a train I didn't see comin'."

"That's the best kind." Winney responded.

"How's that?" asked Chipper.

"Well, let me ask you this. Would y'all rather see the train comin' 'er just have it smack into you while you were whistlin' Dixie 'er somethin'?"

"If I saw it comin', maybe I could up and get off the tracks."

"That ain't the point. If you're goin' to be run over by an incomin' Texas and Pacific, it would be better to not see it comin', thereby avoidin' the terror of it all. If y'all see it comin' then y'all will suffer some before it runs over you. That's what I'm sayin'."

"Well, in my particular train wreck, I didn't see it comin' and I wish I had," J.B. said. "Maybe Chipper's right. There might be some sufferin' all right, but at least a body might be able to do somethin' about it. Influence the outcome, so to speak. Anyway boys, my time's limited and I have a headache I can't put an end to. Let's get down to it."

"What did y'all see, Winney?"

"Nothin', actually. Sorry to say, nothin'."

"Nothin'?"

"Well, I had to take a piss and that wuz when a herd of elephants went up the stairs to the second floor."

"Please explain the herd of elephants if you didn't see anythin'."

"I wuz pissin', like I said. I guess the stairs are above the pisser and they went clumpin' up over my head like a shit full of elephants."

"Well, what about when they left?   What did y'all see then?"

"Nothin'."

"Nothin'?"

"Nope. I got tired and went home."

J.B. rubbed his head. He would need more aspirin. "You went home?"

"I did. I'm not a night owl, J.B. I stayed as long as I could."

"All right." J.B. sighed. "What did either of y'all see, Chipper and Soapy?"

"I seen three kids," Chipper answered. "They wuz drivin' a '39 Studebaker. They up and went into the hotel from its rear. It wuz too dark to tell anythin' about 'em other than that there wuz two girls and a boy."

"Anythin' else? Was there an adult with 'em? Someone carryin' photo equipment and such?"

"Didn't see anyone like that. The kids were alone in the Studebaker. It wuz a pug nose '39, like I said. Had a messed up rear fender and a missin' hubcap. I got the license number. It wuz a Texas plate."

"Good job. No one saw an adult? You Teddy? Y'all's Janey?"

"Nope. No adult unless the kids were adults and like Chipper says, it wuz too dark to tell."

"Not even later? Anyone see anything later? I know for certain the kids aren't takin' pictures of themselves? That wouldn't work. Anythin' Soapy?"

"What say?"

"Did y'all see anythin' from the front?"

"No. Nothin' other than people comin' to wash their clothes. Two families in all. The one feller had three kids with him and he..."

"Well, that's neither here nor there. For gravy sakes, gentlemen, are y'all tellin' me no one saw an adult at anytime either comin' or goin'?"

Heads nodded in the negative. "Maybe Jimmy Friday is the dirty picture taker." Teddy offered.

"I doubt he'd know a camera from a hand grenade." J.B. countered. "Besides, who would be mindin' the store if he's up in the Honeymoon Suite?"

Winney stood. He felt he needed to redeem himself. "After I did my pissin' I went and asked Jimmy Friday who wuz makin' all the noise. He said, What noise? And I said a Goddamn herd of elephants had just gone up the stairs. I said he must be doin' good elephant business on a slow Thursday night. He laughed and said he hadn't heard anythin'. Said he'd noticed that I'd nodded off so I must've been dreamin' or else I must've been hearin' thangs."

"That's good, Winney."

"What's good about me hearin' thangs and all?"

"It means our good owner of the Lone Star is in on the conspiracy."

"What conspiracy?" asked Teddy. "Please explain what a conspiracy is so as I can understand y'all's point."

"We're a conspiracy." J.B. explained. "Anytime two or more people join forces to to do this or that, they conspire. That makes for a conspiracy. Whether it's good or bad is beside the point. A conspiracy is a conspiracy, pure and simple. So, Friday's claimin' ignorance of anyone goin' up the stairs, when in fact they did, means he's in on the picture-takin'. He is profitin' from it one way or another. Why else would he deny the footsteps? You, Winney, say y'all heard footsteps. He, Jimmy Friday, claims he heard nothin'. He's in on the picture takin'. That's good to know."

Winney began to feel better about not seeing anyone although he would have liked to have caught a glimpse of the two girls. He wondered what they looked like. He wondered if one of the girls was the same as the one in Teddy's bombshell photo.

"T.R., how about you and y'all's Janey?"

"Well, the flashin' commenced...I'd say about a half-hour after the kids arrived. Me and Janey saw 'em arrive and park in the back and go into the hotel like Chipper said."

"How long did the flashin' last?"

"Off and on for two hours and twenty-five minutes. We timed it."

"What then? Did they leave shortly after?"

"Yep. They waltzed to the car and drove off."

"I seen 'em do the same thang," Chipper chimed in. "Got into their Studebaker and drove off."

"Which way did they turn on Main?"

"Didn't think to notice," replied Teddy.

"Maybe right or wuz it left? I don't hardly remember," offered Chipper.

"Well, what about you and y'all's boy, James Ray? Did his pictures turn out?" asked Winney.

"Hasn't had time to develop 'em. Things were too crazy last night. That's when I got run over by the train.

"Was it one y'all seen comin'?" asked Soapy.

Chapter 24 - Bedside Pow Wow

Ruth Ann was in stable condition, had regained consciousness, and was able to recall details of her encounter with the cottonmouth but remembered little of her rescue by Rusty.

"I remember being taken somewhere, I think. Funny, I thought Jesus had come to help me. He was strong, I remember that. Nothin' much else...other than how bad I hurt. Scared me half to death...the snake. I turned around and...and there it was. I've never seen, never seen...such an angry sight. It struck me before I knew...it was so fast."

Judith held Ruth Ann's good hand. She had stayed by her side the entire first night at the hospital. She remained the next, but on the third night she left early in the evening. She couldn't drink and be with Ruth Ann at the same time. She planned to go home, have a couple of drinks, and return. Instead, after having her drinks, she went to bed early.

Coach Stillwaters visited each morning. The two talked swimming, topics having to do with past and present acts of valor and discipline, the pool progress and some Mayweather small talk. She also checked the food menu each day to ensure that Ruth Ann was being fed what she called "food decent for an athlete."

On the third night of Ruth Ann's stay, James Ray came calling.

"Hi, it's me. Hope you don't mind me visitin'," James Ray said into the stillness of the hospital room.

Ruth Ann hesitated before responding. "Oh, hi. No, it's fine. You can come in. I should get out of bed and knock you to the ground. What you and your friend did was stupid. Pure stupidity. But I'm willin' to forgive you because I'm bored to death. Mother's gone home for the evenin'. I've read every magazine in the entire hospital. *Look, Life, Time, Saturday Evening Post,* I've read 'em cover to cover and I've only been here three days. I could have been killed by a cottonmouth and now most likely, I'm gonna die from boredom."

"So it's okay? You're not mad anymore?"

"Sure. Mad at you and what's-his-name, your peepin' Tom buddy, and a hateful cottonmouth. Mad at all of y'all."

"May I say I'm sorry for my juvenile behavior?"

"You may."

"Well, I'm sorry. It was, like you say, a stupid thing to do."

"It was."

"And, I...I just hope you will..."

"Don't worry about it. It's over and done. It's probably already all over town but I could have died back at the lake and I didn't. I've decided life is too short to get all wound up about things that don't matter in the long run. Who gives a hoot whether or not you saw me naked? It's just flesh and bone anyway, isn't it? I'm alive and that's all that matters. Right now, anyway. Maybe I'll wake up tomorrow and never speak to you again for the rest of your life. For now, you're forgiven. Rusty, too."

"I'm told he was the one who found you."

"I suppose he did. He must've stuffed me into his car and then driven me to the hospital. I don't know how he found me, actually. Maybe he was at the lake drivin' around or somethin'."

"I went lookin' to thank him but I couldn't find him. We have some old bones to pick and I was hopin'...if I thanked him for savin' you, that maybe, just maybe we could get past whatever it is he has in for me."

"He doesn't like you, does he?"

"Right as rain. Hasn't since forever. I don't know why, actually. Maybe because I beat him out of a startin' position as point guard. Then he up and quit. Actually, it started long before that. I can't figure it out. I've worried over it for a long time."

"Anyway, tell me about y'all's basketball," Ruth Ann said, as she repositioned herself in her bed. "I don't know much about basketball. Tell me about a game when you lost in the last minute or second or somethin' like that."

"How about I tell you about a game we won?"

"No. A want a story about when and how you lost. You, the hero, but you lost despite bein' a hero. You were facin' great odds. Y'all struggled. You meant well, but were facing insurmountable odds. Victory seemed impossible. Undaunted, you pressed ahead only to fall short of your goal. That's the hero quest. I learned about it in English literature."

"I never get to succeed?"

"In the end, but certainly not at first. Never at first. Otherwise, it wouldn't make for a good story, would it? So, tell me about a game in which you, the hero, were rebuffed although you struggled mightily."

James Ray's eyes rolled upward in an attempt to recall a time when victory was lost. Thoughts of the Bloom Bulldogs came to mind. "Well, we almost always get beaten by the Bloom Bulldogs. They're a high school about...I don't know, maybe fifteen miles south of Mayweather and, like I say, they almost always whip up on us. They play basketball year 'round. Nothin' else but basketball. They eat and sleep basketball. Anyway, in one game we were down one point with four-and-a-half seconds to go and Coach, our Coach Mariner, he told me I was to inbound the ball to Colin Harper. We call him Cod, though and..."

"Why Cod?"

"Well, he, he has a ball...excuse me, a testicle missin'. Lost it from cancer. Anyway, he's our center, so Cod was to toss it back to me and Coach said I was to dribble the whole length of the court, drive the lane, and make the winnin' basket."

"Is that heroic? Dribblin' all the way to the basket?"

"Well, there's five on a team and he mostly wants me to do it all by myself with only four-and-a-half seconds left in the game. That isn't a lot of time and you don't know Coach. He's a former Marine and he teaches P.E., and he has no tolerance for failure. Every other word is a cuss word. Mother even turned him over to the school board because of his cussin' and all. I thought I'd have to sit on the bench the rest of the year after she took him on."

"Good. He fits the story nicely. Mayweather basketball coach Mariner, formerly of the Marines. He cusses first thing in the mornin' and cusses after he says his evenin' prayers. I like it. Go on. So what happened to your mother after she told on him? Did the school board do anythin'?"

"Not as far as I know. Anyway, at one game, Coach saw my mother in the stands and pointed his finger at her and scowled. My daddy didn't like his finger pointin' and his scowlin' so Daddy stood up, pointed back at him and scowled back like a cur dog and that was the end of that as far as I know. Come to think about it, that would have made for a good fight, my daddy and Coach. Daddy, the former Navy boxer and Coach, the foul-mouthed Marine."

"So did y'all make the basket?"

"I can't answer that yet, can I?"

"No, I suppose not. So what happened?"

"Well, let me back up. After they scored, makin' it a one-point game, Cod goes and launches a brick of a shot that catches nothin' but air. Coach calls time-out, and he tells me what I'm supposed to do, and I up and say that four seconds or so isn't a lot of time. Coach says we'd have all the blankety-blank time in the world if you, Cod, had the blankety-blank sense not to launch a blankety-blank bomb from blankety-blank twenty-five feet. He said he was gonna remove Cod's remainin' blankety-blank testicle, and that if he had a knife handy he'd do so right then and there in front of Cod's parents and two hundred or so blankety-blank fans. He kept cussin'. He asked if we were gonna let the blankety-blank Bulldogs beat us yet another double-blankety-blank time? Then he said that Cod had better shower in a hurry after the game. Win or lose, he said he'd likely strangle Cod in the shower, relieve him of his remaining blankety-blank testicle, and feed it to the first blankety-blank stray dog that he saw. Then he turned to me. He called me a little turd of a guard, and said it was up to me to save the game."

"So?"

"Well, I was happy to hear the buzzer announcin' the end of the time-out. I was ready for the game to be over, win or lose. If we won, there would be little thanks from Coach. If we lost, we'd have to sit through a post-game session so full of profanity, the air in the locker room would be so dark you couldn't see your locker."

"So what happened?"

"So I inbound the ball to Cod. Cod bounce passes it back to me. I pull a crossover dribble and.."

"What's a crossover dribble?"

"I'll explain it later. After I get the ball, I blow by one of their players...Terry, I think his name is Terrance or Terry, anyway, I blow by him and I fake swingin' the ball to our forward Percy...we call him Purse. Anyway, he's put himself in the corner all waitin' for a shot at the basket. That's what coach wanted 'em to think. Wanted 'em to think that our forward, Purse, would take the shot. He's good from the corner. He'd made two shots from the corner already in the game. So I look for the world like I'm gonna pass to Purse and..."

"How much time was left?"

"I had no idea. I just knew four-and-a-half seconds was all the time we had. So after I faked the pass, I pulled another cross over dribble, thereby evadin' their forward and from the top of the key..."

"Where's the top of the key?"

"Hold on just a second. Their Jolly Green Giant center, rotated over to pester me and kept me from drivin' all the way for a lay-up which was what I wanted to do so I had to launch a floater."

"What's a floater?"

"A shot that's high and soft and to the basket. It's a shot that's hard for a tall center to block. But our center, Cod, was supposed to screen him and keep him from comin' my way but the Bulldog center, I forget his name...I just call him String Bean to get under his skin...he up and elbowed Cod out of the way, but no foul was called. Anyway, the ball left my hand before the buzzer sounded meanin' the game was over. Time had run out but if my shot made good, it would count because the ball left my hand before the buzzer sounded."

"So what happened? Did the shot count even though the buzzer sounded and the game was over?"

"What difference would it make whether or not the game was over if my shot missed? Remember it was good if I made it. If it was good, it was worth two points and we would've won the game by one point. If not, game over. Our goose is cooked. Cotton pickin' Bulldogs win again."

"Good gracious, James Ray. Did you make the shot or not?"

"I can't say yet. Let me continue. You see, String Bean had worried my shot. I had to launch it higher than I would have liked. So the ball goes up and comes down, hits the rim and starts to roll around and around and around the rim of the basket. It finally comes to a stop and I swear, it stood straight and balanced on the rim for a minute or two."

"You lie, James Ray. Tell the truth."

"Well, you said you wanted a good story. So the ball does roll around and around and it stops for a second or two and there wasn't a sound in the gym. Nothin' but silence as both sides waited for a win or a loss. Then, gravity kicks in and the ball falls."

"You scored and y'all won the game? Y'all beat the Bulldogs?"

"Nope. I missed the shot. True to my hero quest, I'll have to wait for this year to try harder, nose-to-the-grindstone hero like."

"That was a great story. Sorry y'all lost the game." Ruth Ann looked down to the sheets covering her bad leg. She looked under the sheet to her wound and frowned. She then turned her gaze to James Ray.

"James Ray, I do appreciate y'all decidin' to come visit me. It's been especially nice for you to come and then tell me a good story. It's the best I've felt since I was bitten by the stupid cottonmouth."

She reached over with her good hand and took a hand of James Ray's. She smiled.

Her touch electrified him. He tingled. He blushed.

"Will you stay for awhile? No one is comin' to visit me tonight. Mother's tired and Bud has a meetin' or somethin' and I'm gonna plain die from boredom. Will y'all stay?"

"Well, I suppose so. Y'all are not supposed to make it too easy on me, though. Hero questin' person that I am and all. Y'all should ring for a nurse and have me thrown out. I'll try to sneak back in through the window. You see mecomin' through the window and crack me over the head with a vase. I fall and break a leg. I'm put in a bed across from y'all's room. I hobble over when the nurse isn't lookin' and I ask you to marry me. You say no at first but I keep askin' and twelve years later, you fold and I finally win you over. I have gray hair by then and no teeth. Quest over."

Ruth Ann laughed. "That's too funny." She looked at James Ray, smiling. "You know, I tried to explain the hero quest to my boyfriend in Fort Worth and he didn't get it."

"That's because he doesn't deserve you. After all, we all can't be heroes. I'll be all the hero you want and need. Fact is, sorry to say Ruth Ann, one hero is enough for y'all."

"I suppose the real hero is Rusty. He's the one who saved me. I probably wouldn't be alive without him. Anyway, y'all sound like you're tryin' to win me over. Is that the case, James Ray? You go watchin' me naked in the shower and then go and try to win me over? I like that. Takes some gall."

James Ray threw Ruth Ann's reference to Rusty aside. He'd focus on the present, the all too precious moment. He felt he needed to move the conversation away from Rusty or the peeping Tom incident.

"Thanks to you, I now know why Coach called me a blanket-blank basketball player after the game and why I have to keep on keepin' on tryin' to beat the Bulldogs. Thanks to you, I now know why I have a limp, why they call me Hopalong or just plain Hop. Thanks to you, I'm Superman just waitin' to happen. I just need a cape, and a good tall window to jump out of."

"Maybe Rusty is the antihero," Ruth Ann said, again bringing Rusty into the conversation.

James Ray drew a deep breath. "What's an antihero?"

"Well, he's a...he's a person who's important to the story but...but he doesn't have...what's the word I'm lookin' for?"

"I don't know," James Ray answered, still hoping to move beyond any talk of Rusty Wickware, whether he had saved Ruth Ann or not. The two were still holding hands.

"An antihero doesn't have...he's without moral values. That's what he is, I think."

"Well, I'm glad Rusty saved y'all's life but he wouldn't recognize a moral value if it walked up and introduced itself."

"How tall are you?"

"Five-feet, eight."

"I'm five-eight and a half. I'm taller than you."

"Not if y'all are barefoot and I'm wearing hero tennis shoes. Not while y'all are flat as a pancake on a hospital bed."

Ruth Ann laughed again.

"Do y'all like bein' a hero?"

"I never thought I was a hero. Never."

"Well, let's say y'all are. Are you a reluctant hero or just plain hero?"

"I don't know what y'all are askin."

"Do you like bein' in charge, bein' the quarterback of the basketball team and all?"

"I'm a point guard not a quarterback."

"It's the same. I was just playin' on words. Y'all direct the team, don't you?"

"Yes."

"Well, then. Do you like bein' in charge? Bein' the person who directs the action?"

"Not really."

"There! That means y'all are a reluctant hero. That's what I thought. You will rise to the occasion, but you do it reluctantly."

"I never thought of it that way."

"Should have had the class I did. Mr. Simms was beyond an interestin' teacher. Anyway, tell me about y'all's polio."

James Ray recounted the saga of his hospital stay and the miracle of his recovery.

"In the end, it was transitory," James Ray said. "One day I found I could move the toes of my paralyzed right leg. In a few days I could move my foot. It was like my foot was stuck ankle deep in mud or somethin' but I kept tryin' to move it and then one day I could actually walk. I walked, hobbled is a better word, down the hall to the nurse's station. The nurse turned white as my bed sheet and hollered for me to get back in bed."

"Did you?"

"I did. I'm good at followin' orders. A hero can do that. They're very versatile. They slay dragons, jump out of tall buildings, and follow orders all at the same time. The heroine, I suppose, although I didn't attend y'all's class, might like a hero who can follow orders while in combat while brushin' his teeth all at the same time."

"You are a funny person, James Ray. Where did you get that from?"

"My daddy's funny. He has a way of lookin' at things from the funny side. I suppose...I suppose it's a way of dealin' with things and, I don't know...maybe its a way of..."

"Coping?"

"Copin' works, if copin' is how a person handles things, problems, situations and such. I don't know..."

Silence enveloped the room. Neither of the two spoke. Ruth Ann looked to the sparseness of the ceiling, James Ray to his feet.

Ruth Ann broke the silence by asking if James Ray wanted to see her snake bites. He did.

"Here's the one on my leg." Ruth Ann pulled back the sheet, carefully covering her private part. She lifted the bandage. He leaned over to see. The bite was high on her inner right thigh. It was crusty, dark crimson, and ugly. Her leg though, was beautiful. From the shower to the hospital, he thought. *What a journey!*

"Can you see the fang marks?"

"I can. Does it hurt still?"

"Yes, despite the medication." Ruth Ann repositioned the sheet over her leg. "I don't know why I should hide anythin' from you, James Ray. You've seen my one hundred percent."

"Well..."

"Well, what?"

"Well, I did catch a little bit of a view. It was from faraway and..."

"As far away as from here to the door?"

"Oh no, much farther. And there were the branches of the tree and the light and all and..."

"So, tell the truth. Did you see my one hundred percent? The truth, James Ray. I'm holdin' you to the honest to God truth."

"I, I did, actually. Yes, y'all's one hundred percent. Front, back, and sideways. Top to bottom."

"Well, I hope you liked the view. I'd be disappointed if y'all didn't. Y'all should've had to pay for the viewin'. You know, like payin' to see a picture show. Want to see my hand?"

James Ray swallowed, "Sure."

"Here it is. Pretty bad, isn't it? Feelin' all sorry for me, James Ray? I've got a worse infection on my leg than my hand, the doctor says. He says he doesn't know why."

Silence again enveloped the room as each teenager accessed their inner thoughts. James Ray referenced his unbelievable good fortune that Ruth Ann had been accepting, kind, forgiving even. *Maybe mother's right. Maybe there is a God in heaven who looks down and fiddles with the affairs of people.*

Ruth Ann, however, turned from worry over her snake bites to accessing thoughts of her mother.

"I'm goin' to help my mother," she blurted.

"What?"

"I'm goin' to help my mother. She's an alcoholic and I'm goin' to help her. I've put it off too long. I won't forgive myself if I don't find a way to help her."

"She's an alcoholic?"

"Yes. She drinks way too much. Has for a long time. She hides her vodka. She'll finish a whole bottle in three days or less. She's unhappy with her marriage to Bud. She, I think...I don't know...I think she hates herself. She's so unhappy. I'm so worried about her and here I am in a hospital givin' her one more thing to be unhappy about."

"Sorry about that. I..."

"It's not y'all's problem. I don't know why I told you in the first place. I'm the one who's sorry. It's back to the copin' thing we were talkin' about. How does she cope? How does Bud cope? How do I cope?"

"What about your...what about Bud? Can he do anythin'?"

There was a soft knock on the door. A nurse entered.

"Well, hello James Ray. Y'all havin' a good talk with our Ruth Ann?" Nurse Jones inquired.

"Yes, and hi back at you. Nice to see y'all again." James Ray stood and shook Amelia Jones's hand. Amelia was with the hospital when James Ray was afflicted with polio.

"Nice to see you, James Ray, somewhere other than our polio ward. How's y'all's family? I hear tell that Seth has up and joined the Marines. Heard anythin' from him?"

"No, actually we haven't, as far as I know."

"Well, I'm sure y'all will. Ruth Ann, dear, how are y'all feelin'?"

"Good. I'm feelin' good. My leg and hand still hurt. They're still swollen and infected, the doctor says."

"All that will settle down over time. The penicillin will work its wonders."

Amelia took Ruth Ann's hand to check her pulse and placed a thermometer in her mouth.

Amelia turned to James Ray. "And you, young man, need to scoot on home. Ruth Ann here needs her beauty rest."

James Ray was still standing. "Indeed so. I will. Goodnight Ruth Ann. See how well I follow orders?"

Ruth Ann smiled through her thermometer-pursed lips and waved goodbye to James Ray with her good hand.

"Well, young lady, seems like y'all have at least a day or two of life left in you. Pulse is good. Temperature's good."

"That's good. I could use another day or so. When can I go home?"

"Most likely in a couple of days, maybe earlier. We'll see."

"The sooner the better. I'm dyin' from boredom."

"I'm sure you are. Fine family, the Turmans. Fine as you can get nowadays. You know, this is just between the two of us, I once had a crush on James Ray's daddy. His mother won out. She roped him quick and good. I was left lookin' on as the train left the station."

"Are you married?"

"Was. Not now. My husband was an alcoholic. He killed himself on Christmas day ten years ago this up-comin' Christmas. Took a shotgun into the garage and arranged so it would go off when he pulled a trip-wire and that was that. I suppose he couldn't deal with his life. Couldn't deal with me. I don't know. Life takes some hard turns sometimes. I don't know why I'm tellin' y'all this. Y'all are so young and with a promisin' future and all. Maybe hard times won't come y'all's way. Let's hope a snakebite will be the worse thing that will happen to you. Let's hope for that."

Amelia sat.

Ruth Ann reached over and took her hand. It was her turn to nurse.

"Sometimes I wish I could start all over," Amelia said, brushing back tears.

"I'm sorry," Ruth Ann managed.

"Oh, don't be sorry. I'm sorry for behavin' like this. What's wrong with me? I have to go. You're fine, sweet Ruth Ann. Take this. It'll help you rest. I'll check on you in a hour or so. Rest well, darlin'."

"I'm sure I will."

"Is James Ray y'all's boyfriend? Excuse me for askin'."

"A friend? As of today, yes. A boyfriend in the meanin' of the word? No. Not yet, anyway. It was nice he came to keep me company. I enjoyed talkin' to him. He made me laugh. It was beyond nice to laugh."

"Well, excuse my sayin', but he's a sweetheart of a boy. The few months he was here I didn't hear one complaint out of his mouth. Well, unless you counted when he was taken off morphine."

"He was on morphine?"

"At night. To help him sleep. He'd get a shot every night to help him sleep. One would think a paralyzed leg wouldn't hurt. Not so."

"Was he addicted to the morphine?"

"Like anythin' else a body sees as necessary to get through the day. Like cigarettes, alcohol and such. A body can over-do almost anythin'."

"Are there treatments for alcohol-addicted people?"

"The first step in treatin' alcohol or any addiction is for a person to recognize they have a problem and actually want to be cured. Without that recognition, without that willingness, nothin' will become of it."

"Nothin?"

"No. Nothin."

Chapter 25 - Toil and Trouble

J.B. stopped the car. It was the place he had chosen to show James Ray the pornographic photo. He led James Ray to a shady spot near a creek that ran almost year-round through the property.

"So, here it is and again, I apologize for the crass nature of all of it." J.B. lifted the Lone Star photo from his shirt pocket where it had been tucked away, face inward, on the trip to Sherman.

James Ray stared, mouth open, eyes wide, at the photograph. "Good gravy, y'all are right about the photo. Holy smokes!"

"Holy smokes indeed. Here's what I need to know if you can answer my concern. I've never seen a picture like this."

"Neither have I. This is a firecracker of a photo, all right."

"Well, I don't mean the nakedness of it all, the sexual hanky-panky. I mean the picture itself."

"The picture itself?"

"Yes, the picture itself. It doesn't look like the ones your mother gets from the drug store. The film she takes to 'em and then, what do they do? Send it off to Kodak or somethin'?"

"Yes. They have a processin' facility in Dallas. Other places, too, but..."

"So why does this picture look different?"

"It's a Polaroid. Is that what y'all are askin'?"

"What's a Polaroid?"

"Well, Carl has one and he..."

"Carl has one?"

"Yes. He says a Polaroid can be used to make sure lighting is good ahead of takin' pictures indoors or somethin' like that. Mostly, though, its charm is that you can take an instant photo and see your image right away. That's the trick part about a Polaroid. But back to its other use. See, a photographer doesn't know exactly what he's goin' to get until the film is developed. Right? So a Polaroid camera lets a photographer know that the light is right or the composition is to his likin' and such because the picture develops right before your eyes. That's the trick. Amazin', actually."

"Have you ever used a Polaroid?"

"Just once when Carl showed me his and how it works. It's a...it's a Land 95, I believe it's called. Only been for sale since 1948 or somethin'. Land is the fellow who invented the camera. It's a one-step type thing. I can't explain how it works exactly. It's like most cameras but you make your exposure and then you up and pull the photo's tab which is stickin' out and all, and when the photo is pulled and squeezed through the openin', the chemicals kick in and the developin' takes place right before your eyes. Like I said, amazin'. We can ask the people at the store in Sherman. They sell Polaroids."

J.B. took the Lone Star photo back from James Ray. He walked to the edge of the creek. The two stood silently beneath the broken shade of a stand of mixed wild pecan, hackberry, and bigtooth maple trees.

"Let me ask you this, James Ray. What does Mr. Malone, Carl, do every third Thursday night of the month?"

"I don't know. Why?"

"Okay. Does he ever develop film of his own? You know, maybe stayin' late or comin' in early to do his own work?"

"Not that I know of. Well, maybe. He lets me develop my own stuff so I suppose he could if he wanted to. I'm not there in the mornings and I leave at five or so in the afternoons unless I'm needed later. Why are you askin' about Carl? What's he got to do with anythin'?"

"Just askin', that's all."

"Just because he has a Polaroid, is that what you're thinkin'? That he's the one who took the picture of the kids at the Lone Star? There must be thousands of Polaroids around. What are you suggestin' anyway? He wouldn't do anythin' like that."

"Look closely. Not at the raw nakedness of it all but at the faces of the people in the photo. You called 'em kids. Do you think they're under eighteen?"

"Well, the girl. Maybe. I don't know. I suppose so. They look like kids I know in high school. Yea, I suppose they could be under eighteen. What does it matter how old they are?"

"There are laws that govern photos like this. The Supreme Court says somethin' that's obscene is somethin' that doesn't comport with normal community standards. I'd have to say, the photo from the Lone Star is a good case in point. Although I like to believe as a whole I'm a live-and-let-live kind of guy, in this case, there's nothin' normal about it and I dare say it isn't somethin' one would want to display down at the post office.

Field of View

Prurient interest, I believe, is the word they use to describe the effect of such images on a person. Appeals to their prurient interest. That's it. Then, there are laws about corruptin' youngsters. Child labor laws. Laws to protect kids from bein' taken advantage of until they reach their age of majority. Certainly laws against havin' 'em taken advantage of sexually and all. If any of the persons in the Lone Star photo are under the age of eighteen, that's also a State of Texas law. I don't know if it differs from state to state. Probably does, although not by much would be my guess."

James Ray tried to follow his father's rambling explanation of what was obscene and the age of majority and why he felt so concerned about the goings on at the Lone Star.

It's a new world all right. Trixie first, and now this.

In Trixie's case, he had retrieved her image from her hiding place more times that he wished to count and each time he willingly succumbed to what his father had just defined as prurient interest. Had he also the Lone Star photo in his possession, he knew he would imagine being with the girl in that photo as well.

Maybe that's what Daddy's talkin' about. I feel guilty about it. But am I a bad person because of it? Is nakedness and what's going on in the Lone Star photo harmful somehow? Carl's Trixie is mild in comparison. Is the Polaroid picture harmful to anyone who happens to see it? It is harmful in some way to me? Does it depend on who's doin' the looking? Is what's going on harmful to the kids in the photo? Is the photographer breakin' the law? Are the subjects?

James Ray asked to see the picture again. He closely examined the photo for its composition. The girl subject, was in perfect focus. So too, was the boy and his appendage. The background, however, displayed circles-of-confusion, thereby softening the background and reducing the visual competition that would otherwise compete with the photo's center of interest. James Ray knew enough to know that the photographer had carefully controlled the picture's depth-of-field. Given Carl's on-going instruction on how depth-of-field was manipulated, James Ray figured whoever had composed the photo had good working knowledge of the concept.

Field of View

"Three things basically affect depth-of-field," Carl lectured. *"First, your subject-to-camera distance. The closer you are to the subject the shallower, the shorter, the depth-of-field. In other words, some light rays come to focus either before or after the film plane and are therefore rendered as circles-of-confusion. Increase your subject-to-camera distance and the opposite happens. More of the light rays fall precisely on the film plane and you get greater sharpness, increased depth-of-field. Second, the lens of the camera. The longer the lens, like the telephoto for your Argus, the shallower the depth-of-field. Use a standard lens or a wide-angle lens, however, and you get greater depth-of-field. Third, aperture. The wider the opening, the shallower the depth-of-field. The smaller the opening, the greater the depth-of-field. Pick and choose but remember, if you can't manage depth-of-field, don't call yourself a photographer."*

Without a shred of hard evidence, J.B. was now more convinced than ever that one big Cadillac drivin', Carl Malone, *Tribune* photographer and entrepreneurial bootlegger, was also a self-employed pornographer, freelancing his tail off.

"Daddy, you didn't answer me. What are y'all suggestin'?"

"Nothin'. You're right. Someone's on the loose, though. We'll see over time how it all shakes out. We need to get on down the highway to Sherman. How do you like the Hudson?"

"It's a dream to drive. No shiftin' gears. No clutch. Hugs the road like a carpet. Like ridin' in a livin' room like y'all said. I feel small in it, though."

"Why so?"

"Well, the Olds is more straight up and down and smaller inside. This, the Hudson, is huge in comparison. Is that why Mother doesn't like it?"

"No. She doesn't like it because I bought it without her permission. Says it looks like an upside down-bathtub."

"You went and bought it without her permission?"

"I did. I thought..."

"Could I borrow it sometime to take Ruth Ann out after she's on the mend?"

"Does a chicken have feathers? Sure. Are you two gettin' friendly? She wouldn't give Seth the time of the day. How is she, anyway? I'd hate to be bitten by a durn cottonmouth."

"She's doin' good. I don't know about the friendly part. I hope so. We had a good talk the other day at the hospital after I thought she'd never speak to me again."

"Why was that?"

"Nothin' really. Just a misunderstandin'."

A one-ton truck carrying watermelons roared past.

"Well, a misunderstandin' will toss a ship for sure. Maybe y'all got past it?"

"I hope so. A bad thing, though."

"What's that?"

"She told me her mother is an alcoholic."

"Don't say. How does she know that?"

"I think that sort of thing is hard to hide, maybe. I don't know. Neither you nor mother drink so I don't know how it all works. I didn't ask her for details. Ruth Ann says she hides her whatever it is she drinks and that she drinks way too much. Says she's gonna help her mother, though."

"Life."

"What?"

"Life. Choices made. Never ceases to amaze me how people make a mess of things whether they mean to or not. Sorry to hear about her problem. Seems like a nice person. Doesn't smile, though. That's a giveaway to a person's happiness, or lack thereof. Anyway, I have a philosophical question to ask you."

"Shoot."

"Are y'all happy with who you are?"

"Yes, why?"

"I don't know. Just wonderin'."

"Well, how about this?" James Ray replied. "Are y'all happy with who you are?"

"Good question. Right now? No. Tomorrow, maybe. Maybe not. Right now I don't have a good grip on it all. These days I feel like I'm singin' off-key. Or, maybe like a car that has a sparkplug wire disconnected."

J.B. picked up a small stone and threw it into a deep part of the creek water. "Here's another question. Are you happy with the way I raised you?"

"What kind of a question is that?"

"Well, I was just thinkin'. You're nearly raised and all. Seth has crossed the Rubicon. In a couple of years, you will too. Off to college or to the moon and stars or wherever. Then there're the girls. It's all over in the blink of an eye, James Ray. The child raisin'. The hope and vision for good things to come their way. First you see currents from stone to water and then, they're gone. First the currents are strong and vigorous and then they weaken and dissipate and over time, they're gone. Vanished before y'all's very eyes. Sometimes, there's little or no trace of what a person thought was supposed to be. Instead, there's somethin' else, foreign tastin' and unwelcome. What you did expect has either vanished or changed in some substantial way. It all becomes a thing of pages past."

"Are y'all upset or somethin'?"

"Maybe. Just thinkin' and all. Mostly, I need assurance that I've been a good father to you. That's important to me. I'll make it if I know that despite everythin' else."

"You've been a great father, Daddy. You've been stern when y'all needed to be stern. You been busy a lot but most fathers are, you know, working and bringin' home the bacon, like they say."

"That's what your mother says. Not the great part but the busy part. Says I've been absent. Doesn't even give me credit for bringin' home the bacon. Claims I haven't been present in y'all's lives."

"What's come between you and mother? Y'all hardly say a word to each other lately."

"Marriage isn't always a walk in the park, James Ray. More like walkin' on hot coals sometimes. Let's go. We've got places to go and things to do and I'm runnin' off at the mouth. Let's go."

Once on the highway, James Ray soon found himself thinking about Carl and how he seemed preoccupied with nudity or sex or a combination of the two. *Trixie's a case in point. There are most likely others like Trixie, I suppose. Once, he even asked if I had gotten into Ruth Ann's panties. When I told him I hadn't, he asked when I was goin' to get around to it. Then, he said after gettin' it on with Ruth Ann, I should make a run at her mother. How crazy is that? He said he'd be happy to help. Said we could switch after awhile and I would take on her mother and he would take on Ruth Ann and if I wasn't up to it, he'd take 'em both on himself. Me with Ruth Ann's mother and he with Ruth Ann? He with both of 'em? Carl with a teenager? I remember thinkin' it was crazy talk at the time. I thought he was jokin' but maybe he was serious?*

And the thing about the locked cabinet in the darkroom. Why did he keep whatever it was inside under lock and key? And why did he have locks on both darkroom doors? Why that? Was he worried that someone would carry off his supplies? They're not his supplies in the first place. He didn't keep the paper's camera and photo equipment in the darkroom so why the secrecy? What's that all about?

Then, there was the Thursday night thing. Now that I think back, he takes off early on some Thursday afternoons. I don't remember which ones. The last time I remember him saying...was it a Thursday night? Said he was going to grab somethin' to eat and then attend an important meetin'. That was the night we were workin' on a deadline and he announced that he'd have to up and leave. It was a Thursday night. I remember because the deadline was noon on Friday. Was it a third Thursday of the month? I'll have to check the calendar. I remember he asked me to keep workin'. Told me to mix new chemicals and not bother cleanin' up because he'd have work to do later. Was it deadline work or some other kind of work?

"James Ray?"

"What?"

"Your mother's movin' to California. I need to tell you that. There, I've said it. She's takin' the girls with her. I don't think the girls know it yet so keep it to y'all's chest. I'm in enough hot water as it is."

"Movin' to California? What are you sayin'?"

"Remember what I said about walking on hot coals? I wasn't jokin'. One other thing, James Ray. The girl on the bed in the Lone Star photo? The pretty girl with the pearl necklace? She's the same girl who jumped to her death from the Lamar hotel in Dallas a couple of months ago. What it all means, I don't know."

Chapter 26 - Gate Keeper

J.B. decided he'd walk to work instead of drive.

It'll be like the good old days, like my life used to be when things were settled, all calm and secure. The walk will give me time to think. I'll have time to figure out how I'm going to fight the next battle with Sarah Mae if a battle is forthcomin', and how to best defend myself without the whole mess of a kettle boilin' over and upsettin' the kids and all. I feel like I'm a heap of pinto beans in a pressure cooker. My head hurts. Where in the world is this all headed? Good grief. Might Sarah Mae change her mind like she did with the new storm shelter, and all of a sudden emerge announcin' that all was good and then say let's get on with our lives? Maybe she'll see the light of day and up and say everything is forgiven? That I haven't been absent after all. In the full light of the day, maybe she'll ask, "What's the fuss all about, anyway?" And then maybe she'll say, "I'm sorry," which she never says, so forget that. She could set a house afire, be caught red-handed, witnessed by a hundred people, be charged, convicted, sent to jail, and never say, "I'm sorry." And now, she's got the gall to end our marriage.

He paused under the shade of an elm tree lining East 9th Street. The morning was already warm and moist. Cicadas were busy doing what cicadas did after seventeen long years underground.

The durn things make a lot of racket while they go about their business of hookin' up with a suitable partner. And given the short time they have to live, perhaps they won't have time to argue once a sturdy and muscular male meets a suitable come-hither female. People are cicada-like come to think about it. Got to find a mate. Not much time. Got to be in a hurry about it. Got to hook up, got to have offspring. Don't have to raise 'em though. Cicada newborns are on their own from the git-go, I suppose. All of it in a hurry. No time to think any of it out.

"We humans don't have big red eyes or transparent wings, though," J.B. said aloud. "Don't make as much racket, either. Or maybe we do. I guess it depends on who's doin' the judgin'."

Field of View

At the intersection of East 9th Street and Center, he noticed several men were busy trimming the elm trees that lined both sides of East 9th. From Center to where the pavement ended on 9th, some wise and pioneering person had planted dozens of elms so that someday, their branches and leaves would afford a pedestrian of the future salvation from the harshness of the overhead sun. However, East 9th Street didn't actually end where the canopy of elms did. Ninth continued, treeless, into colored town. The Johnsons lived three houses from the demarcation between the two supposedly separate but equal towns. The Turmans lived three houses on the white side, but on the mirror opposite side of the street.

At the time, J.B. had a note in his pocket as a reminder that he needed to talk to Booker T. He might have some insight on Mr. Malone, cleaning as he did part-time for the newspaper.

During the day, J.B. deemed himself unproductive. Inattentive also. His shoulders were stooped. He fidgeted, he adjusted and readjusted his oscillating fans. He removed his tie. If he had glanced at his watch once he had done so a dozen times by the time his break rolled around.

Mabel had given up on asking how J.B was feeling. She figured he had a malaise of some kind and guessed he was going through a crisis of some manly nature.

"It's time, Mabel. Time for me to take my break."

J.B stood, stretched and took a deep breath. He waved farewell to Mabel. "Be back soon unless Hoghead arrests me for bein' a vagrant. Some such law may be on the books. Courthouse lawn vagrant law. Probably is such a law."

I need some fresh air. A coke. I need a Coke. I so need a little comic relief. Perhaps the boys will provide such a blessing.

"That what I called y'all and I'll say it again. Y'all are a turd. A shit head. Y'all are the worse kind of company. Me and the others are gonna move our benches. Y'all can have y'all's own bench and keep y'all's own sorry ass company." Winney said.

"My daddy said it takes one to know one," Teddy responded defensively.

"Well, y'all's daddy is a shit head as well."

Teddy rose. His hands were clinched.

"Well, boys. Good stone the crows! What's got you fellows in such a lather?" asked J.B. He had heard Winney's tirade upon his approach. "Why in tarnation is Teddy in such hot water? You spit on Winney's shoes or somethin'?"

Winney was standing and red-faced. Teddy took to his bench; his face pursed, his chin forward in defiance, his arms folded across his chest.

Winney pointed to Teddy. "He's the one who caused it all. He's got somethin' secret again and won't show it to none of us. Says he waitin' fer you. Why can't we get a head start on it without waitin' till doomsday? That's what I would like to know. That's a plain pissy thang fer y'all to do, T.R."

"Well, hold on, Winney," J.B. countered. "Let's see what Teddy has to say or show. Let's get a grip here, boys."

Chipper spat. Soapy had stopped carving.

"Is that so, Teddy?" J.B. asked. "Y'all have somethin' to show us all? Is it somethin' from the Lone Star again? What offerin' do you have on this fine, sunlit of a summer day?"

Winney remained standing.

"A rubber. I've got a rubber. Got it tucked away in my pocket all wrapped up in cellophane."

"A condom?" asked J.B.

"A rubber. Y'all's rubber, is it? I doubt that," Winney interjected. "Only rubber y'all might be able to use is one to decorate Soapy's little, tiny dick of Ivory Soap. Probably last century when y'all were able to manage a hard-on and they didn't have rubbers then anyways. No airplanes. No rubbers. Wooden teeth maybe, but that was about all."

"It ain't my rubber. Janey found it under the bed at the Lone Star. Want to see it J.B.?"

"Who wants to see a used rubber?" asked Chipper. "Keep the dang thang to y'all's self."

"I don't have my Ivory dick with me. I left it at home on the mantle," Soapy offered, tardy of the flow of conversation.

"Everyone hold their horses," J.B. said, his arms and hands providing a non-verbal stop to the chatter. He finished his Coke and forced the empty bottle into his right front pants' pocket.

"Everybody stop. Good. Now Teddy, when did y'all's Janey find the condom, the rubber?"

"After the last cleanin' of the Honeymoon Suite. Must've been left last Thursday. The night we did our stakin' out. She cleans on Fridays, remember?"

"I suppose you mentioned it. Sorry, I didn't exactly remember. Anyway, if you claim to have a rubber and that Janey found it under the bed in the Honeymoon Suite in the Lone Star Hotel, well then, that's even more evidence of on-goin' hanky-panky. Someone got poked and someone did the pokin'. The kids did the pokin' I suppose and someone had to do the picture takin.' And Chipper's right, we don't need to see it. I don't know what good it would be for y'all to parade around the courthouse with a spent condom."

"Maybe I should keep it as evidence, like we did the photo? What about that?"

J.B. sighed. "Maybe so. It's up to you. You keep it. I don't know where's a good place for a used condom to be stored as evidence. I'll leave that up to you and y'all's Janey. She feelin' better after her fall?"

"Limps a little, still. Turned her ankle good the night we staked out the hotel. We wuz tryin' to get a better view of the flashin'. Did y'all ever ask y'all's boy about the flashin' and how it works?"

"No, actually I haven't. I can't believe I forgot to ask him. He did tell me some other interestin' things, though. Things of a photographic nature. Things that might help us in the long run. Will y'all be here noontime? If you are, I'll share it with y'all then."

J.B. left the group and stopped by the concession stand. There, he chatted with Jules Olander about the weather and the upcoming Mule Days.

"Mule Days is always good for business. Pure and simple."

"Indeed," J.B. replied, "good for celebratin'; hard on the wallet. Could I please have two more Cokes? One's for me and one's for my good and honorable secretary, Mabel."

"Hi-do, Mister J.B. Y'all must be mighty thirsty to go and buy two Cokes, or maybe one's for me?"

"Well hello, Book. I was just thinkin' of you. Do you...? Here, take the Coke. I was goin' to give it to Mabel but I'll buy her another one. I know y'all prefer an RC but maybe the Coke will do. Will it tickle y'all's fancy anyway?"

"It'll be mighty fine, Mr. J.B. Just mighty fine. I can do with a change every now and then."

"Good, I have a question for you Book. Can we go outside and talk? Do you have a minute? What are y'all doin' here so early?"

"Well, I have a life other than cleanin' the courthouse. Me and my Eartha are doin' some shoppin'. Mostly, to tell the truth, she's doin' the shoppin'. She's over to Penneys or maybe Woolsworth. She's probably spendin' every dime she made sewin' this week I suppose."

J.B. decided not to correct Booker T. on his pronunciation of Woolworth. He led Booker T. to the south side of the courthouse lawn away from the chewers who were camped on the north side.

"Good to visit with you, Book. How's Eartha?"

"Doin' dandy. Just dandy. Y'all's Sarah Mae and the other children?"

"Oh fine, Book. Thanks for askin'."

"What's y'all's question, J.B.?"

"Well, Book...I, I...was just wonderin' if y'all ever...? Do you still cleanup at the newspaper on Thursday and what was it?"

"Sunday afternoons. Thursday nights. That's when I goes and cleans."

"All right. What I would like to know, if y'all don't mind tellin' me, is if y'all have ever noticed anythin' out-of-order, suspicious and such? Especially to do with the darkroom?"

"Mr. Carl's darkroom? Is that what y'all are askin'?"

"Yes."

"Well, I don't reckon. Why is y'all askin'?"

"I can't answer that. I wish I could. How about this. My boy, James Ray, says the darkroom is locked. Is that so?"

"That be so. Mr. Carl guards his darkroom, that's for sure."

"Why do you thinks he guards it?"

"Well, I suppose it's...it's his, his special place. It's where the magic takes place. Where things are developed and such. He do indeed guard it. Told me to never, ever go inside. Said doin' so would ruin his developin' and such. Said he'd do the cleanin'. Now, it looks like y'all's James Ray is doin' the cleanin' fer him."

Both men finished their Cokes. J.B. had now stretched ten minutes into thirty. He would have to apologize to Mabel.

He'd do it with a Coke. Or a Grapette. He remembered she liked Grapettes. Grapette it would be.

"Who has the keys to the darkroom?"

"Mr. Carl does."

"Who else?"

"I do."

"What? You do?"

"Lookie here, J.B." Booker T. reached into his overall pocket. He produced more keys on one chain than J.B. had ever witnessed.

"The ones on this here ring is keys to our courthouse. Some of 'em are useless since the locks don't work anymore but I keeps 'em anyways. I don't know exactly why. Maybe 'cause throwin' away a skeleton key is bad luck. These here keys," he said fingering another ring, "is keys to the paper's locks. They be new. Mr. Spencer, he up and had all of the paper's locks changed...maybe five years ago."

J.B. rubbed his chin. He looked to his left and to his right. No one was looking as far as he could tell.

"Well, Book, that's a healthy set of keys all right even if some of 'em have retired from their usefulness and all. I wouldn't throw away the skeleton keys either. They're far more handsome than the new keys we all carry around nowadays. Let me ask you this. Does Spencer Shoemaker, the paper's editor, know you have keys to all of his locks?"

"He do. I needs to in case of an emergency. Someone is always losin' or misplacin' a key. Why, J.B.? Why are y'all askin' about the paper's keys? Are y'all fixin' to rob the paper?"

"No. No such thing, Book. I'm just tryin' to put things together."

J.B. sighed. "Let me get back to you, Book. I've got the weight of the world on my shoulders right now. I'd like to say I don't deserve it, but maybe I do."

"Plain hard to say what we deserve and what we don't deserve. I 'spect we are all sinners in the eyes of our Lord."

"Well, I don't know what I've done to upset The Fellow. Well, maybe I do. My failures seem pretty evident these days. Probably seen 'em listed on a newsreel down to the picture show some afternoon."

"You ain't no failure, J.B. Y'all are a good man. Y'all go so far as to accept my kind. You and y'all's Sarah Mae have been most kind and acceptin' and that's the truth."

"Thank you, Book. I need to hear some kind words every now and then." J.B.'s right hand went to his face. He felt stubble. He had forgotten to shave.

"I need to get back to work and I know y'all have things to do. How's Sammy? I haven't seen him for some time. What's he up to this summer that seems as if it will never end?"

"He's over to Little Rock. Got an invite to show off his baseball skill. The Negro League is interested in him."

"Well, good for him. I'll bet you're proud as punch."

"I am. He goin' to be as large as me someday, J.B. Only I do hope he doesn't up and get fat as a cow like his daddy."

"Well, we all carry around a little more weight than we need to as we age."

"I 'spect so. I carry around enough extra weight for any three men."

"Let me put somethin' straight to you, Book." J.B. decided he'd swing for the fences.

"There's some bad things happenin' down to the Lone Star. Troublin' things. Things involvin' kids. Things that are against the law and all. And given the sorry mess of it all, I need y'all's help. I need to ask you to let James Ray and me in late the next comin' third Thursday of this August. The one up comin'."

"Have y'all been taken by an evil spirit? What in the tarnation are y'all talkin' about, J.B.? Why would y'all want me to do that? Are y'all lookin' for me to lose my paper job?"

"No, certainly not that. Never mind. I shouldn't have asked you in the first place. Forget I said anything. I'll figure out how to handle my troubles without involvin' you. I was wrong to ask you in the first place. I'm sorry."

Booker T. stared at his white friend. He had always held J.B. in high esteem. He felt something askew with his friend, what with his talk about the Lone Star and Mr. Carl's darkroom and keys.

"Are y'all feelin' well, J.B.? Tell the truth. Maybe I could help. Or, my Eartha could help. Maybe she could fix y'all a get well potion of some kind."

"I'm fine," J.B. countered. "Are we still on for the upcomin' fight in September? I know it's still weeks away, but it gives us somethin' to talk about. Remember, I've got Jersey Joe and you've got Marciano. I buy the hamburger if Marciano wins; you buy if he doesn't."

Field of View

"I expect I'll win," replied Booker T. "Marciano, he ain't gone and lost a fight yet. The bettin' odds are in favor of Marciano."

"Maybe so. Anyway, I miss Louis. The Brown Bomber was the best of all time in my book. We'll see. When the fight rolls around, want to listen to it on my radio or y'all's?"

"Funny thing about radios J.B. Y'all have a big furniture lookin' thing of a radio and I have my little bitty Philco but they both works the same."

"Better make it your house, Book. Now that I think about it, Sarah Mae thinks boxin' is barbaric. We're barbarians, Book. Put that in y'all's pipe and smoke it."

"I do 'spect so, but my Eartha, she loves a good fight. She'll all roll her shoulders and will punch left and right and so on. You'd think she was in the ring herself."

"I love Eartha. You caught one fine woman when you rounded her up."

"The same with y'all's Sarah Mae, J.B., even though she don't like boxin'. Mighty fine fit, otherwise."

"I'll bring James Ray if that's okay."

"Good. Me, you, Eartha and the boys. It'll be a hoot and holler. When is it again?"

"Twenty-third of September unless the world comes to an end before then. I've got it marked on the calendar."

Chapter 27 - The Red-Lighted Tombstone

"Wait. Run it by me again," Carl said into the red glow of the darkroom. "I had my mind somewhere else."

"Okay. I want to take a picture of a tombstone," James Ray said. "The new radio station in town, KMAY has a red light on the top of its antenna. The light gets bounced off of the tombstone and..."

"I don't want to hear any more unless you use the language of the craft," Carl said impatiently. "Let's talk photographers. First you are a novice. Second you're a craftsman. Third, you're an artist, if you knuckle down and hone the discipline. Now speak to me as if you're at least a craftsman and have working knowledge of your craft."

James Ray became uncomfortable when Carl was impatient. He wasn't often impatient; but when he was, James Ray felt like his mind was being hammered by insecurity and his tongue became thick and weighted down.

"Well...I'll try. The light...the beacon of light from the station's antenna, it bounces..."

"No, it doesn't. It reflects for Chrissakes."

"All right. The light from the antenna reflects off of the tombstone and I want to...to take a...to document the reflected light. I think it would make for a good...a good documentary photo of the graveyard."

"Tell me about reflected light."

"It...it reflects because it's interrupted by some surface and...because light travels...okay, here's the rule with reflected light. The angle of incidence is equal to the angle of reflection. Right? Light arrives at a certain angle and it reflects at the same angle."

"Good. Unless it's interrupted by something."

"Right. So I set up the tripod. I have my cable release and I set the shutter speed to "B" for bulb."

"Good, proceed."

"That's where I need help."

"Why?"

"Because the...reflected light is only there off and on. It flashes off and on, off and on. So how do I capture the reflection?"

Field of View

Ruth Ann agreed to James Ray's invitation to accompany him to the cemetery. He had asked her out the day she was released from the hospital. "I have somethin' special to show you. It'll be good for you to get out for a couple of hours."

"What is it?"

"It's a surprise. I guarantee you'll like it. I'm gonna drive you to the cemetery."

"Oh, great. I love cemeteries. If I hadn't been lucky, I'd be in one by now. Are you kiddin'?"

"No, I promise y'all this. It'll open your eyes to the phenomenon of light. How's that for a big and important mouthful? Also, the story behind the light is scary, but most interestin'."

"All right." Ruth Ann replied. The two were seated in the family's living room. Ruth Ann lay on the couch with both legs extended. Judith was grocery shopping.

"As long as there's no smoke. I'm dyin' from the smoke. I'm thinkin' about settin' up a tent in the backyard so I can breathe without havin' to inhale smoke. The good thing about bein' in the hospital was the fact no smokin' was allowed, at least not in the rooms. Now that I'm home, I could cut the air with a knife."

"Well, there's no smoke if y'all's parents aren't home, right?"

"Right. But the place still smells like a chimney. Y'all can smell the smoke, right?"

"Yes. A chimney it is. Several of 'em. Neither of my parents smoke. My friend Bobby Joe smokes. Carl smokes. A lot of the people at the paper smoke. Everywhere you go there're cigarette butts. Seems like half the world smokes."

James Ray caught sight of a vase of flowers on the kitchen table. "Who brought the flowers? They're nice."

"Rusty. Brought 'em to the hospital. You've made him out to be a crude sort of a person and maybe he is. That was mean of him tellin' on you at the lake even though it was the truth. It was still crude and rude...but he saved me and all. I'm truly thankful for that."

"Well...my experience tells me he is a rat's ass of first order but I'm glad he was on the spot to save you. I do owe him that. That was a good thing for him to do."

James Ray was mortified that he hadn't thought to bring Ruth Ann flowers. Rusty had one-upped him. Two-upped him, actually. He saved her life and had been thoughtful enough to bring her flowers.

"The tombstone is the big one there," James Ray said, pointing in the direction of a massive beige alabaster headstone.

"He must've been an important person," Ruth Ann said into the stillness of the evening.

"She, not he. Ann Carolyn Bloom. Was an early pioneer woman. She, at the time, was married to Bennet J. Bloom. She was young. He was older and rich. He owned half the county. Remember the Bloom Bulldogs?"

"Yes."

"Town's named after the Blooms. You can find Bloom this or Bloom that, here and there all over Mayweather. The family named the county, the town, actually. Story goes that they arrived in May and the weather was great so they named the place Mayweather. Maybe the weather was awful instead. Maybe they were chased by a tornado. May is a good month for 'em. Who knows?"

"Where's Mr. Bloom's tombstone?"

"Behind hers. You can't see it from here. Fell down years ago, I guess, and no one's put it back in place, upright and all."

"That's disrespectful."

"Want to go and see?"

"No. Cemeteries creep me out. So why are we here, again?"

"I'm gonna take a picture of the tombstone. It'll be dark in a few minutes and when it's dark a red light will mysteriously appear on her gravestone. It'll pulse red off and on, off and on."

"We have to wait until dark?"

"Doesn't work unless it's dark."

James Ray went to the trunk of the Olds and removed his camera equipment. He knew approximately where to place the camera and tripod because he had calculated the location the evening before. The red glow of light emanating from the radio station's antenna would travel in a straight line to the surface of the tombstone and reflect from the stone's surface back in a straight line to the lens of his camera. The angle of reflection would be equal to its arrival or incidence.

"I'm not sure I get what y'all are sayin' but go ahead and tell me the story you said you'd tell. About the poor lady who died and her tombstone and all."

"Well, one evenin', she went to her root cellar and..."

"And what?"

"The light isn't right yet. Hold on a minute." The story had to be timed with the pulsation of the red light and it wasn't dark enough. He needed another five or ten minutes to have it all work perfectly.

"So, what are y'all's trainin' plans? Gonna go back to the lake after everythin' that happened?" James Ray asked.

"No. I won't ever put a foot in the stupid lake again. How could I do that not knowin' whether or not a cottonmouth was waitin' for me?"

"I guess you wouldn't know. What does your coach say about it all?"

"After a week or so of gettin' better, we'll drive to Sherman to train. They have a pool there and coach has struck some kind of a bargain with the city to use it."

"That's nice of 'em."

James Ray lapsed into silence. He was still trying to get a grip on the fact his mother and the girls were moving to California. *Daddy's in a sorry state and I have no idea what livin' without mother and the girls will look like. I'm glad Seth is gone. That's good. But Mother and Faith and Hope? It'll just be me and Daddy. Who does the cookin'? Daddy can't cook his way out of a wet paper sack. Then there'll be school and all without mother to pest me to do my homework.*

"What are your plans for school and all? Y'all's basketball and such?" Ruth Ann asked.

"You read my mind. I don't know. You were honest with me the other day about your mother. I should let you know that my mother is leavin' us. Goin' to California. Goin' to take my sisters with her. Daddy and I will stay behind."

"No!"

"Yes. Happened all of a sudden, the decision and all. She's also got cancer of some kind. I should tell you that, too. It's...what do they call it? Malignant. That's it. She says she will get better treatment in California. She's gonna teach fifth grade. Never taught fifth before but..."

"How can she teach if she has cancer?"

"I don't know. Anyway, the light is right now. See the red glow off the tombstone? See it. There. Step here. See?"

"Yes. It's eerie, the light. Glowin' off and on and all."

"Well, here's the story. So the lady who's buried there, on a dark and stormy night, she, that's Ann Carolyn Bloom, went to her root cellar only to have someone stab her to death."

"Good grief. You lie. That can't be true."

"True as the red light you now behold," James Ray replied, in his best story-tellin' voice, authoritative and well-modulated.

"I don't believe you."

"Well, you can look it up. My daddy has a book on the history of Mayweather. There it is, bloody details and all."

"Did the murderer confess?"

"Right before he was hung."

"Hanged. It's right before he was hanged."

"Okay. Thank you for settin' me right. Now, on with the story."

"There's more?"

"She died real young. Only twenty-three years old. An investigation claimed that she wasn't murdered, that maybe she committed suicide."

"No. She wouldn't do that."

"Well, the Texas Ranger claimed..."

"A Texas Ranger?"

"Yes."

"They were around in those days?"

"Been around since Texas was a Republic and all. Anyway..."

"I don't believe she would go and take a knife and stab herself. That couldn't be. That's not natural. She wouldn't do that."

"Well, that's not the worse part."

"It's not? What could be worse than the Bloom lady takin' her own life or most likely, I think...I think that she was stabbed outright by that evil person in her own root cellar. That's what I think. So, what can be worse than that?"

Ruth Ann looked in the direction of the tombstone that pulsated with a soft, red orb of light. The red light from the tombstone continued to throb off and on, off and on.

"Where does the red light come from?" she asked.

James Ray had angled the car's headlights so they provided fill light into the cemetery. Not straight at the tombstone but at an angle that provided some light but not too much for his time exposure. Too much fill light would make it difficult to capture the glow of the reflected light. Carl had suggested the juxtaposition of fill light and subject-matter elements.

"Make it look like the light from a full moon. No more, no less." he had counseled. *"Use Kodacolor. Got to bracket your exposures. I'll give you some suggested settings for night photography. You can send the film off for processing. We don't do color at the paper. Here's my rule for choosing between color and black-and-white. If a photo's dominant element or elements happen to be color, then shoot it with color film. If not, black-and-white will do the trick. In your case, the dominant element will be the tombstone and the glow of the red light. The reflected red light would simply appear as an indistinguishable spot on the tombstone if you use black and white film. Because it's a time-exposure and your shutter will be open for as long as a minute, the repetition of the red glow will appear as if it's steady and not interrupted."*

"The way I see your intended image, even though you'll be using color film, you'll have mostly shades of grey tombstones and the black surrounding them dramatically accented by the red glow of the reflected antenna light. If you can picture a photo before it's taken, you're previsualizing the image. You will get to where you can see your intended image in your head before you trip the shutter. Your camera is just a tool. Put your head and the camera together and you can make art."

Adjacent to the gravestone subject matter, a mass of closely related but dissimilar shapes rose upward, a few leaned so precariously they seemed ready to topple at any moment, thereby unleashing whatever spirits lurked below, uprooted and petulant, into the dark of the night.

James Ray didn't provide Ruth Ann with an answer to her question about where the red light was coming from. Instead, he adjusted the camera and tripod a few inches to the right of where he had initially placed them. He peered through the viewfinder. He lowered the camera' s angle to ensure only the array of tombstones were within view, the red-lighted tombstone his intended center of interest. He would follow the rule of thirds with its placement within the frame. He pressed the cable release and tripped the shutter. The camera's aperture was set at f-3.5, wide open. He held the shutter open for a count of 30 seconds. Then again for 45 seconds, and then for a full minute.

"That ought to do it."

"You'll have to tell me how all that works." Ruth Ann said.

"I will. But now, let me get on with the story."

"James Ray, y'all are gonna scare me to death. Is that what y'all want to do? I survive two bites from a cottonmouth and now you are goin' to frighten me to death here at the cemetery. If you up and yell or somethin' I'm gonna knock you black and blue."

"I bet you could, too. I'm not gonna yell or anythin'. Here's the rest of the story. After she was found in the cellar all dead and bloody..."

"James Ray, skip the gory parts. If a person's stabbed, I know there's blood so don't give me any details I don't need."

"All right. I'm just tellin' you a story. It's told as the truth."

"Everythin' is told as the truth. That's the way gossip becomes the truth. Tell it over and over and, lo and behold, gossip or an outright lie is suddenly the truth."

"I suppose so. Anyway..."

"What happened to the lady's husband? Maybe he did it."

"That's what I'm tryin' to tell you. When he found her..."

"That's it. He did it. He waited for her and then he jumped out from the shadows and stabbed her. It wasn't a stranger, it was her own husband. She never should have married a rich man. Especially one with a knife."

"Everyone has a knife, Ruth Ann."

"Well, anyway, people shouldn't up and marry for money. Or for convenience, for that matter."

"Let me finish. So he found her dead. He goes back to the house and orders a worker to ride for help. A day later, The Texas Rangers arrive. He meets 'em. They go to the root cellar. Then..."

"Then what?"

"Then they find her body's gone. Vanished into thin air."

"No way, James Ray. Y'all are pullin' my leg."

"Which one, the good one or the one with the snake bite?"

Ruth Ann reached over and slapped James Ray on his shoulder. "So now we have a bloody root cellar full of Texas Rangers, a guilty husband most likely, blood all over everywhere, a knife, and a missin' body. Is that what y'all are sayin'?"

"That's a good summary but what of the missin' body? Gone up in smoke. Vanished into thin air. You see, Ruth Ann, that's why her tombstone glows red. They went and had a funeral and all without her bein' there. Buried, without her bein' in her own casket. Her tombstone is all engraved and beautiful in tribute without her bein' all tucked away inside for eternity. That's the tragedy of it all. How can her soul rest in peace when she, herself, hasn't found peace? Think about it. She wasn't even present at her own funeral and buryin' and all?"

"That's the biggest cock-and-bull story I've ever heard, James Ray. But I liked it anyway. You're a good story teller."

"I'd be a better one if y'all hadn't interrupted me a thousand times."

"How does the red glow work anyway?"

James Ray took Ruth Ann by the shoulders and turned her in the direction of the radio station antenna.

"See? The light from the antenna reflects off the tombstone. Throb, throb. Pulse, pulse."

"I see it. It's a good effect and all. Imaginative. I suppose y'all have had a good dozen girls here to see the tombstone and its light. Anyway, I would have changed y'all's story, the story's plot, though."

"Really?"

"I would've had the woman stab her husband instead. That way, she'd inherit all of his riches. The old coot kept her imprisoned. She was guarded by two retired Texas Rangers, night and day. He, the husband, would come and take her when she didn't want to be taken and..."

"Take her where?"

"To bed. Take her to bed. Force himself upon her. Kept her practically chain-bound and would have her whenever he so desired. So one dark and stormy night, she coaxed her lame excuse of a rich, lecher of a husband to the root cellar claimin' she had uncovered a box of silver dollars. Once there, she stabbed him in the back. He stumbled. He turned to face her. She stabbed him in his chest repeatedly. He fell. He was soon dead. With blood up to her knees, she screamed for help and one of the Rangers came climbin' down and entered the cellar.

Field of View

She up and stabbed him too. A knife straight and true to the heart. He fell on top of her dead husband. There they lay, both of 'em in a jumbled mix of lifeless limbs and blood."

"Good grief, Ruth Ann, where do you get such an imagination?"

"Don't interrupt. When the other Ranger heard the fracas—at the time he was in the outhouse answerin' a call of nature—he rushed to the cellar, also. Once there, she calmly claimed the two men had argued and killed themselves, stabbin' each other back and forth willy-nilly like. She, the good lady Ann Carolyn Bloom, picked up the butcher knife with her hankie and handed it to the late arrivin' Ranger. He took it. She fainted and that's the end of the story."

"It's good. Better than mine, for sure. But how could they stab each other back and forth if there was only one knife? And didn't the Rangers arrive later, after they were called to the scene?"

"Good observations. It's called suspended disbelief."

"What?"

"Suspended disbelief. The reader or the listener, whichever case it happens to be, goes along with the story even though some things don't quite add up. Like when you had the young wife bein' killed by who knows whom. What was the motive? Why would anyone do that? She had a far better motive. The reader needs to believe what he's bein' told is...is credible. And stabbin' back and forth when there's only one knife, you're right, that won't fly. The Rangers, too. A person can only suspend so much disbelief and still go along with the story."

"Like the story you made up about the cottonmouth. Who would believe that?"

"Yes, that whole made-up thing. Rusty's rescue and all. By the way, whatever happened to the pictures you took of me before all that made up stuff, the snake and the rescue and the hospital and all?"

"I haven't had time to print them. I have contacts. They look good. Want to see them?"

"What are contacts?"

"Contacts, proof sheets, whatever. You lay the negatives down on a sheet of photo paper and put a piece of heavy glass on top so they'll be flat and then you expose 'em and develop the photo paper and you get little images of each exposure you've taken. You examine the contact and decide which ones you want to enlarge."

"Yes, I'd very much like to see them. See what I looked like before bein' the wreck I am now."

"Okay, let's set a time. I'm usin' my mother's storm shelter as a temporary darkroom."

"Is she okay with that?"

"Not really. Once she threatened to skin me alive if I even thought of such a thing and now, suddenly, she doesn't seem to care much. She says she's gonna live in a place where tornadoes don't happen."

"You don't keep a butcher knife in her shelter do you?"

"No. Actually I'm worried about you and a knife. I suspect that if there's a killin' to take place, you have a better motive than I do."

Chapter 28 - Holdup on East 9th Street

"Who's fault is it?" Hope asked.

"Not anyone's fault. It's just the name of an earthquake fault. It a place where a lot of earthquakes are likely to happen. I don't know whether San Andreas is a person, place or thing. Anyway, it runs all the way from southern California to San Francisco or to who knows where up north," Faith answered.

"Do earthquakes happen all the time?"

"No. Tornadoes are far more likely to happen. With a tornado, a person can sometimes see it comin' like James Ray's tornado when he took a picture of it. An earthquake sneaks up on you. Can't see it comin'. Can't hear it comin'. Then boom! There it is all of a sudden like how we bombed Japan. Boom! One minute all is fine, peachy, and keen. The next, you are swallowed up by an earthquake."

"I'm not goin' if I have to worry over earthquakes. I'll stay here with Daddy and James Ray."

Hope was by far the more timid of the two Turman girls. Faith, had faith. She would leap from a tree limb to the ground as confidently as any boy. She gladly accepted any reasonable dare and some not so reasonable. She sported an inch wide scar on her chin as proof of her daring. One Sunday afternoon, she leaped from a 2 x 6 inch truss beam to the floor of an unfinished home on East 8th Street. Seth had dared her. She had willingly accepted the dare.

Hope, much like her father, suspected something ill lurked around every corner. If the sky were to fall, J.B. would be the first to see it falling and Hope would be there alongside to bear witness. Hope was a literal person. If someone said, as Pastor Pritchard had said many times, or her mother for that matter, that the Devil needed watching, Hope would indeed maintain the sharpest of vigils.

Hope had night terrors about the Devil. He slept under her bed. Hope assumed he could be in any closet, lurking about in any dark room. When she prayed, he would often interrupt her concentration. She had heard her mother talk about spitfire, brimstone, cloven hooves, and other descriptions of the Devil weighted with imagery she wished she could erase from her young and impressionable memory. Now, having only heard her sister mention earthquakes and California in the same sentence, she had a new fear, a new kind of Devil to fret over.

"Can you take a picture of an earthquake?"

"I don't think so. Maybe. Maybe, after it's over? I don't know. We can look 'em up in Momma's *World Book*. Would that make you feel better?"

"No. Probably scare me even more."

*   *   *   *   *

On his way home, J.B. mulled over his chat with the chewers and his futile, should-not-have-asked-the-question conversation with Booker. As J.B. made his turn from Center to East 9th, he noticed that the men, who earlier in the morning had been trimming back tree limbs, were now engaged in hauling them off. Two colored men had joined them in the effort. He tipped his hat as he passed. A sign marked a detour from East 9th. *What's that all about?* J.B. wondered.

He was forced to take to the street because the downed branches blocked both sidewalks. He looked up. The elms looked good. The trees appeared as if they had just received a much needed haircut. He didn't know much about trees other than the blessed shade they provided; but perhaps they felt better after a trimming, like he did after a shave and haircut. Invigorated and renewed.

At the end of East 9th, appearing in the middle of the street directly in front of his house, he calculated, was a house. He squinted to get a good focus. *I've put off getting my eyesight checked for, what is it now, going on three years? A house in the middle of the street? How is that possible? What's going on down there? Is that a sheriff's car?*

J.B. quickened his step. He removed his fedora fearing it would fall to the street. His tie, flag-like, waved back and forth from the unwelcome motion. He decided not to run. He hadn't run since the days when he would race the boys around the house. A fast walk would have to do. He and the boys would race around the house from the sandstone walkway, he on one side, they the other. On the ready-set-go signal, the threesome would speed off with the boys headed in one direction, J.B. in the opposite. He would always find a way for them to win. He would stumble as they met on the back side of the house or slow his pace once he encountered and passed the boys, he in his direction, they in theirs. James Ray would invariably win. Although younger than Seth, he could, as J.B. often bragged, "really put his feet down."

"Jesus wept!" J.B. exclaimed. "Stop! Hey! Stop, Sarah Mae! Stop!"

Sarah Mae held J.B.'s single shot, bolt-action .22 rifle. It was pointed alternately, back and forth, at three men. One man stood with his back to the wall of the house, his hands reaching for the heavens. One was hiding beneath the house, flat on his stomach, watching the unfolding events from the view below the house and its trailer. A third man, a sheriff deputy, stood facing Sarah Mae, his hand on his holster. Three other men, the house movers, had taken cover behind the house, partially out of view from the gun-wielding woman.

"Good God Almighty, Sarah Mae, put the gun down!" J.B. was short of breath. His heart pounded. His face was covered in sweat. He had lost his hat somewhere along the way.

"What in the sapsuckin' tarnation is goin' on here?" he asked.

"Ask her," the deputy replied. "She...is that woman y'all's wife?"

J.B. nodded in the affirmative.

"Well, she up and threatened these here men. Threatened me too. Said she'd lay anybody low if they as much as touched her tree."

"Is that true Sarah Mae? Did y'all say that? Why? Why would y'all go and threaten these movers and the sheriff's deputy? Anyway, what tree are we talkin' about?"

"They were goin' to cut our tree. This one." Sarah Mae pointed in the direction of an elm tree occupying hallowed ground between the Turman sidewalk and the street. "I won't stand for it."

"They're trimmin' trees, Sarah Mae. That's all. Is that all, boys? Is that right? Trimmin' trees so y'all can get this house to wherever it's goin'?"

"Just doin' our job," the man against the house replied. "We're behind. Should've been done yesterday, then the house comes lumberin' down the street and we ain't done with the trees and then y'all's wife jumps out of the house with a gun and..."

"Where is the house headed?" J.B. asked.

"Movin' it to the corner lot down there," the man answered. "The movin' folks are on the back side of the house right now, hidin'. Oughta make 'em come out and speak for themselves but I 'spect they scared shitless. House has come all the way from Honey Grove, they say."

"Movin' it to the corner lot?" J.B. asked.

"Come out and speak fer ya'll's selves," the man hollered to the three hidden movers. No answer was forthcoming.

"They say the vacant one. The one over there," the man replied, pointing to the lot where James Ray and Sammy and other boys frequently put it to use as a baseball field. It was a lot at the end of East 9th in between white Mayweather and colored Mayweather.

"I see. That's too bad. That was a good and decent vacant lot. Sorry to hear that, actually. Sarah Mae, please give me the gun. Please."

"Not until I get a guarantee they won't harm the tree."

"Sarah Mae, they have to trim back the tree to get the house to its final restin' place."

J.B. turned from Sarah Mae to face the sheriff deputy directly. "How did y'all come to attend our street party?" J.B. asked.

"Y'all's neighbor called. Got another from y'all's boy, I think. My boss, Huff, took the calls. I was outside havin' a smoke."

J.B. turned to face Elsie's house. There she was, taking it all in. He waved to her. She took a step back, seeing that J.B. recognized her presence. She was having a hard time taking in the standoff. The angle of the afternoon light fell sharp and harsh on her aged eyes. She couldn't hear a word that was being said, but it made for high drama nonetheless.

"All right. Let me ask you this, Sarah Mae. Why in God's name don't you want the tree trimmed. Why is that?"

"It's got a robin's nest in it. See there? It's plain as day. The branch they were fixin' to cut down."

J.B. looked skyward. "There?" he asked, pointing to what looked like a nest of some kind.

"That's it. I won't have it harmed."

"Look, Sarah Mae. First, it's past a robin's nestin' season. They lay eggs in the spring. It's summer, now. Second, these men have a right to trim the trees like they've done all the way down East 9th. They have a right to relocate the house. I'm sure they have a permit. And, they've rerouted traffic to do so. I saw the sign. The tree trimin' has been approved so they could move the house. They wouldn't be doing what they're doin' if it wasn't legal and all and please, both of y'all...Sarah Mae give me the gun. And sheriff...I don't know y'all's name, but please take your hand off y'all's holster."

"Not until your crazy wife puts..."

"Don't go and call her crazy or you'll have the both of us to deal with," J.B. said in frustration. "She's tryin' to protect nature, that's what she's doin'. She's sensitive to nature and all. She's kept me from pluckin' a pesty owl..."

J.B. stopped in mid-sentence. *I have to regroup, get my head around the problem. I've got to diffuse it, not add to the insanity of it all. The deputy's right. Sarah Mae is crazy sometimes.*

"Name's Dinwitty. Deputy Dinwitty. I've seen y'all around the square. Seen you with those old men that hang around here and there. Y'all work at the courthouse?"

"Yes, nice to meet you Deputy Dinwitty. Name's Turman, J.B."

"I'm on loan from Lamar County," Dinwitty volunteered. I'll be done in three or four months. I don't know. Maybe I'll stay longer."

"Well, good for you," J.B. answered. "I suppose you'll have a good story to tell when y'all get back. Better than a bank robbery, maybe. Anyway, this is my wife Sarah Mae and...and I now see my son's also a witness to this sorry affair."

J.B. looked in the direction of James Ray. He had his camera with him. He was busy documenting the standoff, the holdup of the house, his mother's outright intimidation of the movers, and the arrival of the sheriff, as well. He'd tried to stop his mother but she would have none of it. He thought it important to document the confrontation on film. He hadn't had time to grab his light meter. He used Carl's sunny sixteen rule: *Bright sun? Full daylight? f-16 at 1/125 of a second.*

His mother had asked two men to stop what they were doing. One had positioned his ladder beneath the tree in their front yard and was halfway up when Sarah Mae ordered him down. He laughed. She asked him who he thought he was, insulting her by laughing. The man asked her who she thought she was. Sarah Mae answered that she was the property owner, the owner of the tree, and that he was to get down from his ladder immediately. The man laughed again.

Field of View

Sarah Mae left, went into the house, fetched J.B's rifle, returned to the scene of the intended crime, pointed the gun at the man and again, ordered him off the ladder. This time, the man climbed down, dropped his saw and retreated to the wall of the house facing the Turman yard. He had no time to run and hide. The gun-bearing woman might shoot him mid-stride. Positioned as he was, had his eyes been covered by a bandana, he would look as if he were facing a firing squad.

James Ray had asked his mother to stop what she was doing. She refused. Seeing he could do nothing, he went inside and asked the operator for the sheriff's office. He also placed a call to his daddy's work. J.B. had already left. Two calls were received by the sheriff's office in less than one minute. One from James Ray, the other from Elsie. The operator, Maureen Sumwalt, stayed on the line for each of the calls. She thought it her duty to do so. What if the call wasn't answered? After all, she was central to all calls coming and going. She held the power to connect and disconnect. She figured no one would ever give her credit for all she did for the people of the county. She would press forward, regardless, duty-bound and civic-minded.

The exposure James Ray thought would be best, was the one where his daddy had run into the scene, hat flying to the ground, arms outstretched tryin' to put a halt to the confrontation as the sheriff stood with his hand on his holster, chin forward, while the man who had been on the ladder stood like a coward with his hands up. The light was perfect for such a dramatic scene. James Ray's subject matter was side-lit given the angle of the afternoon sun. Elongated shadows were cast. They contrasted nicely with the sun-ravaged white of the house that was being moved. He was confident his exposures would make for high, abstract, black-and-white drama.

Once again, Carl had been right. He called it the Boy Scout Motto. *Be prepared. Always have your camera. Always have film.*

"What we have here is a Mexican standoff and it has to stop," J.B. said to no one in particular. He figured the gun Sarah Mae held wasn't loaded. He kept the .22 shells hidden on top of a secretariat where Sarah Mae never dusted. Like a lot of other things she didn't like, dusting was in her top ten. He calmly walked over to Sarah Mae and wrenched the gun from her hands, lifted the lever, slid back the bolt and viewed the gun's chamber. It held no bullet.

Field of View

She stared defiantly at J.B., turned, and walked toward the porch. She offered up a frown to James Ray. She stopped her march to the house to give Elsie a hard look. "For once in y'all's life, Elsie, could y'all mind your own cotton-pickin' business? Is that possible?"

Elsie retreated several steps, saying nothing.

Sarah Mae went inside, took to her bedroom, and locked the door behind her.

Noting Sarah Mae's exit, the man against the house lowered his hands. The sheriff's deputy removed his hand from his holster. The men behind the house made their way cautiously back into the scene. They gathered by the sheriff's deputy in case the crazy woman might at any moment leap from the front door of her house with yet another gun.

J.B. couldn't believe his eyes. Down East 9th came a yellow Cadillac, its massive, basket-crate grill leading the parade of chrome and sheet metal. The car parked on the wrong side of the street. Its driver exited the car, leaned over, grabbed what looked like a camera and strode calmly toward the stalled house. Carl Malone was smiling, his Graflex in hand.

"Hello, name's Carl Malone," he said to J.B. Carl switched his Graflex camera to his left hand and offered his right. Reluctantly, J.B. took his hand and shook it.

"Name's J.B. J.B. Turman. This is Deputy Dinwitty. He's our law and order, I suppose. He's here to make sure World War III doesn't begin on East 9th Street."

Carl and the sheriff shook hands.

"James Ray's my boy," J.B. volunteered. "Says he likes workin' for you."

"Doesn't work for me. The paper pays him. I just school him."

"Hello there, James Ray," Carl said, waving in his direction.

James Ray responded in kind and walked toward his daddy and his mentor.

"What are y'all doin' here?" J.B. asked.

"Working. I don't have an eight-to-five like a lot of people do in this town."

"Well, let me ask you again. Why are you here?"

Carl didn't answer immediately. He studied J.B. He knew a little about the man given idle chit-chat with James Ray over the past few months. He calculated James Ray's father to be harmless, gun or no gun.

"The paper got a call from one of your neighbors. Could have been that elderly lady over there. I was told a house was bein' delayed by a gun toting woman. I'm here to see if anyone is dead or dying. Is that gun loaded?"

"No. No one's dead or dyin', so y'all can leave."

"All right. If you say so. I'll just take a couple of photos and then I'll be..."

"You will do no such thing. Photos of this mess aren't necessary. Neither is any kind of a story. We're merely solvin' a problem with a house movin' and a tree cuttin'. That's all. It's all under control."

Carl ignored J.B's. order. Saying nothing, he walked to the location previously inhabited by James Ray. It offered the scene's best perspective.

"Get off the lawn!" J.B. ordered.

"What?"

"I said, get off my lawn. Get off the lawn or I'll remove you from the lawn and you won't like the removin' part."

"Daddy..."

"Hush, James Ray, or you will be part of the removin' as well."

"Listen, you two," managed Dinwitty. "I'll do the orderin' here."

J.B. turned to face Dinwitty and gave him a hard stare. No words were exchanged between the two but Dinwitty decided in the short expanse of an instant that silence was golden.

Carl stood motionless. The two men glared at each other. None of the movers or tree trimmers said anything. The two faced each other defiantly. Less than a hundred years ago, the Yankee and the Confederate would have taken similar positions, facing off at places like Shiloh or Johnsonville or Corpus Christi for that matter. In such a replay of history, one or both of the men would die for causes and propositions neither could fully articulate.

Today, however, in the Turman front yard with Carl Malone occupying grass north of the street while J.B. stood south of the lawn on the pavement of the street, the two men faced off for less grandiose reasons, but reasons they were nonetheless.

J.B. was armed with a chamberless .22 rifle, Carl with a camera loaded with film.

A Yankee on my front lawn. A low-down, dirty-picture-takin', bootleggin', double rat's ass of a Yankee. I should have Deputy Dinwitty arrest him on the spot. Maybe have him skinned alive or burned at the stake. I should gather the townspeople and have him hanged from the elm, and when he's dead, cut him down and leave his body to the first carnivorous animal that comes along.

"I didn't mean to start a skirmish, Mr. Turman," Carl said, breaking the tension between the two men. He walked in J.B.'s direction and off the Turman lawn. "Just doing my duty here, following orders and all. We all have to follow orders, one way or another, don't we, Mr. Turman? If my being present on your lawn offends you, then I'll make my exit. Doesn't look like there's much to do here anyway. Looks like everything's under control. Good day gentlemen. See you at work, James Ray."

J.B. said nothing in reply.

As Carl walked past J.B., he paused and spoke. "Your boy has talent. He's got the sugar. I hope you respect it. He's doing really fine work. It's been a pleasure to teach him what little I know of photography. Now and then, he teaches me. That's the way a teacher and student relationship should be."

"What's the sugar?" J.B. replied, surprised that he had spoken, upset as he was with the entirety of the situation. He recognized that Carl had taken the highroad and had seized the opportunity to defuse the conflict. Carl had won the battle.

"A camera is a tool and a tool only. Your son has both the skill and creativity to use the tool. That's the sugar."

"Well, I appreciate what you've done for James Ray and all. I just hope the sugar part is harmless to all concerned."

Carl left, saying no more.

"Daddy, y'all were rude to Carl. Why'd you order him off our lawn?"

J.B. refused to respond to his son's criticism. He still had a problem to solve and it would be dark in a couple of hours. He was hungry. He was tired. He was fit-to-be-tied over the situation Sarah Mae had created. Perhaps she was losing her senses. Today's confrontation with the tree trimmers and the house movers was testimony to the fact. That and the fact she had decided to move to California leaving him like a tree uprooted, clinging desperately to what used to be the confidence and nurture of terra firma.

J.B. suggested to the movers that they use a rope to bend the tree limb in the direction that the house would travel instead of removing it. The tree trimmers agreed. Anything was better than being shot.

"I think I have some rope in the shed," J.B. announced.

Once the rope was attached to the end of the limb, J.B. and two of the tree trimmers pulled hard to bend the limb back far enough so the house could pass. The truck was started. The house began to move, slowly, foot-by-agonizing-foot. At the point when the house and limb were inches from each other, the limb snapped. The robin's nest flew into pieces. J.B. and the two tree trimmers fell backwards into a heap.

Sarah Mae was watching from her bedroom window. After the limb broke with an agonizingly loud crack, she turned from the window and took to bed. She cried. She cried for the condition of her health. She cried for having made yet another mess of a situation she knew she should have handled differently. She cried because she would be leaving in less than a week and Hope didn't want to come with her. She cried because she loved J.B. despite it all. She cried for what would be whispered in church and around the square and elsewhere throughout the county. She cried given James Ray's ignorance of who his real father was. She cried because of the letter they had finally received from Seth. Seth, the unhappy. Seth, the sufferer. Seth, the boy-child now honed into a callus, fighting machine. She cried because her God was failing her in all aspects of her life. *Where are you? Why do I have to suffer so? Why do I seem to make others suffer so? Where are you when I need you? How can you leave me so alone and so unhappy and so diseased?*

She got out of bed and kneeled to pray as she had done when she was a child. It had worked then, perhaps it would work now.

Chapter 29 - Gravitas

"Are y'all on one of your stop drinkin' campaigns again?" asked Bud as he poured his morning coffee.

"Thanks for your vote of confidence," Judith answered. "That's just what I need, someone to make light of the effort."

"I'm sorry, I didn't mean it to come out that way."

"Ruth Ann's goin' to be fine. That's what I'm focused on. Her life. Her well bein'. Whether I drink or not is neither here nor there."

"Well, I'll get into trouble sayin' so, but it's not a matter of neither here nor there. More like livin' a life or not livin' a life."

Judith didn't respond. She walked to the back door of the house, entered the yard, kicked off her house slippers and sat on a wooden, paint-peeled Adirondack chair. She lit a cigarette. Her bare feet explored the cool of the morning grass. Bud needed to cut the grass before it began resembling a backyard jungle.

Bud followed her into the backyard.

"I'd rather be alone," Judith said, upon hearing his approach.

"Well, not now. Sorry, but we need to talk. I can't go on livin' the way I am, the way we are. Somethin' has to change." He reached for a cigarette. He waited for Judith to say something, anything. She remained silent.

"Can you at least look at me? Can you at least respond in some way that a wife should to a husband?"

Judith said nothing in reply. Instead she inhaled deeply and blew smoke upward into the freshness of the morning air. Clouds were gathering early, she thought. Maybe it would rain.

"You make me feel like I'm irrelevant, meaningless. I took you and Ruth Ann in when y'all were down and out. I adopted her. You have a car you pretty much drive exclusively while I walk to work, whatever the weather. I work. I put a roof over our heads and you treat me like I'm some kind of leper."

Judith remained silent. She closed her eyes. She wished she could close her ears and just be here in the backyard all by herself. *The shade of the tree. A cigarette. Bare feet in the cool grass. A precious, cool drink in her hand.*

"We'll talk about it later," she managed. "Right now I have a headache and I want to be alone."

Field of View

"How many times have you used that trick? Dozens? A hundred? Leave me alone? We'll talk about it later? You know what, Judith? That's why nothin' ever happens. Nothin' gets better. It just gets fuckin' worse. The sore festers. Nothin' happens. Not a Goddamn, fuckin' thing. Nothin' ever gets better."

Bud marched defiantly into the house, slammed the screen door, put on his work shoes, and began walking the eight blocks to work. He carried his coffee cup with him. He had picked up the *Tribune* from the sidewalk and carried it under an arm. He planned to read it on his lunch break. He would be late because he had waited for Judith to shower so he could speak to her. She had a way of always doing something when he was around. She would read. She would go to bed early and then make herself unavailable in the mornings or when he came home or whenever.

But what did being late matter? He didn't even keep watch to see if his employees, all twenty-eight of them, were on time or not. Who cared in the scheme of things? Tardy. Not tardy. Absent. Asleep at the wheel. What difference did any of it make down the road? The pump company could disappear overnight and it wouldn't make a whit of difference in the long run. What about his unfulfilling marriage? What if he gave up trying to make it work? What if he weren't around to be involved in any of it, neither the pump company nor his marriage. What if he were someplace quiet and peaceful?

"I don't want to be disturbed, Samantha," Bud said. "Sorry, I've been here for a couple of months and I haven't even asked if I can call you Samantha. Or do y'all prefer Mrs. Hillside like I've been doin'?"

"Samantha's fine. Some call me Sam. Either way. Samantha or Sam or Mrs. Hillside. Any of it is fine. I appreciate y'all's askin'."

"I've got some paperwork that I've been puttin' off and I have to get it done before I meet with the high-ups from headquarters next Monday. I'm gonna lock myself in my office. Is that all right with you?" Bud asked.

"Certainly is. Of course."

"No calls. No visitors. OK?"

"Got it. How long will y'all be? Should I wait to go to lunch until y'all are done?"

"No, go at y'all's regular time. I won't be long. I'll be done by noon. It'll be...I'll be done soon. Just wait 'till noon. I'll be done by then."

"Sure thing, Mr. Chambers," Samantha replied, returning to her filing. Nice man, Mr. Chambers, she thought. Over the years, she had been subject to good and bad bosses and she would rank Mr. Chambers somewhere in the middle but she didn't know him that well yet. In his favor, he left her pretty much alone to do her job as she saw fit. She liked that. Truth be known, she reflected, most everything she did was busy work she made for herself. And every time Mr. Chambers mentioned that he was meeting with management from headquarters, Samantha worried another layoff could be in the works. Worse, she might be the next to go.

Samantha had been a Reliant Pump employee for going on fifteen years. She remembered when the plant used to be hopping with things to do. There were pumps to assemble, test, package and ship. Accounts receivable. Accounts payable. The plant hummed with activity. People were coming and going, all of them had something important to do. There were people to talk to, important decisions to be made. There were more government contracts than were manageable. Then the war ended. The contracts ended, too. Then came the layoffs. A lot of women, many of them good friends, were let go. They were replaced with men coming home from the war. Imagine that, she thought, men replacing women even though they weren't half as skilled or hardworking as the women who were let go and sent back to their homes, dismissed with hardly a goodbye or a thank-you for helping win the war.

Women always get the short of it all, she figured. *Men manage and posture around like barnyard roosters, like the world owes them a living. Men claim they're head of the house while women do the work of the house and keep the place from falling apart. Women by far make fewer mistakes; they console, they pick up the pieces, even the messes made by men. They soldier on, day after day, unrecognized and undervalued. Always have, probably always will. And what kind of a woman would fire someone without askin' the someone to explain why he or she did this or that? And what kind of a woman would put profit before takin' care of her workers?* "Anyway, name me a woman who ever started a war?" she said quietly to herself.

Field of View

The west-bound Texas and Pacific freight out of Texarkana arrived at 10:45 and began its predictable change of cars, its tedious loading and unloading. Samantha knew the sounds well. They were imprinted deep into her memory bank. She had lived the freight's visitation to its Mayweather stop over for two decades. The train's routine varied little from one visit to the next.

She found the train's sounds comforting: its inbound whistle, its powerful march into town, and the puff and roar of its steam engine. She marveled that the brick and mortar building in which she had labored for so long hadn't completely disintegrated given the assault of vibration emitted by the steam engine's arrivals and departures. However, Reliant Pump still stood. Outside, it appeared as vital as it did during the war and the war before that. Inside, the company little resembled its glory days of activity, promise, purpose, and profit.

The greatest shake and rattle occurred when the train slowly ambled by her building, a mere twenty-five yards removed from the tracks. The resulting vibration was so strong that she could feel it in her chair and in her feet as they rested beneath her desk on the linoleum-covered floor plank.The coffee in her cup would begin to dance, slowly at first, then more rapidly as the liquid submitted to the contentious invasion resulting from the lumbering mass of hundreds of tons of steel and iron. Any pencil or pen left on her desk would begin scurrying about as if it were a Mexican jumping bean desirous to pack up and relocate to a more suitable and stable abode.

Bud stood motionless by the window facing the train yard. He watched as the train slowed and came to a stop. Timed perfectly with the harsh, metallic sound of the first car to be off-loaded, he slowly raised the gun to his head and pulled the trigger.

*   *   *   *   *

The news of the death of Bud Chambers quickly spread throughout the county. Prayers were offered up by pastors of every congregation, regardless of creed. The next morning's *Tribune* displayed a head and shoulders photo of a youthful and smiling Thomas Baldwin Chambers. It was the same photo the paper had used announcing his arrival eight weeks prior. The accompanying article detailed his work at Reliant Pump in Fort

Worth as he moved from shipping and receiving to purchasing to middle management to mid-level manager in product development and finally, his move to oversee the company's meager operation in Mayweather. He had not served in the military. Given his age and critical war time work at Reliant Pump, he and thousands of others like him, escaped the hardship and risk of military service.

Left behind, were his wife, Judith Marie Chambers, a stay-at-home mother and their daughter, Ruth Ann, an upcoming junior at Mayweather High School. Noted also was the fact that the family had relocated to Mayweather from Fort Worth a mere two months prior to his "unfortunate demise."

Judith was both shocked and relieved. Of all the things she had fantasized, Bud's taking of his own life had not been one of them. Now, he was dead. Dead by his own hand. That was that. Nothing could be done to reverse the fact. Nothing. Now she was free to do as she pleased. Mere seconds after learning of his death, she decided to pull the curtains on any and all guilt she might involuntarily conjure because of his death. He pulled the trigger, not she. He should have married someone else, not her.

Ruth Ann would be sorry and grieve; but, in the end, he was not her father. Yes, he had helped them when they needed help but now they could stand on their own feet and make something of themselves. Suddenly, they had choices. Now, she and her Ruth Ann held the power.

"He left us $25,000. It was a life insurance policy," Judith said to Ruth Ann.

"That was thoughtful. That's a lot of money."

"Yes. I knew he had a life insurance policy but that was all. We didn't talk about it."

"Y'all didn't talk about much of anything, actually."

"I suppose you're right. It just shows how important it is to hold high standards, Ruth Ann. Don't compromise. Don't go into a marriage with a little voice in your head tellin' you it's the wrong thing to do. Don't ever do that. Marryin' Bud was the worst mistake of my life."

"He tried hard, Mother. I think you were way too hard on him."

"Maybe so. You're probably right. Anyway, it's a new world without him in it."

"Mother! That's a harsh thing to say. He hasn't been dead for a week yet."

"Ruth Ann, you haven't been married to the man. I'd appreciate some sympathy and less criticism."

"Sorry. I do need to say that I'm happy about your not drinkin'."

"Thank you. I appreciate that. I drank because I couldn't stand my life. You have y'all's whole life ahead of you. You've got promise. You can do anythin' you want to do. Maybe we won't move back to Fort Worth after all."

"I didn't know we were movin' back. I like it here."

"Well, maybe I'll...maybe we'll stay here at least until your graduation. Of course, you're free to follow your dreams after high school. That's only two years from now. Good things will be waitin'. College and all. Scholarships. Just yesterday, I thought your graduation would take forever. Now, I can see it plain as day. I'm sorry to say it, but I'm relieved he's gone."

"That's a terrible thing to say mother. At least wait until the service is over. God! I can't believe you sometimes!"

"He'll be buried in Fort Worth in a day or so. The service will come later. Anyway, I can't believe myself sometimes, to be truthful. Let's hope your life's journey takes a more positive turn. Maybe it'll be full of rich rewards, goals accomplished, wishes attained. We differed, that's all. We never really connected like a husband and wife are supposed to do."

"What does that mean?"

"Look Ruth Ann. We saw life differently, that's all. Had different needs. Had different visions of what we wanted out of life. Parents are people and he wasn't even your father. Biggest thing was that we weren't compatible. There...there was no attraction. You have to be attracted to the person you marry, the person you love. Leave that out of the equation and you'll sink like the Titanic."

Judith felt she needed a drink. She had a bottle of vodka in her panty drawer in case something bad happened. Something good had happened instead. She needed it regardless. Could she resist the temptation? That was the big question.

Ruth Ann announced she was going to James Ray's house to see his photo essay of her training at Devil's Lake.

"He took 'em before the cottonmouth. Before all of it. I haven't seen 'em yet. Is it okay or do you need me to stay with you?"

"No, please go. If you are up to it, that is. I'm fine. Are you feelin' well enough to go?"

"Sure. I'm fine."

"Well then, have a good time. It'll do you good to get out of the house. Bring home some pictures so I can see them."

"I will if I can. I'm not sure how a darkroom works and all. Anyway, I'll be back in a couple of hours or so. May I take the car so James Ray doesn't have to pick me up? I'd walk but my leg is still sore."

"Sure, go ahead. The keys are on the coffee table."

Ruth Ann put on a fresh blouse. She changed her jeans. She played with her hair, what little there was to play with. She thought about lipstick but slathered her lips with chapstick instead. She borrowed a spritz of her mother's White Shoulders. She powdered her underarms. Looking into the mirror, she judged herself to be presentable. She was looking forward to seeing the pictures. She was looking forward to spending time with James Ray.

Following Ruth Ann's departure, Judith walked to her bedroom and removed the vodka. She went into the kitchen and added a few cubes of ice from an ice tray to a high ball glass. She poured a generous amount of the remaining vodka into the glass. She added a large pimento-stuffed olive to her libation. She went into the living room. She sat. She lit a cigarette. She turned on the radio. The vacuum tubes warmed. Sound emitted. She dialed a music station. She imbibed.

The $25,000 whole-life insurance policy Bud left in her name would solve all their money problems. Despite the surprise of the inherited largess, she would accept employment offered to her by a newly-renovated store in town, Sanderson Drug and Cosmetics. It was the only store on the square that was owned by a female. Janelle Sanderson's drugstore would merchandise the standard fare offered by drug stores, but the sit-down soda fountain area was scheduled to be converted into a cosmetic make-up station. It would be a unique offering, unlike any other in Texas. The station would be named "Texas Smile". Judith would provide the consultation and service following completion of two weeks of training in Dallas. During her mother's absence, Ruth Ann lobbied for staying in the house alone.

"There's nothing I can't do by myself while y'all are gone," she informed Judith.

"No, I suppose not. All right, but I don't want the house a wreck when I come home."

"I promise."

"No guests, either. Okay?"

"Okay. I have way too much to do to entertain anyway."

"Good."

"So, I get to stay here by myself? My, myself and I?"

"Yes, all three of you."

Chapter 30 - Seein' Is Believin'

Ruth Ann had difficulty descending the stairs of the shelter. The steps were hard for her to manage given the lingering soreness of her leg. Her hand was healing to the doctor's satisfaction. Her leg, however, lagged behind her hand's performance. Any unwanted pressure on her leg brought pain. The area surrounding the snake bite on her leg was still red, swollen, and blistered. It was caused less from the bite and more from a stubborn staph infection. Ruth Ann was being treated with both an oral and a topical antibiotic.

"Here, let me help you," James Ray offered. Ruth Ann extended her good hand. He took it. Once she worked her way down, the two teenagers stood facing each other, their hands clasped.

"You need to know how sorry I am about your daddy."

"He wasn't my daddy, but I appreciate you sayin' it anyway. He was a good man but he and my mother were like oil and water. In a way, I guess it's for the best. Neither one of 'em was happy. Maybe life isn't worth livin' if a person isn't happy. I don't know."

"Maybe not. You smell good."

"Thank you. It's my mother's White Shoulders. Let me give you a compliment. Your eyes are interestin'," Ruth Ann said into the dank quiet of the shelter. "They're so dark and mysterious. Where did your eyes come from?"

James Ray smiled. He loved the warmth of her hand. He would let Ruth Ann decide when to let go, to part the way of their adjoined flesh.

"I don't know for certain," James Ray replied. "My mother has some Coushatta blood from her mother's side. Anyway..."

"What's Coushatta?"

"An Indian tribe. They were originally somewhere in Alabama but were run off by settlers and ended up in east Texas. They were, are still, I suppose, good basket makers. Good farmers. They weren't hostile like a lot of plains Indians were."

"That's interestin'. I've never known anyone with Indian blood in 'em. So that makes you how much Indian? How much Coushatta?"

"I don't know. Blood's blood, isn't it? I don't know how it all works actually."

Ruth Ann let go of his hand and reached behind James Ray's head and pulled him toward her. She kissed him softly. He was both shocked and overwhelmed by the succulence of her kiss.

"Got a handkerchief?" she asked.

James Ray reached into a back pocket of his jeans. He offered his hanky to Ruth Ann. She wiped her lips, then his.

"Sorry, I've gone and put chapstick all over y'all's lips."

"That's all right, I..."

"Here, I'll get it right this time." Her hand again went to the back of his neck. This time the kiss was firmer, more passionate, even a little wet.

Ruth Ann pulled away and smiled. "Is that better than watchin' me naked in the shower?"

James Ray thought he would faint.

"Well...I, I can't for the life of me imagine anythin' better than that. Could we do it again for a couple of days or so? Or keep it up until we're listed as missin' persons?"

Ruth Ann laughed. Her time with James Ray was living up to her expectations and she had been in the shelter for no more than five minutes.

"Maybe someday I'll watch you naked in the shower. Maybe after a ball game. That would be a good time."

"Land sakes, Ruth Ann. I'm afraid I wouldn't meet y'all's expectations for a naked basketball player."

"Well, what's the sayin'? Beauty's in the eyes of the beholder. I think you're beautiful in a dark and mysterious, Coushatta, basket-makin', dirt farmin' way."

It was James Ray's turn to laugh.

"Am I gonna show you how to develop y'alls pictures or are we gonna kiss until tomorrow? I'll be happy either way."

"Show me. I'm lookin' forward to it."

"All right, here's the contact sheet. Look at all of 'em closely. Here, I have a magnifyin' glass. Let me know which one you like and we'll enlarge it."

James Ray had purchased an entire darkroom setup he'd seen advertised in the *Tribune* for $50.00. He and Carl had driven to the man's home. Carl thought it a bargain especially given the quality and condition of the Beseler enlarger. The man was moving and he was willing to give up his hobby since he needed the money to help pay for his relocation. He said he was headed for the "greener pastures" of California. J.B. ponied up for half of the cost. James Ray was paying him back $5.00 a week in installments.

James Ray had taken a 3/4-inch slab of plywood and had the lumberyard cut it into thirds. He secured two sawhorses and suspended one of the plywood planks between them. There, he set up his developing trays. The enlarger was located on his mother's reading desk, a desk she had insisted upon despite the tight confines of the shelter. J.B.'s insistence on a single bed was also space eating.

Ruth Ann selected one of the head-and-shoulders shots, one of several where she had creatively held the towel above her head.

James Ray located the negative and loaded it into the enlarger. "Emulsion side down. When we expose, a reversal takes place. The light part of the negative will become dark on the paper, the dark part of the image, the sky and all, will become light. James Ray held up the negative. "See your face? It's dark. If it were a picture of my colored friend, Sammy, the face would be light. Anyway, on the paper, because the negative will become a positive, your face will be light, not dark. The dark part of the negative, the sky, is dark because of the light's effect on the film. I know I'm confusin' you. I was confused at first. Let me show you. Just watch and you'll get it over time. I think we need to do this several times a day. I don't think I can live without a kiss every hour or so. How about you just moving into the shelter? There's no smoke down here. It's cool. No closet for y'all's clothes though. If you need to shower, I can soak you with our garden hose.

"I'll take it into consideration. That's a nice invitation. It's good to have a place to hide every now and then."

"All right, here we go. Ready? Ready for another scary red light? There are no tombstones, but remember, we are in a cellar. The question is, who's carryin' a knife?"

"I am," Ruth Ann replied. "I'll stab you when you're concentratin' and not payin' attention. Probably when y'all's back is turned."

"Okay, stab away."

James Ray killed the overhead tungsten light and simultaneously gave life to the safelight. "How's this for atmosphere?"

"I like it. I may kiss you again. Now, with the red glow of the safelight, y'all are beyond mysterious lookin'."

She meant it. She turned, pulled him away from the enlarger and kissed him yet another time. This time her lips lingered in exploration. She pulled him close, then closer still. He felt the firmness of her breasts. Her breath was warming, exciting. She smelled like a garden of springtime flowers. He pulled back given stern and firm notice of his arousal.

"That's it," she said, softly. "I'll behave from this moment forward or else we'll start a fire that can't be put out. Y'all's mother won't like it if we burn down her shelter."

James Ray tried to catch his breath and the runaway beating of his heart. He hoped also, somehow, someway, to calm the excitement of his erection. He moved to the bed and sat. Once seated, James Ray hoped his condition would go unnoticed.

It had not. Ruth Ann had felt it when they were close. She had even pushed against it, her part to his part, separated only by denim and underclothing. She too, was in a state of heightened arousal. Were such a thing capable of being measured, her state would be found equal to his. The condition of her arousal, however, was less directly observable.

"I hope I haven't killed you. Are y'all okay?" Ruth Ann asked.

"Killed me without a knife. That's beyond cruel."

"When's the service for your...for Bud?" James Ray thought if he changed the subject he could get his member to better behave.

"Not sure. He's gonna be buried in Fort Worth, then a service will follow at some point." Ruth Ann joined James Ray on the bed. She sat slowly and stiff-legged. Her bad leg was hard to bend.

"How long did y'all live in Fort Worth?"

"Since I was seven. Second grade."

"I bet you were a knockout even in the second grade."

"I don't think so. Next time y'all are over, I'll show you some of my early childhood pictures. You'll love the one with my front teeth missin'."

"I'm sure I will. Should we get on with the enlargin' and developin' and all?"

"Sure. I'll behave myself and keep my hands to myself all at the same time. Just one more thing," Ruth Ann said, as

James Ray adjusted the enlarger and easel. "you're a better kisser than my boyfriend back home."

James Ray fell silent. He quickly dismissed the 'better kisser' part since she had mentioned 'boyfriend' and 'back home' in the same sentence. *Could she have dual loyalties? Is there a loyalty to me in the first place? Does she still see Fort Worth as her home?*

"You didn't like me sayin' y'all were a good kisser?"

"Well, I don't know what kind of a kisser y'all's boyfriend is. I have to rely on you to put me straight on that one."

"You're mad."

"No. Jealous, maybe. Yes, I'm jealous. I admit it. My daddy told me a person should always own up to his emotions. So there, I've done it."

"Well, don't go and be jealous. We're havin' too much fun. Come here." Ruth Ann kissed him yet another time. "You don't have anythin' to worry about. I've got you on my radar at the moment. You're here. He's there. I'll let y'all know when you have somethin' to worry about. How's that?"

Ruth Ann loved the intrigue and magic of the darkroom. James Ray let her enlarge and develop several of the lake pictures.

"A few days ago my mother stopped a house that was bein' moved," James Ray volunteered as he poured the developing chemicals back into their bottles.

"I heard about that. Mother mentioned it. That was y'all's mother?"

"Had five men and a deputy sheriff scared half to death. Had my daddy's .22 rifle pointed at 'em. Funny thing was, it wasn't even loaded."

"My news is that my mother has stopped drinkin'."

"Really?"

"Stopped cold turkey. I'm proud of her for doin' it. Came just in time 'cause of Bud's death and all. This way she'll be sober for the service with people callin' and comin' and goin' and whatever."

"Good for her. That's really good."

"Anyway, tell me about your mother's holdin' up the house. I want to hear every word of it. Just the facts. Don't go and stretch anything. Remember I know story tellin'. Can you turn off the light again and put on the safelight? That will make for better story tellin'. After that, you can kiss me goodnight. It's your turn, you know. You owe me three or four or five. I haven't kept count."

"I have. I owe you a good dozen, actually. And, sorry to say, seems like I've forgotten the story. It happened so long ago I can't remember. Let's just move on to the kissin' part."

Chapter 31 - South Cow Seance

Carl arrived early. He had left nothing to chance. He believed that good preparation led to good execution. Arriving early also afforded him the opportunity to walk around the abandoned farmhouse and reflect on his plans to move the house to a tree-inhabited, accessible spot adjacent to the highway. Once relocated, he would convert the house to a gas station. It would be his retirement. The house would be partitioned to meet his unique needs. There would be the gas station in front along with an entry way into a large room designed to hold items for legal sale. A smaller, side room would be constructed so that it could be accessed through a locked door where illicit alcohol would be stored. The room would have a door to the outside for convenience. Entrance from the outside would be hidden from highway view by a fence of some kind. He hadn't quite worked that out in his mind.

Available for his personal use would be a small kitchen, a bedroom and a living area. An area behind the house would be cleared for picnic benches. He would save as many trees as necessary to provide needed shade in the summer. A nearby creek ran most of the year. He would clear a path to the creek so people could sample a little nature during their stopover. Awaiting customers would be the great outdoors, a little chit-chat, hand-holding and perhaps some incognito cold beer served in paper cups.

Why, he calculated, would any person drive another three miles to Oklahoma when he could more than service their needs at his store? Or, why would they drive all the way to Ladonia or Dallas, in Lamar County, when he could take care of them? He would name his service station, The Red. He would stock the usual items offered by gas stations anywhere, but he would exclude tedious and nonprofitable service offerings like tire repairs, or lubrication, or oil changes. Instead, his vision was to merchandise picnic items like deli-meats, cold fried chicken, cheese, Fritos, potato chips, coleslaw, dill pickles, soft drinks and so on. After all, people flocked to the Red River like geese to a body of water. Traffic on the highway was heavy anytime of the year.

He'd stock nearly every brand of cigarette and sell them at a discounted price. He'd sell shotgun shells and other ammunition to hunters as well as the beer they would need for refreshment. In his side room, he'd inventory his cold beer and stock an endless variety of spirits. He, and he alone, would hold the keys to the stockroom; one for the first door, yet another for the second. The Red, he figured, would be the stopover of stopovers.

Should Hoghead Albertson ever lose an election, or retire, or be run out-of-town, he'd develop a relationship as secure with the new sheriff as he had with Hoghead, second cousin or no second cousin. He'd win over the new sheriff, if necessary, by paying him more than any of the other run-of-the-mill bootleggers. Pay a premium amount, gain a premium advantage.

He even envisioned hiring some high school girls on the weekends and during summer vacation to entice males of the area from filling their gas tanks in Mayweather. Instead, they would be motivated to drive a few miles out-of-town to be treated to a gas-filling experience never before imagined. The girls would pump the gas and clean windshields. The girls would invite them in. The boys would oblige. Once inside, they would most certainly lose a grip on their wallets.

Also inside the Red, he'd hang three pictures of Trixie. He would go back to his negatives of the comely Trixie and enlarge each to the size of 18 by 24 inches, frame them, and hang the images above the cash register. He'd choose photos where her private parts weren't on prominent display. Suggestive, yes. Complete nudity, no. He would be prudent enough to walk a fine line between prurient interest and respectability.

At The Red, he'd work, play, and sleep.

Judith arrived a little after nine in the evening. She had rescheduled the meeting with Carl twice, once when Ruth Ann was in the hospital, the other following Bud's suicide. Her abstinence had lasted for little longer than it had begun. Now, she was out of liquor and given the stress of Bud's death and having to make long distance plans for his service, she became increasingly more desperate by the hour. Then there were the expenses related to his burial in Fort Worth. How much should be spent to put him in the ground when she and Ruth Ann needed every penny of insurance money above-ground. All and all, the situation called for reinforcement. Her kind of reinforcement. The satisfying, all-encompassing, and senses-dulling kind of reinforcement that alcohol could and would provide.

She could see Carl's Cadillac from the road, just like he had said. Carl noticed her arrival. He could see dust rising from the unpaved road and heard the distinctive throaty hum of the Buick's arrival.

He stepped to the entrance of the road leading into the area and waved her in. She parked, killed the engine, blew smoke out the driver's side window, opened the door, and flipped her nearly-consumed cigarette to the ground.

"Christ, woman. You want me to have to call the fire department? Grass around here is deader than dead."

Judith ignored Carl. She exited the Buick and looked around.

"This place has seen better days," she said.

"You won't believe what I'm going to do with it."

"What do you mean do with it?   Looks to me like it's already done with."

"Nope. Still some life left in the place. I'm going to revive it, Lazarus-like, from the dead. I've made an offer on all 160 acres. Cash offer. I'm offering a little more than half of what they are asking. Cash speaks. I'm pretty sure I'll be the new owner."

"What are y'all goin' to do with a wreck of a farm house and all that land?"

"Here. First off, let's drink to my good fortune."   Carl opened the trunk of his Cadillac, removed the lid of a cooler, secured a cocktail glass, placed ice in it, and poured Judith a drink. He added an olive.

"What's this?"

"A good vodka. On the rocks like you like it. I'm out of Sobieski, like I said. It might taste a little different but it's a another good vodka from Poland. I suspect you'll like it."

"Well, thank you. I didn't expect to be treated so royally. Chilled glasses, ice, and all."

"You're welcome. Now, let me tell you about my plans. Got a minute?"

Carl poured himself a straight bourbon.

"Sure, go ahead."   Judith was free of having to hide anything from Bud. Free to do as she pleased. She had the freedom of time. At least for the moment.

"What kind of palace are y'all goin' to replace the farm house with?"

"I'm going to move the house to the highway. I'm going to salvage it. Knock out some walls, do some relocating of walls, and some fixing up and so on. It's going to sit ass-backwards. Front will be the rear; the rear, with the porch here, will be the front. Going to hang a neon sign announcing The Red. Maybe in the shape of a Rhode Island Red. That will be the station's name."

"Name of what?"

"My gas station, it's..."

"Wait a minute. Y'all are goin' to open a gas station out here in the middle of nowhere?"

"It's not nowhere. There's a lot of traffic back and forth to Oklahoma and I'm going to take advantage of it. Five, ten years from now, the highway will be four lanes. Mark my words."

"Well, if you say so."

"I do say so. Here, let me top off y'all's glass. That's right, isn't it? Y'all's glass?"

"Y'all is a hard habit to break," Judith replied. "I try, but mostly I fail. It's a colloquialism, isn't it? That's the word. Colloquialism."

Judith lit a cigarette. "Can we get on with our business? My daughter's recoverin' from a bite from a Goddamn cottonmouth."

"Yes, I heard. James Ray told me. How is her recovery going?"

"She's seems to be doin' well except for an infection in her leg. She was bitten twice. Once on her...the inner thigh of her leg and the other time on her hand. Was tryin' to defend herself," she said.

"It was out at Devil's Lake, right? Where she trains?"

"Yes. She went past her turnaround point and ended up too close to the south shore. Snake haven on the south side, they say. The bastard cottonmouth must have been waitin' for her."

The two lapsed into silence. Carl walked to the Cadillac, turned on the radio and located a music station. Satisfied with the music, he returned to Judith's side.

"Have some more," Carl offered. Judith offered up her glass. She was drinking quickly, savoring the opportunity to have access to her libation of favor. Carl poured more vodka into Judith's glass.

"Thank you. Anyway, she was found and that's the good news. She could've died out there. The doctor says she should have a full recovery. Said she'd get back to her swimmin' soon."

"Well, I'm glad she's doing as well as she is."

Carl motioned for Judith to sit on the wooden steps of the house while he gathered her order from the trunk of the Cadillac.

"Here, take this while I get your order put together. He handed her the bottle of vodka. "Help yourself. You want some more ice? Another olive?"

"No, thanks. I'm fine. I'm not an olive lover...actually. One olive is enough. Makes the drink pretty. Nice use...nice place to be if you're an olive."

"That's funny," Carl said.

Judith filled her glass to the brim. Some of it spilled to the ground. It was beyond a pleasure to drink again. The vodka thrilled her senses. She loved the warmth of the alcohol as it wound its way down her throat into her stomach. She felt good. Warm inside. Good and warm. Comfortable. Relaxed. She smiled.

"Well, that's a sight," Carl said.

"What?" replied Judith.

"You, that's what. Judith Chambers smiling. It's a rare treat."

"I don't have much reason to smile, so mostly, I don't. Feelin' good now, though. This vodka's good. Is this what I'm buyin'? Is this...whatever it is...is this what I'm takin' home?"

"Wish it was. That's the only bottle I have. Pour yourself some more. It's on the house."

Carl refilled his glass, walked again to the Cadillac and slammed the trunk closed. He then walked behind the barn and once out of sight, urinated. He was soon back at Judith's side. He stood while she sat on the porch steps.

"Y'all know why the little moron took a ladder to the party?" Judith abruptly asked. She lifter her head back and broke into a wide and toothy smile. She ran the fingers of her hand through her hair. "Well, do you? Want me to ask again? The little moron and the ladder and the party? Y'all don't know, do you?"

"Not exactly. I recall a couple of little moron jokes but not that one. Tell me."

"Well, he took the ladder to the party because he was told...," Judith giggled. "He...he was told the drinks were on the house."

Both she and Carl barked a laugh into the still of the evening. Carl coughed from his outburst.

"You know why the little moron slept on his stomach?" Carl asked, as he gave light to a cigarette. This is one I do remember."

"No," Judith laughed. "On his stomach? He didn't...he like sleepin' on his back?" She giggled again. "All right, why did he...the little moron that is, why did he decide to sleep on his stomach?"

"Well, he heard the Japs were lookin' for a new naval base."

Judith laughed loudly. Carl smiled. She asked for a cigarette. She was out. Carl offered her one of his.

"Just who is the little moron anyway?" Judith asked smiling. "Maybe he's plural and not singular. Maybe there are little morons here, there, and everywhere. Like crickets. I feel sorry for all of 'em."

"I don't know. I do know a little comic relief is good for a person," Carl answered blowing smoke toward the barn. "Here's another one I remember. You know why the little moron jumped off the Empire State Building?"

"No."

"To see if he had the guts."

Judith laughed, hard and long. After she recovered, she stared in the direction of the barn, smiling. Carl's car had its headlights on. She hadn't noticed before, but now it was darker and the car's lights illuminated the barn and its near surroundings.

"Y'all left your headlights on," she volunteered.

"Did it on purpose. We have to see, don't we?"

The barn was once painted red, she thought. *A red barn. Maybe that's where he, the braggadocio of a bootlegger, got the idea for naming his gas station, The Red. Or maybe it's because of the Red River. Or maybe because of my red dress which I'm not wearing so that couldn't be it. Maybe because of a red rooster. Who cares anyway?*

Carl waited patiently for the alchemy of the mickey-laced vodka to work its magic. As far as he could see, one fine looking Judith Chambers was well on her way. Her speech had become halting, heavy on her tongue. Her face had become childlike in the fill-light illumination of the Cadillac's headlights. He had parked his car facing the barn and upon Judith's arrival, had turned on the car's lights. That way, the illumination from the car's headlights was softened, diffused, and more face-to-face and conversation friendly.

If everything went the way it should, he'd have her in the back seat of his Cadillac in another fifteen minutes or so. He resumed talking about his plans for the Red. How he would create a different kind of gas station. A gas station where obtaining gasoline was incidental to the experience of the stop over. Judith half listened, half reflected on the condition of her life. Carl faded in and out like a poorly tuned radio program.

"I really need to go," Judith managed. "I...I have to drive back and right now I'm not sure I can. I'm tired. Are y'all tired?"

"Somewhat. Anyway, I've been mistreating a good customer by my inattentive behavior. I'll go to the Caddy and get your order. Y'all's order, right? Y'all's. I'm working on it. I'll get there if I live another two or three months in east Texas. Y'all this and y'all that. Y'all thus and y'all so. Y'all are fixin' to do this and fixin' to do that. Right?"

Judith didn't answer. She was lost in her thoughts.

Carl turned and walked back to the Cadillac and killed the lights. He then moved to the trunk of the car.

"Shit, where are my keys?" he said loudly enough for Judith to hear.

"What are y'all sayin?" she responded weakly.

"I can't find my keys. How can I get home if I can't find my keys? Where are my Goddamn keys?"

Judith looked in Carl's direction. He stood as if planted, as if waiting for some response from her. *His keys are lost? What will he do? What will I do? I don't even know if I can drive home. I'm tired. So tired. What's wrong with me? If I can't get up how can I help him find the keys? If we find the keys everything will be all right. That's what I'll do. I'll get up. I'll help him find the keys. Why, though, did he turn off the lights to his car? How can he find his keys in the dark?*

She stood. She dropped her glass. The glass broke. She stumbled. Carl opened the door of the Cadillac and pushed the front seat forward. He quickly walked back to Judith, secured the half empty bottle of vodka from a step of the porch, picked her up, and cradled her in his arms. He walked heavily to the awaiting Cadillac. He liked having her helpless in his arms. He could feel his arousal. Soon, he would have more of her, all of her. As she lay helpless, he would have her breasts as well as her most divine of feminine offerings.

Carl ushered her awkwardly into the back seat. Unaware of what was happening to her, she complied to his urging. Once inside, he offered her the bottle of vodka. She sat upright with her legs spread, feet splayed on the carpeted floorboard of the Cadillac. She drank directly from the bottle.

Things are moving, she thought. *Everything's moving. It's all moving fast. Too fast for me to clearly focus. I don't feel good. Where am I? Is this Carl's car? Am I in the backseat? What's wrong with me?* Judith fingered the white of the leather upholstery. She drank again from the bottle.

Carl took the bottle from her, reached over and placed it in the front seat. Moving back to Judith, he gently laid her down, unbuttoned her blouse and lifted her bra above her breasts. He unzipped her jeans and slowly pulled them below her knees and then off entirely. Her panties followed.

Judith offered but little resistance. She muttered something inaudible. He put his hand to her mouth to hush her. He stroked her hair. He told her she would be okay.

"You're good Judith. You're good," he whispered.

Judith moaned.

"Now we're better than good," he said, as he entered her. "Good, Judith. Beyond good. Ah, that's a good girl. How's that feel Judith? Feeling good Judith?"

Carl Malone had both captured and disabled his prey. Judith was his.

Judith struggled but was physically and mentally incapable of altering the course of a tragic and sordid memory that would last a lifetime.

Carl had his way with her in the back seat of his Cadillac.

Chapter 32 - Marked to Memory

"County Auditor's office, Mabel speakin'. Yes, one moment please. It's for you, J.B."

J.B. was busy reading through the agenda for the upcoming annual meeting of the Texas Association of County Auditors. The year before, he had been the presenter. He was relieved that was one thing he didn't have to worry about this year. Perhaps he wouldn't even attend; although, if he didn't, it would be his first absence since he assumed office. He readjusted one of his oscillating fans to point in the direction of the telephone. He walked to Mabel's desk, reached for the phone, and thanked her.

"Good mornin', J.B. Turman on this end of the line."

"J.B., this is Spencer down at the *Tribune.* Got a minute?"

"Indeed, what's cookin' Spencer? Someone drown in the Red? Mule Days called off because of a tornado threat?"

"Nothin' like that, J.B. Try a little closer to home. I thought you should know that we're goin' to run a picture along with a short article regardin' the house movin' holdup that took place in front of your house a few days ago and I thought..."

"What? You can't be serious, Spencer."

"Just as I said, the paper's goin' to run a photo...your boy James Ray actually took the picture of the confrontation. I know you're not goin' to be happy about it but..."

"Of course I won't be happy. It's old news anyway, Spencer. Good grief, what gave you the idea to run one of his pictures? You say there's an article that'll run with it? That's even worse."

"Yes, well, we can't run a photo without a caption and I doubt a caption would be sufficient to satisfy our readin' audience. I just wanted to know if either you or Sarah Mae would like to be quoted. You know, tell your side of the story. James Ray says a robin's nest was involved somehow, and a tree and..."

"No, I don't want to comment. It was just a happenstance, pure and simple. The whole thing was merely a problem to be solved. Nothin' newsworthy happened. No one got killed. No birds died. In the end, the house got moved. I'm sorry y'all see fit to run the photo given the history of our friendship but it's a free country, isn't it?"

"Well, it's supposed to be. A free press as well. Look J.B., I'm not happy to run the photo along with the short article but you'll have to admit it's newsworthy when a woman holds up a house bein' moved with a .22 rifle, unloaded or not, all to protect a robin's nest. You sure you don't want to comment?"

"No, I won't comment. Call Sarah Mae. She'll give you an earful. Most likely, you'll need a full page once she's finished. Maybe the entire paper. Spencer?"

"Yes?"

"Did my boy offer you the photos or did you ask for them?"

"He didn't offer and I didn't ask. Carl handed me the film and the proofs of the standoff. James Ray had some other shots on the roll of film, and when they were developed, the ones he took of the standoff came to light. Your boy is a really good photographer."

"Well, you can't blame me for that. Blame Mr. Malone, his tutor."

"Right. You should know that I think James Ray is a little put off by Carl's bringin' me the shots; but, like I say, the standoff is newsworthy nonetheless. It was your neighbor who called in the story. That was how the whole thing came to light."

"Good old busybody, Elsie Cornforth?"

"Yes, Elsie. She's called every day to see if we're goin' to mention the standoff."

"Figures. Well, when is the picture and the article gonna hit the newsstands?"

"Tomorrow, regardless of whether we get Sarah Mae's side of the story or not. I really do wish you would consider providin' some insight into the matter. James Ray says you diffused the situation. Is that right?"

"Spencer?"

"Yes?"

"No comment. And one other thing. I won't hold this against you. You have a job to do and I suppose if I were in your shoes I'd do the same. You'll be pleased to know I'm addin' yet another name to my already numerous names. Maybe you should quote me after all."

"What are you sayin'?"

"My new name will be William Jennings Bryan Laughingstock Turman. I'll be able to thank you for makin' it public knowledge."

*   *   *   *   *

"You're comin' and that's all there is to it. No more cryin', no more fits, no more out-and-out defiance. I need you. Grandpa needs you and Grannie needs you. Pure and simple, y'all are goin'."

Hope caved. She knew of no way out. After all, what power did a child hold? None, really. Hope cried when she said goodbye to her Daddy, James Ray, and the only home she knew. She cried when they drove away from the house. She cried when they left Mayweather city limits. She cried off and on for the entire way to the New Mexico border. She and Faith and her mother were all squeezed into the front seat of the skinny interior of the '38 Oldsmobile. The back seat and the trunk of the car were filled with clothes and things that it was believed unimaginable to live without: an assortment of dolls, childhood blankets, two sets of roller skates, Sarah Mae's wedding album and the time-honored family picture of the Turmans at a more innocent time. Included was Faith's cherished collection of charcoal drawings of trees and wind-swept grasses and birds in flight. There were boxes of shoes plus a random collection of loose shoes that wouldn't quite fit in the box that was reserved for and marked "shoes." There was a box reserved for Sarah Mae's jewelry. There was another for her lotions and potions. There was a box for her hats. Too many hats. There was too much of everything that the three had deemed essential or at least useful in a faraway place called California.

The girls knew little of what California offered. They only knew the state from distant travel memories. Their mother, however, knew it well and sang its praises. She held the Golden State in high esteem: its breadth and scope, the mountains, the ocean and sand, the fresh scent of jasmine and gardenia, the endless orange groves and olive orchards, and the growth and promise and newness of it all. Further, California couldn't muster a tornado if it tried.

Outside of Tucson, Arizona, was a place ironically named, Texas Canyon, a place where over eons of time, wind and water had shaped a seemingly endless offering of sandstone boulders, large and small, round and elongated, plain and misshapen. They were stacked on both sides of the highway for miles, all jumbled together as if deposited by some creative loin of nature. Had James Ray been along for the ride, he would have been in photographic heaven.

No sooner had Faith marked the beauty of the landscape to her memory to use in a future drawing than the Oldsmobile threw a fan belt. The overburdened car had had enough. It rebelled from its task, from the grade of the highway, and from the unforgiving and relentless heat. It was 105 degrees in the shade. An egg would have fried nicely on the asphalt, whether one wanted his or her egg sunnyside up or over easy. The three waited two hours for a tow truck in the minuscule, small-leaf shade of a nearby mesquite tree. Hope figured she would die on the spot either from the heat, or from starvation, or from venomous bites from an angry swarm of rattlesnakes. Or, more optimistically, she'd be kidnapped. That way, she'd die somewhere more forgiving.

Sarah Mae prayed for deliverance. Faith accessed her art paper and charcoal from the car and began to sketch. She saw the thousands of boulders as a sort of family, bound together by some force of nature but somehow separate, each a unique version of the same. Ultimately, she would dub the drawing as her best-ever charcoal effort. More than one art teacher admired the piece. A couple of years later, one of her high school teachers drove all the way from her home in Brea to paint the landscape for herself. Because Faith so loved her landscape of the area, she toted the rendition of Texas Canyon with her when she moved into her dorm at Long Beach State her freshman year.

She was happy to tell the story that went with the drawing. It was a story that described the flight to California because of the break up of the family, the breakdown of the usually trustworthy, but increasingly elderly Oldsmobile, the circumstance of being stranded by the highway, the miserable heat of the day, and the stingy, small-leafed, desert-adapted tree. Despite the hardship, her mother praying and her sister crying, she nonchalantly sketched boulders.

A Samaritan stopped, assessed the situation, and reported the mishap at a truck stop on his way to Willcox. To tow the Oldsmobile back to Willcox plus the car's repair, cost as much as Sarah Mae had expected to pay for motels along the way.

*   *   *   *   *

J.B. had begged Sarah Mae to take the Hudson. It was nearly new. It was strong and reliable and could easily handle the trip. She and his two precious girls would have traveled in style and comfort but no, Sarah Mae would have none of it, none of the Hudson and no more of him. He could remember crying no more than a couple of times in his adult life. Once, when little Charity died, and the fateful day he waved goodbye to Sarah Mae and his two girls.

Sarah Mae left with $200 dollars in her purse. J.B. raided what little was left in their saving's account. He gave each girl a twenty-dollar bill along with a silver dollar for good luck.

"Here's one for you," J.B. said to Sarah Mae.

"A silver dollar?"

"Yes. Look at the date."

"Nineteen thirty-three...it's...what are you tryin' to say, J.B.? That's the year we were married."

"Not much, I guess. Just a reminder of it all--when we were young and idealistic and in love. That's all. Just hopin' it would..."

Tears came to his eyes. Sarah Mae ordered James Ray and the girls to the porch, out of earshot.

"I'm sorry the way it's turned out, J.B. You need to know that."

"You're sayin' sorry? I don't think I've ever heard that word uttered by you before. Not once in our marriage. Not a single, solitary time. And now you're sayin' sorry. I'm...I'm sorry, too. I can't believe y'all are doin' what you're doin'. You're confused...and you're sick. Still, no matter what, you're goin' to cast everythin' to the wind, caution and commitment be damned! Don't rethink anythin'. Don't second-guess. Just go and leave it up to the rest of us to figure our way out of the mess, to pick up the pieces. Well, I'm sorry, too. I'm sick too, sick and sorry."

"I don't need a lecture, J.B. I've made up my mind and you know the reasons why I'm..."

"No, I don't, really. I actually don't. I've given some time to your decision based on y'all's thinkin', but I can't figure it out. I should be the one leavin'. I should be the one upset over the sorry state of our marriage."

"Lower your voice."

"I won't lower my voice. I'll yell like a Comanche on a warpath if I feel like it."

"I wouldn't advise yellin'. I'd advise..."

"You know Sarah Mae, that's somethin' I won't miss. Y'all's endless advice. 'J.B. y'all ought to do this and y'all ought to do that. Pray more. Eat less. Lower your voice. Be more present, whatever.' So go, Sarah Mae. Take the girls and go. Seems I have no say in the matter, just like I've had no say in our marriage."

Sarah Mae motioned for the girls to come. J.B. and the girls kissed and hugged. J.B. cried. James Ray cried. Both girls cried while Sarah Mae waited patiently in the Olds. She had tears as well. As she eased the Olds into reverse, she noticed she still held onto the silver dollar. She asked Hope for her purse. She dropped the monetary memento into its deep recesses.

If J.B. lived to be a hundred, he would never forget Faith leaning out the passenger side front window, waving goodbye, as the Oldsmobile began the first mile of what was surely to be a long, wearisome, summer road trip to California. Given the dark hue of its exhaust, J.B. noted for the first time that the Olds might be burning oil.

*   *   *   *   *

Once the car was repaired, Sarah Mae pressed on to Tucson. She stopped at a motel located on a street named, Miracle Mile. Their tiny adobe-walled room sported what locals referred to as a "swamp cooler." Such a window-mounted, water-fed, air-conditioner worked beautifully in times when the desert sported low humidity. However, it was August. The prevailing winds had shifted in early July, bringing warm, moist air into the Sonoran Desert from the Gulf of Mexico.

It was referred to as monsoon time in the region. As the warm, moist Gulf air reached the mountains surrounding Tucson, the air rose and cooled. Once cooled and uplifted, the promise of rain was at hand. Half of the area's scant amount of rainfall occurred from July through September. Devastating lightning and thunder storms often resulted from the uniqueness of the weather pattern. The storms were isolated, unlike the steady and persistent rain from the Pacific that fell off and on during the winter season. A summer storm, however, might soak one part of an area and leave a neighboring area dry as a proverbial bone. Flash floods often resulted from such downpours. Rainfall that was miles distant could, and often did, result in the loss of both property and life. The Mexican population characterized such seasonal storms as, "Chubascos".

When the rainy season arrived, the air became saturated with moisture. Thousands of heat-escaping, highly-valued water coolers were rendered impotent. Unless one had the luxury of modern, refrigerated air-conditioning, the water coolers no longer cooled, they merely moved around moist air. Hello monsoon. Hello evaporative water coolers, nicknamed "swamp."

On the one hand, denizens of the desert welcomed the rain, its freshness, and the life-giving renewal that came with it. On the other hand, if one desired to live in a high humidity environment, one may as well hang one's hat in Houston, or New Orleans, or Atlanta, for that matter.

In the small confines of their motel room, the air from the cooler closely resembled air one might expect from taking a warm shower.

"It'll be a miracle if we get to California," Faith said dejectedly.

"God will prevail," Sarah Mae offered in return. "God will work his miracles. He rescued us today, after all."

"If God works miracles, why does he put a hardship on a person to begin with?" Hope wanted to know. "Seems to me he'd be better off, and so would we, if he didn't have to rescue us in the first place."

"I'll answer that on the way tomorrow. Now it's time to sleep. Tomorrow, God willin', we'll be in California. Maybe all the way to Momma's. Hold that thought. Tomorrow we'll manage to get to Grannie's."

The three slept on a sagging mattress. Sarah Mae was in the middle, Faith and Hope on the outside. Faith managed early sleep. Hope worried late into the night. In her hand, she held the silver dollar her daddy had given her. When she did sleep, she dreamed of snakes, of thirst, and of privation. Sarah Mae prayed and wept silently.

Chapter 33 - The Gall of it All

"Y'all ought to confer with my brother in Sulphur Springs. He's a Texas Ranger. Was one for quite a spell, anyway. He's retired now. He might be of some help. Y'all could run it by him."

"Maybe I will, Mabel. That's a good suggestion. Perhaps I'll act on it. Where does he hang his hat?"

"In the town of Commerce. I'd do it right away, if I were you. The nasty pornographer might up and leave any day and you'll be left holdin' nothin' but an empty sack. Give him a call."

In an attempt to explain why he had been so distracted at work, J.B. had taken Mabel into his confidence. He revealed his most inner thoughts to Mabel as quickly as a sinner might release his transgressions when offered a promise of leniency. He told of Sarah Mae's leaving and of her cancer and the fact that her moving to California would mean she would receive the best of available treatment. At length, they discussed Bud Chambers' suicide. Before he knew it, one suicide led to another and he found himself detailing the mess at the Lone Star: Rita Fields, youngsters too young to be involved with such a sordid situation, the absence of interest by the county's lazy-do-nothing district attorney, how his distrust of Sheriff Huff Albertson and how the pornography situation might have everything to do with the *Tribune* photographer, a man named Carl Malone.

Mabel was appalled at what she heard.

"My word, J.B., here in Mayweather? Down at the Lone Star? What's the world comin' to, J.B.?"

"Nothin' good, looks like. If y'all's brother is willin' to help maybe we can get to the bottom of the sorry business. I like the idea of talkin' to someone who might be able to help, offer up a suggestion or two."

"You say you haven't talked to the sheriff?"

"No. I chose to leave him out of the loop. He's probably in on the deal, same as he gets kickbacks from the assortment of bootleggers around the county. I do expect I can get a grand jury organized if I can collect somethin', anythin' that directly connects Mr. Malone to the scene of the crime. Keep this close to y'all's chest. Not a word to anybody unless it's to your brother."

J.B. made the long distance call to Commerce from his home. He warned the operator, the Sumwalt woman, that if she stayed on the line he'd march up from his house and shoot holes in her switchboard.

"I should report y'all to the sheriff for makin' such a threat," Maureen countered.

"Well, you have my permission to do just that. After y'all's switchboard is full of holes, go and see if you can wake him up on this fine and lazy got-nothin'-to-do-as-a-sheriff Mayweather afternoon."

There was no answer from the Commerce number.

"Sure y'all have the right number, Mr. Turman? Maybe you'll try again once y'all have finished threatin' me. There are laws against that, you know."

"There are laws about all kinds of things, Maureen, but people go about breakin' them all the time."

An hour later, after the third attempt, each one forcing J.B. to communicate with a woman he detested--a woman he once described as a person with her "busybody head up her giggywompus"--someone picked up the phone at the other end.

"Hello. Charlie here."

"Mr. Biden, J.B. Turman on this end. Y'all's sister Mabel works for me over here at the Mayweather courthouse. Or, I work for her, truth be told. Anyway, I'm the county's auditor. Do you have a minute? Y'all's Mabel says you'd be a good person to run somethin' by."

"I know of you. Mabel speaks highly of y'all. Says you're the best boss she's ever had. What's cookin' in sleepy old Mayweather?"

"Well, I don't know what I'd do without her. She could run the place, that's for certain. Anyway, I hardly know where to start."

J.B. detailed the problem in as accurate a timeline as he could.

"The girl in the pornographic photo and the girl who jumped to her death in Dallas are one in the same. I know that. I checked it out," J.B. explained.

"From what y'all have told me, you don't know that actually. You assume that's the fact," Charlie responded.

"Well, I'll bet my hat on it."

"Hat bettin' won't get y'all's grand jury organized. Look, this phone call is gonna cost you a fortune. Why don't we meet so as we can talk longer?"

"Sure, if you're willin' to spend more time on our unwelcome Mayweather mischief."

"Some mischief. I've never looked into child pornography, if that's what it is. Done everythin' else you could imagine and some you couldn't. It'll give me somethin' to chew over. How many baseball games can a body listen to, anyway? The grass doesn't grow fast enough or else I'd mow it every hour or so. Anyway, I haven't seen Mabel since she was diagnosed with cancer so I'll drive..."

"Cancer?"

"Y'all don't know? That's my little sister. You could cut off one of her legs and she wouldn't complain. She'd be mad-as-a-wet-hen but she wouldn't complain from start to finish."

"She's never said a word to me. My wife has cancer too and I was just tellin' Mabel about it the other day and she said nary a word about her condition. Stone the crows!"

"That's what I'm sayin'. Solid as a rock, that girl. She'll up and hold your hand but doesn't go and expect anyone to hold hers."

"How long...what kind of cancer does she have?"

"Breast cancer. Got the diagnosis back just last month."

"Ah, the day she wanted off a couple of weeks ago. I remember. She's been a little down since then."

"I would reckon so. The biopsy didn't hold good news."

"Good Lord alive! I'm sorry about all that. Suicides, cancer on the loose, child pornography. Next thing you'll know someone will drop an atomic bomb on downtown Dallas or Mayweather or Commerce."

"Could be. So how about I drive up to Mayweather? I could use a day away from the house. I'll get to visit Mabel. We'll talk. Let's set a day and a time. I'd like to see the Lone Star, get a feel for things. From what y'all have told me, the owner of the hotel is in on it all. Y'all's sheriff, too. The Hoghead person. Small town, big fish. It's the same all over Texas. I'll bet my hat that he's on the take as well."

"Well, I don't know who will be doin' the hat eatin'. You or me. One thing is for sure though, we need to put a stop to the shenanigans."

"Maybe you will. Knowin' people like I've learned to know 'em, someone undoubtedly will step up and fill in the gap. As long as there's a market for such business, someone will find a way to answer it."

Field of View

* * * * *

"Don't say no before you hear me out. Okay?"

The day after Sarah Mae's departure, J.B. and James Ray had a long, sit-down, late evening, father-to-son chat in the kitchen.

"You know by now that I suspect Mr. Malone, your Carl, is behind the underage picture takin' at the Lone Star."

"I do, but you don't have any proof of it. I suppose he..."

"You're absolutely right. I don't have any real proof. I have a photo and a this-and-a-that but nothing that absolutely connects Carl with the Lone Star. That's why I need your help. I hate to ask for y'all's help but I need to. I can't get to the bottom of it without proof, evidence, whatever you want to call it, of his involvement."

"So, before you ask me to do whatever it is y'all are gonna ask, let me ask you this. Why do you want to bring Carl down? If you bring him down, I figure I go down with him and lately, everythin' seems to be goin' down. Your marriage to mother and then Ruth Ann's daddy up and shoots himself. Ruth Ann is bitten by a cottonmouth and could have been killed. Does anybody need any more goin' down business?"

"Those are all good points. Sorry about Ruth Ann's daddy...sorry, stepdaddy. One could tell they weren't happily married and..."

"How about you and mother? What happened there?"

J.B. sighed. He got up, opened the refrigerator, and grabbed a bottle of buttermilk.

"Want some?"

"No thanks."

He returned to his seat, and drank directly from the bottle.

"Some things are obvious, others are not. Your mother and I never talked about things that were important. We talked about surface things, like the surface of this tablecloth. You can see what's on top, the oil cloth, its checkerboard, the salt and pepper shaker, the plates we haven't removed from supper, and that kind of stuff. We never went below the surface. We never had the gumption to talk about things that needed to see the light of day. Those issues, those things, were troublesome so they were kept in the dark and unaddressed."

Field of View

James Ray remained silent. He played with a fork with one hand. The other traced around squares of the oilcloth.

"To use your mother's religious way of seein' the world, it was a sin of omission. So, like some organic somethin' that never sees the light of day, the things that were really important got short shrift. They were simply ignored. Over time, I suppose we found ourselves passin' like ships in the night, neither of us talkin' about things that were important to a relationship, things that separated us. So now, we're separated."

"Are y'all gonna divorce?"

"I have no interest in divorce. You'd have to ask your mother."

"Well, seems to me, you just proved y'all's point."

"How's that?"

"You said I'd have to ask mother. I think you should be doin' the askin' or is that somethin' that's all hidden away, like you say."

"You're a smart boy, James Ray. You have a good head on your shoulders. You're right. That's somethin' that's worthy of discussion, if worthy is a good choice of a word."

"So you're tellin' me what? That you and mother have never talked about the difference in bein' separated and bein' divorced. Is that what you're sayin'."

"Well, you've caught us both red-handed. No, we haven't discussed where we're headed. I thought all along she would change her mind. You know, like women do with dresses or their hair and such. I thought..."

"Daddy, I don't think marriage is simple like that and I think comparin' your marriage with mother to changing clothes is a...what's the word? Disservice. That's what I'm tryin' to say. You comparin' marriage to clothes changin' isn't fair to either of y'all. I hate havin' mother and Faith and Hope gone. I hate it. And there you sit Daddy, without liftin' a finger to fix things."

James Ray began to cry. He put his face in his hands. He got up to leave.

"Please stay, James Ray. Please. These days I have to think of reasons to smile. I can't deal with anymore failure. If I fail you, what else do I have left? Please hear me out. My plan is to ask her back. After she gets treatment for her cancer, maybe she'll want to return. Maybe she'll come back after the first half of the school year is over. Maybe around Christmas. We could have the house decorated and the tree up and all. She would like that. The thing is, her whole family is there. She has a new job. Maybe she'll like it so much she'll want to stay. Your grandpa's mind is failin' along with the rest of him. If we are to work things out, to be honest, maybe I'd have to go there. I don't know if I can do that."

"Seems to me you should have stopped her in the first place instead of havin' to ask her back after she's already gone."

"Look, James Ray. I couldn't have stopped her anymore than she was able to stop Seth from joinin' the Marines. No more than I could have stopped you from workin' with a person for whom I have low regard. Sometimes, you have to wait things out and hope for a good outcome."

"Well, that doesn't fit with the advice you gave me about Rusty, does it?"

"What do you mean? How so?"

"You told me that appeasin' him and hopin' for a good outcome or however y'all put it, would only encourage him. Said I'd have to stand up and face him and all. Is that right?"

"I believe I did say somethin' like that."

"And how does not tryin' to stop somethin' have to do with Carl and whatever's goin' on there? Why are you so wound up tryin' to stop him and yet you couldn't muster the effort to stop mother?"

"Well..."

"Seems to me, Daddy, y'all are not bein' consistent with things."

"'Consistency is the hobnob of small minds,' Emerson once said. Yes, I've been inconsistent. So, in a way I've been small-minded. I honestly don't know. When I look back, I do know that I've failed as a husband. I'll admit to that. What I won't admit to is bein' a failure as a father."

"I don't think any of us would say that, Daddy."

"Good. I need to hear that. Now, let's get back to my inconsistency of dealin' with Mr. Malone. I'm gettin' some help from a retired Texas Ranger. He says we need hard evidence down at the Lone Star. He suggests we avail ourselves of a roll of film from a Thursday night session. That's where I need your help."

"A roll of film?"

"Yes. A roll that he's taken at the Lone Star. The upcomin' third Thursday of the month."

"Well, I can't up and ask him for a roll of film that he's maybe taken at the Lone Star. Is that what y'all are askin'?"

"No. You can't ask him for anythin'. You can't suggest anythin'. You have to act like all is well with the world, your work, your relationship with him. All of it has to be peachy-keen."

"So how do I get a roll of film? Steal it? Y'all are puttin' me in a hard place. I could lose my job and I'll most likely lose a friend. He's been a friend, Daddy. He's changed my life for the better. Thanks to him, I know what I want to be. I don't want to lose that. I don't want to see him in jail either, even if he's what you say he is. I still can't believe it all. I don't know why he would do such a thing."

"Money, that's why. Money, and a lack of an ethical code of conduct. My new Ranger friend says people do bad things and think they can get away with it because they think there will be no consequences for what they are doin', or they think they can escape the consequences, or they don't know what the consequences are in the first place. Mr. Malone is smart enough to know there are consequences for what he's doin'. He just figures that he can get away with what he's doin', pure and simple. He figures someone has his back, thinks he has friends in high places."

"Why don't you just let it all be?"

"Well, sometimes in life you have to take the high moral ground. Believe me, I've given the mess at the Lone Star a lot of thought. Keeps me up at nights. That and your mother's leavin', the splittin' up of the family. What's happenin' at the Lone Star isn't a case where a body has to tolerate the worst of things in defense of the best of things."

"What's that mean?"

"I'm sayin' that there's freedom of expression and free speech and so on. That's all well and good. But there's also, like I said, the high moral ground where a person has to stand up and be a citizen, give a hoot about the common good, the moral fabric of our society even if it costs him personally. What good is a life if one turns one's back on tough moral issues?"

"You've lost me Daddy, I..."

"What if the girls in the Lone Star photo were your sisters? Would that change the way you think about it?"

"They wouldn't ever..."

"The point is, James Ray, the girls are someone's sisters, daughters at least. Don't they deserve savin'?"

"Maybe they don't want savin'?"

"It's possible they don't. How do we know how compromised they are, whether they do or do not want savin'? The Lamar Hotel girl, the Fields girl, the girl who jumped to her death, she was a model for Mr. Malone..."

"You don't know that."

"I pretty much do, but let me finish. She was a model. Now she's dead. Took her own life. Is it possible, even likely, that she committed suicide because of what was goin' on at the Lone Star? That maybe she carried around enough guilt that she saw no way out? That our good Mr. Malone was more than an employer? That he had a role in her death? Maybe even, that she was pregnant with his child?"

"I don't think we'll ever know the answer to that since she can't speak for herself."

"That's the point, James Ray. That's what I'm talkin' about. Young kids often can't speak for themselves. That's where the law and morality come in. I feel called upon to do somethin' about it and I will, whether you help me or not."

"So what do you want me to do?"

"Steal a roll of film."

Chapter 34 - Planetary Alignment

"First the daughter, now the mother? In between, the father blows his brains out? I've never seen anythin' like it."

"Dixie, let's focus on what we can do here and not dwell on some kind of planetary convergence if that's where you're headed. Can we do that?" asked Doctor Kearshammer.

"Of course, it just seems inexplicable that..."

"The explaining will be done by the authorities. We're responsible for the treatment."

Nurse Dixie Horseman was a staunch believer in astrology. Given the exact moment of Judith Chambers' birth, armed with an astrology chart and other tools of the trade, she was confident she could identify a reason or reasons why the Chambers woman should not have left the house that evening. At the very least, her horoscope would have told her to exercise extreme caution should she choose to do so. Without that knowledge, the woman could have been easily victimized, and victimized she was, no matter what the doctor believed.

Earlier, she had also made an effort to read the victim's palm shortly after Judith was admitted. It was an old habit that was hard to break. Perhaps the patient's palm held some clue that would be helpful. She had only gotten to Judith's lifeline when the doctor had reentered the room and interrupted her. The lifeline news wasn't good.

"We're done for now, Dixie, Dr. Kearshammer said. "Thank you for your help and please keep a close eye on the patient in room seven. Keep him sedated. He tried to walk out of the hospital last night. You weren't here. What a brouhaha that was. Anyway, I need to talk with the Chambers' daughter. Sorry, who was it again that brought her in?"

"Well, her daughter and the Turman man and his son. The three of 'em, actually. I suppose the boy and his daddy are friends with the Chambers... what's left of the family. Anyway, the daughter found her mother in her car. It was parked on the street outside their home. She must have called the Turmans for help. I don't know. You can ask them."

"Thank you, Dixie. Oh, will you ask the daughter to come in?"

"I will."

Dixie walked to the waiting room. She introduced herself. She hadn't had the opportunity when Judith was admitted to the emergency room.

"Y'all's mother will be fine. A day or two and she'll be in shipshape. The doctor wants to see you."

"I see Ruth Ann is y'all's name. What a nice name. Sorry about y'all's daddy. Now your mother. It was you, just a week ago. Your family sure has had a hard run lately. When were y'all born, if you don't mind me askin'?"

Ruth Ann looked at Dixie for several seconds before answering. "I'm sixteen, if that's what you're askin'. I'll be seventeen in three months."

"Actually, I need the day and month and year. And, the exact time of your arrival would be most helpful, I..."

"Excuse me. Nurse Dixie. Dixie is it?" J.B. interrupted. "I don't for the life of me see what relevance Ruth Ann's...are y'all into astrology? Is that it?"

Dixie blushed, craned her neck, and didn't respond to J.B.'s inquiry.

"May I see my mother?" Ruth Ann asked.

"Certainly, follow me." Dixie gave J.B. a stern look.

J.B. and James Ray remained behind. "A hard run. I don't know whether a hard run is a good description of what's happened to 'em," James Ray offered.

"More like an apocalypse than a hard run." J.B. said. "And then the Dixieland nurse starts to probe for astrological information. What kind of hospital is this? Was she around when you were here?"

"No, I don't think so."

James Ray changed the subject. "Do you think Ruth Ann's mother drank so much she passed out? Ruth Ann says she has a problem with alcohol."

"I remember you mentioned that fact. I don't know much about how much a body can drink and still stand up or, in this case, drive home from wherever she was. I don't know. Actually, I'm convinced she didn't drive herself home. I wonder if it could have happened right in front of her house, on the street and all. Anyway, drivin' seems out of the question. She would have ended up on the side of the road or in some cornfield somewhere. I imagine the doctor can figure out what it was that caused her to be so sick and pass out and all."

The two fell into silence. It was two in the morning. J.B. had to report to work in another six hours. James Ray had until noon to show up at the *Tribune*.

"I noticed y'all were holdin' hands. How's all that goin'?"

"Goin' good, I think. She likes the pictures I've taken of her. I took her to the red-lighted tombstone. She got a kick out of that."

"Well, good. I'm glad y'all are here for her in her time of need. I hope that..."

"Excuse me, gentlemen," Nurse Dixie said. "The doctor wants to talk to you both."

"To see us?" J.B. responded.

"I believe that's what I just said."

"Well, all right. Do you need to know my date of birth before we follow you?"

Dixie frowned, but said nothing in reply.

James Ray and J.B. fell in line behind the side-to-side, path-clearing sway of Dixie's hips. *Enough backside for any three women,* thought J.B.

Dixie opened the door to a small conference room. She motioned them in and left without saying a word.

"I'm Doctor Kearshammer. Please be seated." Again, names were exchanged. J.B. was surprised he didn't know the doctor. Perhaps he was new to the hospital.

"Ruth Ann has asked that you two be present. It's unusual, but given the circumstances, I've agreed to her request."

"Thank you for bein' here," Ruth Ann said. She reached over and took James Ray's hand. She began to cry. "The...the doctor says...he says...he says mother was a victim...a victim of ill intent."

"Well, can you be more specific?" J.B. asked the doctor.

"It appears she had nonconsensual sex. Let me back up. Here's what we know. She overdosed on alcohol and perhaps, a barbiturate of some kind. There's evidence that she's had sex and given her overall condition, someone has had his way with her."

"Rape, you're sayin'?"

"Yes. Ruth Ann, are you sure you want to hear all this?"

"I do. I need to know. How can I deal with...with it all if...if I don't know...don't know what it is she's been through?"

J.B. handed Ruth Ann his handkerchief.

"Ruth Ann, does your mother take drugs? How about her alcohol use?"

"She...she drank too much, but she stopped. At least I thought she had. Stopped after my stepfather killed himself. Drug wise, she's never taken anythin' but aspirin as far as I know."

"Unless she was getting help, changing a dependency is a difficult thing to do by one's self. Maybe she relapsed."

"Doctor...I'm sorry, I think I've missed y'all's last name," J.B. said.

"It's Kearshammer, as in curse and hammer. Doctor Robert Kearshammer."

"May I just call you Doctor Robert?"

"Most do. Yes, that's fine."

"Well, seems to me, Ruth Ann's mother couldn't have driven in her condition. How's that explained?"

"I don't know. That's for the authorities to determine. I need to ask you, Ruth Ann, if you want me to notify the sheriff and report what I've found, or do you wish to do that?"

Ruth Ann looked to J.B.

"I think we should talk to your mother first," J.B. said. "Let her decide what should or shouldn't be done. Is that okay with you?"

Ruth Ann nodded in the affirmative.

"What's her prognosis, Dr. Robert?"

"We pumped her stomach. She's resting well for now. We'll watch her closely throughout the rest of the night and into tomorrow. If all goes well, she might be able to go home in a day or so. If not, we'll keep her as long as she needs our help."

J.B. spoke. "May I ask a question, Ruth Ann? It might not be pleasant."

Ruth Ann nodded her head. She and James Ray were seated. She wiped another tear from her face. She leaned over and put her head on James Ray's shoulder. She fixed her gaze on a full-figured rendition of Jesus that hung on the wall. He had sandy looking hair. In his fixed gaze, he appeared calm and confident in who he was. He wore a flowing robe and sandals. She wondered if he was a carpenter at the time or was it from a period when he was out running around in the hills with his disciples.

"So what you're sayin' is that she was raped," J.B. said. "Taken against her will. Is that right?"

"Without revealing details, I'll tell you what I told Ruth Ann earlier. Things are out of order on her person, if you get my meaning. There's evidence of her having been with someone and the someone, whoever it was, was not careful with how he...how he put things back together."

"Back together?"

"Yes. I don't know any woman who would not try to repair herself after being with someone."

"Repair?"

"Ruth Ann," Doctor Kearshammer asked, "may I speak privately with Mr. Turman?   Do I have your permission to do that?"

Ruth Ann said yes, and she and James Ray left the room.

"We've taken a blood sample and we've frozen what we believe to be semen. Might be needed as evidence later on," the doctor informed J.B.

"I see. What lab do you use?"

"There's a lab we use in Dallas and a new one in Dennison. We'll use the one in Dallas although it might take a day or two longer to get the results."

J.B. scratched his chin and his eyes wandered. He wondered who would do such a thing. Then, he put two and two together. *Judith has a drinking problem and Mayweather's bootleggin' Carl Malone supplies her. I'll bet that's it. Carl Malone. He's the one who's raped Judith. I'll bet my life on it.*

"Mr. Turman?"

"Yes."

"The question you asked earlier?"

"What question did I ask?   Sorry. I got lost in my thoughts."

"About why I believe it wasn't consensual sex."

"Yes, well, what about it?"

"You saw the state she was in. Like I said before, a woman puts herself back together after having consensual sex. Mrs. Chambers has been roughed up. She is missing her undergarment. And..."

"What do you mean? Her panties?   Sorry, I didn't mean to interrupt."

"That's okay. Yes. What woman wouldn't replace her panties after sex unless she was going to bed. Most likely, she'd replace them even then. From what I am able to tell, the perpetrator also engaged in anal penetration. She was sodomized."

"What? How do you know such a thing?"

"Semen. From where you would expect it and from elsewhere. Whoever it was, he took his time with her."

"Good God. Her husband's dead from a self-inflicted gunshot and now this."

"Seems whoever compromised her didn't wear protection."

"Mr. Turman?"

"Yes."

"What's your relationship with Mrs. Chambers?"

"Why do you...what are you implyin'?"

"Nothing, other than that anyone who knows her will be questioned if she decides to report the incident."

"Yes, I'm sure they will be. I'll be more than happy to help in any way I can."

"Which room were you in when you had polio?" Ruth Ann asked after they were in the hall. A groan emanated from room seven.

"For a few days toward the end, the one your mother's in. The one with the picture of Jesus. I looked at that picture until I was sick of it. He just stood there, lookin' on, and sayin' nothin', and doin' nothin' for weeks on end."

Nurse Dixie noted the two as they returned to the waiting room.

"Let's go outside," suggested Ruth Ann.

"Okay. I wish somethin' was open. I'd buy you a banana split or somethin'."

"You know I can't have such a concoction. Coach would have a conniption."

"I like that."

"What?"

"New name for a banana split. The conniption concoction. That's good."

The night was black and radiant with starlight. Given the hour, there was no coming or going, either in the hospital parking lot or on the streets adjacent. A crescent moon hung over them.

"I wonder why they say there's a man in the moon," Ruth Ann said.

"Why do you ask?"

"I don't know. Just a question. All of a sudden it seems I live in a world full of questions with no answers."

"What do you mean?"

"Bud. My mother. Me. Why all of the misery and heartache? What did any of us do to bring on such misery?"

Ruth Ann began to cry again.

"I'm so sorry, I..."

"Don't need to be sorry. It puts watchin' me naked in the shower in perspective. I'd let you do it every day if it could help remove some of the misery."

James Ray didn't comment. He liked the idea but thought it wise not to participate in subject matter that reflected poorly on his character, even when given an opening.

"My boyfriend in Fort Worth is no longer a boyfriend," Ruth Ann volunteered. "I thought y'all might like to hear that."

"I'll say. That's good news indeed. What happened?"

"He dumped me. I was goin' to give him the boot but he beat me to it. Guess I'm too slow on the draw."

"Does he have his head screwed on wrong or somethin'?"

"Not really. He's datin' twins. Twin blondes. He has 'em fightin' over him. They think he's the cat's meow."

"Well, good for him. Meow and all. Tell him to keep up the good work. For me, I'll settle for you fightin' over me. One Ruth Ann Chambers is all I need. Two of 'em would be far too much for me to handle."

"You're sweet, James Ray. That's what won me over. Your patience, and your sweetness, and y'all's sense of humor. And you tell a good story too, once you stop and get it straight and all."

James Ray held her close. They kissed. "I thank you for the compliment. Maybe I'm some kind of cat's meow myself. I'll have to go look in the mirror."

Ruth Ann smiled and looked at the moon overhead.

"What's goin' to happen with Bud's service now that he's...sorry, I shouldn't have asked that question."

"It's all right. I don't know. When mother is better we'll find out. It'll be in Fort Worth, I know that. Might be held without mother there. I really don't know."

"What about tonight? James Ray asked. "Where're you gonna sleep? Are you afraid to be alone?"

"I'm not afraid but I'm goin' home with you and your daddy anyway. It wouldn't be proper for you to stay with me. The town has enough to talk about."

"Well, you're welcome to stay with us. My sisters, well, they're gone as you know, and you could have one of their beds. Would that be good?"

J.B. found the two outside.

"Ruth Ann is comin' home with us, Daddy. Is that okay? She doesn't want to be alone."

"Just fine. We'll be mighty pleased to have you. Do you need to pick up anythin' at your house?"

"Yes, my nightie and some this and that girl stuff."

The three walked to the hospital parking lot. "I like your new car," Ruth Ann offered. "James Ray drove me in it the other day. A couple of days after we went out to the red-lighted tombstone. Scared me half to death with his story-tellin'."

"I expect he did. Thank you for likin' the car. It got me into a heap of trouble with my wife. I suppose I was in trouble already and the car just added to the pile."

James Ray and Ruth Ann were seated in the cavernous back seat of the Hudson, she close by his side. They held hands.

"Sorry to hear about y'all's situation. I don't know what it is about marriage. My mother and Bud fought all the time."

"Well, Sarah Mae and I didn't fight. I don't know which is worse. There were things in our marriage that needed to be fought over but they always ended up festerin' instead. Festerin' over time isn't good. I think it's better to get things out in the open. Throw the saucer. Get red faced. Whoop and holler and get it out. For better or worse, that wasn't our style. We kept things tucked away, darker than the inside of James Ray's mother's storm shelter."

Chapter 35 - Same Difference

"Booker, all you have to do is turn your head," J.B. pleaded. "That's all. I'll take full responsibility. If it comes to it, I'm willin' to go to jail to solve this problem. First the Lone Star and now Judith Chambers. Who's next, Book? We've got to put a stop to the madness."

The two men were in Booker T.'s backyard. Booker T. looked skyward. What his friend J.B. was asking put him at risk. There were two sets of rules in his world; one for white folks and yet another for colored people. What a white person might do, illegal though it was, would be met with far less punishment than if a colored person did the same thing. There were consequences...and then there were consequences! He didn't want to be on the receiving end of any kind, white or colored.

"Mr. J.B., I don't know why..."

"Book, you haven't called me Mr. J.B. since we met. I asked y'all not to. We're friends. We go back. We've shared good times and bad times. Our relationship is, I'm proud to say, reflective of a standard that should and will over time be seen as normal, not out-of-place or unusual. I hope we both live long enough to see the day."

"I do know that. I do appreciate what we've had together, we Johnsons and Turmans. Dignity is hard to find in my world, J.B., and y'all make me feel like I have some worth. I so do appreciate it. It's just that y'all are puttin' me in between a rock and some hard place. What if Mr. Carl finds out you went and stole his film and up and wants to know how y'all got into his darkroom?"

"I'll simply own up to takin' your keys and to enactin' the whole crime. Thing is, Book, he won't be askin' any questions from behind bars. The law will put him in his place, take away his camera and darkroom, his bootleggin' and the rest of whatever he's involved with. The man's a criminal, through and through. He's done despicable things. It would be hard to list all the bad things he's done. All I need is evidence of his wrong doin' at the Lone Star to hit him with the sledgehammer of justice. That's all."

J.B. detailed his plan of action as the two stood in the shade of a tree in Booker T.'s back yard. The one that still held their boys' tree house.

"I'll even mow y'all's lawn. Twice a week, if you want."

Booker T. laughed. "That'd be a sight. A white man up and mowin' a colored man's backyard. Now y'all are talkin', that just might make me change my mind."

"I would do it. I would..."

"J.B., why would you want to go and ruin y'all's reputation in town?"

"My reputation is sunk anyway. Went to the bottom when Sarah Mae left, takin' the two girls with her. I can claim that she left because of the cancer but I know people are talkin' like they always do. I see the way they look at me and there's nothin' I can do about it. Then the paper's gone and run an article along with a picture taken by my own son callin' attention to Sarah Mae's holdin' up some house movers. So much for my reputation. If I get into trouble for sneakin' away with a roll of film, it's petty theft anyway."

"If I can be honest, J.B., I think y'all are on a fool's errand. Y'all are puttin' you, y'all's boy, and me in a spot with no wiggle room. I do fear there'll be nothin' good come from it. I guarantee my Eartha will think the same."

"Maybe so. But maybe she'll be proud of all of us for doin' the community a favor by gettin' rid of a worse than bad character. Besides, I have a friend who's helpin' me. He's a retired Texas Ranger. He says authorities, people charged with enforcin' the law, go about bendin' the law all the time when they have a need to gather evidence. They pretty much do what they have to do to bring a criminal to justice."

"J.B., I'm no expert on thievery but it seems to me that Mr. Carl will figure you got the keys to his darkroom one way or the other. Mostly, I 'spect he'll figure you got 'em from me whether my head was turned or not."

"Well, like I say, once we have proof of his law breakin' he'll get..."

"That may be in y'all's white world. Maybe he'll get what he deserves. In my world, breakin' the law is breakin' the law no matter what. We colored folk don't get the breaks y'all white folk do. I might get accused for bein' an accomplice or somethin'. You would likely get let go but me bein' colored and all, I'll go to prison or get horsewhipped or some such."

"I understand y'all's worry but you're an innocent in all this, Book. There's absolutely no need for you to worry. You'll have done nothin' to be accused of. Like I said, if it comes to it, I'll take all the blame for whatever happens. Book, look. You've not said no to my takin' the keys when you're busy cleanin' so I'm takin' y'all's no answer for a yes answer. James Ray knows which ones open the darkroom. He'll be with me. We'll be in and out before you can say Jack Robinson."

Booker T. didn't answer. He reached down and picked up a baseball Sammy had left in the grass which appeared to be too tall to be easily mowed. He tossed the ball into the air, catching it on the way down in his leviathan hand.

J.B. followed the motion of the ball; its toss upward and its gravity-driven descent back into Booker T.'s hand. Up with the whiteness of the ball, down to the darkness of Booker T.'s hand. Up and down, black and white, white and black, down and up.

"I have grave misgivin's about it, J.B. Mighty grave misgivin's, but yes, y'all can take 'em when I'm not lookin'. I don't like hearin' about what's goin' on either. It's a shame, all of it. It would be easy for me to say y'all white people make a mess of most things and that what's goin' on is none of my colored, segregated, keep-to-my-own-kind business, but I won't. You can borrow the keys when I've got my back turned. Maybe I'll be in Mr. Spencer's office cleanin'. Don't let me see you take 'em. That way I can tell the honest to God truth."

"He has two locks, doesn't he? One for each door?"

"He do. James Ray knows the keys. When are y'all goin' to rob him?"

"We aren't goin' to rob him, Book. We're just relievin' him of a roll of film, that's all. One single, solitary, little roll of film. Nothin' more. He won't even miss it, never know it's gone."

*   *   *   *   *

"He told me he hit a ball over four hundred feet. Imagine that. It was a tape-measure home run," James Ray said.

"He must be proud of himself. Is he plannin' on playin' in the Negro League?" Ruth Ann asked.

She and James Ray were seated on the front porch of the Chambers house. Judith had been released from the hospital and was resting inside. Sheriff Albertson had come and gone. He had picked over Judith's Buick, then returned to his office. Rape got special attention throughout the south. There always existed the possibility that a Negro might be the wrong-doer. In 1943, a colored man from Farmers Branch outside of Dallas was convicted and executed for just such a crime. He met the infamous "Old Sparky" in Huntsville at the ripe old age of twenty-one. He claimed innocence from beginning to end.

"Major leagues. He'll be the next Jackie Robinson except he's bigger and taller. Jackie might be faster but Sammy can hit a ball a country mile. Says he wants to play first base. Bein' so tall and all, I think that would be a good position."

"Why?"

"He can stretch out and catch balls, puttin' runners out before they reach the base." James Ray reached out with his arm, stretching it toward the steps as if they were first base in some famous major league ballpark. "He should be here shortly. I'm anxious for y'all to meet him."

"Eager, is the word. Y'all are 'eager' to meet him. If you were 'anxious' to meet him y'all would be, well, anxious, nervous maybe. See the difference? Or, maybe y'all are anxious after all."

"I'm not. Correction noted. Where do y'all teach English?"

"Right now? On my front porch."

"I see. Well, let me ask you this. Are y'all sure you're all right with havin' Sammy over? I asked you before, but I need to be sure. Maybe y'all are anxious about meetin' him. I don't want to embarrass him. We've been friends since forever."

"Like I said, it's fine. My mother used to have a colored friend."

"She did?"

"Yes, when she was in college. Before she had to drop out. I remember him. He was nice. I remember he made my mother laugh. Bud never made her laugh. That's one reason I like you, James Ray. You make me laugh."

"If y'all don't mind me askin', were they more than friends, if you know what I mean?"

"Of course I know what you mean. Maybe. I don't know. I was only eight or nine at the time. What does a child know at that age about parents anyway? I do remember someone took chalk and wrote, "Nigger lover" on our front door. That I do remember. It took mother some time to get rid of the markin'. I can't remember his name. Otis? Anyway, he was nice to me and to my mother."

"Things must be different in Fort Worth. I can't imagine a colored man around here bein' able to even visit an unmarried white woman at her house. Especially one as pretty as your mom."

"Well, I don't know. Prejudice is prejudice, I suspect, no matter..."

Ruth Ann stopped in mid-sentence. James Ray froze. The hair on his arms rose and the back of his neck stiffened. He heard the reprobate car before he saw it. At its wheel was a smiling Rusty Wickware, his teeth reflecting white inside the darkness of the car. Inside, James Ray could see members of his gang. The Dodge coughed and snorted as it came to a halt behind Judith's Buick. Rusty exited. His tagalongs remained inside. Rusty was carrying a bouquet of daisies. James Ray stood.

A mere half-block away from Ruth Ann's house, Sammy too, observed the Dodge's arrival.

*   *   *   *   *

Dear J.B.:

We are here, finally. It was a very long and difficult trip, but our Savior Jesus Christ saw us through the journey's shadow. The girls are fine. Faith loves California. Hope not so much, but she will adjust. A church neighbor took the girls to the beach yesterday. They both came back with sunburns even though I oiled them well. They are both so fair.

Daddy just sits and stares. I tried to take him out yesterday for a walk but he doesn't want to go anywhere, anymore. It's sad, but we are doing everything in our power to help him. I have an appointment with my doctor tomorrow. I now have three lumps. Seems like I'm growing them like turnips. Anyway, I drove by my new school. It's only two years old, and in a beautiful setting. The air isn't very good here, though. They call it smog. Anyway, the school is where an olive orchard used to be. If you hear from Seth, I'd appreciate it if you would forward his letter. Please tell him to use mother's address if he wants to contact me here in California. It's crowded at mother's house but it will make-do until I can get a place of our own. She appreciates me cooking and helping with Daddy. She loves having the girls around. How is James Ray?

Bye for now, Sarah Mae.

J.B. placed the letter on the kitchen table. "Bye for now?" he said aloud. *Good gravy. Bye for now. No mention of me whatsoever, other than a salutation and a carefree, chatty bye for now. By now I could've been taken by one of her tornadoes, dead and gone for all she knows or cares.*

J.B. needed to talk to James Ray about specific plans for bringing light to Carl's misconduct by absconding with a roll of his film. The third Thursday of the month would be on the twenty-first. If things went according to past example, the kids would come in from wherever it was they came from, Carl would do his illicit picture taking and he would, J.B. hoped, drop off the exposed but undeveloped film at the paper's darkroom. He and James Ray would ask Booker T. to let them in through the paper's back door. James Ray would claim to have left his wallet in the darkroom in an effort to provide Booker T. with plausible denial.

Booker T., of course, would know what they were up to, but neither J.B. nor James Ray would say or do anything that would implicate him. He could swear on a dozen bibles he had no knowledge of anything except that on the night of the twenty-first of August, J.B. and his son had shown up at the paper looking to retrieve James Ray's wallet. He could swear that on that fateful night, if it came to it, no one asked him for keys to the darkroom. That and nothing more. He saw nothing. He and J.B. had talked. He would say he did not see James Ray either enter or exit the darkroom. James Ray would find his wallet somewhere and as far as the darkroom was concerned, maybe it had been left unlocked. Booker T. had been told by Carl to never enter the darkroom, and he had honored the request. And if an open door possibility existed, keys would be of no concern. Maybe James Ray would simply enter the darkroom, find his wallet, and that would be the long and short of it.

Charlie, his Texas Ranger friend, had warned J.B. that it was entirely possible Carl might simply take the film home with him and develop it at a later time. What then?

"Well, I don't know," J.B. had replied. "My boy says he doesn't have a darkroom at home, so I know he has to develop the film at the paper. I don't know how he has time to do his work for the paper and time leftover to do his mischief work as well."

"Maybe he does. People can make it look like they are busier than they are. I worked with some people who took days to do what a motivated person might do in half the time. I was one of 'em sometimes. Especially toward the end of my career."

"Well, here's my guess given what James Ray has told me. I'll bet he takes the film to the paper and either develops it right then and there, or he sets it aside somewhere to develop at a later time, like you say, when things aren't too busy and all. My boy has shown up to work a couple of times and Carl has sent him away, sayin' that he doesn't need him. Or, could it be that he doesn't want him instead? Maybe those are the times he goes about developing and printing."

"Could be. Could be he doesn't either develop or print his work."

"What are y'all sayin'?"

"Let's say he tucks away the film, and then at a time that's convenient, he sends it off to someone, somewhere, for processing."

"I hadn't thought of that possibility. How'd that work?"

"Don't have a clue. This is as new to me as it is to you. Maybe he's got connections. Maybe he pays someone to do the grunt work. Simple, really. That would make for a much cleaner operation. He's the artist, the pornographer. From what y'all have told me, he uses a Polaroid camera so he knows he's gettin' good results. So, when he takes the for real pictures, maybe he simply mails 'em off for someone else to take the time and energy to develop and print 'em and distribute them. That way, other than the risk he assumes at the Lone Star, and seems to me that's a big one, he reduces the likelihood that he'll be discovered."

"I see, but what about turnin' away my boy from work?"

"Could be he really didn't need him. I don't know. Anyway, we'll know on the night of the twenty-first whether he takes the film to the paper or takes it home. My guess is he'll drop it off. By the way, how are y'all goin' to gain access if he has a locked cabinet? You'll have keys to the two darkroom doors, but how about the cabinet?"

"When James Ray was cleanin' up one day, he noticed a single key on the top of a shelf. We're bettin' that's the one that opens the cabinet, if that's the place he puts his film. Maybe he just leaves the film on a shelf. I suppose we'll find out."

"So you're gonna observe from the roof of the drugstore, right? And I'm staking out the Tribune to see what happens there. You'll document when he leaves the hotel and I'll note the time he arrives at the paper and when he leaves for that matter. If you need to join me for some reason, I'll be in my car on the corner of Elm and Fourth Avenue. Maroon '49 Nash. You can see right into the back of the buildin' from there."

"Right. And this time, we're goin' to be early gettin' to the rooftop. Last time, we caught no sight of anyone who looked like he was a photographer type of person. No yellow Cadillac, no nothin' other than the kids comin' and goin' and the flashin' from the window. My guess is he arrives early and sets up and is ready for the kids. No wasted time. That's my guess. James Ray says it takes time to set up artificial light situations like that because it takes light stands and light reflectin' umbrellas and whatnot."

"So y'all watch from the roof of the drug store," Charlie mused. "Y'all see what y'all can see. And your boy will take pictures again?"

"Yes. He'll hopefully get one of Carl or the kids, I don't know. We may as well try even though The Lone Star is pretty far away for his camera."

"No matter. Documentation, a picture in this case, can be highly prized as evidence. There are ways of enhancing images on film. I don't understand it all but things can be blown up from the original size and all. I'd suggest y'all's boy do what he can do. What he comes up with will hopefully go along with our eye witness account. If all goes well, y'all's good judge, what's-his-name, will be satisfied."

"Well, I hope so."

"J.B. y'all know that if you come up with a roll of film, no matter what it reveals, it can't be used as evidence. Much of what we're doin' can't be used. You know that, right? Not havin' a search warrant. Us not bein' official and all."

"I do. Judge Schmid told me that's why we can't stage a raid when he's there at the hotel doin' his picture takin'. We don't have a search warrant. Can't go and round all of 'em up like a herd of wild horses. I know that. But, if I do have somethin' other than the one pornographic picture I already have, and I have eye witnesses to the comin' and goin', y'all's testimony included, he said he'd authorize a grand jury investigation. That's my goal.

Bypass our sorry excuse of a sheriff, bypass our lazy and incompetent district attorney, get a grand jury organized, then I'll be done with the whole matter. I can go back to my life, such as it is."

Chapter 36 - Disarmed

"It's all organized. Next Thursday we'll stake out the Lone Star again."

"Again?"

"Yes, again. This will be the last time. I'm sure of it. I also need you to take pictures again."

"Daddy, from that distance I can't get..."

"Don't worry about what you can or can't do. Just take the pictures. If I'm right, I think at the end of the day we'll have our man."

"And that man, you think, is Carl?"

"We've got help, this time. A retired Texas Ranger is goin' to help us. Here's what we're goin' to do."

J.B. detailed his plan to James Ray. James Ray was most worried about his father's brash idea to steal a roll of film from the paper's darkroom. Would Carl drop off the film in the first place? A bigger question was whether or not Carl was the picture taker. James hoped beyond hope that he wasn't. It was that hope that gave him reason to say yes to his father. If Carl wasn't taking pictures at the Lone Star, he wouldn't be arrested and charged with pornography. Further, James Ray wouldn't lose his job.

"OK, I guess so. Seems crazy to me. The whole thing. I'd like to be done with it. It's hard workin' with Carl with you thinkin' he's a criminal and all. Makes me nervous."

"I expect so. You need to know I hate havin' to put you in such a situation. Makes me feel like a sorry rear-end of a daddy askin' my own son to steal."

"Well, it's good, I guess, that we have a Texas Ranger to help. That makes me feel a little better."

*　　*　　*　　*　　*

No sooner than he was out of his car, Rusty noted Sammy's approach. Motionless, he watched Sammy's long, confident strides. He was discomposed to see James Ray's colored friend enter the scene.

"What do you want, Rusty?" James Ray asked. Ruth Ann rose and stood along side James Ray.

"Didn't come here to talk to you, Turman. I've got business with Ruth Ann." He turned to face Ruth Ann. "I brought y'all some more flowers. I'm guessin' the first ones I brought y'all have seen their glory days." He smiled his best of smiles.

"That's nice. Y'all are right. The others you brought me when I was in the hospital are pretty much done, but I have a question for you?"

"What's that," Rusty asked, maintaining his expansive smile.

"Are you here to offer me flowers but can't find it within yourself to be pleasant? If that's the case, I'll ask you to leave."

Sammy reached the house and stopped on the grass, facing Wickware. His arms were folded. He said nothing. He stood on the upper edge of the sloped lawn above Rusty.

From Rusty's perspective, down-looking-up from the sidewalk, Sammy appeared larger and stronger than he had when Rusty had spied him on the sidewalk and yelled "nigger" from behind the wheel of his Dodge.

Carl had explained the nature of such a perspective.

If you want a subject, say a child, to gain visual importance, get down into their world. Shoot them straight on or from a down-shooting-up camera angle. That way, your subject will communicate a stronger visual image. The subject will seem bigger than life, more meaningful, more powerful, more expressive.

Rusty couldn't muster words to answer Ruth Ann's question. Yet again, in James Ray's presence, he found himself disarmed and flummoxed.

The four were like remaining pieces in a game of chess. The match had come to a halt while moves were considered or rejected. No one spoke. Silence enveloped Ruth Ann's front lawn and porch.

Ruth Ann broke the silence. "This is James Ray's friend, Sammy," she said to Rusty, pointing in the direction of Sammy. "I invited him over. Pretty soon, I'm goin' to make some sandwiches. Would y'all like to join us?"

"Me, eat with a nigger?"

Sammy dropped his arms from his chest and clenched his fists, but said nothing in reply. He was on white property in the white part of town. He would remain silent and let Ruth Ann or James Ray do the talking.

"You can leave now, Rusty," James Ray said. "I don't take kindly to insults directed at my friends."

"Is that so? Now, do tell, what are y'all going to do about it, Turman? Get fierce with me? Step down from the porch steps and clean my plow?"

"Rusty," Ruth Ann asked, "what exactly is it that makes you so angry?"

"Oh, I'm not angry. I just don't like bein' provoked. There's hell to pay when I'm provoked."

"Seems to me, from what I've heard, y'all are pretty much provoked twenty-four hours a day. Where does that come from? That's what I'd like to know. Does your daddy beat you or somethin'? If that's the case, maybe that's why you parade around town with no end to y'all's bullin' ways.

"No. He don't beat me no more, I'm too big..."

"So he did beat you when you were little. When y'all were a boy? Is that right?"

"I ain't here to discuss..."

"And how did y'all learn to dislike people of a different race. We were all born pure as the driven snow, but somewhere along the way, some of us are taught to fear and to hate people who aren't exactly like ourselves.

"What's that supposed to mean? Look, I brought you flowers. I saved y'all's life and now you up and..."

"Am I goin' to be next on y'all's list? If so, I'm sorry about that. I appreciate y'all's savin' my life. I really do. I told you so. And I appreciate y'all bringin' me flowers. What I don't appreciate is the hostility toward James Ray and his friend Sammy. This could have been a friendly time. You bringin' me flowers. You saying hello and bein' nice to someone y'all have been goin' to school with since first grade. You gettin' to know someone from a different race, lettin' bygones be bygones, but no, you have to turn it all into some kind of cockfight. Kick and peck until someone goes down bleedin', mortally wounded either by words or deeds."

"Well, that's some sermon," Rusty said in response.

"I didn't intend a sermon. You brought it on, though. Please leave."

"You need the flowers or not?"

"I don't 'need' the flowers. The question is whether or not I 'want' the flowers. The answer is, no thank you. I appreciate y'all's offer. I only wish it could have been made with generosity beyond the flowers. Someday when I tell my kids about y'all savin' my life, I wish I could say that the Samaritan who saved me didn't have a lifetime chip on his shoulder. That's somethin' y'all have to work on, Rusty. Less a chip on y'all's shoulder and a little true generosity. Less anger, more acceptance, and more generosity. Y'all will live longer if you can manage that."

Rusty turned and threw the flowers to the sidewalk. "Fuck you, Turman!" he yelled as he left. "Fuck you, you coon lover! Y'all's days are numbered, hear me?"

James Ray shrugged. "Last time I heard tell, all of our days are numbered."

He turned to Ruth Ann after watching a chastened Wickware depart. She was beautiful in the soft fill-light of the porch. He took in the resolve of her jaw, the fold of her arms across her chest, the strength of her character, her Wonder Woman grit and resolve. He loved her more each day. She was smart, beautiful, and could use words in powerful and meaningful ways. He had always thought his daddy was skillful with words. On many an occasion, his daddy had left an adversary stunned by a steady stream of either sarcasm or outright logic or a hefty one-two combination of both. Ruth Ann, James Ray figured, although not half his daddy's age, could, if put against his daddy in some kind of verbal see-who's-left-standing challenge, more than hold her own.

*   *   *   *   *

J.B. sat by Judith's bed. She was home. Ruth Ann had begged J.B. to come and talk to her mother; to try and unravel what had happened to her, and to persuade her to agree to report the incident if a rape had indeed taken place.

Ruth Ann and James Ray were in the kitchen adding a pinch of sugar to a pitcher of iced tea.

"Here's the thing," J.B. said. "I know it's a hard subject but..."

"I really don't want to talk about it. I told Ruth Ann. I told the doctor and now I'm tellin' you. I don't want to talk about it."

"I know that. I know it must be hard for..."

"No you don't. You don't have any idea, bein' a man and all."

"I'm sure you're right. I don't have any idea and I wouldn't be here if Mr. Chambers were here, but y'all's Ruth Ann wanted me, implored me, to come and talk to you. Just look at what y'all as a family have gone through in the last couple of weeks. I dare say..."

"Don't dare say anythin'. Please go away."

"Look, Judith. What's happened to you is nothin' short of tragic and...and I'm goin' to be completely honest here, and if you throw me out, well then, throw me out. At the very least I will have honored your daughter's request. She's a good girl and she is worried beyond worried about you."

"Well, get on with it and then please leave. I want to be alone."

"Were you victimized? The doctor says you were."

Judith turned her head from J.B. and the searing heat of the question. "You mean was I raped?"

"Well...yes, I suppose that's..."

"I don't want to talk about it."

"You asked me to get on with it. Judith, if you were victimized, raped, we need, sorry, you need to report it. If you give me permission, I'll report it. The longer it goes unreported the less weight it will carry. Immediacy is important. Tonight will mark the third night followin' what happened to you. Any further delay will work to your disadvantage, and really, too much time has already passed."

"Like I said," Judith replied, turning back to face J.B., "I have nothin' to say about the matter. Ruth Ann?"

"Yes." Ruth Ann walked from the kitchen to her mother's bedroom. James Ray didn't follow.

"Please ask Mr. Turman to leave." Judith requested.

Ruth Ann thought, blinked her eyes, and turned to look at J.B. "Will you stay?"

"Only if..."

"No. Stay for me and stay for mother, too, no matter what she says. Please stay."

Ruth Ann sat on her mother's bed. She took her mother's hand. She began to cry. "Mother, please...please hear us out. This is all so terrible and we have to stand up and face it, no...no matter what. Mr. Turman was the person I called in the middle of the night when I found you in your car. He took you to the hospital. He took me in for both nights while you were in the hospital. He's only tryin' to help. Actin' the way you are won't help anythin'. Please talk to us, please. If not to me, then to Mr. Turman. Please, mother. Let's get a grip on this whole thing. Enough is enough."

Judith closed her eyes. She recalled being at the old farmhouse. *I remember Carl offered me a drink. Several was it? And I remember breaking a glass. There was a red barn. I remember that. I remember the light was on in the ceiling of his car. The dome light. Yes, the dome light. That's what it's called. I remember bad things started to happen. How did I get into the car? Why would I have done that? That was stupid of me to do. I don't know...I don't really remember. Bastard of a person. Son-of-a-bitch bastard. He raped me. He must have doped me and then he raped me.*

"How did I get home?" she said, opening her eyes.

"From where?" J.B. asked. "Where were you that night?"

"I was at an old farmhouse. No one lives there. Carl is goin' to buy the place. At least that's what he says."

"Carl? Carl Malone? You were with Carl Malone?"

"Yes, the bastard. The lowlife, son-of-a-bitch bastard. Sorry, for my language. I'll have to watch my language. I'm just so angry and upset over it all."

"You should be, Mother. Is he the one who raped you?" Ruth Ann interjected.

"Yes. Who else would it have been? We were alone. It was gettin' dark. I was...I was buyin' some alcohol. I'm a weak person. I...I am..."

Judith reached for Ruth Ann's hand. "Ruth Ann darlin'. I know I promised you I wouldn't drink anymore but with you bein' in the hospital and then Bud takin' his own life...well, it was too much for me. I tried, but it was too much. I'm so sorry."

Judith began to cry.

For a minute or so no one spoke.

"So you went to the farmhouse and then what?" J.B. finally asked. "You don't have to say anythin' that would embarrass you, but what happened in a chronological sort of way? That's important. You went to the farm house. Did you go there together? Did..."

"Please. Stop. May I answer one question at a time?"

"Yes. Sorry. I'm just tryin' to help."

"I met him there."

"You met him there so he could sell you some alcohol. Then what?"

"Well, he offered me a drink. He had a whole setup in the trunk of his car."

Judith asked Ruth Ann for more Kleenex. "Just bring the whole box. He had a travelin' bar of some kind, all in the trunk of his car. I thought it strange but I hadn't had a drink in a few days and I was all strung out mentally and I didn't give it much thought so I went along with it. Stupid me. Anyway...I think...I think he must've put something in my drink. I thought it tasted different...a little sweet but I drank it anyway. I thought it was just the taste of a different vodka. He talked about how he was goin' to move the house to the highway and open a fillin' station and all."

"What then?"

"I had a couple of drinks. More actually. Too much. It sounds stupid, but I was happy to be drinkin' again. Anyway, I don't really remember it all that well. Pretty soon, I got so I couldn't think or stand. It's all a blur after that. He must have gotten me in his car and that's when he...that's when the bad things happened."

"Mother," Ruth Ann interjected, "do you remember what he did to you when you were in his car?"

Judith covered her eyes with both hands. She paused before she spoke. "Some of it yes, but I just couldn't muster the will to resist. I was so weak, so tired, so out of it. That's when he forced himself on me. He was so strong and I was so weak. Then, then he turned me over. I really couldn't...I couldn't stop...I couldn't stop him. How could I have been so stupid? I should...should have known better. That's when I vomited. I remember vomitin' in the back seat. That's when it all stopped."

Judith continued to weep. She turned her head from J.B. and Ruth Ann. The bed soon shook from her convulsive sobbing.

Ruth Ann cried with her. She leaned over and kissed her mother's face. Then, Ruth Ann sought a position on the bed next to her mother; the way her mother had done when Ruth Ann was a child and hurt emotionally. She put one arm around her mother while the other stroked her hair.

"You'll be all right, mother. We'll get through this just like you told me when I was bitten by the snake. Like the time when I broke my ankle jumpin' from a swing. Remember that time? And like a hundred other times when I was wounded by words or deeds. We're here to help you. We'll make it through the storm. We'll make it. I promise you. There'll be a better tomorrow. Today's not so good, that's for sure, but tomorrow will be a better day. I love you. I love you so much. You mean the world to me and you need to be happy in your life. Let's choose happiness. After all the sorrow, let's have some hope and happiness. You've held out hope for me and my swimmin' for how long? Years. Now it's time for me to hold out hope for you. Is that all right Mother? It's my turn. Let me hold out hope for you."

J.B. stood and left the room. He, too, had tears. He walked into the kitchen. James Ray had overheard some of the bedroom conversation. He had heard Carl's name mentioned.

"Is Carl the one who raped her? Tell me Daddy. I need to know the truth."

"Yes, that appears to be the case. The big question is whether or not such a thing can be proven. In a rape situation, a question that's likely to rise is whether or not any woman, Judith included, had it comin'. You know, a woman puts herself in harm's way and then cries rape. That would be his defense, I suppose, if Judith decides to press charges. Anyway, that man has more lives than any dozen alley cats. Guilty as sin for any number of things up to and includin' rape."

"May I have some of the iced tea," J.B. asked. He noticed his throat was dry.

James Ray poked around until he opened a cabinet door containing water glasses.

"Here's the question. When is enough, enough for some people?" J.B. asked.

"What do you mean? I don't follow."

"I don't know that I can answer my own question," J.B. said as he gulped the iced tea and asked for more.

"Here's a man who has a job. He's not down and out. He's employed. Then, he has an unlawful job on the side. He provides who knows how many Mayweather citizens with their desire for alcohol. And then, he runs yet another highly immoral operation down at the Lone Star, possibly involvin' underage kids. And aside from all that, if he doesn't get what he wants, and I assume that's what it was with Ruth Ann's mother, her havin' a need and all and his bein' able to answer that need, he takes advantage and rapes her. That's what I'm tryin' to say. When is enough, enough?"

"I'm sorry I've tried to defend him. I guess I've a lot to learn about people, who they appear to be and who they actually are."

"Well, good luck with that. Take me and y'all's mother as an example. Married for nineteen some years and all of a sudden you wake up and you're married to a stranger."

"Well, I still hold out that y'all will get back together. Mother is goin' through a hard time, not like Ruth Ann's mother, but still, she's got cancer and maybe she's not thinkin' straight."

"Maybe. Anyway, as soon as Mrs. Chambers calms down, I'm goin' to ask her if I have her permission to notify the authorities, such as they are."

Chapter 37 - The Long and Short of it

Judith agreed. There would be accountability. J.B. would accompany Ruth Ann to the sheriff's office and notify Hoghead of the rape. Judith would have to file the official complaint and that would be that. Or maybe not, justice being what it was in Mayweather, thought J.B.

J.B. recalled the day when Booker T.'s dog had been shot by a deputy sheriff, the same sorry excuse of a sheriff who was now toes up from smoking himself to his grave. Sammy was but a baby at the time. The dog, Prince, was a German shepherd. He was kept chained because he had a tendency to bark and menace white people who were careless enough to enter colored town. Dogs on the white side were guilty of similar sins. The Turman's former dog, Soldier, was among them. One day an inebriated white person ambled down East 9th Street and forged forth across the demarcation. It registered not to his addled mind that he was in foreign territory.

Prince barked at the intrusion. The white man barked back. Prince became enraged. He strained the chain to its limit. The man approached and stood within feet of Prince and the confine of his chain. The man continued to taunt Prince. Prince was beside himself. The chain broke from its mooring. Prince's charge caused the man to fall. Prince bit him several times. The man was finally able to right himself and run away. An hour later, the deputy sheriff arrived. He was accompanied by the man. Prince began to bark again. The man pointed in the direction of the dog which had been re-secured by Eartha. The sheriff aimed a double-barreled shotgun at Prince. He shot twice. Prince fell in a heap. Eartha watched from the porch steps. Booker T. was at work. Sammy awoke suddenly from his nap. Given the mayhem of the shotgun blasts, he lapsed into an emotional and shrill fit.

"We have a complaint to bring to y'all's attention," J. B. said to the deputy sheriff. "I do believe we've met."

"Yes, I recall our meetin'," Deputy Dinwitty responded.

"It was down on East 9th," J.B. replied. "My wife was the one who held up the house that was bein' moved. Y'all are here in Mayweather on loan, right?"

"Right. That standoff. Yes, well, that was a crazy situation. There she was, the mite of a woman armed with a shotgun all ready to shoot me because of a little shit of a nothin' robin's nest."

"Mind your language, please. There's a young girl standin' nearby in case you haven't taken note. Anyway, it was a .22, not a shotgun, and it was unloaded if y'all recall which it seems you haven't. Anyway, it's good it worked out as well as it did but we're here to report a serious situation not to rehash an event that's now an inconsequential matter of the past."

J.B. turned to Ruth Ann. He put his hand on her shoulder. "This is Ruth Ann Chambers. She has a charge to file. It's a serious matter. It has to do with more than a house delay on East 9th. Is Huff in?"

"I suspect he is although he's engaged in things of an official nature. Are y'all the girl who was in the paper? The one who was bitten by the cottonmouth? I seen y'all's picture in the paper. Y'all were in a hospital bed. It must've been..."

"I am. Sorry to say, but I am. May I ask what I need to do to report a crime?"

"Just say the word. Tell me what happened. What kind of a crime? We've got all kinds to choose from."

"I didn't know we were at Penneys," J.B. said. "We're not pickin' and choosin' among an assortment of sweaters for the upcomin' winter. This is serious business and we expect a serious response. I'm not in the mood for flippancy."

"Flippancy?" Dinwitty said. "I'm a flippancy? Is that what y'all are sayin'?"

"No. I'll explain the use of the word later. Will you please tell our good sheriff we're here, if he's here. Is he? Or is he off somewhere pickin' and choosin' among any number of crimes at the moment?"

"Like I said, the sheriff is in." Dinwitty gave J.B. a long, hard stare.

"Good. May we please see him?"

"It's that important that y'all have to see him and not me?"

"It's that important. He needs to hear from Ruth Ann. And we'll need a place where it's private. Not out here in the open."

"Well, we got an interrogation room."

"If it's private, it'll do."

"All right, I reckon I can see if he's available. Wait here."

"I suppose we will," J.B. said in response.

Dinwitty frowned and walked in the direction of Huff's office.

Sheriff Albertson was well into a crossword puzzle. For the life of him, he couldn't come up with a five letter world for 'bizarre' beginning with 'q.'

"Got a complaint out front," Dinwitty said after gaining permission to enter Huff's office. "It's the ass wipe of a man whose wife held up the house movin' a couple of weeks ago. His wife was the one who tried to shoot me with the shotgun. Remember that?"

"Just scared the shit out of you, that's all," Hoghead answered. "What kind of complaint? His name's Turman. That's who he is. He's the county auditor. He's the one who messed up the Mule Days celebration last year. Went and reduced the number of turkeys released from the top of the courthouse from four turkeys to a single, solitary one. Claimed four of 'em released at the same time caused too many accidents, just because one old fool of a woman broke her leg chasin' down one of 'em. So what does he do? Releases just one turkey with everyone now on the south side of the courthouse instead of bein' all spread out on all four sides. Was a mess of pushin' and shovin'. Fisticuffs and all. We had to arrest one fellow for pissin' on the courthouse steps. Another for snatchin' a woman's purse. Yet another two for fightin' over a parkin' spot. It was a sorry mess and he caused it all."

"How could he cause someone to piss on the courthouse steps?"

"That's not the point. He caused all of it one way or another."

"Sassy son-of-a-bitch, too," Dinwitty replied. "Says he has somethin' so important y'all need to be on it from the git-go. Anyways, he's got that there girl with him that wuz bitten by the cottonmouth down to Devil's Lake. She's the one who wants to report the crime. I think Turman's just with her for support or somethin'."

"Don't go thinkin', Dinwitty. If you do, y'all will most likely lapse into unconsciousness."

Huff rose from his chair and reached into his desk for a cigar. "Jesus Christ, when can a man catch a little peace? They call us peace officers but don't give us an iota of peace. Wait a minute, Dinwitty. I'll get my shoes on and I'll be there shortly.

Havin' them wait will do 'em some good. Maybe they won't file a charge after coolin' their heels."

Hoghead went back to his puzzle. What's a nine letter word for 'pus' beginning with a 's', he wondered.

"He'll be here directly," Dinwitty said to J.B. upon returning.

"Good, thank you," replied J.B.

He and Ruth Ann located a bench and seated themselves. James Ray was asked by J.B. to remain at home. He was to be on call should Judith need anything.

Ten minutes later, J.B. rose and approached Deputy Dinwitty.

"Is he here or not?" J.B. asked. "Or is he takin' his well-deserved afternoon nap? Or maybe he left through the back door for a sandwich over to Linde Bees? Could it be that a gang of criminals have stormed the courthouse, with hostages taken, and he's engaged in intense, life-and-death negotiations while handlin' the situation single handedly?"

Dinwitty looked up from a paper detailing his evening assignment. "He'll be here directly, I reckon. No need for sarcasm. He had some business to finish."

"Well, would you kindly ask again if he's available? We both would greatly appreciate it, and let me know what 'directly' means exactly. 'Directly' today or 'directly' in a month or so or 'directly' before the end of the world as predicted by the Mayan calendar?"

"No need to get y'all's back up," Dinwitty responded. He rose and once again walked back to Huff's office.

"Come in," said Hoghead, in response to the knock on his door.

"Man's gettin' ouchy and all. Gonna set fire to the place in a minute or so. Are y'all ready to see him and the girl or do I have to put up with his shit for another hour or two?"

"That's what y'all are paid to do. All of us. Put up with shit. I can't seem to find a word for bizarre that begins with a 'q'."

"'Q' as in queer?"

"That's it! Shit sakes alive! Good for you, Dinwitty. Good for you. Come on, let's see what's so fuckin' important that it can't wait 'till tomorrow."

* * * * *

James Ray had driven Ruth Ann to Bud's service in Fort Worth. He was buried a week prior. There were but eleven people in attendance. Present were Bud's wheelchair-bound mother, an older brother who had driven in from Clovis, New Mexico, James Ray and Ruth Ann, several pump company co-workers, a former neighbor, and a retired Presbyterian minister who specialized in such events. Judith remained back in Mayweather. Ruth Ann would explain that her mother had taken ill and couldn't manage the drive. No word was to be mentioned of her real situation. Bud's suicide was enough of a family mishap. Bud's brother said a few kind words and the service for Bud Chambers was over almost as soon as it started.

On the way back to Mayweather, James Ray and Ruth Ann stopped at a Dairy Queen. James Ray parked the Hudson under the shade of a tree. They held hands as they approached the small, take-out building. Ruth Ann ordered a child-size cone. James Ray followed suit but asked to have his dipped in chocolate.

They moved to a wooden picnic bench which was partially covered with shade from the same tree that shaded the Hudson. They sat at the bench's shady end.

"Daddy says life is short. Enjoy it while you can," James Ray volunteered.

"Lately, the enjoyin' part is hard to get a handle on. About as easy as it is to keep this thing from drippin'." Ruth Ann answered.

"How's y'all's mother doin'?"

"Fine. She's up and around. I told Bud's mother that my mother has the flu, flat on her back and all, sick as a dog. That part's true. Was true, anyway. I said that's why she couldn't attend."

"Do you think she believed you?"

"Probably not. Anyway, here's some good news. Mother's got a job offer at a new drugstore in town. The one they've been redoin'."

"The old Mayweather drugstore. What'll she do there?"

"Gonna sell cosmetics, make-up and stuff like that."

"Could she do anythin' for me?"

"Not hardly. Y'all are a lost cause."

"Thought so. What's happenin' with her case? Daddy hasn't heard a word."

"Us neither. Don't know. Mother is so embarrassed about it. It took her almost a week to be seen in public. It's hard on her but I'm proud she's not had anythin' to drink since the happenin'."

"That's really good news. How'd that come about?"

"Took the advice of the doctor, the cursin' hammer doctor. He referred her to a group that helps people with addiction. So far, so good. I'm tryin' to get her to quit smokin' but the doctor says one thing at a time. It would be nice though, to have a house that's not full of smoke. Coach says it's bad for me. Calls it second-hand smoke."

"Well, a body gets second-hand smoke everywhere. The only place I can think of where no one smokes is church. Outside they do. Inside, I suppose they are as anxious as I am for..."

"Eager, not anxious, remember? Y'all are 'anxious' about the whole church goin' thing period. Once there, y'all are 'eager' to get it over with so y'all can go outside and light up. That's twice now I've had to school you on the difference."

James Ray laughed, nodding his head in the affirmative. "I remember. You should have married my Daddy. The two of you would be quite a couple. Y'all could have contests about who's the best with words."

"He's better with sarcasm and innuendo. He'd win hands down. You..."

"What's innuendo?"

"Ah...something someone says that's...that's disparagin' I think. Maybe insinuate somethin' without havin' to say it directly? I don't know. Sorry I used the word. Anyway, y'all should have been with him at the sheriff's office. He cut up the deputy sheriff like he was guttin' a fish. Y'all's daddy thought the sheriff made us wait on purpose so he went on about the Mayan calendar and maybe how the sheriff was busy fightin' off criminals who had stormed the courthouse and so on. He schooled me good on the use of sarcasm."

"Yes, I know. I've been on the receivin' end of that. Mother hated it. I think he uses sarcasm as a kind of...as some sort of..."

"It's a way of doin' battle without actually goin' for someone's throat, I think. You subdue them with words. Use words like knives. Cut 'em to the quick."

"Yes, that's it. Mother would just walk away. For the most part, I didn't get a lot of it."

"That's the point, really. I think usin' sarcasm is often like fightin' someone who's blindfolded. Or has their hands tied behind their backs. For the most part, they're taken aback and pretty much defenseless."

"Sort of the way y'all took on Rusty. I don't 'need' the flowers nor do I 'want' 'em, you said. You knocked him clean out of the ring."

"Maybe. Maybe that's sarcasm and maybe it isn't. It was just an English lesson for a lunkhead. I don't exactly remember what I said, I was so mad. The nerve. Callin' Sammy a nigger. Always pushin' you to the limit. Throwin' down the flowers. Usin' the 'F' word. That boy needs a serious head adjustment."

"Needs more than that. Needs to be hogtied to a fence post 'til the buzzards set on him leavin' nothin' but the sun-bleached, bare bones of an asshole Wickware."

"I can see it now," Ruth Ann mused. "He's dead and buried. His gravestone reads, 'Here lies a bully and a coward... none could match his abject and wretched nature."

"Abject? I know wretched. What's abject?"

"Bad. Bad, and wretched. Downright awful, and wretched. Wretched and...and hateful? I don't know about hateful."

"Well, I have it anyway. Let's be on our abject and wretched way. Daddy and I are goin' to Sammy's house for supper tonight."

"Y'all are so liberal. I love it. Goin' to a colored person's house for supper."

"Well, we go there and they come to our house, or did before mother left. I suppose it's unusual but honestly, I don't even think about it unless Rusty up and yells nigger-lover from his car. Then I'm reminded. Otherwise..."

"I wish I was comin' with you..."

"Want to?"

"Oh no, I wasn't invited and I need to be with mother."

"Ask her. Please. Y'all said she was up and about. Maybe she'd like to come also. I..."

"Slow down, James Ray."

"I know it'll be okay with the Johnsons. They're great people. You haven't met either one of 'em. Sammy's Daddy is Booker T. My Daddy calls him 'Book' sometimes. Anyway,

Booker T. is the size of a movin' van. Eartha, Sammy's Mother, is the warmest person on the planet. Her touch can cure the worst of ills. Of course, y'all know Sammy now. Please ask your mother. When I drop you off, you'll ask permission?"

"Not before you ask if it's okay with the Johnsons. If it is, I'll ask. I owe you that for watchin' me naked in the shower."

"Good. Great. I told you, you can watch me naked anytime you want. I'll take a shower that will last an hour or so. I owe you that."

James Ray opened the car door for Ruth Ann. She entered and slid over to be next to the driver's seat.

James Ray gave life to the Hudson. He leaned over and they kissed.

"Which do y'all prefer?" Ruth Ann asked.

"Prefer?"

"Chapstick or Dairy Queen?"

"So far, I'll take the Dairy Queen. But I need more examples to choose from."

"How about fried chicken lips?"

"Now y'all are talkin'."

"Well, let's stop on the way back and get some fried chicken. I'm hungry. Once I start trainin' again, fried chicken will be plain off the menu."

"Okay. Fried chicken it is. How about fried chicken lips followed by pecan pie lips?"

"I'm all in. Let's do it. How fast will the Hudson go?"

*   *   *   *   *

Carl showed up for work on Friday morning following the photo session at the Lone Star. He entered the darkroom and immediately had a feeling something was wrong. He was an organized person. He set goals. He outlined steps to reach those goals. He believed in a place for everything and everything in its place.

He counted his rolls of film. One roll was missing. He had shot eleven, now there were ten. "Which one is the missing roll?" he said to himself in a hushed voice.

A quick inventory indicated that the number eight roll was the roll absent. He lit a cigarette. He sat down on his stool. He got up and looked around on the floor of the darkroom. *Someone took the roll. I know I exposed eleven. I numbered them. Who has keys to the darkroom? Who could want to gain entrance in the first place? Booker T. has keys. He works Thursday nights but why would he want a roll of film? What would he do with it, assuming he took it? I'm a cooked fuckin' goose if that roll sees the light of day. Now what?*

Carl was disappointed in himself. He had been careless. It had been a long night at the Lone Star. He should have locked up the film in the cabinet he had built for just such use instead of leaving all eleven rolls on the counter.

All in all, he figured the session the least worthwhile in the two years he had been shooting at the Lone Star. The new, male, Negro model was raw and took a lot of coaching. One of the girls was fine with him, the other, not so much. Still, mixed race, nude teenagers engaged in shameless sexual behavior would sell regardless. Maybe not in Mayweather or the South but elsewhere, the photos would be enticing and erotic, if not entirely acceptable.

Carl missed Rita. She had been great to work with. She was willing to do anything, at least at first. Then she claimed she was pregnant. Not long after that, she had committed suicide. Such is life, he thought.

Looking back on the evening's session, Carl figured that by roll eight, the three models had pretty much hit their stride. The one girl, Mindy, insisted that the boy wear a condom when penetration was called for. Carl had resisted the request. Condoms cost money and they took away from the raw reality of the coupling. A man's penis wasn't the same wrapped up in a condom like a banana in its skin.

Surprisingly, Carl found that he didn't have to do much coaching with either girl when it came to the oral sex scenes. Those images, he thought, might just would turn out to be the best of the evening's exposures. *Could the missing roll be the one when one of the two girls was on her knees orally servicing the boy's worthy endowment while the other, the smaller breasted of the two, sat on the bed, legs spread wide, eagerly pursuing her own pleasure? Or, was it the roll when the two girls took turns pleasuring themselves while the boy tried to recover from an unfortunate second ejaculation? He wasn't sure.*

Carl locked up the ten rolls of film and left the darkroom. He walked to the rear of the newspaper building and stood in the sunlight to think. He noticed a bird had deficated on the top of his Cadillac. The car's interior still smelled of vomit despite his effort to rid the car's carpet and backseat of the unpleasant odorous reminder. With the windows down, there was little odor. Windows up, the smell was a reminder of an evening gone awry.

He lit a cigarette and inhaled deeply. *Things didn't go well out at South Cow either. Maybe I'm slipping. I shouldn't have tried to take her from the rear. That's when she threw up. I gave her too much of the Mickey, too. Jesus. I half thought she would be so drunk she'd enjoy fuckin' me. Oh, well, it looks like she hasn't reported it. I didn't think she would. My word against hers if she does. Anyway, Hoghead's my trump card. He's had my back the whole way. I don't know, though. If he gets wind of the Lone Star business, he won't be happy about being left out of that. Oh well, we'll see. Right now I have to wait until Sunday for Booker T. to show up. He and I will have a little chat. I hope I can wait that long. Today's Friday. Another day, and then I'll jump his case on Sunday when he comes in to clean. No. I'll take him for a ride in the country instead. Get him to tell me what he knows. He has to know something.*

Chapter 38 - South Cow Revisited

"It's nice y'all are home early to have supper with us," Lucy said.

"Don't start with me," Huff answered.

"I ain't startin', I'm just sayin'."

"Then don't say. You know I need time to unwind. Work's been crazy lately."

Hoghead's habit was to leave his office a good half hour ahead of the end of his shift and head over to the Prince Domino Hall where he would play a couple of rounds of dominoes, have two or three cold beers, smoke, and have some fun with the other men who frequented the parlor. Women weren't welcome.

The beer was kept in a large cooler in the rear. It was available due to a handshake financial agreement between Hoghead and the parlor's owner. The only rule concerning the beer drinking was that the alcohol be consumed in paper cups. The parlor's owner once complained to Hoghead about the cost associated with having to buy so many paper cups. Hoghead's answer was that the cost was merely an expense associated with doing business. Would he, Hoghead had argued, rather go back to selling just soda pop?

The Albertsons lived well. The supplementary income from the illegal alcohol sales of a half-dozen bootleggers had long benefited the family. The largess of the illegal enterprise enabled their only daughter to attend Southern Methodist University, drive around Dallas in her own car, and live in the Chi Omega sorority house.

"A woman got raped and now I have to go and deal with all that that entails," Huff said, while trying to subdue a tough chunk of pork chop. "Can't y'all cook a pork chop without takin' it beyond the limit of reasonable chewin'?" he asked.

"The woman that was mentioned in the paper?" Lucy asked.

"Yes. That new woman in town. The woman who's married, rather was married to the feller who shot himself down to the pump company. Same family as the one where the daughter got bit by the cottonmouth at Devil's Lake. Plain run of poor family fortune. Never seen anythin' like it."

"That is terrible news. Is she all right?"

"Who? The daughter or the mother?"

"Well, both I suppose. But who raped the mother?"

"That's what I'm paid to find out."

"How did it happen?"

"How? A man dicked her. That's how. I just don't know the who part of it. I know the when but nothin' else. I don't know the who yet," he lied. But I have my suspicions. Anyways, it'll end up as rapes always do."

"How's that?"

"The woman will claim innocence and all, sayin' the man dicked her for no good reason while all the time she was gettin' him hot and bothered and then after he dicks her, she yells rape. It'll be her word against his. If it goes to trial, most juries won't convict 'cause once again, it's he says and she says."

"I don't think that it's always the woman's fault. Men have a way..."

"Maybe not in all cases, but my experience tells me most of 'em are that way. Too bad it ain't a buck nigger. That would make for a good arrest and conviction. That way, the woman wouldn't be questioned about her end of the business, if y'all know what I mean."

"How do you know it's not a colored person?"

"Well, I don't. I'll have to see. Maybe it will end up being a nigger after all. There's plenty of 'em around to blame. Who knows?"

*   *   *   *   *

Hoghead had driven to Judith's house after the rape had been reported. She told him as much as she could remember. She asked for J.B. to be in the bedroom with her. In the beginning, Sheriff Albertson was on his best behavior. After all, he was in the company of a beautiful bedridden woman and he was the county's on-the-ground legal authority. He would be kind, gentle, and polite.

James Ray and Ruth Ann sat in the kitchen.

Ruth Ann noticed that the kitchen's electric clock was off by a good ten minutes according to her wrist watch.

"What time do y'all have?" she asked James Ray. She was holding his hand bearing his watch.

"Twenty minutes after two."

"We should get an electric clock that actually keeps time," she said as she rose to make the adjustment.

"How long do you think they'll be in there?" James Ray asked.

"I don't know. Mother must be hatin' it. Havin' to go over it all again."

"I'm sure she is. Daddy will keep Hoghead in his place, though. I'm sure of that, if that gives y'all any comfort."

"Why does everyone call him Hoghead?"

"You've seen his nose, right?" James Ray said, lowering his voice.

"Yes."

"Well, put the nose of a hog on a fat, squatty person and you have a Hoghead. That's why."

J.B. left the bedroom, closed the door, and entered the kitchen. He sat. Hoghead continued asking questions about her ordeal. J.B. didn't want the sheriff to think he was coaching Judith. She would call for him if she needed him.

He stared blankly at the kitchen wallpaper. The repetitive floral pattern reminded him of a Japanese sushi place where he had dined when on leave in the Navy. *Flowers, birds and leaves. Leaves, flowers and birds. Birds, leaves and flowers.*

"Nothin' untoward goin' on there," J.B. said out loud.

"What?" asked James Ray.

"The wallpaper. Flowers, birds and leaves and then more flowers, birds and leaves. The same ones, over and over again, but they just sit there all of 'em behavin' themselves. No treachery, no ill will, no one thing takin' advantage of anything. The world as it should be, I suppose."

"In photography, it's called repetition. A single subject standin' alone is often without visual importance but let the subject be joined by more of its kind, time and time again, and you have a different, more powerful statement," James Ray lectured. "Leastways that's what I was told."

Ruth Ann locked eyes with James Ray, saying nothing.

"Like for example, a clothesline. Nothin' there. But add a dozen or so clothespins on the line and choose an angle that traces 'em front to back, all 'em hangin' there, one after the other, waitin' for somethin' to be hung on 'em, and you have a kind of statement. Or tall grasses wavin' in the wind. Ever see a stack of metal pipes all bundled together? Look at 'em end-on and you have the openings of the pipes, all in circles, creatin' a beautiful and interestin' pattern, if you follow my meanin'."

"I do. You've learned a lot from your coach, James Ray. Maybe you should teach photography someday. I'm plain sorry about the rest of it, though," J.B. offered.

"Me, too."

"How come y'all don't talk about him anymore, James Ray?" Ruth Ann asked. "It used to be Carl this and Carl that, but even before he did what he did to my mother, y'all stopped mentionin' him by name. What else is goin' on between the two of you?"

"Nothin' really."

"Well it all makes sense now," Ruth Ann said. She stood and looked out the kitchen window and then turned back to face James Ray and J.B.

"What are y'all sayin'?" asked James Ray.

"Y'all's long-time girlfriend, Melissa? The one who says she's gonna marry you."

"Yes, that's Melissa for you. She's got her life all planned out month by month, year by year."

"Well, good for her. Anyway, she told me a month ago or so that she saw my mother ridin' with a man in a yellow Cadillac. I told her I didn't think so. Didn't make sense to me. But now, y'all's Carl has a yellow Cadillac, right?"

"Yes." James Ray answered. "Let's be quiet. Hoghead might hear us."

"OK," Ruth Ann answered in a hushed tone. So y'all's Carl...he's been plannin' to rape her for some time. The bastard. I see it all now. She was buyin' liquor from him because she can't get liquor in the county. James Ray, you told me he had a side job that was illegal and all. Your Daddy told you that. Right, Mr. Turman?"

"Well, I shouldn't have said anythin' without havin' proof, and James Ray shouldn't have said..."

"But you did and he did, and mother's been raped by the bastard of a man. I know it. Maybe he's like Melissa and had it all scripted out. He got her out to the country and no one was around and he raped her. Anyway, what is Sheriff Hogface, or whatever his name is, gonna do?"

"I don't know for sure," J.B. said. "Your mother knows who raped her and so do I. Now, so does the sheriff. So does James Ray and so do you. The thing is, we have to proceed cautiously. I can't tell you more, but you have to trust me. Other things are in the works. If Carl gets wind of the something else, he'll take off and go unpunished. He probably thinks your mother won't report the rape. If she does, it'll be his word against hers, and then there's the embarrassment of makin' it public which your mother has had the courage to do, but Carl doesn't know it. Let's let things work themselves out. Maybe somethin' good will come of all of it over time."

"How could something good come of my mother bein' raped?" Ruth Ann asked.

"Sometimes good things are brought about by things that aren't so good. I...I know I'm havin' a hard time explainin' myself but maybe...maybe y'all's mother will benefit from her misfortune by bein' able to kick the alcohol habit. Maybe that's the good that will come from the situation."

Ruth Ann sighed. "What a way to come to that realization," she said.

"Ruth Ann, you're smart like your mother. It'll all come to some focus over time. Justice will be served," counseled J.B. "I'll see to it, if it's the last thing I do."

The door opened to the bedroom. Hoghead exited.

"I'm goin' to have a hard time solvin' this thing if she won't say much beyond that she was raped," he announced. "Anyways, I've got her deposition, she..."

"I thought a deposition was something said under oath," J.B. said.

"Well, call it a statement, whatever. Let's just say that she corroborated what y'all said down at the office except she was shy on the details."

"I suppose the details are painful for her," J.B. countered. "Rape is rape. One doesn't have to divulge every last this or that of it."

"If it goes to trial, I expect she will. Her laundry will be seen throughout the county. Maybe the state."

"Her laundry?" J.B. replied, his arms folded. "Her laundry?"

"Look, Turman. Here's the problem. No matter what she says, or her daughter here says..."

"Her name's Ruth Ann," J.B. said.

"Could I speak without an interruption?"

"Please continue and forgive me for my impertinence, if you see my words as such."

"Well, as I was attemptin' to say," Hoghead said pulling up his overburdened belt, "it's gonna be her word against his.

Pure and simple. Always is, in a case like this whether there's no details or a encyclopedia full of details." Hoghead looked directly at Ruth Ann. "For the life of me I don't know why y'all's mother would go through the humiliation of it all. Why..."

"May I speak for you, Ruth Ann?" J.B. asked.

"Please."

"Mrs. Chambers is goin' to go through the humiliation because she was humiliated. Because someone, and we know who, took advantage of her in a criminal way. I would think, Huff, that y'all would get the picture bein' the county's worthy sheriff and all. Keeper of the peace. Our guardian against uncivil acts like the one who took Mrs. Chambers down. That's why she's willin' to speak up. A grave injustice has been done to her as a person and as a woman. She didn't go out to the country askin' to be raped. She went out there on business."

"What she done was against the law."

"It's against the law to sell liquor in every nook and cranny in Mayweather County other than the fine hamlet of Ladonia. We know that to be a fact. Yet liquor is asked for and liquor is delivered. Who's the law breaker, Huff? The buyer or the seller? Where does the law come down on that? And how many bootleggers are there, gainfully employed in our fine example of a county, runnin' around all hours of the day satisfyin' the people's thirst? Have y'all ever done an inventory of such illegal activity?"

"Look, Turman, I'm tryin' to help here and y'all are bein' an asshole about it. Please excuse my language, young lady."

"I think you should answer his question," Ruth Ann interjected. "How does all of that work? Is a blind eye turned to bootleggin' in Mayweather County? I think that's a question that needs to be answered."

"Couldn't have said it better," J.B. added. "Let me put it to you this way, Huff. Does the sorry business of bootleggin' benefit y'all in any way?"

"Go take a flyin' leap, Turman! I don't know what y'all are talkin' about. The very idea. I come and try to help with a sorry situation you asked me to help with, and y'all up and accuse me of coverin' up for bootleggers. I'll have you know I made an arrest just last month."

"Well, good for you, Huff. Good to know you're vigilant and all. I suppose y'all will charge you know who with rape as well as illegal alcohol sales. Double whammy. Should make for some good press down to the *Tribune*. And I don't know how I'll be able to do what you just asked me to do. A flyin' leap from where? The top of the courthouse, turkey-like. So do I have to wait for Mule Days to roll around?"

Saying nothing, Hoghead stormed from the house, shutting the front door loudly.

Ruth Ann rose and went into her mother's bedroom. Judith was near sleep given the weight of her medication. Ruth Ann sat beside her, turned to face the bedroom window, and managed a short, silent prayer.

"I suppose we should go now," J.B whispered through the doorway.

Ruth Ann turned to face him. She got up and walked through the doorway, closed the door gently and gave J.B. a hug. She leaned into his barrel of a chest.

"Thanks so much for y'all's help but you know you may have made an enemy out of the sheriff, don't you?"

"Well, I have a hard time keepin' my mouth shut when I get cranked up. Thing is, he's got more comin'. A lot more comin'."

"What if he won't help bring the Carl man to justice?"

"I don't know. I'm hoping there are some good citizens who will help me make sure justice is served."

Ruth Ann turned to James Ray. "Can you stay? I'm goin' to tell you a story about an ordinary law-abidin' citizen who, despite his hesitation, took on a corrupt sheriff. How the hogface of a sheriff drew his gun, but given the kitchen knife sharpness of the citizen's words, he fell to the ground bleedin' and was forced to retreat. He tucked his tail and ran, all coward-like."

"Sounds like it would make for a good read," J.B. said. "Maybe I'll find a copy in a bookstore or run across it someday in *Reader's Digest*."

Chapter 39 - Smoke Signals

"Collect call for a J.B. Turman."

"He's outside. I'll run get him," Mabel answered.

She raced out the office door, scooted past the concession stand, and broke into the afternoon sun and the burden of heat it carried. She squinted given the intensity of the overhead sun. Finally, she located J.B. with his gang of oldtimers.

"J.B.! J.B.! There's a collect call for y'all. Hurry!"

J.B. put his new German made Hoffritz Stag Handle pocket knife back in his pants pocket, excused himself, and ran to his office, catching up and passing Mabel on the way.

"Hello, J.B. Turman here," he answered breathlessly.

"Will you accept a long-distance call from a Sarah Mae Turman?"

"Yes...yes I will. Yes, put her on."

"J.B.?"

"Yes, it's me. What's happenin'? Why the collect call?"

Sarah Mae began crying. Upon hearing J.B.'s voice, she broke down. She was unable to form distinct words.

J.B. motioned for Mabel to leave the office.

"Sarah Mae, what is it? What's wrong? Are the girls okay?"

"Yes...yes, they're fine. Let me catch myself. They, they're doin' well. It's about me. I'm...I'm afraid I'm goin' to die."

"What? Sarah Mae, what are y'all sayin'? Tell me what's happened."

"I need you to come to California. I need you, please come."

"Look, Sarah Mae. Listen to me. Tell me what's wrong. I need to know what's happened."

"I...I went to see the doctor. He, he told me... said I'll have to have radon treatments. I won't be able to teach. The cancer has spread. I'm sick J.B., and I need you. I made a mistake leavin'. We...we should have worked things out. I don't know what I was thinkin'. I pray God will forgive me for my transgressions."

"How about askin' me for forgiveness? Frankly, I'd appreciate it. Look Sarah Mae, as usual, you leave me speechless. I don't know what to say. I'm very sorry to hear about your situation. I don't know what to do. I can't come to California right now, I..."

"Yes...yes you can. I may die, J.B. Are you tellin' me you can't come when I'm dyin'?"

"Good Lord, Sarah Mae, why does everythin' have to be life and death with you?   Why can't you come back to Mayweather?"

"Did I hear you say what you said? That's all you have to say? I'm y'all's wife and I have cancer spreadin' all over me like ants after a summer rain and that's all you can say? Come home? Do y'all think comin' home will cure my cancer?"

Sarah Mae slammed down the phone into its receiver.

J.B. stood motionless, phone still to his head.

The operator informed him of the charges for a long-distance collect call. He said thank you and hung up.

He walked to the hall, located Mabel, called out her name, and motioned for her to return to the office.

"Don't look up," he said, "the sky is fallin'. Probably be good if it does. Be an end to everybody's misery."

"I'm guessin' the call didn't bear good news."

"Not at all. Sarah Mae says her cancer has spread. Said she won't be able to teach. Now she wants me to come to California. Want's me to move there."

"Sorry to hear her cancer is spreadin'. How do you feel about movin' and all?"

"I'm not movin' and I don't know how I can leave everythin' and drive or fly or crawl to California. I simply can't do it right now."

He walked to his desk, picked up a pencil and made note of the collect charge.

"Do y'all have some aspirin? I'm out."

"I believe I do."

"I'll pay you back as soon as I find out how to pay for the long-distance collect phone call."

Mabel offered J.B. her thin tin of enclosed aspirin.

"What is her doctor sayin' about Sarah Mae?"   Mabel asked.

"Just that her cancer has spread. She got mad and hung up on me so I don't have any details. Has to have radon treatments. I don't know what I could do to help her in California."

"You could hold her hand, J.B. That's what y'all could do if you could figure out a way to do it."

She and J.B. locked eyes. J.B. blinked, and looked to the floor.

"I don't know about that. She's never been one for much hand holdin'. By the way, how's your cancer ordeal?"

"How did you know about that?"

"Charlie told me."

*　　*　　*　　*　　*

Charlie had been of great help. Not only on the night of the second stake-out at the Lone Star, but also in figuring out what happened to Judith as well. Fact be known, he and J.B. knew more of what happened at the abandoned farmhouse than Hoghead.

Their trip to South Cow road and the farmhouse was revealing. Charlie walked up and down, examining car tracks, and footprints, and within an hour had pieced together the sequence of cars and people coming and going by virtue of what he read Indian like in the dirt left behind.

"You learn that everythin' tells a story. What we have here is Carl's Cadillac," he said pointing to a set of tire tracks. Those are Double Eagle tracks. They come standard on all Cadillacs. See the diamondback rattlesnake like tread? Carl was here. No doubt about it. These are the Chambers lady's car tracks. Here's where she stopped her car. Carls was pointed at the barn over there. I'll come back tomorrow and make a cast of both sets. Then, when it's time, they can be used as evidence. The chain of custody is a problem. We'll see how it goes."

"Chain of custody?"

"Yes. Evidence being collected here and there by unofficial hands. The movin' and storin' of evidence and what might have happened to it over time. Maybe none of what we find will stand up in court, if it comes to all that. Same with stolen film and such. But again, it'll probably be enough to get y'all's grand jury summoned."

"Well, be that as it may. The callin' of a grand jury is all I'm lookin' for at this point. I've got to hold hope that enough of what we discover will be enough for a modern day equivalent of bein' tarred and feathered. By the way, do all Texas Rangers have such a good set of eyes?"

"Some do. Some don't. Back in the day, some Rangers could track as well as a Comanche warrior. Lost art now, mostly. What's that?"

"What's what?" J.B. asked.

"Over there. Broken glass?"

"Where?"

"By the steps of the porch. Wait. Walk around those footprints. I need to see if they have anythin' to tell us."

Charlie and J.B. walked in a half-circle to the steps of the porch.

"Now we have some real, solid-as-a-brick-wall piece of evidence. Don't touch. That's a broken glass of some kind. Look at its bottom. Rounded and thick. It's a high-ball glass. Dollars to doughnuts, its got both Carl's and the victim's fingerprints all over it."

"Oh, my."

"Oh, my indeed."

Charlie took out his handkerchief. "Y'all have one?"

"Yes. Here."

"Is it clean?

"Yes."

"Open it up and hold it so I can put the pieces into it without 'em falling out. We don't need the tiny pieces. The big ones will give us what we want. They'll tell the story." Charlie carefully picked up the various pieces of glass using his handkerchief and placed them one by one into J.B.'s awaiting hand.

"Probably dropped the glass when she was overcome by whatever it was he put in her drink. If she was pretty heavy into drinkin' like she said she was, three or four drinks would've done her under conscious wise. Could've killed her. She was fortunate as far as that goes."

J.B. said nothing in return. He tried to mentally reconstruct the scene. An almost uncontrollable anger swept over him. Judith Chambers had ceased to be just someone who was victimized by a rapist. She had slowly but surely positioned herself as being something special to him. Very special. He put his hand to his jaw and drew a deep breath.

He finally spoke. "I guess he knew what he was doin' all right."

"Funny thing about crime," Charlie answered. "everyone thinks they know what they are doin' until somethin' goes wrong.

Then all the plannin' and the executin' and the thrill of it is over and if somethin' did go wrong, consequences kick in. At least they do sometimes."

"I suppose so. I don't know. I haven't been much of a law breaker in my life. Pretty much go about my life followin' the rules and bein' Mr. Predictable. Except for the Lone Star business. That's been different. I wonder what the somethin' wrong might be with all of that?"

"Hard to say. Has y'all's boy developed the film yet?"

"Goin' to when he gets back from the funeral service in Fort Worth. He's pickin' up some supplies in Sherman on the way back. Was out of developer for the film or was it for the photo paper? I forget. Anyway, are y'all goin' back to Commerce tonight?"

"Tomorrow. I'll stop by the courthouse before I go. We'll go over what needs to be done goin' forward. I'd like to hear from you when the film's developed. If the images are anythin' like the one you already have, it'll make for another hot time in the old town of Mayweather."

*　　*　　*　　*　　*

Charlie and J.B had beaten Hoghead to his mark by a full forty-eight hours. By the time the esteemed Mayweather sheriff drove to South Cow to investigate, they figured they had all they needed. They had Judith's testimony, secure in the knowledge that she had provided them with more detailed information than she had Hoghead. Charlie had made a cast of both cars' tire tracks, and most helpful of all, thought Charlie, he would take the broken glass back to Commerce to be dusted for fingerprints. He, and the city's police chief, had gone to high school together. Charlie was the fullback; Buzz, the quarterback. Judith's comparison prints could be easily obtained. So, too, he figured, could a comparison set of Carl's.

Charlie had also noticed a woman's footprints leading to the steps of the farmhouse, but none leading back to the car they assumed to be Carl's Cadillac. He paid particular attention to an area of dirt next to the car. The dirt had been sorely disturbed.

"It's where he had trouble loadin' her into the backseat of his car," Charlie said.

"How do you know?"

"I don't know, just surmisin'. Try loadin' a hundred and twenty pounds or so of dead weight into the backseat of a car. No easy task. I'm assuming, given the dirt's disturbance, that he had some difficulty doin' just that."

"Look. See there? The tire tracks stop there. They stop, don't they? Those tracks are from the front tires. Now look to the dirt here. This would be approximately where the backseat of the car is located. Door opens here. Victim is placed, with great effort, inside."

"I never would have been able to figure that out. Never would have thought to..."

"Yes, you would. Just trainin' and experience and all. Knowin' what to look for. Like you do when goin' over books and records and such."

Charlie searched further around the area where the Cadillac had been parked.

"Lookie here. Back here. This is the rear of the car. Dirt's been messed up here also. This is where he accessed his liquor supply from the trunk of the car. Tracks comin' and goin', all of 'em from a man. Big feller, too. How tall is he?"

"Tall. Over six feet."

"Wears a size twelve or so. I'll make a cast of his footprints along with the Chambers woman's."

"Charlie, I can't thank y'all enough. I..."

"Best murder I ever solved was solved by footprints. That, and fingerprints on a pocket watch. Left the watch behind, stupid asshole. Must have been worried about how much time he had, and he goes and sets the watch down on a coffee table. There's more to it than that, but that's it in a nutshell. The ol' boy is still doin' time."

"Well, remind me not to break the law while you are around."

"You did break the law. You and y'all's boy. And I'm an accomplice. We'll all hang."

*   *   *   *   *

Hoghead couldn't make much sense of the farmhouse rape scene. What bothered him most was the abundance of foot prints all over the back yard of the house. *Different size prints. Someone was wearin' cowboy boots. Several people were walkin' back and forth, one of 'em with cowboy boots although there're only tire prints from two cars. One of 'em Carl's, the other, hers. What the fuck is that all about?* The best he could ascertain, there were footprints from three men and one woman.

The Chambers woman said she was raped by one man. It wasn't a party of men. Even though she wouldn't detail the juicier parts of the encounter, one Carl Malone was, beyond a doubt, the doer. *Who else has been out here?*

"Double Eagles," he said aloud. *These here tire prints are Double Eagles. Distinctive tire tread. Diamond like pattern. I think Cadillacs come outfitted with Double Eagles. No question Carl's the one who dicked her. He told me he's put money down on the property. Has big plans for the place. No one's ever out here 'cept for the old coot we ran off after he decided to make the farmhouse his hangout. That was a year ago or so. But where do all the footprints come from? These here belong to Carl. Big man, big foot. But someone else has been out here. A cowboy type?*

Hoghead found little to disprove Judith's testimony. He would have to have a sit-down with his second cousin, Carl, and come up with some kind of strategy to deal with it all. He had taken a risk bringing him into the county in the first place. He had afforded Carl special treatment, never threatening him with arrest, nor asking for more money given his successful and growing bootleggin' enterprise. Now, a rape has been reported and he was sure Carl was guilty of the crime.

How do I cover that up? If that comes to light and it looks as if it will, so too may the bootleggin' business and my profitin' from it. I can't risk that. I can't lose that income. I'll have to put the blame on someone else, but who?

Chapter 40 - Friday Afternoon Throw-down

James Ray and Sammy lamented the loss of their make-do baseball field. The house that now occupied the hallowed childhood space was on its foundation, plumbed, wired, and ready for occupancy. A widow from Pecan Gap, a small town a few miles northeast of Commerce, had purchased the property for far below market value because of its proximity to colored town. The home, abandoned during the war, was bought for little more than a song. Her plans included living out the rest of her life at her new location while writing an historical fiction novel or two or three, if it all worked out. She had already begun the first of what she envisioned to be a trilogy. The books would trace several generations of Negros from slavery, to emancipation, to reconstruction, to segregation, and finally, to the so-called separate but equal era.

Dr. Kay Beatrice Hardy, retired English and anthropology professor at East Texas State Teacher's College, in Commerce, was an author of some regional note. Her book titled, *Westward to the Hills of East Texas*, detailed the forced evacuation of the Coushatta people from their ancestral home in the Alabama region. It was published by the University of Texas Press. Another, examining the negative economic and social impact of Jim Crow laws in the south, was to be released in the fall. The concluding sentence in her book read: *When we decide to fully employ the talent, the vision, the energy, and the creativity of the Negro race, our nation will benefit. Until then, we will remain an imperfect union.*

She was eager to begin talking to her new neighbors, especially the ones of color. Her Ampex magnetic tape recorder would be put to good use collecting oral history.

*   *   *   *   *

The two boys entered the playground-intrusion-of-a-home from its back door. It had been left open. They walked around the vacant home, trying to calculate which room would serve which purpose. The home had two bedrooms, one upstairs and one at the lower level.

"Just got one bathroom," James Ray said.

"Who's got more than one bathroom?" asked Sammy. "We still have an outhouse. Can't put in a flushin' toilet unless the white-powers-that-be put in a sewer line. If they do, my daddy says they want us to pay for the puttin' in."

"In California, lots of homes have more than one bathroom. They have garages, too, and everyone puts up a fence, my mother says."

"How's she doin'?"

"Not well. My daddy may have to go. Her cancer has spread."

"I'm sorry to hear that. Mighty sorry."

"Me, too. A year ago everythin' seemed all perfect and then all of it came crashin' down like a tower of dominos. Remember when we used to build the domino towers with a plunger at the bottom, and then we'd hit the plunger and the tower would fall down? Once it made so much noise when they came fallin' down, y'all's mother thought we'd broken some dishes. She ran us outside to play. Remember that?"

"I remember."

"Sammy, I have somethin' to tell you."

"What?"

"Well, this mornin' I ran into my favorite asshole."

"Y'all's Wickware?"

"Yes, my Wickware. Actually, as usual, he ran into me. We exchanged words which means he called me this and that so I up and told him to meet me here at five this afternoon and we'd finally have it out. Right here In front of this house."

"Why here? What else he say to y'all?"

"Doesn't matter what he said or I said, I'm sick of havin' to have him pop up here and there all over the place no matter where I go. He's like a bad case of head lice. I chose here because, well it's not downtown. If I get my ass whipped I don't want the whole world watchin'."

"James Ray, it's four thirty. He'll be here in less than an hour."

"I know. I'm a coward for trickin' you to be here with me. I'm sorry for that. I was hopin' that you would hold off his thugs while Rusty and I finally have it out. Just hold 'em off. Wickware will be enough for me to deal with. I'm just askin' for a fair fight, that's all. I also didn't want it to be someplace out in the country where...where if things went wrong, I couldn't get help. Or like I say, in town where everyone would be witness to it all. I feel safer here. It's daylight. Your house is three houses away and mine is just over there. I don't know why I feel safer, but I do. Daddy told me to pick my place and I have. He also said for me to be in control of the situation. I'm gonna be."

"I'll be back in a minute," Sammy said.

"Where are y'all goin'?"

"You'll see," he said over his shoulder. "Be right back."

James Ray remained inside the house. He wondered why a wall had been knocked out that used to separate a living room from a parlor or maybe a dining room. The new expanded room was lined wall-to-wall with shelves. *Maybe the owner has a lot of books. Maybe the new owner is a large person like Booker T. and needs a lot of room to move around.*

He heard a car approach. He froze. He looked through the window to the street. The car rambled on into colored town.

He looked at his watch. He tried to calm himself. He began to run his daddy's words through his head.

Take the fight to Rusty. Be the aggressor. Don't wait for him to strike the first blow. Keep calm. Keep your emotions in check. Think. Know where you are. Choose a place where you're comfortable. Taunt him. You do the insulting. Confuse him. Let Rusty lose his cool.

"I'm here," Sammy announced, as he ran into the back of the house.

"You've got y'all's baseball bat?"

"Indeed I do. It's my Louisville Slugger. I call it 'The Beast.' It's thirty-six inches of a pitcher's nightmare."

"Well, don't go and remove anyone's head. Just keep his gang out of the way."

"You can bet on it. I bet they won't even get out of the car when they see me holdin' my Beast."

"Hope so. Anyway, let's get on out to the sidewalk so we can be waitin' for 'em. Daddy told me to pick my spot. Like linin' up for a free throw. Know my territory. Be calm and calculatin'."

Rusty was late. His car quit on him on East 9th Street like it had the night when he had tried to get James Ray to fight on the Turman front lawn. It was the same place where he had flooded the car after James Ray had cursed back at him. That was the night, he remembered, that James Ray's shit-ass of a father had spoiled the evening. This time, a dirty gas filter had brought the car to a halt.

"I can't Goddam believe it," Rusty exclaimed. "Same Goddam street. Same fuckin' result. Fuckin' car quits on me for no good reason. Out boys. We'll have to walk the rest of the way."

James Ray and Sammy waited. James Ray took advantage of the extra time by reviewing his strategy once again.

"They ain't here. Maybe y'all should hightail it," Sammy offered.

"No. Not this time. Mother nature's gonna be on my side. You, too."

"Mother Nature?"

"Yep. Good old Mother Nature."

"How's that?"

"Ever hear that the angle of incidence is equal to the angle of reflection?"

"What are y'all talkin' about?"

"You'll see."

"Here they come," Sammy said. "There, see 'em? They ain't in his wreck of a car. They're hoofin' it. All four of 'em. The son-of-a-bitch Rusty's leadin' the parade."

James Ray motioned Sammy toward the house. He took a deep breath. He would do as he did before a game. He would try to calm himself. He would be conscious of his breath. He began to manage slow and deliberate breaths. He walked to the sidewalk. Once again, he mentally rehearsed his plan that he hoped would disadvantage his adversary. He looked toward the harsh angle of the afternoon sun and how it reflected off the sidewalk. He walked over and touched the trunk of the elm tree occupying space between the sidewalk and the pavement of the street. He walked in a counter-clockwise circle, taking careful note of the sunlight as he did. He again noted the difference in the light's intensity when the sun was to his back, and then, when the sun shone directly onto his face.

Light is either your enemy, or your best friend, Carl had said. Hard, direct light will work to your advantage in some situations, ruin your effort in others. Same with soft, diffused, indirect light. Good in one situation, not so good in another.

Your shot of Ruth Ann with the towel above her head is a winner. Could be on the front cover of a magazine. No hard light there. It was softened by the interruption of the towel. Clever, but think back to the dozens of photos you've taken where your subjects were facing hard, hammer-like direct light. Dozens, right? And so what did you get, given the fact your subjects were tortured by the harshness of the direct light? Squinty eyes, nose shadows, deep, dark, eye sockets, and all that mess, right? That kind of light for that kind of a situation, puts your subject at a real disadvantage. Uncomfortable subjects make for uncomfortable and shitty photographs.

Having spied James Ray waiting on the sidewalk, Rusty picked up his pace. He began to smile. James Ray watched him approach. He readied himself. Again he tried to calm his breathing. His heart was beating drum-like. Rusty soon arrived. James Ray moved in the direction of the porch steps allowing Rusty to solely occupy space on the sidewalk.

James Ray thought Rusty looked like the Joker in a Batman comic, smiling and evil to the core.

"Don't hardly believe it, I didn't think y'all would be...what the fuck is this?" Rusty said, as he looked to the house.

Sammy stepped from the shadow of the porch with his Beast casually resting on his right shoulder. He walked into the daylight of the weed-inhabited scrub of the front yard. He stood next to James Ray. He said nothing.

"I believe you've met my friend Sammy," James Ray said. "Maybe not formally. Y'all have yelled 'nigger' at him several times."

"I don't need to meet him. A nigger one day is a nigger the next. Why bother?"

"Excuse me, white trash, you call me nigger one more time and you'll be missin' y'all's head. I'll knock it clean to the Red River. Wouldn't be a bad thing, either. Y'all without a head. There'd be less shit comin' from y'all's white-trash mouth."

Rusty's eyes narrowed. "I see," Wickware replied. "You think you and your cripple friend here can take on all four of us?"

"Don't think so, know so," Sammy answered.

"Wickware, this is between you and me," James Ray interjected. "Leave Sammy out of it and I'll leave your fuck-alongs out of it. Is that fair? Isn't that what y'all want? Beat the shit out of me and take another bully of a scalp? Then go on a tour of downtown tellin' everyone how you whipped the two of us even though both of us had baseball bats?"

James Ray stepped toward Rusty, but then turned and walked around him in the direction of Cecil, Will, and Smiley.

"Good afternoon gentlemen," he offered. "You stay where y'all are and my friend Sammy stays where he is. Any of y'all decide to participate and one or more heads will go missin'. See that hedge row yonder? Step up to it and stay there. Any questions?"

None were forthcoming. The boys dutifully walked to the side of the hedge and stopped.

James Ray turned and walked back in the direction of Rusty, stopping a mere two feet from where he stood. Rusty was facing the west. He was shading his eyes from the sun.

"Y'all ready to do some scalp takin'?" James Ray asked.

"Fuck yeah. Let's get on with it."

James Ray didn't reply. Instead he stepped to the side and began to walk in a wide circle around Rusty.

"What kind of fuck-up are y'all, Turman?" Rusty said, turning in concert with James Ray. "What are..."

"Just doin' what the Comanches used to do with the cavalry."

James Ray continued his full circle march around Rusty. "They used to form a circle. The circle over time would get tighter and tighter. The cavalry, they were sittin' ducks, all encircled, while the Comanches were a movin' target. Advantage, Comanches. Disadvantage, cavalry."

James Ray was now into his second turn around Wickware. It was as he had hoped. When Rusty faced west, when the sun both shone and reflected intensely into his eyes, he squinted. He shaded his eyes with his left hand when he faced west. James Ray took note.

Rusty was no longer smiling. He was confused. He was forced to follow James Ray's rotation. Rusty thought James Ray might attack him from his rear, when he wasn't looking, whatever good that would do him.

"Comanches showed no mercy to their enemies, Rusty. Thought y'all would like to know that. Would scalp their enemies alive or for a little fun, cut off the bottoms of their feet and make 'em walk around 'till they fell dead in their own pool of blood. Cut off their dicks and stick 'em into their victim's mouths."

"Hear that boys? Geronimo Turman, here, is givin' us a history lesson."

"Geronimo was an Apache and y'all are an ignorant son-of-a-bitch, cock-suckin-bastard."

"If you say so." Rusty lost his smile. "I suppose Indians know fellow Indians like niggers know niggers. Y'all are some sight, Turman, all prancin' around in y'all's girly, little Indian circles. This is more fun than the county fair. Are we gonna..."

James Ray suddenly stopped in front of Rusty. Rusty ceased his rotation. He faced James Ray. He also faced the blinding and unwelcome glare of the afternoon sun. As his hand rose to shade his eyes from the sudden intrusion of direct and low-angled sunlight, James Ray landed a vicious right hand to his face, propelling him to the ground. The force of the blow broke Rusty's nose.

Rusty was stunned and speechless. His hand went to his nose. He tried to focus. Blood flowed freely down his face. His nose looked like a dogleg, left turn on a short, par three golf course.

Cecil made the mistake of moving in the direction of his fallen leader. Sammy lowered his bat and stepped toward him. Cecil retreated. Will and Smiley took steps backward until they were stopped by the hedge.

Rusty struggled to regain his feet. He hurt. He wasn't sure, but perhaps James Ray might have hit him with a bat. Righting himself, and somewhat regaining his focus, he still faced the burdensome glare of direct light. He identified what he thought to be James Ray, or was it one of his boys? It was hard to tell in the intensity of the unwelcome light. Like an enraged bull he charged the image regardless, arms wide, head down, chin extended.

James Ray had hoped for just such a reaction. He gave a shoulder-and-head fake to his left and stepped deftly to his right, much as he would have evaded a pesky, opposing guard. As Rusty charged past him, catching nothing but air, James Ray grabbed his left arm and like a sling-shot, threw him head first into the trunk of the elm.

Rusty fell in a heap. As he struggled to bring himself to a standing position, he placed both hands on his wounded face. He was dazed, hurt and confused. James Ray approached him and hit him hard in the stomach. Rusty's breath left him. Suddenly, he couldn't breathe. He fell to his knees. There, he fought to gain his breath. His arms hung by his sides, limp and useless. A torrent of blood poured down his face. James Ray took the stricken and helpless Wickware by the shoulders and placed him on the ground, face up. Rusty offered no resistance.

Nearly unconscious, Wickware realized he could finally breathe. That is good, he thought. *Everything else is bad.*

Field of View

James Ray mounted Rusty. That's when the storm cloud released its fury. That's when a downpour of accumulated resentment and outright hatred rained down on the town's bully.

James Ray began to pummel the face. The hateful face. The racist face. The bully face. Left, right, left, and right again. Blood covered James Ray's hands. Rusty's face became featureless, save the blood that covered it.

"Low-life bastard! Goddamn son-of-a-bitch! How does it feel, Rusty? Feelin' good now?"

Right hand, left hand, and then right again.

James Ray knew not who he was, nor where he was. He lost track of time and space. He was in a dream-like state; he was in a war, but he didn't know where or what kind. In the war, he knew he would either live or he would die. Something told him he had been chosen to live. *I must make sure I live. I'll kill my enemy. Kill him. Kill the enemy! Kill him forever!*

"Enough, James Ray. Enough!"

Sammy pulled James Ray from the carnage he had wrought on Rusty.

Sammy quickly removed his T-shirt.

"Over here," Sammy commanded. "Any of y'all, over here. Take him to the hospital. Use my shirt to help stop the blood. Git over here! I ain't gonna hurt y'all." Sammy had left his Beast at the porch steps.

"We ain't got a car," Cecil said as he approached his stricken leader.

"Well, then pick up y'all's piece of shit white trash and start walkin'. We don't have a car neither," Sammy replied.

Rusty moaned as he was lifted from the ground. Cecil applied Sammy's T-shirt to his disfigured face. They began to slowly walk back up East 9th Street, the blood stained sidewalk marking their exit. The hospital was ten blocks from the battlefield. A lifetime of bullying was over in less than two minutes.

"I think I've broken my hand," James Ray said, in the wake of Rusty's departure.

"Broke his face and broke y'all's hand. I'd have to say that was somethin' to see. That was real smart. Y'all confusin' him by circlin' him like a band of hostile Indians. Making him look into the hard light and all. Y'all landin' the first blow. Mighty impressive if I do say so, and I'm sayin' so. Y'all whipped him like a rented mule. Mighty impressive. I ain't never gonna piss you off. You just might up and whup my black ass and go and ram my head into a tree and all and then beat up my face until it looked like mincemeat."

James Ray laughed, then he began to cry. He sobbed uncontrollably. He moved to the steps of the house and sat and cried. He cried because of the emotional relief he felt, not from the hurt of his hand. The fight with Rusty was finally over. At last, he was free of his childhood nightmare. Despite the odds, he had been victorious. He had won the battle and he hoped he had won the war. He also cried because he'd been scared to confront Wickware, but in the end he had prevailed. He cried because he missed his mother. He cried, too, because he was on the verge of losing a job he cherished. Carl had said little at work for the last couple of days. He suspected Carl knew a roll of film was missing.

"I guess I broke it when I hit him in his stupid lookin' face," James Ray said, reflectively. He looked closely at the hill-like swelling in the middle section of the top of his right hand.

"Does it hurt?"

"Not much. A little. It feels funny. I suppose it'll hurt more later."

"I 'spect it will." Sammy stood before him, a shirtless, bronze Adonis.

"I wish I had y'all's body," James Ray said.

"You'd want to be black like me?"

"I wouldn't care. No wonder y'all can hit a baseball a country mile."

"Well, thank you. Someday a Louisville Slugger will have my name on it. Y'all watch and see. That's my way out of Mayweather. My way out of being called nigger, or coon, or havin' to drink out of fountains marked 'colored', or havin' to take a shit somewhere separate from where some white person shits their holy white shit. Shit's shit. We're all the same inside. Understand what I'm sayin'?"

"I do. I do. It's a shame. All of it. I think I hit Rusty an extra three or four times just for callin' y'all a nigger."

"I appreciate that. Come on. Let momma see to your hand. I'll call y'all's daddy if you like. He could come and take you to the doctor."

"Let's have Eartha look at it first. Let's go. I won't be cryin' like a sissy by the time we get there."

"Well, y'all ain't no sissy. What I saw was a person who did what he had to do whether he liked it or not. A bully and a fuckin' racist got the shit kicked out of him. Y'all should be proud of yourself. Like I say, I ain't never gonna say a harsh word to y'all, ever. Maybe I should take to carryin' my Beast with me when I'm around y'all."

"That's the strange part of it all."

"What strange part?"

"I didn't like havin' to do what I just did. You're right about that. I didn't look forward to it at all. I hated havin' to face him. But here's the thing, Sammy. In the end I liked it. I liked it more than I should've liked it. I like it right now. I'm sorry to say, I'll probably like it tomorrow. There's a word for how I'm feelin' but I'm too tired and hare brained to know what it is."

"It'll come to you. Come on. Let's go see my momma."

"Vindicated. That's the word. Vindicated."

"Is that the same as victorious?"

"Maybe in some way. I don't know."

"We've got a dictionary. I'll look it up while Momma tends to y'all's hand."

Chapter 41 - Of Feet and Feathers

"We could meet at the domino parlor. How about that?" Carl asked.

"Nope," Hoghead replied. "Got to be somewhere where we ain't seen together. There's a nothin' much cafe in Bloom. The Nest, it's called. On the right side 'bout a quarter mile past the post office. I'll meet you there tomorrow at noon."

"I'm working tomorrow. I can't drive to Bloom and have you sing a sad song, us eat, and me get back to work."

"Tomorrow at noon. Be there. Figure a way to take a couple of hours. You take time whenever y'all want too. I see you here, there, and everywhere at all hours of the day answerin' the population's need for a little of somethin' that goes down easy. Tomorrow at noon."

*   *   *   *   *

Judith asked J.B. to fetch her purse. "It's in the living room. I need a cigarette."

J.B. rose from his chair, walked to the couch in the living room, and secured her purse.

"Here. Y'all sure you need to smoke?"

"Usually have one first thing in the morning. Almost noon now."

Judith sat on the edge of her bed. She was wearing the see-through nightgown that so tormented Bud. She was barefooted. Her legs were crossed.

"Thank you. Sorry for my appearance. After what's happened to me I suppose I don't have any shame left."

J.B. swallowed. He fought his desire to peer beyond the bare fabric of her gown, to take in the white, fleshy swell of her breasts and the contrasting dark punctuation of her nipples.

At the same moment that Judith looked to the ceiling and blew a smoke ring upward, he managed a glance. He found himself without words.

"Y'all need to know how much I appreciate your help," she said. "With me. With my Ruth Ann. I so do appreciate it," Judith said after deeply inhaling again. Smoke scattered randomly as she exhaled while speaking. "I'm sorry I gave you such a hard time at first. I was humiliated by the whole thing. Still am for that matter."

"No need to apologize. I dare say y'all's Ruth Ann and my James Ray seem to have somethin' goin' on between 'em," J.B. said, changing the subject.

"She speaks highly of y'all's boy. Her boyfriend back in Fort Worth was a loser. That's one good thing that's happened since movin' here."

"How's that?"

"Her breakin' up with him and her meetin' your James Ray."

"Well, I..."

"It's strange how that happens."

"What?"

"Girl meets boy. Boy meets girl and somethin' happens between 'em. Some unexplained chemistry. Either it's hello and goodbye or it's I'm goin' to make you mine if I have to move heaven and earth."

"The whole mutual attraction thing, I suppose," J.B. offered.

Judith rose. She stood before him in all her endowments. She took his hand.

"Follow me to the kitchen. I'm hungry. No, I'm starved. Come on, I'll make us a sandwich."

Judith released his hand and J.B. followed in her wake. He observed her through her gown and panty-covered backside. As he did, the rhythmic sway of her hips stirred him to carnal thoughts. He averted his view for a moment and then his eyes returned to the visual feast that lay just ahead of him.

James Ray and Ruth Ann had gone for a drive. She had asked to be taken to Devil's Lake for the first time since her encounter with the cottonmouth.

"Will you join me? Are you hungry?" Judith asked.

"Sure. I could manage a bite of somethin'. With Sarah Mae gone, James Ray and I find ourselves either skippin' meals or eatin' way too much when we do eat. We've become regulars at Linde Bee's. Mostly I don't have much of an appetite, period."

"Anyway, sorry to hear about Sarah Mae and her cancer. How are y'all copin' with her being gone?"

"We're doin' reasonably well, I suppose. As well as can be expected given the circumstances."

"Balogna and American cheese okay for you?"

"Sure. That would be mighty fine."

"Want a tomato on yours?"

"Sure."

"Mustard and mayo?"

"Sure. Mighty fine again."

"I'll make one for me that's minus the baloney."

"I'll help if..."

"You're helpin' by bein' here. That's the biggest of any kind of help. When I'm alone, I have dark thoughts."

"I'm sure y'all do."

After they ate, Judith steered the conversation back to the mystery of how a person was either attracted to or not attracted to a member of the opposite sex. She mentioned Darwin and his work at the Galapagos Islands and J.B. was eager to extend the conversation.

"Are y'all referrin' to those islands off the coast of Ecuador?" J.B. asked.

"Yes. The Galapagos. Darwin's place of study for much of his book. Fascinatin'."

"Have you read Darwin? His...what was the title?

"I believe it was *On the Origin of the Species.*"

"Yes. Well, I read some of it. Fascinatin', like I said. His natural selection and survival of the fittest and all that. That's what I was referrin' to earlier. What causes, or forces, or whatever come into play in all of that?" Judith asked. She lit another cigarette and cast a long gaze at J.B.

J.B. found himself shifting in his chair. He noticed its hardness. He took note of how the design of the chair caused him to sit taut and upright.

"Well," Judith offered, "Darwin claimed that natural selection has to do with the environment and all. The things that are in the environment go to work on the mating process, over time, of course. The other thing is artificial selection, or sexual selection of...those are the things that are seen...are seen as desirable by the mating couple. The woman sees that the man could protect the cave. He's big and strong. He brings home the bacon or a wooly mammoth or such. The man wants to sow his seeds with a woman who...well, he's sexually attracted to. So, on the Galapagos, Mr. Blue-footed Booby meets woman Blue-footed Booby. Male booby likes what he sees in female booby. On her part, she wants to make sure male booby is up to her expectations, so she takes a little while to be convinced so she can collect her thoughts about the matter."

Judith continued looking directly at J.B.

"His blue feet are a fine color of blue. The blue is just right. He approaches her and starts prancin' about, liftin' one foot up and down, and then the other, up and down. She likes what she sees. The up-and-down foot business. The just right, perfect blue of his feet. Over time and after more dancin' around on the sandy shore of the ocean, she's smitten, and accepts his approach and his seed. Time marches on. Eggs hatch, little boobies abound. Over time if left alone in isolation, given the environment and sexual attraction and things like that, things change. Things change for the better, if survival is at stake, and it always is. Legs get longer or feathers change color or beaks get stronger or whatnot dependin'. Then survival of the fittest comes in by way of a creature being stronger or smarter or havin' characteristics that are somehow more useful. Maybe the winged creature adapts to his or her environment and by skill or whatever becomes the best fish catcher on the island. Other creatures of its kind don't fish as well so their genes don't get passed on. I don't know, I'm just ramblin' on. I read the book so long ago."

"Well, seems you know more about evolution than I do. I wish Pastor Pritchard could work a little evolution into a sermon or two. If he painted a word picture the way you just did, I doubt there'd be a single soul asleep by the time he finished. Could be that he'd be stoned by his parishoners after the sermon. Anyway, it won't happen. Evolution's a bad word with people around these parts. Ranks right up there with Republicans or Catholics or Jews. Mention any of those subjects includin' evolution and you'll have to adopt some kind of defensive position. Up and defend your territory. Survival of the fittest, Mayweather style."

"I suppose you're right. Take y'all's James Ray. He looks Indian to me. His skin color. His high cheek bones. It's interestin' how genes get thrown together and all, and which ones get expressed and which ones take a back seat. None of y'all's other children look Indian. Why him? Ruth Ann says y'all's Sarah Mae has Indian blood in her but why then does James Ray's genetic heritage, the same as the rest of y'all's kids, get so differently expressed and all?"

J.B. didn't immediately respond. Instead, he reached into a jar for another pickle. He looked outside into the afternoon light through the kitchen window. He looked again to the pattern of the Oriental-looking wallpaper. He rubbed his forehead and then his chin. He noticed that for the second time that week, he had forgotten to shave.

"I've got to tell him at some point." J.B. muttered.

"Tell him what?"

"Well, it's, it's somethin' that's hard for me to talk about. Can you keep a secret?"

"I can. Here I sit before you nearly naked. I have nothin' to hide anymore. It's like we're an old married couple who've been married so long things cease to be new. Y'all know all about me. You know the good and bad of me. It's like you know everythin', have seen everythin' I have, and more. You've come to know all about any possible anythin' about me and my family in the short expanse of a couple months or so. I've been to y'all's house for dinner. Y'all know I'm an alcoholic; you know I've been unhappily married, that Ruth Ann's step daddy blew his brains out mostly because of me, and now you know I got stupid and was raped. I dare say you've been witness to it all, one way or another. I guess that qualifies me to keep y'all's secret. I'm confident you're keepin' my secrets, least as much as y'all can."

"He's not my son."

"What? What are y'all sayin', J.B.?"

"Well, he's Indian all right. Sarah Mae is one-eighth Coushatta. James Ray is more Coushatta than his mother. What would Darwin say to that? How does a boy who's mother is only one-eighth Indian have more Indian blood in him than his mother?"

Judith reached across the table and took J. B.'s hand. The one not holding a yet-to-be-consumed dill pickle.

"She was unfaithful? Someone...an Indian took her?"

"I suppose that's as good an explanation as any. I guess it's called a betrayal of the flesh."

"Was the person a...what do you call it? A Coushatta?" asked Judith.

"I suppose. I don't actually know. She has relatives on the reservation. I never asked."

"I suppose I'm guilty of betrayal as well. The flesh and all."

"How's that?"

"Do you want somethin' to drink?   Sweet tea or somethin'?"

Field of View

"Love some tea, thank you."

Judith got up and walked to the refrigerator. She reached inside for the pitcher of tea. She opened a tall cabinet door and stretched upward for a glass. J.B. noted the uplift of one of her partially-covered breasts, the muscled calf of her leg, the curvy sweep of calf muscle to ankle, the spread of her toes on the linoleum. She returned and offered the tea to J.B. and sat.

"I made vows. I promised this and that, but I reneged. I didn't commit adultery, I just withheld what a husband...I withheld the pleasures a husband is entitled to in a marriage. So I'm guilty too. I suppose that's a betrayal as well. Your Sarah Mae and I are both birds of a Galapagos betrayal feather."

"Maybe you're right. I don't know. It gets so complicated. Let me ask you this. Would you feel better if you were...were taken the way you were, but didn't know the who of it all? Know what I'm sayin'?"

"Good question. Knowin' the who of it does make for a lot of hatred. That's true enough. I don't know. I can see his face. I hate his face, his monster of a face. Maybe I'd feel better if someone had jumped me down at Piggly Wiggly, masked and all and I didn't know who it was. Maybe I would feel better if I didn't have a face to remember. I don't know."

Judith reached for another cigarette. "I need to stop smokin' at some point. I know it's not good for me. A poor and nervous habit, I suppose."

J.B. hated cigarette smoke. Cigar smoke even worse. But Judith had taken smoke to the level of some kind of art form. It was sexy. Her inhale, the purse of her lips, the oval shape her fleshy lips took when she released the perfect and tantalizing slow spiral of her smoke rings.

"But, back to y'all's James Ray, does he know that he's more Indian than his mother? Second, does he know that you aren't his biological father, and third, does he even know who his real father is?"

"No to all of those questions. I just hope that there's some royal blood in him. That his biological father is worthy, that he's from a long line of warriors, that his daddy is someone who's looked up to by the tribe. Maybe James Ray's better off havin' that someone's genes than mine."

"Well, that explains it." Judith formed another pursed oval with her lips and blew a smoke ring toward the kitchen's light fixture. Bull's eye. By the time the ring reached the ceiling, it completely encircled the fixture. After hitting the ceiling, the smoke ring lost its shape and form as it joined the lingering family of cigarette smoke that had already worked its way upward.

"Explains what?"

"His eyes. Those dark and mysterious eyes. Ruth Ann loves his eyes. She says that his eyes have a thousand stories to tell. I won't say a word to Ruth Ann or anyone about what you've told me. I promise. You have my word on that."

"Thank you."

"When are y'all goin' to tell him? He has a right to know. How long have you known? When..."

"I don't know when I'm goin' to tell him. At some opportune time, I guess. Sarah Mae told me of her infidelity before she left for California. Guess I'm plain stupid for not suspectin' sooner. Anyway, I know I need to tell James Ray but I never seem to find the right time. Everythin' all of a sudden has reached some kind of climax of sorts. One thing happens right on the heels of somethin' that's just happened and so on infinitum. Things seem to line up for attention.

"Yes, and I'm among them. Anyway, there may not be a right time to tell him. I've found that waiting is pretty much a losin' game. Better out with it. Keepin' it all inside is harmful to your health and well bein'. Pretty soon, you'll wonder if you have anything left inside you. You'll find yourself lookin' for a substitute for your soul like I did with alcohol. Numb the senses. Soothe what's left of your shriveled soul with alcohol. Pretty soon, you can't live without it. Your soul and alcohol become one and the same."

"Was that the way it felt to be married to Bud? Did y'all feel shriveled and all?"

"Yes. I never should have married him in the first place. I had...I felt like I had too, and once I did, I felt like I had to keep my unhappiness to myself. I took the vows. I said 'I do.' I agreed to the better or worse part, and so on, but I was miserable from the beginnin' to the end. Plain miserable. I never saw the better part, just the worse part. If there was a better part, I didn't lift it up or even recognize it. I just focused on my misery. Now, I feel guilty that Bud most likely killed himself because of me. Christ! How screwed up can life get? Talk about a battin' average gone sour."

"So, you married Bud for convenience? It wasn't the brilliant blue of his feet?"

Judith smiled and inhaled deeply from her cigarette. She didn't answer immediately, instead she looked intently at the man who sat beyond her in her kitchen. The man who was sitting upright in her kitchen chair while he still held a pickle. *He isn't what you would call handsome, but he's pleasant looking in a boyish sort of way. He's five, maybe ten years my senior? He seems comfortable in his own skin and he doesn't mind challenging authority. He's both smart and funny. Good with words, too. He's been kind and supportive throughout my mess of an ordeal and right now, he's doing what I need most. He's keeping me company. I have someone to talk to.*

"Convenience. Simple, really. I thought he would take care of Ruth Ann. Me too, for that matter. He'd bring home the mammoth, all Darwin-like. Problem was, there was no sexual selection part involved, at least on my part. No blue feet. No display of colorful peacock-like feathers. There was none of that. Other than his income, that is. I saw him as a provider, nothin' else."

"Speakin' of alcohol. If y'all don't mind me askin', are you goin' to take the advice of Dr. Curse His Hammer?"

"Yes. My first meetin' is Saturday evenin', comin' up. I've got to get a grip or y'all will have to help me identify a new bootlegger. I'm supposed to begin work when the drugstore is finished."

"That'll be good. Good for you. I'm proud of you."

"Will y'all come with me to my meetin'?"

J.B. looked directly into the hazel of Judith's eyes. He leaned back in his chair and bit into his pickle.

Chapter 42 - Ricochet

Carl feared he would have to put up the windows of his Cadillac. It looked like rain. He parked in the newspaper's rear lot and walked through the open back door. He looked around for Booker T. It was Sunday afternoon. Booker T.'s shift would end in a half-hour.

He found Booker T. in Spencer Shoemaker's office.

"Booker T., how're you doing?"

Booker T. was startled by the sound of Carl's voice.

"Oh...well, I be fine. How about y'all, Mr. Carl? What brings y'all to the paper on a Sunday afternoon?"

"So you like Ike?"

"I do. You noticed my button. I wear it all the time."

"You vote?"

"I do. Faithful to the polls. That's me and my Eartha."

"You vote despite the poll tax?"

"I do. I see it as my civic duty. Time was when we colored folk couldn't vote. 'Spect I'd better honor the fact I can vote, poll tax or not. Be a disgrace not to."

"Glad to hear it, Booker T. You think Eisenhower will do anything to end the condition of Negroes residing in the time-honored but prejudicial South?"

"Maybe so. Maybe not. I'm not privy to such knowin'."

"Hate to be negative, but my guess is southern Democrats will stop him like a chain link fence stops a cur dog."

"Maybe so, Mr. Carl, maybe so. Time, I 'spect will tell."

"Southern whites are a sorry lot, all in all. That's my Yankee opinion. Never got over losing the war and they hate bein' told by the federal government to do anything. It's state' rights this and states' rights that."

"Is the north where y'all came from different?"

"Is in some ways. In others, no. If you're referring to race, there's prejudice everywhere. In the north, it's just not so obvious. No Jim Crow. Not so in-your-face, I'm-in-and-you're-out, sort of thing but underneath it all, probably so."

"Well, I ain't never been to the north, I..."

"You done with your work?"

"I be. I just has to dump this trash and I be done."

"Good. I want to take you on a ride in my Cadillac."

"Y'all's Cadillac, Mr. Carl? Take me for a ride?"

"Yes, indeed. Might rain, but who cares. Come on. We'll take a ride to the Red River."

Booker T. thought he understood the reason behind the invitation. He had feared a confrontation with Carl since the evening when J.B. and his son confiscated a roll of film from Carl's darkroom. He paused before answering. "In all respect, Mr. Carl, I needs to decline y'all's fine offer. I needs to be home. My Eartha will have supper waitin'. I needs to..."

"Don't need to do anything, Booker. Look. Are you worried about being home for dinner, is that it?"

"I do appreciate y'all's kind offer but..."

"Have I ever done you any harm, Booker?"

"No suh, I..."

"Have I ever caused you to think ill of me?"

"No suh, never."

"Then are you asking me to beg you to ride in my Cadillac?"

"No suh. I don't mean for y'all to beg for anythin'."

"Well, then?"

"What y'all are askin' is unusual, that be it. It ain't like a white person to up and invite a colored person to ride in his fine example of a car. That's it. I just ain't never been invited to ride in a white person's car."

Booker T. thought it unwise to mention that he had often ridden in J.B.'s car.

"Let's leave race out of this, Booker. I'm asking you as a friend. As a co-worker and all. We work for the same newspaper. We live in the same town. The same county. Race has nothing to do with it. I'm a friend asking another friend to go for a ride. That's all."

"I do know that. Y'all have been a friend. And I appreciate how y'all have treated James Ray with respect and kindness and all here at work. Y'all have been patient with him. I have seen it. Y'all have treated him like a son. I know Mr. J.B. appreciates that. So do I. Do y'all know that my boy Sammy and James Ray are best friends, no matter the difference in their skin color. It's good for youngsters to have someone be kind to them, to help them along the way."

"No problem. I'm glad he's friends with your boy. What is his name?"

"Sammy."

"Yes, Sammy. Anyway, I don't know about your boy, but James Ray has talent. He'll do fine if he applies himself and if photography isn't a passing fling. But we weren't talking about James Ray and your boy, Sammy. We're were talking about my asking you kindly to take a ride in my Cadillac."

"Yes suh, I was just..."

"Good. Come on, let's go for a ride.

"I suppose I will. How long will we be? I'll need to tell my Eartha that I'll be late comin' home."

"We won't take long. Have you home in thirty minutes. Most likely it takes you twenty to walk. Ten minutes late isn't going to worry her."

Booker T. locked the rear door to the building and got into Carl's car. The car tilted to the right and down given his prodigious weight. Carl lit a cigarette. He turned the radio on. It was tuned to his favorite station.

After the radio tubes had warmed, Tennessee Ernie Ford and Kay Starr were in the middle of a duet titled, *I'll Never be Free.*

"Folks around here call that music, Hillbilly," Booker T. offered, thinking small talk would help in some way.

"Rockabilly. Hillbilly. It's all the same. Ten years from now it'll be called something else."

Carl accelerated after he left much of the town behind. The sky was growing dark. It began to rain. Carl had to put the windows up. He noticed the faint odor of vomit from the backseat carpet. He had meant to get over to Sherman where they had a full-service car wash. While the car was being detailed, he planned to take the short walk to a BBQ joint known for their pulled pork.

Carl activated the windshield wipers. Lightning ripped overhead followed by a loud clap of thunder.

"We gone far enough?" asked Booker T. "We might get caught in a forty day and night flood, Bible like and all."

Carl didn't respond. He began to worry about his plan. He was going to drive Booker T. to a spot he knew which could only be reached on a dirt road. He had photographed a wedding there. It was a beautiful location for an outdoor wedding. He loved using existing light for wedding photos. They were much superior to the indoor church photos where artificial light had to be used. He remembered that the bride was unattractive. Innocent and unattractive. When photographing weddings, he always wondered if the bride had any idea of what she was getting into. Or the groom, for that matter. The wedding had been short and sweet. A little talk about Adam's rib, and a little warning to the bride that she needed to be deferential to her husband, and it was over. The minister was one of his customers and had remained so to this day. He drank gin. Large amounts of gin.

Maybe it wouldn't be raining there, he hoped. If it were, his car would be a mess from the mud and gravel. He would have to take the road, regardless.

"We'll turn around in a couple of minutes. I know a good turnaround spot. Just relax, Booker, enjoy the ride. We need the rain, don't we?"

"I reckon so, Mr. Carl but..."

"Ever gone a hundred miles an hour?"

"No, suh, never."

"Well, hold on to your hat. Here we go."

The highway was clear ahead. The rain had subsided. Carl urged the Cadillac forward into the wind and rain. He noticed the car's slower acceleration given the extra weight of his passenger. The Cadillac's soft suspension swayed left to right, and top to bottom, given the thrust of the car and the unevenness of the pavement.

"Ninety...ninety-five. Here comes one hundred."

"Lawdy, Mr. Carl. Slow down or we be killed. The road's slippery and all."

"There it is. One hundred fucking miles an hour! Carl let his foot up from the accelerator pedal. The car slowed. The roar decreased. Booker T. relaxed his grip on the armrest.

Back at highway speed, Booker T. welcomed the blessing of an engine unchallenged. At sixty miles an hour, he felt as if he could simply step out of the car uninjured, so slow did the car seem to be traveling.

"How was that? Was that a kick in the ass or what?"

Booker T. knew he had made a mistake. *Getting into Mr. Carl's car was a foolish thing for me to do. White people, most of 'em anyway, are plumb crazy. I can't wait to get home. Watch and see, he'll up and ask me about the film. What will I say? Wonder what Eartha is makin' for supper? I'll tell her all about my bein' so stupid.*

"Here's our turnaround."

Carl brought the Cadillac to a halt. That was good. Booker T. hoped upon hope that he'd be home in fifteen minutes or so.

"Why ain't we back on the highway, Mr. Carl? Where we be goin'?"

"Got something to show you. Just take a minute."

The dirt road had received some rain. The road was puddled in spots. He'd have to get his car over to Sherman for a good wash just like he thought.

Carl stopped the car alongside a cottonwood tree. He immediately noticed the tree was partially uprooted. Probably by the same storm James Ray had documented.

Carl exited the car and walked around to the passenger door. He opened the door and ordered Booker T. from the car.

"I said get out of the car."

"What we be doin', Mr. Carl? Y'all promised me..."

Carl leaned into the car and opened the glove compartment. He reached in and secured his .38 snub-nose revolver.

Booker T. was stunned by what he saw.

"Now will you get out of the car?" Carl asked, pointing the gun at Booker T.

"Mr. Carl..."

"Get out of the fucking car."

Booker T. slowly worked his ample weight from the car. Carl ordered him to the cottonwood. Booker T. thought that any moment he'd be shot. He'd be shot in the back. He was destined to die alongside a cottonwood tree. He began to pray.

"Turn around and face me."

"Yes, suh. Mr. Carl, y'all don't know what y'all are doin'. Why you be treatin' me this way? Why are y'all goin' to shoot me dead. Why...?"

"Stop talking, Booker. I'll ask the questions. Where's my Goddam roll of film?"

"What film you be talkin' about, Mr. Carl?"

"You know Goddam well what I'm talking about. Let me paint a picture for you. Someone has taken a roll of film from my darkroom. No one has keys to the darkroom but me and who else? Who might the other person be, Booker? Who?"

"I don't rightly know!"

"You do rightly know! Now, do I have to shoot you or are you going to tell me who it was who took the film? I have keys, you have keys. Either you took the film or you let someone else take the film. So, what's your preference? You want me to shoot you or do you want to tell me who's the thief? Simple choice. Die, or tell the truth. Tell the truth and you live. Tell the truth and I get my film back and I take you home and I say nothing and you say nothing. It's over just like that. Ready to go home or are you ready to die?"

Booker T. resumed praying. He bowed his head. His hands went to his face. He felt that his end was near. *Any second I'll be dead. Please Lord, please deliver me. I ask your forgiveness for anythin' I may have...*

"Stop the Goddam muttering."

A shot rang out into the still of the country side. A flock of blackbirds took to the air from a nearby field.

"The next shot, you go down, Booker. The next one will be for real. Who took the fucking film?"

Booker T. didn't answer. His throat was dry. Sweat poured from his forehead. His hands shook. His legs trembled.

Fire spit from Carl's revolver a second time.

Booker T. fell to the ground. He reached for his leg. Something burned in his leg. It was unlike anything he'd ever experienced. The searing pain clawed at his consciousness, unrelenting and abusive.

"Sorry, Booker. I didn't mean to shoot you. In fact, I didn't shoot you. The bullet must've ricocheted from the tree or a rock or something. I was just trying to scare you."

Booker T. didn't hear a word Carl said. Blood poured from the back of his leg. A lot of blood.

"Mr. Carl, they be laws agin killin' folks. Lordy. Whether they be colored or white. Y'all can't up and kill...Lordy. I never done y'all a lick of harm, Mr. Carl. Never. Don't go and kill me...please, Mr. Carl."

"Christ. Now what?" Carl said aloud. "I'm not going to kill you. Never intended to but...but I can't put you in the car, Booker. You're bleeding too much. Who took the film?" Carl asked, thinking a wounded Booker T. might now be willing to talk.

"I don't know. I told y'all...Lordy, I hurt."

"Shit, fuck! I'm leaving. You walk to the road. Someone will pick you up. Here's my handkerchief. Forget all this happened. You got shot by accident. Make up a good story. One that's believable. Not a word to anyone, you hear? Or I will kill you."

Carl got into the car. He replaced the revolver in the glove compartment. He started the car. He left, the Cadillac's distinctive finned taillights marking his exit.

Booker T. struggled to right himself. He looked at his hand that had been tending to the wound. It was covered with blood. The ground too, was bloody. He hurt. The pain in his leg was excruciating. The wound was in the back of his left leg, not the front. It all happened so suddenly, Booker T. couldn't make sense of the situation. He couldn't figure out how to stop the bleeding. He wondered if this was the place where he would die. He recalled the time his father had informed him that there were two mysteries of life. One, a person didn't know when they would die, and two, how they would die. But die they would.

He applied Carl's handkerchief to his leg and managed to stand. It was of no use. He couldn't hold the handkerchief to his leg and walk at the same time. He reached up to the tree and ripped a dead branch from its mooring. He would use the branch for support.

He prayed as he began his stumbled walk back to the highway. Although only a few hundred yards distant, the highway seemed miles away, too far, too unattainable.

He fell. He found he couldn't rise. He managed to get to his hands and knees, but no further. He felt weak, exhausted. He lay down on his back in the wet mud of the road. The cool wet of the road was refreshing. He thought that maybe someone would come along and save him. Maybe a farmer didn't care if blood got on the bed of his pickup.

He looked skyward to the clouds. The sun's rays shone through. It was a beautiful sight: the clouds, and the rays of light that filtered through them. He prayed, but he didn't finish his prayer. His mind wandered back to his youth when he was whipped by a white rancher in Arkansas. The whip stung, but nothing like what he was feeling now. Enraged by the sadistic act, Booker T. had taken the single-tailed snake whip from the man and had choked him with it. He let the hateful man live. The man never bothered him again.

A peaceful calm came over Booker T. Johnson. He was now too weak to feel his pain. He left Arkansas and returned to his prayers. He asked for God's forgiveness for being such a fool. He prayed for his beloved Eartha. He prayed that his son Sammy would some day play alongside Jackie Robinson. He prayed. And, he died.

Chapter 43 - Fit to be Seen

"It's developed. Film's still wet though." James Ray informed J.B.

"May I see it? I'd like to catch a glimpse of what sorry business he's been up to."

"Sure, but let me handle the film. Can't touch the emulsion 'cause like I say, it's still wet."

J.B. rose from the kitchen table and followed James Ray to the storm cellar.

"Be careful. Here, just hold the film with the clothespin. I don't know what you'll be able to make out, though. When the film's dry, I'll make a contact sheet and then you'll have a better look."

To air dry the film, James Ray had pinned the roll with a clothespin to some kite string he'd strung from one wall to another. J.B. looked at the film from beginning to end. He said nothing.

"There's three of 'em. Seems he's upped the ante. Come the next third Thursday he'll have the room full of kids.'

"Well, this is just one of his rolls of film," James Ray said. "Who knows what the others would show."

"A white boy and two colored girls?" J.B. asked.

"No, the boy's colored. The girls are white."

"I don't understand."

"You're lookin' at a negative. The white you see is because his skin reflected little light. The girls are black, because they reflected a lot of light. When I make the contact, it'll all be reversed. We'll have a positive. The two girls will be seen as white and the boy will look like Sammy."

"So what y'all are tellin' me is that Carl has a colored boy and two white girls goin' at it, at least in this roll of film."

"There's a French word for it. I think it's called a menagerie or somethin' like that."

"I don't think that's the right word to describe a get-it-on-threesome-sexual-horseplay situation, but in a way it is a menagerie, I suppose."

"Anyway, I..."

J.B. interrupted. "So there are three models. Chipper is the one who said the boy was colored but no one believed him. Maybe he's light-skinned, but colored just the same given the way those things are judged. Do you think we'll be able to tell whether or not they're underage?"

"They all look young to me. That was what I was goin' to say."

"All right. And we know Carl was there. He arrived early. He left late. He was seen by everyone. We have good, solid eye witnesses to his presence. He walked early to the Lone Star. He left his prize of a Cadillac in the paper's parkin' lot. Must have all of his whatever-he-needs at the hotel already locked in the closet. We have witnesses to Carl leavin' the Lone Star and walkin' to the *Tribune* to drop off the film. Now, we also have film evidence, thanks to you. And maybe at some point we can determine whether or not the kids are underage. Once we get a grand jury organized, we can have the license plate of the car traced. Who knows where that will lead? All in all, I think we'll have enough evidence corralled to get Judge Schmid to call for a grand jury. Good job all-around. I think we have as much as we need."

"Daddy, Carl's been actin' very strange lately. I'm sure he knows a roll of film is missin'."

"Probably thinks he's misplaced it."

"Not Carl. Remember, the roll was numbered."

"Well, just go about things as normal. We'll have this wrapped up soon. At least I hope we do."

"Me too. It makes me nervous."

"James Ray?"

"What?"

"You've done the right thing. Without your help, we couldn't have gotten to the bottom of this mess. I've got to believe that good will come of it eventually."

*　*　*　*　*

"Look at it this way," Charlie said. "If y'all's sheriff, Hoghead, tries to cover up the rape or pin it on someone else, we have enough to bring him down as well."

"Boy, I don't know about that. I don't see..."

"Well, try to see. He's in on the take from the bootleggers. They pay, he receives. He protects 'em, they operate safely. At least, for the most part. Anyway, it's a business arrangement that works. It's well-oiled and mutually beneficial all the way around. Now, to make sure the mess of bootleggin' and the rape doesn't hit the front page of the paper, he'll try to figure a way out of it all, to cover it up in some way. I don't know how exactly, but always look for the motive behind the behavior. It's basic investigative science. We know all about the Lone Star and we know who raped the Chambers lady. All in all, once the grand jury is summoned, we'll have evidence on both fronts. And once we get the fingerprint analysis back, there will be Judith's prints and Carl's prints. Once we get the ball rollin', we'll figure out a way to collect fresh prints from Carl or leave it up to the authorities. Fingerprints speak. Can't beat 'em when you're tryin' to fix a person to a crime once we have a comparison. We can get 'em from anythin' he touches. A water glass, a magazine, the steerin' wheel of his car, anythin'."

"I suppose that's what's called incriminatin' evidence."

"Yes, indeed. Also, I'm havin' the glass shards chemically analyzed for evidence of a barbiturate of some kind, somethin' that would've depressed her central nervous system, somethin' that Carl would have added to the drinks to bring her down. Now, armed with all that, we're in good shape. And if y'all's sheriff, like I say, goes and tries to cover up the rape, well, he'll come down like Carl is gonna come down. Two birds with one stone, as the sayin' goes."

*   *   *   *   *

"Oh, J.B., I'm so very worried. He's not home and he's always home for supper after work on Sundays. It's been two hours now."

"Come on in, Eartha. Let's try to figure this out."

"Thank you, kindly." Eartha entered the Turman house, and sat on the chair that was seldom used. The chair that had served as the prop for the family photo years ago. She was wearing slippers and an apron. The apron was worn. How many meal preparations had it accompanied? It displayed a faded print of an ocean scene of some kind, waves crashing onto rock, sea gulls in the air. It caused J.B. to think of Sarah Mae and his girls.

"When does he finish work?" J.B. asked.

"Six in the afternoon. Goes in at three."

"And he hasn't called? Didn't say he'd be late when he left this afternoon?"

"No." Eartha began to cry.

"He doesn't stop and shop on the way home? Could he have had some reason to be late that maybe..."

"Sammy's on the way to the paper right now to see if he's still there. I tell you, for certain J.B., it's not like him to be late. Especially for supper. Somethin' bad has happened, J.B. I can feel it in my bones."

"We'll find him. A man as big as he is can't easily get lost."

"Did you know y'all's James Ray had it out with the bully boy. I don't remember the bully boy's name."

"Rusty Wickware? They fought? What happened?"

"My Sammy says he whupped the bully boy mightily, but our James Ray broke some bones in his right hand. I mended his hand as best as I could and sent him to the doctor to get it fixed proper. Y'all didn't get a call from the doctor?"

"No. Not yet, anyway. I've been away from the phone, workin' in what's left of the garden, given the heat. Is he okay, other than the broken hand? When did it happen?"

"Just this afternoon. In front of that new house that's been moved. Blood all over the sidewalk. Sammy showed it to me. Showed me how our James Ray threw the bully boy head first into a tree. Busted his head up somethin' terrible."

"Good Lord. They fought right down the street while I'm weedin' the garden?"

"Seems y'all's James Ray did a little weedin' of his own."

"Sammy said they went lookin' for y'all after the fight, and hollered and all, but y'all didn't answer. 'Spect they thought y'all weren't home."

Sammy rushed through the Turman front door. He had run all the way home from the newspaper. "Mama, I've been lookin' for you. Daddy ain't at the paper. It's closed shut."

"Mercy. Now what do we do J.B.?"

"I don't know, Eartha. I don't know. We can go lookin' for him, I suppose."

A painful remorse came over J.B. Booker T.'s missing might have something to do with Carl and the missing film. *Good God, now what?*

*   *   *   *   *

Field of View

A dead man doesn't talk, thought Hoghead. That's good. The nigger janitor was dead. He was found in the general vicinity of South Cow. That's all good. He figured he had his rapist. All he had to do was plant some kind of evidence back at the farm house, and go from there. No matter what the Chambers woman would claim, assuming she didn't give up on the whole idea, there'll be evidence to the contrary. He would see to it.

"How long would y'all say he's been dead?" Hoghead asked Murray Singletree, the mortician.

"Not long. I'd guess last evenin' or so. Did y'all talk with the teenagers who reported findin' him?" Murray asked.

"Not yet. Maybe he's the sorry son-of-a-bitch who went and raped the Chambers lady," Hoghead speculated. "Y'all know that family that moved in from Fort Worth? The husband is the one who shot himself down to the pump company. She's the wife, the good looker. Ever seen her around town?"

"Can't say as I have. But I recall workin' on the husband. Put a small caliber bullet clean through his head. Chambers. Bud Chambers. Don't get too many suicides around here. Maybe one every other year or so. Somethin' like that. Anyway, as I recollect, his wife was raped. Makes for a pure run of misfortune, doesn't it?"

"Probably by the dead nigger here. Look at the size of him. No woman could resist if he up and decided he wanted a little refreshment."

"Well, that might be a stretch too far, Huff. What do y'all have that..."

"Was found by the kids within a couple of miles from the location where the Chambers lady was raped. Found on a back woods county road. Got shot and died. Was probably on the prowl. Got caught by someone packin' a pistol. The Nigger rapist ran from the scene of the crime and got shot in the leg and then he bled to death. Makes sense to me. Probably would have raped the girl who was with the boy if someone hadn't taken him down first."

"All in all, I think that's a pretty much a stretch, Huff."

"Well, what I know is that we've got a dead nigger janitor. I think it's more than likely that he's a rapist. Was anyway. So now I have yet another crime to solve. Such is the life of a sheriff."

"I do wish y'all would stop callin' the Johnson man a 'nigger.' It's disrespectful. Inside...take away the skin color...and I've found all of us are the same. Anyway, somedays I think I'd like to trade jobs with you. Y'all deal with death every now and then. I get to deal with it on a daily basis, rain or shine, sleet or snow, regardless of the season. People dyin' from natural causes and then I also get the ones who don't. I'm mostly numb to it by now. Goin' on thirty years of gettin' people presentable for their viewin'. It's the ones I can't do much with that are the hard ones."

Murray returned to his work.

Hoghead walked over to a basket containing Booker T.'s personal items. He reached into the basket, and retrieved Booker T.'s pocket watch by its chain. He calmly placed the watch in his pocket.

The watch was an heirloom. It had been Booker T.'s grandfather's. His grandfather had spoken fluent Spanish and had worked for most of his adult life helping build railways in Panama, and throughout much of Latin America. He and his Mexican wife returned to his home state of Arkansas when he was unable to continue the physical aspects of his labor.

The war was over after all, the thirteenth amendment in place, and he was, supposedly, a free man.

Chapter 44 - Long Time Comin', Long Time Gone

Unlike almost all Negro deaths, Booker T.'s obituary was given two full columns on the front page along with a picture James Ray had taken of him a few weeks before. Booker T. stood at the rear entrance to the paper, holding a broom. He was smiling. He was framed by the doorway. James Ray's exposure was spot on. He had followed Carl's advice and had overexposed to ensure Booker T.'s image revealed detail given the scant amount of light his face reflected. The headline read, *Courthouse and Tribune Employee Found Dead.* Its subhead: *Mystery surrounds shooting death in rural Mayweather.*

Spencer Shoemaker refused to follow Huff's suggestion that the paper describe Booker T.'s death as retribution for a possible rape attempt. Huff had walked to the *Tribune* to discuss the matter. His walks around town allowed the good citizens of Mayweather to see that their tax dollars were well spent. He always made an effort to greet the ladies with a smile and a tip of his Stetson.

"Absolutely not. There's not a shred of evidence, as far as I can see, that he was engaged in any such activity," Shoemaker replied. "That's pure wild speculation on y'all's part, if I may be forgiven for sayin' so. The man was a gentle giant. There wasn't an ounce of immorality in his entire body. His death is a tragedy for our community. He was a good man, and now he's dead, in all probability by malicious means."

Hoghead sat back in his chair. "Don't say. Now who's guilty of wild speculation? I'll agree we don't know for certain at this point but..."

"Please excuse the interruption, Huff. My reporter told me a bullet was removed from his leg. What do you have on that front?"

"Nothin'. Bullets from a gun like that is as commonplace as crows in a cornfield."

"Well, it seems to me you should be trying to ascertain why he was out on that country road in the first place. He doesn't drive. Someone must've driven him to the place where he was shot. Have you given that any thought?"

"Of course I have. The man's dead. I can't ask him, can I?"

Field of View

*   *   *   *   *

James Ray sat at the kitchen table. One minute he was rid of Rusty Wickware. The next, Booker T. was dead and now he was being forced to quit a job he loved. He was near tears when J.B. entered the kitchen. James Ray immediately began protesting his daddy's instance that he quit his job at the paper.

"I know what y'all are sayin'," James Ray said. "It's just that..."

"I can't have it, James Ray. One day you'll be an adult and you can call your own shots. You're not there yet and as your father, I can't have you in harm's way. I don't know how else to put it. Booker T.'s dead, and dollars to doughnuts, Carl is behind it. I feel terrible. I know I...I'm complicit in his death. I'll never forgive myself. I'm goin' to have to tell Eartha and Sammy soon."

J.B. buried his head in his hands. He sat. Tears came to his eyes. He lapsed into silence. James Ray drew a deep breath and wiped tears from his eyes. J.B. rose and reached for a Coke inside the refrigerator.

"Want one?"

"No, thanks."

"Come here," he said to James Ray. James Ray rose. They hugged. They both cried.

Later, J.B. drove James Ray to the *Tribune.* They parked in the rear lot. J.B. accompanied his son inside. He had arranged an appointment with Spencer. They would talk while James Ray delivered his message to Carl. J.B. sat in a position allowing him a clear view of the entrance to the paper's darkroom. James Ray had been warned not to enter the darkroom, to make sure he talked to Carl outside so the two could be seen from the editor's office window.

"I know this hurts," J.B. said to James Ray. "It's not the way you intended things to work out. Life is like that. Life is often unfair but I won't have you in harm's way, not now, not ever, although to be honest, I suppose I already have. You and Booker T. both."

*   *   *   *   *

"What happened to you?" Carl asked. "Is that why you haven't been to work for, what is it, three days?"

"Broke my hand. Still hurts. The doctor reset it. Hurt more when he reset it than it did when I broke it."

"How did you break it?"

"Had a fight."

"Who got the worse of it?"

"The other guy did. I think I told you about the guy. The town bully? Rusty Wickware? Anyway, that's all over with finally, thank God. Leastways I hope it is."

Carl looked at his young apprentice. He now saw James Ray in a new and unwelcome light. The missing film was still missing. Everyone at the paper was in mourning given Booker T.'s death. Things hadn't gone well, hadn't gone well for a week or so. The remaining question was what role did James Ray play regarding the absent roll of film. He would have to find out.

"We're headed to California to see my mother and then school is gonna start and I have so much to do I don't think I can handle it all," James Ray told Carl.

"Didn't figure it would end like this, James Ray."

"Me neither."

"Sorry to hear about Booker T. He was a nice man."

"Yes."

"What's your father doing here?"

"Oh, he and Mr. Shoemaker are friends. They went to college together. Daddy and Booker T. were real good friends. Daddy drove me. I can't drive with my bad hand."

"So, that's why you're quitting, James Ray? Taking a trip to California, and then when you return, you'll be too busy to help out?"

"Well, like I say, I have so much on my plate and..."

"So you've told the man?"

"Mr. Shoemaker? Yes, I called him last night at his house."

"You haven't seen a roll of film laying about, have you?"

"No, why?"

Carl narrowed his eyes. He tried to read James Ray's nonverbal behavior. He figured it was possible James Ray knew more than he was admitting.

"Just asking. I'm missing a roll. I always number my film, and one roll must have grown legs and walked away. It's a mystery how a roll of film can just disappear. There one minute; gone the next."

"Well, I lost my key to the house the other day. It..."

"Losing your key and having a roll of film placed on a shelf one day, and the very next morning it's gone, are two different scenarios. You know I lock the darkroom."

"I'm sorry about the film...I, was it somethin' worthwhile? Somethin' you can't replace?"

"Of course it's worthwhile. I don't record any images unless they're worthwhile. You've been around long enough to know that. By the way, been doing any developing or enlarging in your mother's storm shelter darkroom lately?"

James Ray paused before answering. He looked over his shoulder to the editor's office. Both J.B. and Spencer were furtively watching. "I'm finished with my photo essay of Ruth Ann."

"You laid her yet?"

"No. Actually we..."

"That's neither here nor there. Let's get back to the subject of the missing film."

"Like I told you, I don't know anythin' about a missin' roll of film."

"Then say hello to sunny southern California and get the fuck out of my life."

*　　*　　*　　*　　*

"Here's my problem, Carl," Hoghead said. "I've got a woman cryin' rape and now I've got a dead nigger custodian on my hands." Interestin', all of it. You service the woman's need for alcohol and you work with the nigger custodian. Lo and behold, the woman is raped and the nigger custodian is found dead."

Carl remained silent. Hoghead had asked for a booth in the corner of the cafe out of hearing distance from anyone other than someone going to the restroom.

"The Chambers woman is serviced by you. You take care of her need. All of a sudden, someone meets her at the place y'all are tryin' to buy and then someone liquors her up with some concoction and he dicks her good against her will. In any book, that's rape, Carl. She's filed a charge and she claims y'all are the person who raped her. Imagine that. Says y'all tricked her to come out there, put somethin' in her whatever it was she was drinkin' and fucked her. Front and back. Must've been a horny night for you, Carl. Front and back?"

Field of View

Carl remained silent. He lit a cigarette. He held the cigarette between his teeth. He stared at Hoghead. He reached for his belt and pulled upward on his jeans. His pants were loose. He had lost weight. He chased a fly from the rim of his water glass. Hoghead played with a cigar but didn't attempt to light it.

"Now," Hoghead said. "I have to deal with a fuckin' dead nigger. A nigger who worked with you since you arrived in town some two-and-a-half years ago. A nigger who is looked well upon by the paper's publisher...and the whole fuckin' county for that matter...whether he is, was, colored or not."

Carl said nothing. Their hamburgers arrived. Carl removed the tomato from his sandwich. "I asked her for no tomatoes. Fuckin' stupid waitress."

"Don't jump to conclusions, Carl. Could have been the cook who put in the tomatoes. Maybe he doesn't read well. Anyways," Hoghead asked with a mouthful of burger, "what kind of a grudge did y'all have against the nigger? That's the question. What would bring y'all to shoot him? In the back of the leg and all. That's a funny place to shoot someone if you're out to kill someone. Shoot 'em in the back of the leg and let 'em bleed to death. Interestin'. Maybe y'all have a good excuse for why he's dead. Maybe he jumped you or somethin'?"

"I don't know what you're talking about." Carl hadn't touched his burger. He snuffed his cigarette and lit another.

"Sure you do. I've matched tire prints from both crime scenes, the farmhouse and the country road nearby. Both places are crime scenes, Carl. They bear a heap of evidence. Tire tracks belong to a spiffy Cadillac seen around town. Yellow, Cadillac Coupe deVille. Goodyear Double Eagles for tires."

"Could have been someone else's Cadillac."

"Could have been. Yes, sir. Problem is, the Chambers lady says it's y'all's Cadillac and you were drivin' it and you're the one who raped her. Then, there's the bullet that was removed from the janitor's leg. It's a .38 caliber. Blew away the main artery to his leg. Might have to go and match the bullet to the gun y'all keep with y'all in case someone tries to jump you and steal your liquor, or money, or whatever y'all see as valuable. Remember when y'all showed me the gun? A cute little snub-nose Smith and Wesson, was it? Do I have to go to all the trouble to do that?"

"What the fuck do you want, Huff? What are you trying to tell me?"

"Let me be as direct as I can be. Are y'all listenin' with both ears?"

"Get on with it." Carl finally took a bite of his burger.

"I got wind a grand jury's bein' formed. The good citizens of Mayweather are gonna try to sort out who knows what. It's all kept secret what they're up to but I can assure you that they will be lookin' into both the rape and the death of the nigger custodian. So, a grand jury's bein' convened. I've got a good and reliable source that says so. Someone who's privy to matters like that. Grand jury's got a lot of power, Carl. Transcends the usual law and order peace-keepin'. A bunch of citizens who get to play God. So, like I say, they'll be lookin' into not only the rape but the nigger custodian's death as well."

"What does any of that have to do with me?"

"Do you have y'all's head up your ass? Shit, Carl. You know fuckin' well what it all has to do with you. Or maybe y'all are deaf. Or maybe you're stupid. Look. There's nothin' an ordinary run-of-the-mill citizen loves better than bein' on a grand jury and callin' for an indictment. They'll up and indict the Father, the Son and the fuckin' Holy Ghost if they get a chance. That puts me in a hard spot. You too, Carl. Are you beginnin' to see the light?"

"Just spell it out. What do you want?"

"Oh, one other little thing. My source tells me, of course, this is secret and all, that somethin' is goin' on down to the Lone Star. Interestin' stuff. Has to do with underage kids fuckin' their brains out while bein' photographed. You wouldn't happen to know about any of that business would you?"

Carl wasn't surprised by Hoghead's revelation. *The missing roll of film. Of course. The film and its images. James Ray was the one. The little shit. I spend countless hours teaching him a craft and he turns on me. Probably developed the film in his shelter of a darkroom and then passed the film on to his do-good daddy. But what turned them on to the Lone Star in the first place? Fuck a duck.*

"I asked y'all a question. Do you know what's goin' on at the Lone Star? I'm disappointed Carl. I take you in. I protect your bootleggin' business and then you up and leave me out of the dirty picture-takin' at the Lone Star? Not that I would want to have anythin' to do with tainted monetary gain, pornography and all. There's some talk about the models bein' underage. Holy, fuckin' shit, Carl. Holy, fuckin' shit!"

Hoghead leaned forward and narrowed his eyes. He glared at Carl.

"Let's be truthful here, Huff. You'd take money from anywhere as long as you figured it could be kept on the quiet. You're as much of a law breaker as I am."

"Not hardly. Not even in the same league. The Lone Star business is a pile of deep shit and y'all are standin' waist deep in it. Shit, that'll have the whole town in a fuckin', Devil's-upon-us conniption."

Carl looked down at his hamburger. He then looked over at the waitress who had gotten his order wrong. Her back was turned to his table. He had failed to even look at her when he had placed his order. He noticed she had nice legs. A nice round and tight rear end as well. She leaned over to take an order from a man who looked like a farmer. She was partially silhouetted by the cafe's picture window. He began to mentally arrange the visual elements: what he would include, what he would exclude, what camera angle would be best. Given the contrast between the brilliance of the outside light and the relative dimness of the interior of the cafe, the scene would make for a tough exposure. For sure, he'd expose for the interior light and bracket as well. The photo would, as all of his images did, capture a moment in time and space.

"Are y'all listenin' or trollin' for a piece of ass?"

"Fire away, Sheriff. Fire away."

"Well, then we've got the issue of murder or manslaughter, nigger or not, ain't we? I don't know which it'll be, but the grand jury will figure all that out, won't they? I won't have to go to the trouble. I was gonna cover it all up but why fuckin' bother. The Goddam train has left the station with a load of shit that carries far more punishment than bein' busted for mere bootleggin'. And if y'all have been foolish enough to send your Lone Star naked-picture-takin' creativity out-of-state, the Feds will shove the Interstate Commerce Act straight up y'all's entrepreneurial ass. Y'all are in deep shit, Carl. Just like you were before, back east. Mighty deep shit."

"You're in it too, Huff, if the bootleggin' payoff comes to light, and it will."

"Maybe, maybe not. The Chambers lady may mention buyin' alcohol from you but everyone knows about bootleggin' around here. It ain't just alcohol we're talkin' about here Carl. She's cryin' rape. Anyways, half the county are customers one way or another and you won't be here to answer a single Goddam fuckin' grand jury question. I'll bust a couple of bootleggers to show that I'm on the lookout for 'em and conveniently, you'll be long gone."

"What are you saying?"

"I'm saying, I want y'all's underage, picture-takin', nigger-shootin', rapist ass out of town. Tonight, Carl!"

*   *   *   *   *

Judith invited J.B. and James Ray to dinner at her house. She desperately needed something to do, and having something to do inside, as opposed to being seen around town, met her goal nicely. She was going to serve up an Indian curry dish. It would be vegetarian, of course, but it was a dish she thought would please the worst of carnivores, J.B. and his son among them. She had found the recipe in a year-old *Better Homes and Gardens* magazine when she had been in the hospital.

J.B. was asked to bring carrots and garlic.

"Let me see what else I need." Judith said. She laid the phone down and walked back to the kitchen and returned with the magazine. "Anythin' really. All vegetables are good. What else do you have ready to harvest?"

"Beets, greens..."

"What kind of greens?"

"Cabbage, mustard greens..."

"No. It calls for cilantro. Do you have any?"

"What's cilantro?"

"Sort of a Mexican parsley, I think. If you don't have any, I suppose parsley would do."

"I've got a ton of parsley."

"Good. Have any okra?"

"I do. I have enough okra to choke a horse."

"Good. Bring enough that would half choke a horse. Got potatoes?"

"Maybe, I'll have to go and dig around. Should have some by now. Probably just be fingerlings."

"That's fine. Let me see. Oh, of course, I need onions."

"Red or white?"

"Calls for one white onion, but I think red would be better. It'll add a little color."

"OK. Anythin' else?"

"Well, I'm missing turmeric and ginger. Maybe I can find somethin' that will substitute. The big thing is where can I get my hands on some coconut milk?"

"Coconut milk?"

"It won't work without coconut milk."

J.B. thought. There was a foreign food market in Sherman of some kind. The town possessed some descendants from the Chinese who had immigrated to east Texas in the last century. He remembered passing the market at some point but he couldn't remember where it was located exactly. South Sherman somewhere.

"Are you there?"

"Yes, just thinkin'. There's a little market in Sherman. Chinese, I think."

"Curry is Indian, as in Columbus was sailin' for India. Not as in our Indian, the misnomer of it all."

"Well, I'm not sure exactly what kind of..."

"It's early. Will you take me for a ride? I've never ridden in y'all's new car. Let's drive to Sherman. Is that all right? Maybe they'll have coconut milk and maybe the spices I'm missing. I need some fresh air, regardless. Will y'all take me?"

"Does a horse have feathers?"

"No."

"Well then, looks like you'll have to take a cab."

"And y'all are fixin' to be scalped."

The dinner went well. J.B. was pleased to have such a beautiful woman cook for him but overall, he wasn't sure about Indian cuisine. Aside from the ingredients that he was familiar with, and could easily discern in the mix of orange-like broth, he thought it would be nice to fork into a piece of pork or chicken, perhaps. The jalapeño pepper most disturbed him. He grew sweet and delicious bell peppers. He did not grow peppers that were hot enough to set fire to a stack of wet timber. Then, there was the pungent and foreign tasting cilantro. Judith had made him take a bite of it raw. And who ever thought to put coconut milk into anything? If one cracked open a coconut, one ate the coconut and drank the milk. He had never heard of anyone putting the nut's milk into a stew-like mixture of vegetables.

Following supper, James Ray and Ruth Ann left to go to Devil's lake. They took Judith's Buick. She said it needed a run. Ruth Ann was going to force James Ray to dance. He was terrified.

"Y'all get out on the basketball court in front of hundreds of people and you run up and down the court not givin' a care to your infirmity, scant though it is."

"That's different."

"No, it's not. It's just that you're used to it. That's all. Over time, you will get used to dancin', too."

"Well, I don't know."

"Yes, you do. You hang on to me and listen to the music. Move your feet to the music. Hold onto me and feel the music. That's all there is to it. You still have to lead, though. I'll teach you how to lead. Lead, feel the music, and hold on to me."

"I like the idea of the holdin' part. Music, too."

"You are the startin' guard on the basketball team, right?"

"Yes...but I..."

"Well, then you can lead or I'll bench you. Y'all will be left with the bench and the music."

*   *   *   *   *

"We'll be gone on Thursday." J.B. said, as much to the wallpaper of the kitchen as to Judith. "We're packed and ready to haul out."

"How long will you be gone?"

"I don't know. Two weeks most likely. I can't take more time than that. Sarah Mae isn't doin' well. Her prognosis doesn't shed good light. She's started her radon treatments."

J.B. looked out the kitchen window. Then he closed his eyes and tried to get a handle on where he was headed, where anything was headed. He had finished drying the dishes.

Judith approached and thanked him for his help, and he once again thanked her for the interesting, though somewhat questionable, curry dish.

The two returned to the kitchen table and sat. Judith lit a cigarette.

"What about the grand jury and your testifyin'?"

"Old Judge Schmid said it would be a week or so just to put the grand jury together. Then, there'll be another couple of weeks before evidence is presented, witnesses called, and so on. I'll be back by then."

"It's a funny thing."

"What's funny?"

"I'm goin' to miss you."

"Me?"

"Yes, you, Mr. William Jennings Bryan Turman. You. Then there's Ruth Ann and James Ray. Her coach warned her about havin' a boyfriend and no sooner does she shuck her boyfriend in Fort Worth and recover from a snake bite than she corrals a another boyfriend who just so happens to be y'all's son. Or did y'all's James Ray corral her?"

J.B. rose and moved to Judith's side. He leaned over to kiss her. She hesitated but then accepted his advance. His hands briefly held her face. After their lips parted, she placed her cigarette into the ash tray. She looked him in his eyes. She surveyed his face. Their hands joined. They kissed a second time. It was both forceful and exploratory.

"Thank you for that." J.B. said. He returned to his seat. "A foreign vegetarian meal and a delightful kiss from the cook. Free, all of it, although I'm out some precious vegetables."

"No, I thank you, but please don't make light of the moment. Somethin' just happened here and I'm not sure what to make of it. Given what I just went through, I shouldn't get within a hundred yards of a man."

J.B. didn't respond. He looked intently at Judith. He thought her beautiful in the smoke-filled light of the kitchen. A beautiful yet forbidden fruit.

"Anyway," she said, "all of a sudden maybe it could be that y'all will have some reason to make your way back from California after all. You never know, you might get hungry for Indian food, grow so many vegetables that you can't eat 'em all, and you'll bring 'em over here for cookin'. Or, maybe you'll get as far as Sherman and turn around. Or, maybe y'all won't as much as leave your driveway. Never make it to California in the first place."

J.B. laughed and smiled. "Now look who is makin' light of the situation."

"I suppose I am." Judith shrugged her shoulders and smiled. "You caught me red handed taking somethin' serious and puttin' it in a flippant, J.B. Turman kind of way. You've taught me well."

She stood. "I know you need to go to California. Y'all's Sarah Mae needs you." She blew smoke toward the ceiling. "After all, you're a married man. I suppose things will develop one way or another over the passin' of time, won't they? Lots of possibilities, actually. In the end, after they've played out, whether they're good or bad depends on who's doin' the judgin'."

At that precise moment, J.B. wasn't concerned with possibilities. He simply figured he was in nirvana, or perhaps someplace near nirvana, wherever nirvana was, if there was such a place or state of mind. He wasn't sure of the word's correct definition. He thought it to be Indian. If nirvana had anything to do with curry, he'd get used to it, in the same way the sensation of Judith's lips trumped the chimney-like taste of cigarette smoke. If curry and smoky cigarette lips were to play a role in his life, he decided then and there, he would be open and accepting. Cilantro, too. Even jalapeños."

"Y'all's mind is racin'. A penny for your thoughts," Judith said.

"Just a penny?"

"That's all."

J.B. paused before answering. "Well, I do have a load on my mind." He adjusted himself in his chair and folded his arms across his chest. "There's California for starters. My marriage, or what's left of it. Then there's my good friend Booker T. and the wagon load of guilt I have from that. There's the mess at the Lone Star. My kids. You. Everythin', it seems. My mind is like Dagwood's closet. It's chock full of personal issues and I'm afraid to open the door."

"Well, if you're Dagwood, I'll be Blondie. I think you should open the door anyway. That's one of the twelve steps in AA. Do a personal inventory. Find out what the issues are. Make amends if you've wronged someone. Admit to your shortcomings. Blondie also suggests that you don't try to solve all of the problems at the same time or you'll get buried when you open the closet door."

J.B. sighed. "Well, thank you, Blondie."

"You're welcome, Dagwood."

"I suppose I should be goin'."

"Yes, tomorrow's another day."

"Yes, it is."

"Remember what Gandhi said."

"He said a bunch of things."

"He said we must become the change that we want to see."

"He was trying to rid India of colonial rule."

"Yes, and you're trying to rid yourself of doubt and guilt. Am I right?"

"Yes. Doubt and guilt. I'd rather be fighting the cotton-pickin' British."

"Well, fate would have it that you have to deal with your closet, not the British."

"Yes, the closet."

"One issue at a time."

J.B. reached for Judith's hand. "Mind if I send Blondie a postcard from California?"

"Of course not. That would be nice. Do you have my address?"

"No, I actually don't."

"Then the postcard will have a hard time gettin' here, won't it?"

Judith located a pencil, ripped a blank page from a binder and wrote her address. "Here. Now the postcard has half a chance of reachin' me."

On his way home, J.B. turned his thoughts to California. He would go, but he would return. In his mind it was a given, not a possibility. Coming home to Mayweather would be a big step in being the change he wanted to see.

Chapter 45 - Sister Twister

Carl left in the middle of the night. Other than his few personal possessions, he packed his camera equipment and clothing. He boxed up several albums containing negatives, proof sheets, and enlargements, along with an aging portfolio. Trixie would make the trip with him.

Trixie had been good. It would only be a matter of time before he'd find another Trixie, or several Trixies. He'd strike out for somewhere different, somewhere more accepting of changing times and shifting values. And, he'd be more careful. He knew he'd taken unnecessary chances. How the Lone Star operation had come to light, he might never know. Further, he figured, he could have had Judith if he'd been more patient.

His plan was to move beyond still images. Sixteen millimeter film would be his new visual medium. Still, black-and-white, and even color nude images were static. Movement was called for. Audio too. That was where the market for pornography was headed and he'd be a pioneer. He only had to find the right location, make the right connections, and solve the logistics behind such filmmaking. He had the money to do so. He'd go where people were more accepting of graphic depictions of sex. Pornographic customers were overwhelmingly male. He would court a female audience, as well. He planned to add interesting story lines to his work. He would create drama and tension between and among participants. When the plot worked its way to unabashed sex, women would be as eager to get it on as their male partners.

"California," he said out loud. "I'll create a new kind of Hollywood."

He drove straight until he reached Wichita Falls. He arrived mid-morning, had a late breakfast, and then paid a visit to the town's Oldsmobile and Cadillac dealership. An obese waitress with bad teeth and dyed red hair informed him of the location.

"Corner of 5th and Broad Street. Head up Broad. It's on the north corner of 5th and Broad."

There, he spent a good two hours trying to convince a cowboy type sales manager into accepting his Cadillac in trade for a used but presentable 1950 Plymouth Deluxe fastback.

"Look," Carl argued, "It's your good fortune to take my Caddy in on trade. Never mind the why of it. It's paid for. I have the title. I know I'm trading down. The Plymouth will do me fine. You'll make money on the Plymouth and you'll screw some hapless soul when you sell the Cadillac. You should be jumping with joy. You ask me one more time why, and I'll go to a Buick or Pontiac dealership and have them jump for joy."

"Car's got a funny smell," the man said after he had driven the Cadillac around the block.

"A kid threw up in the back seat. I haven't had time to clean the carpet. For shit sakes, shampoo the goddam carpet and you have a low mileage, slick-as-a-whistle, nearly new Caddy on your hands. Won't last a day once you put a for sale sign on it."

From Wichita Falls, Carl drove west to Vernon, had lunch, and got a buzz hair cut, military-style. He bought a carton of cigarettes and continued driving west. Just outside a small outpost of a town named after Quanah Parker, a half-white, half-Indian Comanche Chief, he pulled off to the shoulder of the highway to watch what he took to be the formation of a tornado. The radio had warned of severe weather. So, too, had the pimple-faced teenager who sold him the cigarettes.

"That's what they're sayin'. Could be a Johnny-come-lately," the boy said.

"Get many this far to the west?" Carl asked.

"Oh, yeah. Maybe not this time of the year but we get our share, that's 'fer sure. Radio said might be a squadron of 'em. Said conditions were right for storms and all."

"A squadron? Well. That'll make for an interesting drive."

Carl reached for his bottle of bourbon resting on the passenger side of the front seat. He lit a cigarette. The wind had picked up, the sky had darkened and he saw ahead that a tornado had indeed formed. He stopped the Plymouth, walked to the car's rear and opened the trunk. He retrieved his Exacta single lens reflex camera. He decided not to bother with his tripod and cable release. He'd use the stability of the car to steady his camera. The wide open spaces of the plains provided him with a great view of the storm. By now, it was fully formed. Its path, Carl calculated, should cause the tornado to intersect the highway a few miles ahead. It was headed north, so he saw no problem in attempting to photograph the storm.

He got back into the car and drove closer. He drank and he smoked. He guessed he was within a mile of the tornado. Ahead, he noticed a barn to the right of the road. From his perspective, the barn appeared to lie directly in the path of the tornado. If he was fortunate enough for that to happen, he would document the coupling of the barn and tornado.

He drove ever nearer. He had another drink. He snuffed his cigarette in the car's ash tray. The wind blew so hard he had a hard time opening the door of the car. Once outside, he braced himself against the car's front fender and spread his feet for support. He placed his elbows on the hood of the car. He began to pre-visualize his intended image, to arrange the visual elements within his field of view. He would place the barn in the lower, right third of the photograph. He would allow for two-thirds sky, and one-third land. The tornado would have space within the frame to 'move' prior to impacting the barn. He needed a fast enough shutter speed to capture the debris that would result from the collision and also fast enough to eliminate the possibility of camera shake.

The light was good despite the dark of the sky. Distant sunlight shone beneath a cloud, and fell on the barn at an angle, both highlighting the barn and the snake-like funnel of the tornado. Adding drama to the scene, was the fact that the tornado was grey in appearance, not black as he would have imagined. He couldn't have hoped for a better combination of dramatic visual elements abetted by quality light.

The gray, rope-like tail of the tornado advanced more slowly than he had anticipated. He moved from the hood of the Plymouth to its door and reached inside for his bourbon. He drank from the bottle.

Carl patiently observed the severe-weather phenomena's progress. The tornado finally crossed the highway and continued its mindless but persistent march toward the barn, just as he had hoped. He figured he was no less than two hundred yards removed from the base of the storm. He wished he had a longer lens. His 135mm telephoto lens would have to do. If need be, he would enlarge the image later.

As the twister neared the barn, it lost its shape and form. The tornado was spent. Its funnel separated at the bottom. The decaying base of the tornado became disjointed, appearing like a frayed and frazzled end of an earthen-colored and diabolical rope. The upper tip of the storm's funnel, however, was still anchored to the roiling and ominous sky above.

The barn disintegrated from the tornado's remaining power. Carl ducked as a piece of timber from the barn sailed overhead. He was finished with his photography. He figured he had captured several worthy images. He hoped each of his seven exposures, when linked, would document a kind of tornado timeline. It would move in lock step from full fury to exhaustion. Strangely, he noticed, the wind's velocity had accelerated, not diminished, despite the storm's discontinuation.

Given the rush and thrust of the wind surrounding him, Carl was unaware of the thrust and swirl of another tornado directly overhead. He tried to open the car's door but failed. Flying bits of gravel and roadside debris stung his face and hands. In an effort to protect the camera, he turned its lens inward to his chest. He shielded his face with his other hand. Crouching, with his back to the pummel of the wind, he reached for the door's handle again. He jerked hard on the door's handle. The door opened. The force of the wind whipped the door against his body, slamming him hard to the ground. He lay on his back. He managed a look skyward. He looked directly into the eye of the maelstrom. The tornado was upon him.

Epilogue

"Well, no sooner were the words out of my mouth and she forgave me," said J.B. in response to James Ray's question. "Said It could have been me or you for that matter who got shot and killed. She said Booker T. was called to heaven. He had work to do there, she said. I don't understand how a person can be so forgivin'. I really don't. What I did in contributing to his death should be deemed unforgivable in anyone's eyes."

James Ray slowed the Hudson as they found themselves behind a truck carrying a load of hay. The two were in west Texas. Both were getting hungry.

"You had no way of knowing what would happen to Sammy's daddy," James Ray replied. "I think you thought you were tryin'...tryin' to make somethin' right by doin' what you did...what we did, but then a bad thing happened along the way that you didn't think would happen, never gave a thought to, if that makes sense. Anyway, I think Sammy has taken it harder than his mother. I've never seen him so down. He didn't say a word to me at the service."

"The same with me. I tried to talk to him but he just walked away. You're right, I don't think he has the same faith his mother does. My guess is he thinks it's a ridiculous thought that his daddy has been called to heaven for some kind of work. Be careful if you decide to pass or we'll end up bein' buried out here with the buzzards and tumbleweeds."

"I will."

"You know," J.B. continued, "the whole Christian concept of grace is an interestin' concept. Just ask for forgiveness and it's granted. Sure, you have to say you know Christ and that he's your savior and all but then, just like that, you're free of your sin, whatever it may have been. Just like that. So, all Mr. Malone has to do is to ask for forgiveness. Magic like, he gets off free as a bird, at least when it comes to heaven or hell. It's never made any sense to me. Heaven and hell doesn't make any sense either. I wonder whatever happened to the poor folks who came before the Jews and the Christians? The ones who were unfortunate enough to have walked the face of our lovely planet before the concept of heaven and hell, before there was a single all-powerful, all-knowing, and judgmental God? I say if you take the Bible, either the old or the new, and believe in a literal interpretation and all, you've got your head screwed on backwards. Anyway, maybe I'm the one who needs to ask for my share of grace. Of course, it won't be forthcomin' if I don't get down on my religious hands and knees."

James Ray remained silent as J.B. droned on as if he were an unbelieving Pastor Pritchard. It was as if his daddy were a slow-moving freight train with a cargo of accepted truth, but as the train's conductor, he elected to remain defiant and askew of the commonly accepted and ethical path forward.

James Ray marveled at the vastness of the west Texas landscape: treeless, shapeless, and formless, with only an endless horizon upon which to focus.

"Slow down," said J.B. "I don't want to have to attend another funeral, yours or mine."

"Sorry. I do wonder how fast the Hudson will go. Think it can do a hundred?" James Ray asked.

"Maybe, but I'm not in the mood to find out."

The Hudson slowed. J.B. opened his map of Texas.

James Ray tried to find a radio station that he could bring into good reception. He failed to find anything interesting. The two stopped to have lunch at a diner named Honeysuckle's in Wichita Falls.

They ate. J. B. snared a discarded copy of the *Wichita Daily Times* and asked for a refill of coffee. James Ray got up, walked outside, stretched, and wandered up and down the street while he waited for J.B. to be finished. He noticed that the women on the street looked much like women in Mayweather. Many of the men, however, seemed to prefer cowboy boots to dress shoes. Later, they stopped at a gas station, then continued their drive through town.

"Well, I'll be hogtied," J.B. remarked.

"What?"

"There's a Cadillac, just like Carl Malone's. See? Over there. Identical to his. My, oh my. I suppose someone else will parade around town like the sorry excuse of a Mr. Malone did in Mayweather once the someone makes the car theirs."

"Wonder how many Cadillac Coupe deVilles GM made this year?" James Ray wondered.

"Good question. And how many of 'em will be yellow?"

"So what will happen to him if they catch him?"

"Bring him back to Mayweather to face charges, assumin' the grand jury indicts him. Manslaughter or outright murder. Rape. I don't know about the bootleggin' business. That's as common an activity as buyin' a loaf of bread down to the Piggly Wiggly. Anyway, it's up to the grand jury to define the charges, to figure it all out. Certainly, the whole mess at the Lone Star will be a thing of the past. Jimmy Friday, the owner, will probably go down. I don't know about Hoghead. Maybe he was in on it and maybe he wasn't. Anyway, I hope he'll be voted out come the next election. Hard to tell."

"Funny, Carl was so good to me. At least he was up until the end."

"Well, he was good with a lot of things. But bein' good at things and doin' good are horses of a different color."

"Do you want to drive for awhile, Daddy?   I'm gettin' tired."

"Sure, pull over when it's safe to do so."

"Maybe we should go back," James Ray said, after he and his father switched seats.

"Why?"

"The Cadillac could be you-know-whose. Besides, I'd like to photograph the Cadillac in with the mix of other cars for sale. The Caddy will appear white and the others dark in a black-and-white photo. It'll make for great contrast both as..."

"No, I'm not turnin' back."

"You know I'm doin' a photo essay of our trip."

"Yes. Look. I agree it's a possibility the car's his. Maybe not probable, but it's certainly within the realm of possibility. I agree with y'all's reasonin', but I'm not turning around. He's no longer in Mayweather and that's all to the good. Let him do his mischief elsewhere."

J.B. accelerated as they left the town's city limits. He continued driving west.

"Y'all aren't goin' to turn around and see if the Caddy might be Carl's?   Check it out?   Maybe he traded it in on somethin' else so no one would recognize him? You spend all the time and energy to sleuth him out down at the Lone Star and..."

"I'm not turnin' around, James Ray. I'm done with tryin' to be a poor man's Dick Tracy. I'll leave Carl Malone to a higher authority. Let the Texas Rangers ride to the rescue, or the FBI, or have God intervene if he's in your religious tool kit."

"Y'all mention God a lot for you not to believe in God."

"Maybe. If anyone wants to believe, let 'em believe. If you do, or your mother does, or anyone else does for that matter, then by all means believe and then put the fellow to work. Have God determine the outcome of a baseball game. Have God save the starvin' children in China. Have God cure polio. Have God bless us with fewer tornadoes. Have God have at our Mr. Malone. Have God send a tornado his way and send him straight to hell. Let God do the work. Personally, I'm done with makin' a mess of things."

Following J.B.'s rant, the two fell silent as the Hudson inched further west into what James Ray felt was landscape devoid of fertile subject matter.

Slowly, the Hudson gained on a west-bound train. James Ray spied two hobos seated in the open door of an empty freight car. He reached for his camera. He quickly set his shutter speed to 1/60th of a second and choose F-11 as his aperture. He decided to try something Carl had suggested when photographing a moving object. The relatively slow shutter speed would be fast enough to reduce camera shake but slow enough to communicate a sense of movement between the train and the landscape upon which it moved. The landscape alongside the train would be blurred while the image of the train and the men would appear sharp and recognizable. Given the fact the Hudson was moving at the same speed as the train, there was little relative movement between the two modes of transportation.

"Hold your speed, Daddy. Stay even with the train."

James Ray waved to the men. They waved back. He recorded his image. He waved again to the men and again, they waved back. Again, he tripped the shutter. Again, he encouraged the men to wave. The man wearing a baseball cap lifted his cap and waved. The other man remained motionless, his hands in his lap.

"Did you get 'em?" asked J.B.

"Yes. I got 'em." James Ray put away his camera.

"Daddy, so what was it with the girl who jumped to her death in Dallas? Will we ever find out why she killed herself and how she got involved in the Lone Star mess?"

"We don't know why she killed herself. Left no note. Nothin' to go on but speculation. She was pregnant. Maybe by Carl. Seems as if he's a man who can't keep his peter in his pocket. I don't know, she was...what's the word? Wish I had my sister here. Your aunt is the queen of vocabulary. Want a word and she can bring it to mind like flippin' a light switch. She'd know. The girl was a...a harbinger. That's it. A harbinger."

"What's a harbinger?"

"Someone who initiates things, I think. Someone who or something that leads to other things. I don't know. I'll have to look it up. But it's somethin' like that. She was a precursor of sorts. That's another fancy word. It all began with the girl and her death. If I hadn't paid so much attention to it all and hadn't linked her picture in the *Dallas Morning News* to the face of the girl in the Lone Star photo, same girl and all...I don't know that I would have taken so much interest, gotten so involved. Lookin' back, it all happened so fast. Maybe if I hadn't been such a busybody, Booker T. would be alive today, and you'd still be workin' at the paper, and Carl would still be takin' pornographic pictures of teenagers down at the Lone Star."

"Well, I guess that's true. You were sort of possessed by it all."

"Yes. Possessed is an apt word for it."

"What have you done with her picture? The first one. The one that the old-timer's wife found."

"The grand jury has it along with the roll of film we took. It'll be used as evidence."

"Mr. Shoemaker called before we left."

"He did? What did he want?"

"Wants me to fill in after we get back from California. Wants me to work in the afternoons after school now that's Carl's gone."

"How do you feel about that?"

"I like the feelin' of bein' wanted. I don't know that I can do as good a job as Carl, but I'll try. He said I could work as many hours as I want 'till they find a full-time person."

"Well, good for you. I'm proud of you."

"May I ask y'all a personal question?"

"Fire away, my boy, fire away."

"What's goin' on with you and Ruth Ann's mother?"

J.B. jerked his head to face James Ray and then back to the road ahead.

The Hudson had finally left the train in their wake.

"To be honest. I don't know. That's another good question. Like I say, I don't know. I've always tried to map things out in my life. Know what to expect and all, know what's around the next corner, or over the next hill. Looks like I've lost my touch. The last several months have been close to chaos. There were times when I thought I was losin' my mind. There were times I thought I should go underground all cicada-like and pop back up in seventeen years to see if the air had cleared."

J.B.'s fingers nervously strummed the outer edge of the steering wheel.

"I suppose I'm guilty of puttin' what I believed to be urgent ahead of what was truly important. I achieved my goal of puttin' an end to the Lone Star mess but lost my best friend in the process."

James Ray changed the subject. "How's Ruth Ann's mother dealin' with her problem?"

"The drinkin' problem?"

"Yes."

"Good, so far. She's in with a group...a support group. Alcoholics Anonymous. Maybe with Bud gone and Ruth Ann doin' well, and her new job at the drug store, maybe she'll be good in the long run. I hope so. Here's a question for you. How about you and Ruth Ann?"

"Well, since we're bein' honest and all...I think I love her. I know I'm supposedly too young to be in love, but that's the way I feel." James Ray sought a more comfortable position in his seat.

"Nothin' to be embarrassed about. You feel the way you feel. Just be careful. Don't push anythin'. Push too hard and she'll resist. Just be there for her. That's my best advice."

"Like y'all are bein' there for her mother?"

J.B. swallowed hard. "I suppose. His fingers increased their strumming. "Yes. After all she's been through, someone needs to be there for her. Is Ruth Ann back in trainin'?"

"Yes, starts today, actually. Daddy, another question. What about you and Mother? Are you two goin' to get back together? Seems to me y'all ought to put your energy to work tryin' to solve whatever came between the two of you. I miss her, Daddy. I miss her a lot. It's not the same with the two of you in two different states."

"More like two different worlds. Have been for a long time. I suppose I wasn't payin' attention. Your mother says I was absent in the relationship. I thought I was there, but accordin' to her, I wasn't. It's not a good feelin' to see our marriage in tatters, all threadbare. Maybe it's in such a condition it can't be mended."

"Why can't you can try to mend it?"

J.B. didn't respond immediately. He sighed. "Honestly, James Ray, I think it's beyond savin'."

"Will you try?"

J.B. gripped the steering wheel hard with both hands. "Look James Ray, things are different now. Things turned on a dime. I never gave a single, solitary thought to life without your mother. Then, lo and behold, I find myself in an entirely new situation, one that I didn't call for let alone anticipate. Lookin' back, I suppose I should have done things differently. I suppose I wasn't meeting your mother's needs as a husband. I've told you that already. Who knows what she's been thinkin' for all these years. It's a puzzle to me. At first I was taken aback when she announced she was leavin', I didn't know what to think. Then, I was confused. Then, I got angry. Now, I don't know. To be honest, if she weren't so sick, I suppose I'd have to say I'm relieved. I know it sounds terrible for me to say; but, in some ways, I feel free. In other ways, I feel like a failure. I know people are talkin'. I can tell by the way they look at me. Even more revealin' is what they don't say, the questions they don't ask, if you know what I mean."

"Do you think she's gonna die?"

"I hope not. She's a good person. She, she...she just..."

"Just what?"

"She's not satisfied with how her life has turned out. Let me put it that way."

"How do you know she isn't satisfied?"

"You'd be better off askin' her that. Or, maybe not. You know how she can get riled."

The two didn't speak for an hour. James Ray tried to sleep but couldn't, given his ruminations concerning his mother, the horrible way Booker T. died, the Lone Star naked picture-taking by his friend and photographer teacher, his fight with Rusty, his obsession with Ruth Ann, and the start of school and what that would look and feel like.

His father began humming indistinctly. James Ray looked to the outside of the car. The air entering the Hudson was slightly cooler given evening's approach. The drabness of the flat land disinterested him. He was already missing the rolling, oak-studded hills and lush green of Mayweather. He missed Ruth Ann. He missed not being around to help Sammy with his grief. He hoped upon hope that Sammy would remain his friend. He missed his work at the paper. He would try not to miss Carl. He had learned so much from him. Carl had changed his life.

"Quanah's just up the road," J.B. announced. "Not much of a town but it's a town. The paper I grabbed back at the cafe in Wichita Falls said a spate of twisters passed through a few days ago. Look down to the road and you can still see puddles of rain alongside the road. The paper said there was some property damage but that no one was killed. Said a person was missin' from a car they found overturned in a field. Car was found in a field alongside this highway somewhere around here. Said no road led to the field so it had to have been picked up and dropped there by a twister. Anyway, back to Quanah. The town's named after a great Comanche chief. Last of the bunch of 'em. Ever hear of Quanah Parker?"

"Yes. My history teacher told me about him. I checked out a book in the library about Quanah, and the Comanches and the Texas Rangers and all."

"Good for your teacher and good for you. I suspect that little is taught about Indians aside from them bein' so called savages. At least it wasn't taught when I was a teacher."

"You taught math and science."

"Yes, but you get to know what's being taught and what isn't. Thing is, no one could stand up to the Comanches. No one. Not the Spaniards, not the Mexicans, not the Apaches, not even the cavalry, or the Texas Rangers, at least in the beginnin'. I suppose you know that. Quanah was half-white and half-Comanche. His father was a also a Comanche chief. You probably know that also."

James Ray nodded in the affirmative.

"His white mother was very young at the time when she was stolen from a pioneerin' family, the Parkers. So, she was raised Comanche. Years later, in her adult years, she was rescued, but she never wanted to be returned to white civilization. Did y'all know that too?"

"Yes. I sometimes wonder what my life would have been like if I'd been born a hundred years ago. You know, a full-blood Comanche or Coushatta."

J.B. looked over to James Ray. "Well, if we're comparin' you to Quanah Parker, you have more Indian blood in you than he does, or rather did."

"What are you sayin'?"

"My son, there's somethin' I've been meanin' to tell you for sometime. Somethin' that's weighed heavy on my mind. Somethin' that has to do with me, and your mother, and someone else and everythin' to do with you. I suppose now's as good a time as any to tell you. It won't take long to tell because I know little of it except for one simple, yet painful, fact. Your mother has all the details. The who, what, where, how, and why of it."

"Mother?"

"Yes, your mother."

"Well, tell me whatever it is you want to tell me."

"Okay. Like I say, it won't take long to tell. I imagine I can tell everythin' I know in about the time your camera's shutter was open when you photographed the freight train."

J.B. swallowed and again looked over at James Ray.

James Ray looked back at his father. Above the roar of the road noise, J.B. spoke. As he spoke, he alternately looked to the road ahead and to his son.

"You, my son, aren't my son in the biological sense of the word. You're more Indian than Quanah Parker. Your biological father is or was, I don't actually know which, Coushatta. However, in all other respects, you are my son. I love you. I cherish you. I'm here for you no matter what."

"Daddy, what in the world are you sayin'?"

"Just what I've said. I know no more than that. If you have questions, you'll have to take them up with your mother. She'll most likely be highly agitated with me for tellin' you but I felt I had no choice. Mostly, I didn't think it was fair for you not to know. You have a right to know the facts of your heritage although you or I may never know or fully understand the 'why' of it all."

James Ray suddenly felt burdened by an emotion that, if asked, he would be unable to articulate. He now realized that there was more to his mother's and father's separation other than his father being so called "absent". Much more. He hadn't felt so fearful, so alone or so helpless, since being diagnosed with polio. His father's revelation left him speechless. He felt disoriented, disoriented by his father's words and disoriented by the featureless, mundane landscape. A landscape that visually offered nothing but a seemingly endless and empty horizon. He turned from his father who, in little more than an instant, wasn't his father. James Ray peered out the car's window to the nadir beyond. His eyes were wet.

Storm clouds had gathered on the distant horizon. He wondered how long they had taken to form. He wondered how long they would last.

About the Author

First time author Jack Pirtle was born and raised in northeast Texas. He attended segregated schools during the Jim Crow forties and fifties. "I was walking around with this story in my head for much of my adult life," he says. "Further, I was eager to have my youthful, teenage experiences take the shape and form of regional fiction."

Pirtle holds a masters degree in education from the University of Arizona. He taught social studies and photography at Sunnyside High School and Pima Community College in Tucson. His high school photography students won local, state and national awards for their creativity. He is the father of six children and grandfather of eleven. He lives in Tucson, Arizona, with his wife Klaire.

For more information on Jack Pirtle, please visit
www.jackpirtleauthor.com

the story continues…

Circles of
Confusion

(the sequel to Field of View)

Coming this fall
by

Jack Pirtle

www.jackpirtleauthor.com

www.ingramcontent.com/pod-product-compliance
Lightning Source LLC
Chambersburg PA
CBHW072107250626
47159CB00007B/2332